# A Match for *Mary Bennet*

### Can a Serious Young Lady Ever Find Her Way to Love?

D0167476

## EUCHARISTA WARD, O.S.F.

SOURCEBOOKS LANDMARK™
AN IMPRINT OF SOURCEBOOKS, INC.®
NAPERVILLE, ILLINOIS

Copyright © 2009 by Eucharista Ward, O.S.F.
Cover and internal design © 2009 by Sourcebooks, Inc.
Cover Design by Renee Witherwax
Cover Image © Christopher Wood Gallery, London, UK / The Bridgeman Art Library

Sourcebooks and the colophon are registered trademarks of Sourcebooks, Inc.

All rights reserved. No part of this book may be reproduced in any form or by any electronic or mechanical means including information storage and retrieval systems—except in the case of brief quotations embodied in critical articles or reviews—without permission in writing from its publisher, Sourcebooks, Inc.

The characters and events portrayed in this book are fictitious or are used fictitiously. Any similarity to real persons, living or dead, is purely coincidental and not intended by the author.

Published by Sourcebooks Landmark, an imprint of Sourcebooks, Inc.
P.O. Box 4410, Naperville, Illinois 60567–4410
(630) 961–3900
FAX: (630) 961–2168
www.sourcebooks.com

Library of Congress Cataloging-in-Publication Data

Ward, Eucharista.
  A match for Mary Bennet : can a serious young lady ever find her way to love? / Eucharista Ward.
     p. cm.
  1. Young women--Fiction. 2. England--Fiction. I. Title.
  PS3623.A7318M38 2009
  813'.6--dc22
                            2009018721


Printed and bound in the United States of America
CHG 10 9 8 7 6 5 4 3 2 1

# Volume One

## Decided

ONE MIGHT SAY THAT USING THE DIVINE GIFT OF HUMAN memory for the recitation of three-month-old annoyances represents talent misspent. Mary Bennet thought, as she sat with her hand poised over the silver tea urn, that not even all four evangelists together had documented Jesus's public life as thoroughly as her mother insisted on recounting Mary's social life. Mrs. Bennet sat in an upright chair opposite the tea caddy, continuing her catalogue of Mary's behaviours at Meryton's midsummer Assembly. Mary placed the heated china pot, with its fair quantity of precious Twinings tea, below the spout of the new urn, a gift to the Bennets from Mary's sister Elizabeth Darcy. When she sensed that the recitation was nearing its end—she had heard it twice previously—Mary released the boiling water. She then concentrated on timing the brew and, finally, pouring it carefully into Mrs. Bennet's cup. She knew well that if she sloshed any onto the saucer, her mother's long-suffering sigh and roll of the eyes would be followed by, "How I miss dear Jane!" This time, Mrs. Bennet paused in her admonitions long enough to peer at the saucer, taste her tea, and smile. Mary relaxed and poured her own cup.

Mrs. Bennet then set her tea down and ignored it, fixing her eyes on her daughter's calm expression. "You sat so creep mouse in a corner with, of all things, a book! What a way to comport yourself at a dance! Why, you might as well scream to all the world that no man is good enough for you. Oh yes, I saw you stand up with Russell Mortenson, but you did not smile at him once! Dancing is not torture, you know, and your face should not declare it so. What am I to do with you? Will any gentleman ever take an interest if you continue in such a fashion?"

Mary managed a "yes, Mama," but it was not an answer to her mother's question. She smiled inwardly at her mother's description of her dancing, which put her in mind of a pair from *Pilgrim's Progress* her father had remarked on—Ready-to-Halt who dances with Despondency's daughter. As her mother ended her midsummer's tale, she launched into warnings for the upcoming Michaelmas assembly. Perhaps, Mary mused, Despondency's daughter had also been daughter to another character her father mentioned, Madame Bubble. Mary reprimanded herself for this lapse and listened to her mother's rules for the harvest dance.

"Take no book... no sheet music... try to avoid Mrs. Long's nieces. You know they always seek you out so that their smiles, by contrast with your sober mien, will invite dancers. At least watch the dance as if it interests you. You know, tap your feet, smile... are you listening?"

"Yes, Mama." Mary finished her tea and eyed her mother's, which was growing cold. How she missed Jane and Elizabeth! Nobody had cared a whit about her actions at dances while her older sisters lived at Longbourn with them.

Her mother began on Mary's attire. "You did not need another grey gown. Could you not find more eye-catching material?"

Mary liked grey muslin and it was certainly more practical than the flimsy pink and lilac materials so easily soiled. Mary also liked feeling unnoticed, except at the pianoforte. She glanced through the open sitting room doorway to the drawing room where her beloved instrument sat against an inner wall, inviting her to ignore her mother and leave the room. She did so only in her mind, and even then briefly. Her mother came finally to her reason for this sudden interest in Mary's ball behaviour.

"And according to his letter, Colonel Fitzwilliam means to visit exactly on Michaelmas on his way from Kent to Derbyshire. If he attends the dance, he will surely stand up with you. Remember to smile at him. You are not at all bad looking if only you would refrain from screwing up your face in a frown or a squint."

Mary thought longingly of Catherine's imminent arrival from her London stay with Aunt and Uncle Gardiner. With Kitty home, her mother would have a daughter more to her taste: a lively, smiling, dance-loving daughter. And likely, she would come with a pretty new gown and some ribbons from Bond Street shops. Her mother would have something to talk of besides Mary's plainness.

Mrs. Bennet finally stopped to sip her tea again. "Hill! Hill! This tea is cold! Please put the kettle back on the fire!"

Mrs. Hill bustled in, lightly touched the hot urn, methodically emptied the teapot and Mrs. Bennet's cup into the slop bowl, and brewed more tea. All the while Mrs. Hill explained, as she had done before, that this new tea urn was just like Pemberley's, though of course not as ornate. "It contains an iron that is heated red hot to retain the water's heat." Mrs. Hill gave Mrs. Bennet a steaming cup of tea, and as she did so, she asked, "When do you expect Miss Catherine back, ma'am?"

"Mr. Bennet must have reached Gracechurch Street two days ago, Hill. I expect them back tomorrow or Sunday at the latest." Then, remembering to drink her tea between her comments, she happily discussed Kitty's last letter and her plans for the harvest ball.

Mary's attention drifted out the window, beyond the shrubbery to the rutted track she could not see, the one that led to Netherfield, where Jane had once lived with her beloved Charles Bingley. Good, kind Jane whose baby Beth was two years old now.

Shortly after their baby was born though, the Bingleys moved to Nottingham. Jane said they wished to be nearer Elizabeth and Fitzwilliam Darcy in Derbyshire, but Mrs. Bennet did not believe it. According to her, it was all Caroline Bingley's fault. Charles's sister lived with them, and it was true that Caroline did at times appear to scorn Hertfordshire society and spoke of it as being not varied enough to suit her. But Mary had visited them in Nottingham, and they seemed to be as much in the country as ever. Mary did not understand how one quiet country manor became more varied than another, though she could understand their wanting to visit so grand a place as Pemberley.

Mrs. Bennet spoke of the dance to Mrs. Hill as the very place to find husbands for her two unmarried daughters. Mary did not understand that either, since her mother always insisted that Elizabeth had married Darcy to provide for her sisters. Why else would Lizzy accept in marriage a man she once declared she would not even dance with? The ways of society puzzled Mary greatly. She sat, chin resting on her hand, and looked off toward Meryton and Netherfield, regretting their lost visits to that fine manor. The new tenant, Mr. Grantley, did not care to show the stately house with its trellised porch, large rooms, and fine, wide avenue. Rumour had it that he did not even care to hunt the land. He had turned out to be the most un-neighbourly neighbour in all of Hertfordshire. Mary knew it was unchristian to complain, even in her mind, and truly she did not mind that Mr. Grantley ignored her as he did all the young ladies, but oh, she did miss gentle Jane, good-humoured Bingley, and their charming baby.

Her mother rose and left the room with Hill, saying she would approve the menu for tomorrow's dinner with Mr. Bennet and Kitty. Hill took the tea things out with them, leaving Mary free to go to her pianoforte. She played her favourite pieces, still thinking of the great changes her sisters' marriages had brought. While she played softly, she tried to imagine how her sisters themselves had changed since marriage. Had their marriages been an instrument of happiness for them? For dear Jane perhaps it was so. While she lived close by, Mary thought that the bloom of her skin, the sparkle of her eyes, and her air of contentment had spoken eloquently of her happiness. Only, in the months before they moved, the Bingleys had seemed preoccupied, a bit distant. It may have been Jane's reluctance to go, especially if it had been to satisfy Caroline. But still, Elizabeth was Jane's closest sister and friend, and Mary did not think that Jane would be hesitant to go nearer Lizzy. The baby was young for such a journey. Perhaps that had worried them.

The soft music soothed Mary's wandering mind, and she thought about Lizzy, whose marriage puzzled her more. How brave she was to accept such a man, and no one expected her to find her happiness in him. She wondered that her father had seemed content with Lizzy's choice. The few times Mary had visited Pemberley, Lizzy certainly did not seem unhappy, and how surprisingly easy she seemed with Mr. Darcy! Was marriage some magical step to happiness? This might be the clue to Mrs. Bennet's urgings to her daughters to enter the state. Well, Mary felt she could be content without such a change in her life, and she was grateful for Lizzy's sacrifice that made it possible to choose against it.

Mary turned to another music book and practised her new études. Her mind turned to the coming harvest dance. She rather hoped that Darcy's cousin, Colonel Fitzwilliam, would choose not to attend. She hardly knew him, having seen him only at Lizzy's wedding and at Pemberley's Christmas balls. On these occasions, he had not shown any particular interest in the Bennets. She wondered greatly why he proposed a visit now, one that would delay his return to Mr. Darcy. Was it possible that even he found his proud cousin daunting and wished to prolong his journey?

# Chapter 1

A MAN OF MODERATE FORTUNE STILL SINGLE INTO HIS THIRTY-second year, who has manoeuvred past temptations to imprudent matches and has slid guiltily past prudent matches devoid of temptation, usually views "someday" a likelier wedding day than "next month" or even "next year." Thus, it surprised Colonel Darcy Fitzwilliam, second son of the earl of Norwich Mills, to find himself mentally rehearsing a proposal of marriage, though the exact object of that proposal remained uncertain.

After a month in Kent with his ailing aunt, Lady Catherine de Bourgh, the Colonel might have been preparing a report for his cousin, Fitzwilliam Darcy, who had requested his journey. Darcy's wife being so near to her lying-in and still inclined to keep up her usual active life, Darcy had remained with her to urge continued rest. Mrs. Darcy's friend in Kent, Charlotte Collins, had written that Lady Catherine, who was by far too stubborn to be ill, nevertheless had suffered a "serious indisposition." Though the redoubtable Lady Catherine had all but divorced her nephew, Darcy did not return the sentiment, and he wanted a firsthand account of her health. His amiable cousin had obliged him and had spent a month attending Lady Catherine in the company of her daughter, Anne, and the local surgeon. Now he mused, to the rhythmic swish of carriage wheels, on all his female acquaintances.

The Colonel rather enjoyed the diversions of Rosings Park until Lady Catherine's strength returned. Then, having faced the prospect that she could actually die like other mortals, that dowager set about preparing her world for life without her. Her daughter, approaching thirty and unlikely to meet anyone worthy to marry a genuine de Bourgh, occupied her first concern. She strongly urged Fitzwilliam to marry her.

The suggestion appalled the Colonel, who had for years pitied his cousin Darcy for no other reason than that Lady Catherine asserted to all the family that Darcy was "destined for Anne." No sooner had he transferred that pity to himself than he resolved to follow Darcy's example and take a bride of his own choosing.

True, Anne de Bourgh would inherit great riches, but no wealth of land and its rents could make palatable a life yoked to that mousy, sickly, cross, and simpering young woman. And to Fitzwilliam, even her fortune presented no asset. He had grown too fond of his own moderate estate of Castle Park adjoining the charming village of Castlebury in Norfolk. He could not face becoming slave to the de Bourgh estate at Rosings Park.

Consequently, at Lady Catherine's odious suggestion, he had frowned and said he doubted such a course would be possible for him. Now he faced a problem Darcy had not encountered. Darcy's immense holdings in Derbyshire had made possible the courtship of lively, lovely Elizabeth Bennet, whose chief fortune was wit, charm, and character. Fitzwilliam, on the contrary, had to support his estate, and after his military career, he hoped for a wife with some dowry—at least ten thousand pounds—with interest sufficient for comfortable living.

The Colonel looked out of the carriage window, briefly caught the reflection of his chiseled features, pushed back the flop of hair that persisted in hiding his forehead, and judged that he would not likely attract some new acquaintance quickly enough to escape Miss de Bourgh. He must court someone who knew him well enough already to appreciate his character and overlook his unprepossessing countenance. He smiled at the reasonable ten thousand pounds he now estimated as his need. A few years ago Mrs. Darcy, then still Miss Bennet, had teased him, asking the price of an earl's second son. The sum he had then, and even recently, envisioned had shrunk appreciably at the moment of Lady Catherine's proposal.

Without the luxury of choosing for love, he examined the possibilities his present social circle provided. He thought of the young women he knew in Castlebury. Quickly he dismissed Miss Reed, who was far too frivolous, and the cripplingly timid Miss Gribble. Alas, many other neighbours lacked even the modest portion he felt necessary. He turned to wider circles. Did any of his fellow officers have amiable sisters? Yes, but unfortunately none that he knew possessed much of a dowry. But the idea of sisters brought him to his cousin Darcy and Darcy's good friend Bingley. Georgiana Darcy and Caroline Bingley captured his first attention. Georgiana, only recently of age, had been under his and Darcy's guardianship since her father's death. He knew she loved him as cousin and guardian. Since living at Pemberley with Elizabeth, Miss Darcy had shed some of her childlike timidity and had blossomed into a charming, even witty maiden, though of late he had seen moments of melancholy. He felt sure Darcy would not oppose the match, and though her fortune of thirty thousand pounds as well as her beauty of face and character made her fit for a nobleman, Darcy had no such ambitions for her. If she could but learn to like him more intimately, as courtship might evoke, he had some hope of winning her.

And what of Darcy's new sisters, the younger Miss Bennets? Might Darcy not offer even them some dowry their own family could not manage? Fitzwilliam resolved to make himself agreeable to them in Hertfordshire, just in case.

As for Caroline Bingley, he knew not for certain the extent of her fortune, but her provident father had done well in trade and would have extended his generosity to her as he had for her sister, Louisa. Besides, Darcy's genial friend Bingley was as openhanded as anyone he knew, and he would certainly approve the match. Caroline had stately beauty, ease of manner in society, and musical talent. If she occasionally spoke sharply, chiefly to or about women, she at least showed energy and ready wit. Being closer to his age than Georgiana, she may have more in common with him, and the rougher edges of her wit may well mellow with marriage.

A raucous clatter of wheels told the Colonel he was in London, and when the carriage slowed to a stop at the Bell, he had time for a bit of beef and ale before taking the post to Hertfordshire. He dashed past a small knot of men loitering under the swaying sign of a greying and scratched bell. He soon had his simple fare before him, and he spent much of the quiet mealtime recalling last year's Christmas ball at Pemberley. It had been the second one since Darcy's marriage. How much more festive it was than the first, when the lovely Elizabeth tried to be all things to all her new neighbours and grew tense over it. That second one, nine months ago, displayed an Elizabeth comfortable in her position as mistress of Pemberley. Besides, the presence of the Bingleys, recently moved from Hertfordshire, had obviously added to Mrs. Darcy's joy, Jane being her most beloved sister. Mrs. Bingley exuded a grace and calm presence exactly complementing the witty charm of Mrs. Darcy. Bingley himself, Darcy's oldest friend, had likewise enhanced Darcy's pleasure, so that even the stateliest guests joined in the merriment. The Colonel himself had danced—and even sung noels—with a pleasure he experienced anew as he thought of it. Georgiana charmed him with her slightly timid smile and new-found ease and grace of movement. She even teased him a bit as they danced, crowing that he no longer had license to tell her what to do since her coming of age. Caroline Bingley, houseguest of the Bingleys, amused him greatly at that ball also. Fitzwilliam's dances with her were altogether enjoyable, and he was much taken with her fine dark eyes and stately, almost majestic manner. Yes, either young lady would grace his homely estate. Caroline's imperious good looks pleased his military nature. Her fortune, likely adequate, could not reach a proportion which would render his own modest Norfolk estate inconsequential. On the other hand, Georgiana's new sparkle and burgeoning womanhood appealed to him, and Georgiana may well prefer being lady of the house in her own right to remaining at Pemberley, where she resided only as sister of the master.

He tried to recall the Bennet girls at that ball, but only the younger one came to mind. He had danced with her, he knew. What was it she was called? Kitty? Probably Catherine, a name not happy in its nuances for him. Of the other sister he remembered nothing. He knew he had not danced with her.

Fitzwilliam entered the carriage bound for Meryton, still certain of his course yet undecided as to its exact object. He hoped to explain satisfactorily his visit to the Bennet family by offering to collect any messages the family might wish him to carry to their married daughters in the North. It would be pleasant to provide some missive more palatable to Mrs. Darcy's taste than the note from Lady Catherine, which burned in his pocket. He knew not what it contained, but Lady Catherine's grim and rigid expression as she wrote and handed it to him led him to fear that it would not please the recipient. He meant also to glean some homely news from Longbourn to retail to Jane Bingley and Elizabeth Darcy, sure that it would be more welcome than what he had to tell of his stay in Kent. He might even mention his own just-forming plan to be married by next year, in order to see how the idea fared. The more he thought of marriage, the more comfortable he grew at the prospect. Marriage had done his cousin's companionability a great good: Darcy's concerns had deepened, his compassion extended beyond his estates, and his ease as both host and guest had visibly increased. Fitzwilliam sighed. "May my own future be so bettered by taking on a helpmate!"

A T LONGBOURN, HALF OF THE BENNET HOUSEHOLD BUSTLED gaily from the large sitting room to the hall mirror preparing for the next day's assembly. Gowns had been brushed and aired, and fussing over hairdressings now occupied young Catherine Bennet, while Mrs. Bennet called for Hill every few minutes to have her freshen a bit of lace or press yet another ribbon. Catherine set three ribbons and some gems on the table before her and fastened the gems carefully onto one ribbon and then another, twisting each into her hair and frowning, unsure which looked the most elegant. One by one, she took them to the mirror and returned, dissatisfied, to exchange ribbons or to rearrange the gems.

Not far from the sitting room table, Mary sat quietly rereading a small volume of Pope's essay-poems that her father had lent her. At Kitty's every moan of displeasure, Mary sighed and frowned, distracted from the reading she depended on to improve her mind. Each of her sighs invariably brought on a volley of reproof from Mrs. Bennet, along with a reminder that Mary too would be dancing on the morrow and might profit by entering into the preparations. The expected arrival of Colonel Fitzwilliam increased Mrs. Bennet's anticipated pleasure in the ball, and she showed deep resentment at

Mary's studious indifference. "It is a special blessing of Providence that he is coming just at this time, and you know he will feel obliged to partner you in the dance. Why do you not take interest enough to look your best?"

Mary responded laconically, "Oh, Mama, Kitty can entertain the Colonel far better than I can anyway. Why should I not try to improve my mind?"

Mr. Bennet, safe in his customary retreat of the library, contemplated his delinquent correspondence. The Colonel's generous offer to stop on his way to Derbyshire prompted him to answer Elizabeth's letter, so full of delight, awe, and trepidation over her expected first child. He easily addressed himself to her, perhaps his favourite daughter and certainly his wittiest. Upon completion of this labour of love, however, he sat back in his cosy leather chair and turned to the letter from Jane, his oldest daughter, which gave him pause. He reread it, enjoying Jane's genuine delight in the antics of little Beth, Bennet's only grandchild at present, and her expressions of genuine joy in her husband Charles, so loving and good-humoured. He set the letter aside. Much as he missed the Bingleys since their move to Nottingham, he knew they had done well in buying their own estate near the Darcys. He also knew that even life so close to Pemberley could not be as rosy as Jane contrived to portray it, and her failure to mention Charles's sister Caroline conveyed more than Jane had intended. Sweet Jane, who never said anything where nothing good could be said, spoke a silent complaint to which Bennet could hardly respond. No, he would refer that letter to his wife, who would likely not notice the omission. Whenever Mrs. Bennet tired of urging Hill to the height of frenzy over the ball, which Kitty and she would enjoy and Mary would endure, she could write to Jane. Then the Colonel, due to arrive on the day of the ball, would carry letters to both daughters in the North.

Bennet glanced at the other letters before him. Lydia's request for an advance of her per annum allowance showed only her persistence in a vain pursuit and her ignorance of the meaning of annum. He would copy his previous terse letter, as he had no intention of honouring such a request. At any rate, he knew Mrs. Bennet would send her whatever the household could spare each month.

He turned to the more amusing notes. Wickham, the ever-ingratiating erstwhile military officer who had carried off Lydia and subsequently been paid to marry her, had sent yet another preposterous scheme. The project purported to be like all Wickham's others: "absolutely certain to double their money" in a few years. It offered Bennet an "investment opportunity." Wickham and his cohorts proposed to buy up old post horses, spruce them up, and sell them at London fairs. Bennet decided to answer that one in a carefully expanded panegyric on the evils of speculation. Wickham would not, of course, read it, but if sufficient papers were inserted, Bennet could picture his son-in-law frantically searching through them under the illusion that a cheque was included.

He smiled as he picked up Mr. Collins's last epistle. That pompous clergyman cousin of his had written from Kent to announce the birth of his daughter Louisa, named for Charlotte's mother. Mr. Bennet surmised that this, like the name of the Collins son Lucas, represented a hope for lucrative attentions from the children's grandparents which were unlikely to ever materialize. Especially of interest in the letter was the sermonet on the "grave responsibility of raising a daughter in the fear of God, instilling modest and seemly behaviour so as to avoid any hint of scandal as she approaches womanhood." He recognized this reference to his Lydia, and he momentarily wished upon poor Louisa a spitfire temperament like Lydia's. He would answer Collins later, with many pointers on raising daughters to encourage their adventurous spirits that they may become as gracious and charming as Elizabeth. That may remind Collins that his Lizzy had had the good sense to refuse his offer of marriage.

In the morning room, from time to time, Catherine importuned Mary to join her in concern for her ball attire. Mary declined, preferring to continue copying couplets she meant to memorise and use in conversation. Her father's cousin, Mr. Collins, had recommended this method of proceeding in society, and she liked to take the clergyman's advice.

"Mary, how do you like this pink ribbon now?" Kitty asked as she twisted it before her, its rhinestones sparkling.

"Very nice, Kitty." Mary barely looked up.

"I have a new pink gown, you know."

"I am sure both will look fine on you." Mary read on: "In all you speak, let truth and candour shine."

"And what will you wear?"

Mary finally looked up. "My grey muslin is brushed and aired. It will do fine." She went back to her book.

"Oh, Mary! You always wear that. Everybody will think you too poor to afford better. And what in your hair?"

"Oh, I will wear the combs Lizzy gave me for Christmas." Mary watched her sister put forth another adorned ribbon for inspection. She could not help wondering how many dressings Kitty meant to wear at this ball. She added, "And everybody at this ball knows us perfectly well and probably what we can afford, to the last farthing. What does it matter?" She returned to her reading.

Catherine expressed her yearning for the sister who would have shared her enthusiasm for finery. "If Lydia were here, she would love a fine gown."

Mary smiled over what she read, developing a kinship with Alexander Pope. "They'll talk you dead." But all she said was, "Vanity of vanities; all is vanity."

Catherine seemed not to hear. "Do you think Lydia will come?"

Mary bit her lips tight and did not reply. She neither spoke of nor acknowledged her youngest sister since Mr. Collins had admonished them to consider Lydia as one dead.

Catherine grew impatient. "Really, Mary, you might as well say something."

"Oh, I hear you, Catherine. I choose not to recognize the person of whom you speak."

Mrs. Bennet left off stewing over Hill's long absence in pursuit of their shoe roses. She burst out, "For heaven's sake, Mary. Stop judging Lydia. She at least did what she should do—she got a husband! When will you manage that?"

The acquisition of a husband would not ever trouble her, Mary decided. She wanted to assure Mrs. Bennet that her happiness did not depend on marriage, but she knew that her mother would deny the possibility. One day Mary might find herself living contentedly at Derbyshire with Elizabeth and Darcy, just as Caroline Bingley lived with Jane and Charles at Nottingham. What could be simpler? She did not understand such persistent anxiety over beaux. Perhaps it was a mere habit that Mama could not break.

Exasperated, Mrs. Bennet again looked for Hill and, not seeing her, turned on Mary. "You will look to please a young man if you know what is good for you. You act this way only to antagonise me! Consider my poor nerves!"

Mary looked up from her reading and spoke calmly. "To me it seems that I act from a spirit of order. I try to accomplish what I have set out to do each day. I keep a schedule in my head." Perhaps it steadies my own nerves, she thought.

If anything, her answer further enraged Mrs. Bennet. "Oh, Mary! Forget your silly regimen! Such nonsense you talk. With your head full of schedules you will never find time for anything important."

At this point, Hill hastened in with the shoe roses, and the assessment of them took the full attention of Mrs. Bennet and Kitty. Mary returned to her pursuit of sagacity.

*Chapter 3*

Arriving at Longbourn before noon on Michaelmas as scheduled, Colonel Fitzwilliam learned of the ball at Meryton's assembly hall. Though tired from travel, he found himself pleased at the prospect after his sombre month at Kent. Mrs. Bennet rejoiced to see him immediately turn to secure Mary for the first two dances. She held her breath and then rejoiced even more as Mary accepted. One never knew about Mary. Having seen three daughters successfully married, Mrs. Bennet frequently opined that securing husbands for the remaining two would free her to relax quietly at home for the remainder of her days, resting her poor nerves. She could count on Catherine's full cooperation, but Mary, she realized with a sigh, seemed to want to go to each ball as if determined to ignore it and everyone present. She might as well be a hermitess. What great good fortune that Colonel Fitzwilliam would take her quiet Mary into the dance. Only too often her sister, Mrs. Philips, observed, "Poor Mary. What a pity she has not the beauty and liveliness of her sisters. Whatever will you do with her?" This assembly could prove different.

In some respects, this assembly proved different indeed. The afternoon clouded over, and a dull rain persisted into the evening, nullifying the whole advantage of the full moon and discouraging Catherine from wearing any of her ribbons, lest they run and stain her hair. Sighing, she too wore the combs Elizabeth had sent from Pemberley. Mary opined calmly that life is not meant to be all pleasure, and Kitty scowled at her ribbonless hair.

On arrival at the brilliantly lit hall, Mrs. Bennet groaned to see Mrs. Long advance toward her with her two plain nieces bent on sitting near Mary. Of course, they would expect to be introduced to Colonel Fitzwilliam. Mrs. Long did in fact show great interest, especially on finding him to be the cousin of Mr. Darcy, the almost legendary, rich landowner who had carried off the "jewel of Hertfordshire," Elizabeth Bennet. Her joy might have been tempered indeed had she learned that he was not nearly so rich as his cousin, but Mrs. Bennet judiciously withheld that information.

Almost immediately upon hearing the music that announced the dance, Catherine was claimed by the oldest Lucas boy and Mary went to the set with the Colonel. Mrs. Bennet smiled triumphantly at Mrs. Long's two nieces and beatifically at the good Colonel, even as she mouthed in Mary's direction "smile."

Mary, however, who liked to concentrate on her feet while dancing, could not smile because the Colonel dismayed her by his great willingness to converse. Worse, he insisted on asking questions. "Is this the room where Darcy first saw your sister Elizabeth?"

"Yes, sir, and refused to dance with her." Mary counted in rhythm to herself, a rising alarm unsteadying her.

Fitzwilliam laughed good-naturedly. "Darcy is not so stuffy these days. Your sister has done wonders for him. You must be very proud of her."

Mary, reminded of Elizabeth's sacrifice in marrying Darcy, said truthfully, "I am indeed proud of her."

Colonel Fitzwilliam found Mary a good listener and sounded her out on the subject of marriage. She tersely referred him to Kitty as one who took more interest in the subject than she did. Surprised at her seeming indifference to the state, he opened his mind to her, conscious that she knew two of the ladies he had been considering for marriage. "Do you know Miss Georgiana Darcy?"

"Yes. That is, I met her at Elizabeth's wedding and again at both of Pemberley's Christmas balls." She closed her eyes and willed him to stop questioning her.

"Do you like her?"

"Very much. She plays the pianoforte beautifully." Mary glanced down to watch her feet.

"And do you know Miss Caroline Bingley?"

Must this tiresome patter continue? "Oh yes, even better than I know Miss Darcy. She lived with Charles and my sister Jane at Netherfield before they moved to the North." She hoped her longer answer would satisfy him.

But no, he kept on. "And do you like her as well?"

"Oh no, not as well as Miss Darcy." Mary knew she was frowning, and she saw that he was too. She must have disappointed him. What could she say? Pope's words about "truth and candour" swam in her mind with her mother's dictum to smile while dancing. She hastened to add, "But Miss Bingley tries to be pleasant, in a regal sort of way." She had almost said "haughty," but she caught his eyes on her and did not wish to displease him. "And she plays very well also." Music was important to Mary's assessment. The dance went on and on, and so did Fitzwilliam. Mary's being able to talk at all while dancing must have been the result of rhythm acquired at the pianoforte. But must this man tax her so?

"I confess, I mean to ask someone to marry me, and I really cannot decide." Fitzwilliam had not intended to reveal so much, but his brain was more tired than his feet.

To Mary, this was an utterly perplexing problem. "And… must you marry?"

The sour, dispirited face of Miss de Bourgh leaped to his imagination. "Oh yes."

Mary's feet actually stopped entirely, and she regarded him, eyes wide. It had never occurred to her that a *man* must marry, at least not unless he had incurred the wrath of some lady's family, as Wickham had with Lydia. But this could hardly be the Colonel's situation if he knew not whom to marry. Finally she recovered the rhythm of movement, and after awhile she asked, "And the lady does not matter?" The music drew to a merciful close, and Mary relaxed. She curtsied.

The Colonel took her hand and they walked the long way around to where her mother sat. "Well, more than one would suit my purpose equally well."

He looked at her and seemed to request a response, but Mary was at a loss. Logical as she wished to be, the problem eluded her. "Then… then I suppose you must choose the lady who would be most pleased to marry you." She hoped that was reasonable, but she feared his puzzle was beyond her powers and a bit unfair, as it seemed one in which reason played a small part.

Happily, the Colonel smiled as if pleased. "A wonderful solution! You have helped a great deal." And his gracious thanks as he returned her to her mother rang so genuinely hearty that Mrs. Bennet smiled her pleasure after him.

As he went off to find Catherine, Mrs. Bennet turned her radiant geniality to Mary. "What a noble conquest you have made!"

Mary kept to herself the exact nature of her "conquest," which would not have pleased her mother. At any rate, the smile soon faded from Mrs. Bennet's face as Mr. Grantley entered the brilliant hall from the dimly lit foyer. "Oh no. There is that odious man!" The young MP who had taken Netherfield's lease irritated all the doting mothers, but as he was not thought handsome, few young ladies minded not receiving his attention. He strutted in as usual, head in the air, preceded by the firm tapping of the walking stick that invariably announced his arrival. Why he bothered to attend every assembly mystified the populace, as he never danced and ignored all the ladies. Worse, he often monopolized more congenial gentlemen who could be escorting some lady; and according to Sir William Lucas, his talk was of spies, informers, and pronouncements of the foreign secretary. According to Mr. Robinson, when Sir William once suggested that Mr. Grantley dance, that strange man had responded dolefully, "I prefer not to encourage young ladies in dangerous frivolities which they seem quite capable of initiating on their own."

Mrs. Philips joined Mrs. Bennet, and they exchanged sisterly pleasantries at the expense of Mr. Grantley. His sharp nose, his thick spectacles, his long head, the incessant tapping of his stick all came under their scrutiny as defects that would have been overlooked had he made himself more agreeable. Finally they turned the subject to Mary, and Mary slipped away as she heard, "Your Mary danced very well just now. Did I not see her partner at Elizabeth's wedding?"

"Yes. He is Mr. Darcy's cousin, Colonel Fitzwilliam."

"He does not greatly resemble his handsome cousin, does he?" Mrs. Philips asked and then sniffed.

Mrs. Bennet could not let her sister disparage a man who had so gallantly appreciated her daughter. "No," she said, "I believe he resembles his father, the Earl of Norwich Mills." She spoke without knowing anything of the resemblance, just conscious that the title would impress. Soon after, Mrs. Philips found reason to rise from her place, and not long after that the information spread generally through the hall. Mothers of presentable daughters came to be introduced, blissfully unaware that the Colonel was a second son. The Colonel's popularity grew apace, and he found himself dancing with more young ladies than he had ever before squired in one evening. Mrs. Bennet soon regretted her unfortunate impulse, as this left Mary at her usual occupation of observation from her post near the refreshment table. Mary did not mind this at all, and that only added to Mrs. Bennet's distress. Mrs. Bennet and Mrs. Philips went into the supper room with Lady Lucas, but Mary had enjoyed tea, fruit, and buns from the refreshment table, and she stayed where she was.

Soon a doubly surprising encounter took place. First, Mr. Grantley left his cronies and their political palaver, tapped his way over to the straight chair next to Mary's, sat down, and addressed her. The second surprise was that Mrs. Bennet missed the whole incident and did not even hear of it until the next day.

That august gentleman commented on Mary's having proved that she could indeed dance. "I assumed all these months that you had not learnt, though your sister dances readily enough. Now I wonder if you find it, as I do, a trivial occupation."

Mary, not sure whether she had been complimented, insulted, or neither, replied, "Dancing has its place, and a gracious partner can even render it pleasurable. But I am content to watch also."

His solemn regard wandered off to the few remaining dancers, and he nodded his long head sagely. "For myself I refrain, conscious that young females look upon the activity as a step leading to a husband who will meet their needs and feed their greeds; and even for successful ones, it may easily be an exercise in futility."

Mary plunged into a silence in which she examined her motives and those of her sisters, and she frowned deeply. Her sisters had met their husbands at such gatherings, of course, and for two of them the marriage had resulted in their needs being met. But she steadfastly refused to ascribe greed to either of them. Jane sincerely loved Bingley, even when she thought he had forgotten her. Elizabeth, it is true, called Darcy proud—insufferably so—but she married him without thinking of herself. Rather, she atoned for having refused Mr. Collins, which forfeited the living of Longbourn. No, it was never greed that led Elizabeth to accept the rich Darcy but contrition and concern for her family, and Mary applauded her selfless action. And what of Lydia, the not-to-be-mentioned eloper? If anything, she married a man who looked for her to feed his greed.

Mr. Grantley raised his eyebrows over his glasses. "You say nothing. Have I offended you?"

"No," Mary said slowly, "but I question the justice of ascribing greed to all young women. I reviewed my sisters' marriages, and not one of them could have been so. It is a pity you did not know them."

"And your sister Catherine, does she not seek a well-to-do husband?" He stared at the dancers, possibly at Kitty, whose pink gown whirled prettily, its gossamer net flaring.

Mary glanced at his profile, struck by his pronounced nose, and she followed his gaze to her sister. "Certainly not by dancing with the Lucas boys." The thought made her smile. "In fact, she has known all the men here since we were children, except for Colonel Fitzwilliam and you, sir. She danced with the Colonel, as I did, because he is a house guest, but surely she would not think of marrying him. He is over thirty!"

"So she does not dance to find a beau? Do you really think so?"

"She does not tonight, certainly. Kitty dances because she enjoys dancing. She has more energy for it than I do, and she finds the exercise agreeable."

"Perhaps you are too kind in assessing your sister. To me she seems like all the others, smiling ingratiatingly so as to bewitch her partners."

Mary shrugged. "I speak truth as I see it. But why not be kind? It has often been said that charity begins at home." What a strange man he was! Had not her mother told her so? She recalled that his first arrival drew curious glances despite his long face, until his melancholy temperament caused most ladies to ignore him as fully as he seemed to ignore them. Even Lady Lucas, who rarely paid attention to any but her family, denounced him as a destroyer of the merriment one looked for at assemblies. He seemed now to be musing solemnly to himself, fingering his watch fob thoughtfully.

He murmured, "And over thirty is too old?" He looked at Mary. "Pray, tell me, what age do you fancy me to be?"

She studied his stern face, judged his question to be serious, and mumbled, "I really could not say. I am no judge of ages."

Grantley considered that, again eyes on the dancers, and said, almost to himself, "And likely could not care."

At this moment, Richard Lucas skipped over to Mary and asked her to dance. "Kitty won't dance with me again. She says I was clumsy and broke one of her shoe roses. Miss Mary, won't you?"

Mary sighed and stood, surprised to find that Richard was now almost as tall as she. "Richard, you must first beg Mr. Grantley's pardon."

Richard did so, with careful politeness. Mary also excused herself, and she took the floor with Richard. He danced well, if anything more carefully than she, and thankfully without talking. Afterward, she complimented him on knowing all the figures and performing them so smoothly. Then she made her way to Maria Lucas, who had beckoned. "Tell me about Colonel Fitzwilliam. Is he really the son of an Earl?"

"Yes. The second son; he is no viscount. But for a cousin of Mr. Darcy he is a remarkably pleasant man." As Mary spoke she led the way to the supper room, where Maria reported to her mother, whence the question had originated. Mary found her mother, and they called Kitty, as it was time to order the carriage.

Not until the following day did Mrs. Philips relay to Mrs. Bennet what she had learned from Mrs. Long about Grantley and Mary. Mrs. Bennet called Mary to ask the nature of their conversation, but Mary could recall little. "He just criticized young ladies who dance, as if they all were setting their caps for a husband." Even as Mary remembered it, she realized that his conjecture fit the young ladies' mothers more than them, but of course, she did not say this.

"What an odious man! He comes to assemblies to talk of government and pass judgement on dancers, does he? Well, he ought to follow Mr. Bennet's example and stay home if he feels that way. Why punish himself and the rest of us by deliberately coming to watch what he abhors?"

Mary had no answer but that did not keep Mrs. Bennet from going on about it for twenty minutes.

COLONEL FITZWILLIAM LEFT THE NEXT MORNING FOR Derbyshire, bearing Mr. Bennet's letter for Elizabeth, Mrs. Bennet's note for Jane, the assurance that the Bennets meant to be in Derbyshire for Elizabeth's lying-in, and a certainty concerning his own plans. He hoped the news he carried from Hertfordshire would soften the blow of what he supposed he carried from Kent. Within his hearing, Lady Catherine had never spoken a kind word about "that upstart girl who stole Darcy from my Anne," and he feared that the note he carried to Elizabeth Darcy would bring her little joy. He mused on the possibility that the same formidable lady may soon feel equal rancour toward Miss Caroline Bingley, assuming that Miss Bingley accepted him. Mary Bennet's fortunate advice had settled his hopes on Miss Bingley who, he immediately realized, would welcome his attentions more readily than would Georgiana Darcy, who perhaps still thought of him as a guardian.

As he travelled, he wondered how the stylish Caroline would like his modest Norfolk village, and they her. But he firmly believed that she would welcome having a home of her own, no matter where. Could any woman really fancy dependence on a brother or her married sister for a lifetime? Better for Caroline, he trusted she would feel, to have her own home and family than to be attached to a brother, be he ever so amiable. As for the younger Georgiana, she would have many suitors, especially if she grew out of her shyness; and even if none were found suitable for her, Pemberley could supply the needs of many family members with little loss to anyone's privacy.

When he had mentioned Elizabeth's condition to Lady Catherine, he wondered if she had thought, as he did, of Anne de Bourgh's frailty. Could she ever endure or survive a pregnancy? More likely, a husband to Anne might well be little more than caretaker of his wife and of her property. Of course, he assured Lady Catherine that he and Darcy would always do whatever they could for Anne, thinking seriously that she might be better off by forgoing marriage entirely.

At Lambton he left the post house and found Billum, the horse Darcy had promised to leave at the livery stable in time for his return. Mounting, he raced to Pemberley, the hour being late. Almost as soon as he arrived, he was greeted by Georgiana, who had waited up hoping he would come. Upon his enquiry, she assured him that Elizabeth was fine. "There is no sign that the baby will come early. The doctor reckoned it will come by Martinmas or a little earlier but surely no sooner than late October," she said as she led him to the small parlour.

"You will be happy to know," said the Colonel, depositing his packet on a low table, "that you need no longer refer to the child as 'it.' Lady Catherine has pronounced it a boy." He tried to imitate the dowager's regal tones. "The Darcys *always* had a boy first."

Georgiana laughed. "Lady Catherine has decreed: a boy it must be." Then she posed the serious question she had waited up to learn. "Did Aunt Catherine soften toward my brother? Has she forgiven Elizabeth? Will she be able to come this year for Christmas?"

Fitzwilliam squirmed a bit, wishing for an assurance he would dearly love to give her. "At first, I had greatly hoped so. She took Mrs. Darcy's note calmly, nodded at the invitation as if it was to be expected, and enquired about Elizabeth's health. But later, when she grew stronger, she turned her whole attention to Anne, as if nothing mattered but to take care of Anne, although Anne seemed fine to me." He did not feel free to mention the note he held for Elizabeth, and he certainly would not bring up the offer Lady Catherine had made concerning her daughter. Briefly he wondered how the Darcys would have accepted such a project, which would prevent Darcy from ever inheriting Rosings Park.

Georgiana had ordered a substantial, cold collation, which two footmen now brought him. "My brother has persuaded Elizabeth to retire early, and he thought you would be tired. He will meet you at breakfast to discuss your visit." The Colonel was grateful for this.

In the breakfast room the next morning, after hearing of Lady Catherine's concern for Anne and of her suggestion to the Colonel, Darcy chuckled. "Really? Do not decline for my sake, I pray you. I never coveted Rosings. Even if I have many sons, I would not wish to send any as far as Kent. Consider your own future."

Fitzwilliam opened to Darcy that he had indeed considered his future, one in which he did not function as agent to another's property. He rather thought about a woman willing to attach to him and his own property, modest as it was, and he ventured to mention aloud the name of his choice: Caroline Bingley.

Darcy raised his eyebrows at this. "I believe that such a proposal would meet with pleased acceptance, not only with Caroline, but with Charles and Jane as well. My only concern…" He paused to express it as carefully as possible. "Do you feel she would brighten your home?"

Fitzwilliam briefly reflected. "I do. Surely she will be happier as mistress of her own home than as a dependent sister, and she is bright enough when happy."

Darcy nodded thoughtfully. They turned then to consider the apparent failure of the reconciliation Elizabeth's note to Lady Catherine had invited. Darcy showed little enough concern. "She cannot forgive my breaking a promise my mother made for me. Did you assure her that, but for Elizabeth's being with child, I would have attended her in her illness?"

Fitzwilliam acknowledged that he had done so, and he also recounted his hopes in her relenting during the worst of her illness. "Only with her returning strength did she dismiss all concerns but for Anne, for whom she showed the deepest anxiety for some reason. She seemed to want to only see her provided for."

Darcy responded with something like amusement. "Poor Lady Catherine! She has grown so fond of running other people's lives that a brush with death serves only to affront her with the vision that, when she is gone, others may decide for themselves."

Fitzwilliam, glad to see that Darcy did not suffer greatly from the disappointment, disclosed his errand to Mrs. Darcy. "Lady Catherine sent a written reply to Mrs. Darcy's invitation. Perhaps all is not lost."

Darcy, visibly surprised, considered this. "You may be right. She has not written one word in reply to Lizzy's other letters. I will see Mrs. Darcy later, when she rises. Shall I tell her you will come to her sitting room for tea this afternoon? I fear we have much business to consult about before then."

The Colonel, always glad for Pemberley's hospitality, agreed readily. He rose from breakfast, walked to the window, and admired the yellowing witch hazel shrubs near his favourite trout stream. Perhaps he would visit it later that morning. His fingers touched the notes in his pocket, and he turned back as Darcy sliced another piece of ham from the sideboard. "Oh yes. I also stopped at Longbourn. Mr. Bennet sent a note for his daughter, which you may wish to give her."

Darcy replied that both missives could wait until afternoon, when Fitzwilliam may present them himself. The Colonel relaxed. "The Bennets assured me they would be here in mid-October—that is, Mrs. Bennet and Miss Mary will attend Mrs. Darcy's lying-in, while Mr. Bennet and Miss Catherine will stay with the Bingleys until the Christmas holidays. Mrs. Bennet claims she stayed with Jane for her firstborn, and she wishes to be with Elizabeth for hers. And she seems to like having Mary with her."

For Darcy, this furthered his wish for the reconciliation Elizabeth worked so perseveringly to obtain. Miss Mary Bennet, at her last visit, had expressed dismay at "such a gross rift in a Christian family." Mrs. Bennet, he had to admit, made little of it. And though she tended to speak a bit too much for his taste, he welcomed her coming to be with Elizabeth. He daily found himself becoming more concerned about the coming event, remembering too often that his own mother had not long survived Georgiana's birth. Fortunately, Elizabeth came from hardy stock, and it could not hurt to have the advice of Mrs. Bennet, who seemed lively enough after five births. Jane too, he recalled, had grown strong after Beth's birth, even consenting to a strenuous move from Hertfordshire to Nottingham—he took this as further encouragement that all would be well.

The Colonel went looking for fishing tackle, and Darcy mused on the coming visit and on the visits of the two previous holidays. Having grown more accustomed to his acquired family, he acknowledged that he liked them far more than he had ever anticipated. The first year, they stayed but a fortnight because Jane was still at Netherfield and Mrs. Bennet insisted on seeing the new year in with the Bingleys. Mr. Bennet had spent the entire time watching his "beloved Lizzy" as if trying to discern any hint of unhappiness. Darcy had grown anxious lest Bennet notice her discomfort at hostessing so large a gathering, mostly neighbours she had hardly met before. But on the whole, Bennet had left content.

By the second Christmas, Bennet had stolen a few intermediate visits on his own and had opened up to Darcy, who warmed to him as he had previously warmed to Mrs. Bennet's brother, Mr. Gardiner. In fact, on one occasion, the three of them had fished together most companionably. Mrs. Bennet, whose concern for the Bingleys had occupied her first Pemberley visit, relaxed for the second one, when the Bingleys, having settled in nearby Nottingham, were present at Pemberley's Christmas ball. Consequently, Elizabeth's mother spent her time exploring Pemberley, exclaiming like a child over each luxury. "Oh Lizzy! The avenue!" "Oh Lizzy! The silver!" "Oh Lizzy! The carriages!" Later they learned that she had returned to Longbourn with a sizable list of items to describe for all of her Hertfordshire neighbours. Also, by that second Christmas visit, young Catherine no longer pouted over the dearth of military men in the area. Having visited the Bingleys often in the meantime, she had gained a touch of Jane's serenity, and she found delight in surveying the grounds on fine days and exploring the grand house on wet ones. And by that time, Darcy had found Mary a bit less rigid. Perhaps, having spent some months at Longbourn alone with

her garrulous mother during Catherine's Nottingham visits, she had
come to read and ponder less. He had to admit too that Georgiana
warmly welcomed Mary, who shared her joy in music. He hoped
for a deepening of that friendship in the longer visit that had been
proposed that year. While Mary had been with Georgiana to listen
and play duets with her, Georgiana had not so frequently hovered
dreamily at her instrument, fingering a melody she seemed to strain
over. He did not recognize it himself, and once he'd asked her if she
composed it. Georgiana then shook her head, saying it was in her
memory somewhere, but she could never finish it. At least with Mary,
they both played tunes they knew or had music for, and Georgiana's
moments of quiet melancholy over the lost song disappeared.

It was Georgiana who pointed out that, on the whole, the Bennets
treated the servants with respect and appreciation for their extra
holiday duties, and in that, they did far better than did Bingley's
sisters, who seemed to operate on the premise that ordering around
servants established their superior elegance. And, amused as Darcy
was at Mrs. Bennet's counting stairways and touching furniture to
assess materials, the whole family had worked their way into his
heart. The one comment he had bristled at was Mrs. Bennet's, "Oh
Lizzy, you have done so much better than Jane—except that Jane
has given us a grandchild." Well, this Christmas that annoyance
must disappear. Theirs would be a long stay at Pemberley, and he
determined that Pemberley would welcome them heartily.

Delia interrupted his thoughts, as she looked in at the breakfast
room to tell Darcy that the mistress was up and breakfasted and
awaiting him in her sitting room. He jumped up. "And how does
she look today?"

Delia giggled. "Bloomin,' sir."

Chapter 5

Upstairs, Darcy tapped at Elizabeth's door and entered. Elizabeth, her head bent over her needlework, waved him over. He kissed her cheek, saying, "You can look at me, Lizzy, unless you fear such a sight may turn the child ugly."

Elizabeth smiled at him. "I may as well—it is probably too late to worry about such things. It has been kicking for days."

"Your mother arrives soon. Shall we pamper her in the grand orchid room?"

"What a capital idea! She will spend all her time memorising it to describe for the astonishment of Mrs. Philips and Lady Lucas."

"And Mary?"

Elizabeth thought awhile. "She would like something not too handy to Mama and very handy to the library. The blue room?"

"Fine. I'll tell Mrs. Reynolds." Darcy pulled up an ottoman near her chaise, sat on it, and told her of Colonel Fitzwilliam's trip. "He has some letters for you, and he desires to see you himself."

Elizabeth set aside the white christening robe she worked on. "Since you forbid the stairs to me, he will have to come up here for tea. Or would you prefer to carry me down?"

Darcy surveyed her girth with a look of exaggerated dismay. "I will send him up. I may even join you." He pulled his perch closer. "Lizzy, I need your advice. Until yesterday, I thought I knew exactly what I wanted for Kympton's new vicar. Like my late father, I looked for a gentleman of good character, settled in marriage, experienced in divine services, unconcerned about tithes, and able to afford three thousand pounds for the living. I interviewed six young clergymen and had practically settled on Edward Smythe, who answered all my requirements. Now, as it nears the time Reverend Wynters means to retire, I become unsure."

Elizabeth met his eyes, her own eyes sparkling and her mouth a playful upturn. "You had not listed indecision among your vices before we married."

His gaze echoed hers. "If I had enumerated them all, would you ever have relented and agreed to marry me?"

Elizabeth looked down, red-faced. "Now you remind me how worthless my opinion must be on important matters. I was at first so wrong about you."

"Not at all." He admired her fine eyes, thanking God he'd had the good sense to love her.

More serious now, Elizabeth asked, "And yesterday, what happened?"

"There came young Steven Oliver, the son of an ostler educated by a sympathetic vicar. He has been but two years in orders and has spent the whole of it as curate at Ramsgate under Reverend Leighton, who grew up near Kympton and recommended that Oliver try for the post. But Oliver is unmarried, has saved very little toward the living, and sorely needs the tithes. Also, none of his letters of recommendation mention his sermons or his knowledge of ritual."

Elizabeth waited patiently for him to define his dilemma. He continued, "Yet, this man spoke lovingly of his parishioners at Ramsgate and was sympathetic to their needs. Unfortunately, he saw little opportunity there for a vicarage. His letters say chiefly that the people will miss him greatly, and he acknowledges that he will miss them. He asked about the people of Kympton, had already visited the church and the village, spoke enthusiastically about my collection of early church Fathers in the library, told of some young people he had met in Kympton—the Langley girls and Fred Hooks, by his descriptions—and when he left, Mrs. Reynolds took his cause as her own. How can I ignore him?"

Elizabeth did not know. "So… are you changing your requirements?" Mentally, she recalled that his father must have done the same when he proposed young Wickham for the post, but she did not care to mention that name.

Darcy frowned. "As soon as he left, it struck me that Mr. Smythe had never asked about the villagers nor did his recommendations contain the warmth I discerned in Oliver's. He had been far more assured than was Oliver, yet he appeared to have noted nothing of Pemberley, and he had not even visited Kympton. Oliver's manner, more tentative and halting than Smythe's, may better fit the country people he seeks to serve. He also mentioned a desire to serve for a time under Reverend Wynters, whose reputation the Reverend Leighton had esteemed."

Elizabeth reached again for the christening robe and the lace she meant to attach to it. "Mr. Smythe may have reasoned that competence was your only concern. Or he may wish to meet the people and judge them for himself. Surely some of his references came from ordinary parishioners?"

Darcy stood and paced the room. "They were, comparatively, most literate ones… and Mrs. Reynolds said he sat waiting for me while she dusted the foyer, and he never said a word to her."

Elizabeth looked up smiling. "You have Mrs. Reynolds's opinion, and that should suffice. After all, it was Mrs. Reynolds's praise of you that first caused me to question my prejudice against you."

Darcy's eyebrows raised in surprise. "Really? I must raise her salary." He rubbed his chin thoughtfully, and Elizabeth felt his quandary. She knew that deep-seated convictions about requirements for a position—as for a husband—altered only with great effort. Darcy frowned. "When I invited him to question me, Oliver asked about the elderly and how they were served, and he wondered if the young people had ready means of involvement. Also, he hoped, if chosen, to spend some hours in my fine library." He studied Elizabeth's calm face as she worked deftly. He went on. "Oliver is not yet thirty and is unmarried. I question whether he is mature enough. What do you think, dear?"

"That he could get over it." She pressed with her fingers the embroidery and lace at the hem. "And he knows the rites of the church, surely?"

Darcy nodded. "And now you seem to favour both."

"Observe how I have reformed. My prejudices now tend toward the favourable." She smiled as she held out the robe to admire her work. "But, Darcy, if you know what you prefer in a vicar, choose the one more likely to accept your influence and grow. Does that help?"

Darcy stopped pacing and regarded her with pride and love, looking for all the world as if she had made his choice. "Very much. I will write to him." He left for his study.

Elizabeth wondered at his sudden decision, musing on whether Bingley's penchant for precipitate choices had been contagious.

Then she watched the late morning sun filter into the upper chamber she had grown, perforce, to enjoy. Was it her mother's five pregnancies, she wondered, that had taught her to spend times of crisis in her sitting room? It could not improve upon a walk in the woods, but the place had nevertheless a calming, meditative effect. What manner of mother would she make? She had achieved no great obedience as a wife, for twice last week fine weather had enticed her down the forbidden stairs and out to the gardens. Even in the yellowing autumn, a walk invigorated her, as a walk—or in her case a waddle—had always done. Elizabeth mused also on the pros and cons of confinement. She had been spared some months of hostessing her at-homes, a blessing she would have loved in those first trying months of receiving Darcy's neighbours and acquaintances, most of whom dropped in out of curiosity to see his bride. She vaguely remembered stately, white-haired Lord Exbridge and jolly Lady Exbridge, who had amused and teased her into relaxation on one of her first at-homes. They had finished by inviting her to their country residence some ten or fifteen miles west of Pemberley. She and Darcy never returned that visit, as not long after that first meeting Lady Exbridge and her son were killed in a carriage accident on an icy bridge. Excepting only the funeral, even Darcy had not seen Lord Exbridge since then. He had vacated his country house for his London seat with its better memories and had remained in solitary mourning ever since, discouraging all visits. For a while, Darcy worked to bring him out of his sadness but was always refused entrance by a sympathetic but solemn servant. Lizzy deeply regretted the loss of those neighbours who had been the lone bright and saving grace of her first days as mistress of Pemberley.

She turned her thoughts to more familiar neighbours who had come to be regulars: Mrs. Langley of Kympton had seemed as nervous as Lizzy on that first visit. She stayed only long enough to present the new bride with a jar of excellent plum jam. How Lizzy praised it when next she came, until she noticed that poor Mrs. Langley accepted her praise most uneasily, making Lizzy wonder how the mistress of a manor should comport herself. She simply broke down and told Mrs. Langley of her own nervousness, assuring her guest that she never intended to spread her unease around. Then they laughed, relaxed, and became friends.

It was harder with Lady Elliott, Georgiana's mentor and friend in London. When she first visited, Elizabeth detected some jealousy, possibly arising from Georgiana's praise of her new sister. Or perhaps Lady Elliott feared that Lizzy would usurp the lady's role in Georgiana's life. Elizabeth sighed. She hoped by now Lady Elliott, whom she liked well, saw that Lizzy meant to be a sister to Miss Darcy, and certainly no companion in London, a place Lizzy had never learned to appreciate. She knew that Lady Elliott could teach Georgiana far more about fashion and manners than she ever could.

Had she ever grown accustomed to being mistress of Pemberley? She felt so, but still she did enjoy these weeks of respite from the social duties, and she was glad Georgiana had agreed to act in her stead. She would like to be able to peek in on her as hostess, fearing that Georgiana must miss the help of Mrs. Annesley since her coming of age. Now she must offer refreshments while Mrs. Reynolds provided protection when Miss Johnstone visited. Oh, Alicia Johnstone had been an education indeed for Lizzy.

Elizabeth adjusted the pillows at her back and stretched a bit as she thought of that fateful first visit from the rosy-faced, lumbering, and strange Miss Johnstone. To this day, she wondered how Miss Johnstone's voice would sound if she did not mutter, head down, in an apologetic whimper, "Oh, the fortunate Mrs. Darcy... I knew him first, you know. He might have married me." There had been no one like Miss Johnstone in Hertfordshire. And how many "souvenirs" of Pemberley had the lady managed to sneak out in her oversized reticule before Mrs. Reynolds caught on? By now a harmless game had developed, the sharp-eyed Mrs. Reynolds following the wandering visitor into nearby parlours to see her chubby hand snatch some small ornamental piece and later cueing Lizzy to retrieve and replace the item as she quietly showed the lady to the door. There was never a hint of shame, nor did that strange neighbour resist being shown out. But always the inevitable, "It might have been mine, you know. I saw him first." Elizabeth had offered to let Delia do the search-and-retrieve act, but Mrs. Reynolds, noble soul, insisted that she did not mind at all, that in fact, it somewhat enlivened the day.

"How have I managed to get used to all this and even learn to enjoy it?" Lizzy asked herself. Darcy, that was how.

# Chapter 6

THAT AFTERNOON, COLONEL FITZWILLIAM THANKED ELIZABETH for receiving him and tried to retail all the news from Kent. "Charlotte Collins sends her love. She keeps busy trying to adopt all Lady Catherine's prescriptions for raising children. I believe she did not appreciate Lady Catherine's returning health as much as Mr. Collins did." Fitzwilliam took time to admire the fine work on the nearly-finished christening robe. Then he sat fidgeting until Elizabeth asked what bothered him.

"I did not tell Darcy, but I do worry about Lady Catherine. During her illness, she called for him urgently, as if he were needed for something. Then after recovering, she spoke no more of him."

"Returning health brought returning stubbornness as well?"

"Perhaps. She spoke of the de Bourgh estate as if it were falling into danger, and she wailed incessantly about Anne's future, uncertain about her daughter on account of what she called the 'wretched old age' of both herself and Mrs. Jenkinson. She even asked me to consider marrying Anne."

Elizabeth's eyebrows went up. "What a fine offer! And it is a pretty property for an earl's second son."

He laughed. "Not so pretty to my mind. And I couldn't help thinking she deliberately ignored Darcy—possibly even intending to spite him by alienating the estate from him. At least there was something, I felt sure, that she withheld. When I told her that truly Anne did look well and appeared in fine spirits, she looked away, coughed, and said it did not matter. That was not like her. At any rate, Anne is of age, but I have no intention of becoming the steward of her property—which is about all her husband will be."

Elizabeth nodded wisely. "Actually, since last year's holidays, I have been half expecting to hear that you had proposed to Miss Bingley. She certainly smiled on you all through the ball, and I thought you got on well together."

Fitzwilliam snapped, "Did Darcy tell you that?"

She started, surprised, and examined his chiseled features, again trying to find some resemblance to her handsome husband. "No indeed. He told me only that you carried letters for me."

Fitzwilliam apologised then, both for his ungallant reaction and for forgetting the letters, and he drew out the packet just as tea was brought in. Elizabeth stifled her wish to tease his secret out of him and let the subject of Caroline Bingley drop. She poured his tea and offered plum cake and fruit. After pouring her own tea, she opened Lady Catherine's letter.

A few moments later Darcy arrived, poured his own tea, greeted the Colonel, and stared at Elizabeth, who seemed in a trance, her letter resting on her sorry excuse for a lap. "What is it, darling?" Worry crept into his voice.

Elizabeth looked up and smiled. "Oh! I was still doing it homage. Here." She held out the short note. "I believe I am ordered to serve you a son." She watched, amused, as Darcy read his aunt's note, his teeth growing tighter and his face darker as he read.

"What kind of reply is this?" he thundered.

Elizabeth put a gentle hand on his. "After all, it is an answer, even an acceptance. When we have been ignored for two years, this has to be an improvement. Let us enjoy the progress."

Colonel Fitzwilliam looked from one to the other. "An acceptance? What does she say?" Then he flushed and asked pardon for his boldness.

Darcy put him at his ease, cleared his throat, assumed a stance of despotic authority, and intoned, "'Finally you give my nephew an heir. Anne and I will arrive to see the boy on the Wednesday before Christmas. Prepare the orchid room for me and the gold room for Anne. Our two maids and a footman need rooms above us, and Mrs. Jenkinson will stay next to Anne, as always. We stay until Candlemas. Have your son christened during that time. Lady Catherine de Bourgh.'" In his own voice, still determined, Darcy added, "Those rooms are taken."

Elizabeth, laughing at his performance, shook her head playfully. "No. Mama will like to be nearer our rooms, and Lady Elliott will never know she has been moved."

Darcy held the note cushioned flat on his hand and relegated it ceremoniously to the grate, where it burst into flame.

Elizabeth gasped in mock horror. "Have you no respect for my letter?"

"Of course. I merely assured that it adds warmth to our home." He relaxed, sat to drink his tea, and told them both of his choice for vicar of Kympton. "Young Oliver will stay until year's end in the gardener's cottage. I will be glad to have it occupied again." He turned to Fitzwilliam. "Brooks, you know, married a widow last year, and now resides with her in Lambton, coming daily to tend my gardens." He looked again at Lizzy. "Oliver can use Billum to reach Kympton as often as he wishes to consult Reverend Wynters and acquaint himself with the parish."

Elizabeth thought briefly of the choice, praying that Mr. Oliver would prove better for the parish than Mr. Darcy senior's choice, Wickham, would have been. Then she read her father's letter, learning of Mr. Collins's concerns for his daughter, as if the raising of her would not be principally Charlotte's responsibility. Somehow that sensible Charlotte managed to quietly keep Mr. Collins from realizing how little the household order depended on him. What a clever woman she was! As Lizzy finished her letter, she laughed aloud, and Darcy looked up in interest. She responded to his unspoken question, "Papa says he gave Mary one of Pope's essays to read, hoping she might profit from the line, 'To err is human, to forgive, divine.' He deplores her habit of ignoring Lydia as if she did not exist. But he says that as she read, she found many snippets to note and quote, but that one was not among them. Finally he came out and asked her what she made of that line. She said, quite solemnly, 'Forgiveness is the prerogative of God Himself and of Him alone.' Papa felt properly foiled in his attempt to guide her reading."

Darcy shared the humour of the item, and then, reminded of his own sister, he said, "Lizzy, you would enjoy watching Georgiana as she entertains visitors on your at-home days. I almost think she has studied your manner to imitate it. She tells me you warned her about the acquisitive Miss Johnstone, and she has calmly helped Mrs. Reynolds to confront her on two occasions, rescuing a vase and a small mirror. I am quite proud of her."

Elizabeth agreed. "She does well indeed." She grew thoughtful. "Poor Alicia Johnstone! She told me she came here as a child once and saw you and Wickham playing by the stream. From that time she dreamed of being mistress of Pemberley and likes to pretend that she is even now. Mrs. Reynolds, who is fully aware of her propensity to assume ownership, simply cues the hostess to perform the confrontation."

"That lady was a hoyden from her childhood! Why on earth do you permit her visits? Surely you would be more at ease if she were forbidden from visiting the manor?"

"No. I visited here once myself after refusing you. By then I had read your letter and felt differently about the honour you had offered, and this place gave me a wistful feeling because I thought it was forever lost to me. Miss Johnstone seems so wilted of spirit when I speak to her. I prefer to have more compassion than distaste for withered lilies—or even withered hoydens."

Darcy said, "That prodigious lady's resemblance to a lily or indeed to anything withered is a contradiction of the highest order." He exchanged a look with Fitzwilliam that shared his esteem for the charming mistress of Pemberley, grateful anew that she had at last accepted Darcy's proposal.

## Chapter 7

THE BENNETS ARRIVED AT PEMBERLEY, AS PROMISED, IN MID-October, though Mr. Bennet and Catherine stayed but a day. Mr. Bennet visited Elizabeth in her sitting room, stifling his discomfort at the delicate elegance of its furniture. He sat on the edge of one ornate chair, as Elizabeth tried to keep back her smile at his unease. After asking about her health, Bennet voiced his request. "I leave Mary to you, hoping you may instill in her a few social graces. She has made a conquest in Hertfordshire: an unusual young man who currently leases Netherfield. His name is Grantley—the Honourable Lewis Grantley, M.P.—and I believe our neighbours all agree that she is the only young lady he has singled out for conversation." Bennet attempted to sit up straighter, found he almost tipped the chair, and resumed his former perilous perch. "Before we left Longbourn, that stiff young man called on me, ostensibly to interest me in a bill he plans to support in Parliament, something about the flogging of soldiers. He means to introduce legislation that will proscribe all physical punishment for any offence short of treason. After his discourse on that subject, he began to hem and look uneasy, and finally, he produced a small book and asked me to give it to Mary, in whose mind he is interested. The essays in it were by American authors, and they all extolled the joys of freedom. I cautioned him that Mary's propensity to read serious works did not include the likelihood of her understanding them in quite the way authors intended. "He actually seemed heartened by the idea that the interpretations will be all her own, as he esteems her mind an original one, and left in a sanguine frame of mind." Bennet took Elizabeth's smile as agreement and so finished. "See if you can prepare her to be the wife of an M.P.—just in case."

It amused Elizabeth that her father now played her mother's game: jumping to thoughts of marriage over any insubstantial hint that her daughter might have a chance. But she fully intended to do his bidding, and she mentally reviewed the yard goods she had on hand, meaning to interest Mary in needlework. She did not see why hands so good at the pianoforte should not also ply the needle more often than Mary's did, and she meant to devote an hour or so of each afternoon making linens and other items for a trousseau— just in case! Perhaps, Elizabeth mused, marriage had made her a matchmaker like her mother.

Mr. Bennet and Catherine left the next day with the Bingleys to settle at their estate, which Catherine called "Otherfield," chiefly because, she said, it was so much finer than Netherfield. Then Mrs. Bennet, as soon as she was settled in the room near Elizabeth's, began proposing a regimen of exercises for her daughter. When told that Mr. Darcy seemed rather to recommend almost constant rest, Mrs. Bennet kept right on showing her how to tighten muscles and stretch her arms and legs. Though usually much in awe of Darcy, Mrs. Bennet sniffed. "What do men know?" She hastened to add, "Oh, humour him, of course, when he is present. But otherwise, do all you can to strengthen your back and torso. You will need much strength." She went on demonstrating, moving Elizabeth's arms and legs, and urging her to breathe deeply. Elizabeth felt a sense of entering a mother lore that may have come from Mrs. Gardiner—the grandmother she never knew—and she complied readily.

On the accustomed at-home day when Georgiana received morning callers, Elizabeth asked Mary to assist her. Not knowing exactly what to do, Mary told Georgiana she would sit in a corner and watch her for a while. She soon noticed that many callers seemed familiar to both Georgiana and Mrs. Reynolds, and Mary had her first taste of an at-home day in a fine manor. Soon little knots of guests extended even into her corner, and she became privy to their conversations. A very pretty young matron spoke her unmitigated approval of the absent lady of the house. "I always enjoy calling here, and Miss Darcy is an excellent hostess, but I do miss Mrs. Darcy. I feel so at ease in her presence."

The large, rather square lady to whom she spoke could not agree. "Miss Darcy is real gentry and was born to the manor. Mrs. Darcy is from Hertfordshire. She does not know our ways."

Mary watched as the lovely lady sipped her tea daintily, and her companion reached out for the scones that had been offered, spilling her own tea into its saucer. Mary turned her attention to the newcomers Georgiana greeted as Mrs. and Miss Langley. She studied their faces to see if she could remember them, hoping to attach names to them should they meet again. For a while she followed them with her eyes as they made way for even later arrivals, took tea, and went off to sit near the fireplace.

When Mary returned her attention to the two near her, the large lady was complaining of a shoulder ache. "I can hardly extend my arm, you know. I fear the intense pain will cripple me entirely. The surgeon prescribed hot packs, you know, and Katy applies them regularly, three times daily, but to no avail. Soon I fear I must give up the use of my right arm entirely. Even to hold a teacup sends rays of pain through me from elbow to neck." Her companion made sympathetic sounds and said something about a change of physicians. "Oh no, indeed, Mrs. Jennings. I quite depend on Mr. Williams." The tray of cakes went round, and as they were offered to the pretty lady, the other reached for one, attaining it before the tray came to her. As she used her right hand, Mary winced for her, but the lady herself seemed hardly discomposed at the motion.

Mrs. Jennings refused the desserts politely, adding to her companion, "I will wait for the fruit if you please. I try to limit my sweets, Miss Johnstone, which I find make me a bit slow of foot about my work in the garden."

Miss Johnstone agreed. "I quite know what you mean. I find myself winded at a mere stroll in the shrubbery. I am ever so careful of what I eat, and yet I notice no improvement. I am sure it is the fault of my constitution. My dear mother was the same. Oh, there is that sour-faced Mrs. Leighton. One should not aspire to be thin if it deprives one of a talent for happiness!"

Mary again turned her attention elsewhere, admiring Georgiana's aplomb while conversing with all her guests. She thought Mrs. Reynolds seemed intent on watching the two closest to her, Mrs. Jennings and Miss Johnstone, the whole time. Then Miss Johnstone excused herself, extricated herself from her chair with some difficulty, and headed for the adjacent parlour. Mrs. Reynolds followed her there. As other guests too began to take their leave, Georgiana brought Mary to her and introduced her as Mrs. Darcy's sister who would be visiting them for a while. They all smiled and welcomed her. Later, when most were gone, Mary realized she had seen nothing of Miss Johnstone. Mrs. Reynolds hurried in then, whispered to Georgiana, and took her place with the remaining guests, while Georgiana hurried to the small parlour. Mary felt glad indeed when she too could excuse herself and seek out the library. At-home day at a great manor did not much appeal to her.

Slightly ahead of schedule, on November the eighth, the Darcy boy arrived in a painfully long ordeal Lizzy could never have imagined, and she appreciated all the work at strengthening her muscles. The surgeon, who had been requested to stay in the house just the day before, assisted the birth, as did an attendant nurse-midwife, Mrs. Kaye. Finally the doctor handed a bundle to Mrs. Kaye, who washed and wrapped him, and called for Mr. Darcy. Darcy had been right outside the door, had not liked what he had heard from the room until then, and accepted his son a bit gingerly, craning his neck to look at Lizzy, who was being cleaned up while the bed linens were changed beneath her. Having been assured by the doctor that Elizabeth was fine, Darcy relaxed somewhat and regarded his perfect little son. Leaning over Elizabeth, he solemnly asked, "May we call him Charles?"

As Charles squalled and jerked his fists in the air, Elizabeth said, "I'm not sure he likes it." Mrs. Reynolds came in with Mrs. Downey, who was to be the baby's wet nurse, took the baby from Darcy, and handed him to Mrs. Downey, who knew just how to quiet the babe.

"See? He likes it fine." Darcy grinned.

Elizabeth, tired and spent, murmured weakly, "Not Fitzwilliam?"

"Oh no. I never used that name. Why should I give him what I did not like?"

Elizabeth nodded and whispered, "Charles."

Darcy sat next to her and took her hand. "To keep peace with Aunt Catherine, I welcome the boy, else I would have loved a little

Elizabeth and watching her grow. However, Lady Catherine would have blamed you if we had produced a girl, or possibly would have accused us both of intransigence." At this point, Georgiana and Mary were permitted a glimpse of the baby and Elizabeth, who was just nodding off to sleep. The serene picture the room now presented made childbirth a sweet prospect indeed for the young ladies.

In the weeks following, Elizabeth rejoiced in her gradually returning strength, even with the new call in her life for patience, responsibility, and sweet needfulness. She asked Mary to join her in her sitting room each afternoon for an hour of needlework, and Mary, thinking she was helping Elizabeth, gladly did so. She even began to enjoy working the needle and grew adept at it, her fingers strong and disciplined from her musical practise.

When she was again permitted stairs, Elizabeth ventured down to the breakfast room, leaning on Darcy's arm. After breakfast, Callie, the official nursemaid, brought little Charles to place in her arms, and she nursed him, as her mother had urged her to do, despite Mrs. Downey's ministrations. Darcy, who had breakfasted earlier, spent the quiet time reading the day's mail, exclaiming over the many answers to the invitations they had sent for the Christmas ball. "The Gardiners say they will not miss it." "Lady Elliott looks forward to it." "The Langleys gratefully accept." Then an exaggerated groan introduced, "Miss Johnstone will gladly attend." Later, after a long pause, in a sad voice, Darcy read, "Lord Exbridge regrets that he cannot leave his London apartment." Darcy sighed. "Again this year! He cannot seem to accept life without his wife and son. I do wish he would not continue this mournful solitude."

"Has he ever taken your suggestion to invite his daughter-in-law and grandson to live with him?" Elizabeth's voice echoed his sorrow.

"He does not say so, though the invitation included them." Darcy grew determined. "Lizzy, if you are well enough in the spring, we must try to visit him again and urge him to it. He cannot continue to live as if he too died on that icy bridge."

Mrs. Downey and young Callie came in then to take Charles back to the nursery, and Elizabeth reluctantly yielded him to their care. Mrs. Bennet came in frowning as they went out with the child. "Do you not nurse him yourself?"

"Oh yes, Mama. It gives me such a tranquil half-hour to do so. But we must not let Mrs. Downey feel she is not needed."

"Do you think that young Callie is able to handle such an important charge? She cannot be much older than Lydia!"

"Mama, Lydia is old enough and married long enough to have a child herself."

"But she has none, and that is good. She is really too young. And so is that Callie."

Elizabeth shook her head dismissively. "Mama, Callie has cared for three younger brothers of her own. She has more experience with boys than I do! Please do not make her feel incompetent."

Music wafted into the breakfast room from the music room, and Elizabeth hoped Mrs. Bennet would stop to listen. But the lady just said, "Oh, carols," and walked out.

Elizabeth loved to hear Georgiana and Mary practising noels and dances for the coming festivities. The friendship of the two musical members of the family had been good for both. It kept Georgiana from playing that doleful snatch of melody which seemed to haunt her, and Mary no longer played the endlessly droning études she practised so often at Longbourn.

Mrs. Bennet, having spent two weeks nervously and needlessly instructing the long-suffering Mrs. Kaye on midwifery, had of late spent hours pestering the fair-haired, wide-smiling Mrs. Downey with her opinions and her misgivings about young, rosy-cheeked Callie. Fortunately Charles, a healthy, even a robust, child, thrived despite all the fuss. After a time, the nursery routine became established, dampening Mrs. Bennet's spirit so bent on excitement, and she transferred her attentions to the chambermaids preparing rooms for the coming Christmas guests. After all, some of the rooms were for the Bennet and Bingley families, and who better to know what they would want than Mrs. Bennet? She ignored the great buzz over Lady Catherine's requirements, which Mrs. Reynolds struggled to recall from that lady's last visit so long before. Mrs. Reynolds well knew that any item overlooked would constitute the very pivotal necessity that would set Lady Catherine against all the servants. "Remember to tend the fireplaces before seven every morning, put double washstands in their rooms, and each morning at nine bring in two ewers of hot water and two of cold." Mrs. Reynolds cued the chief chambermaids on each idiosyncrasy that she remembered.

Mary elected to stay well out of the way. After a morning hour in the music room, she repaired to the library for an hour or so. It was so handy to her room—just down the hall to the great ballroom and across the dance floor where a small door opened onto a balcony surrounding three sides of the immense library. It was on that balcony, right near her door, that she had discovered a copy of Bunyan's *Pilgrim's Progress*. She would settle in a comfortable, leather chair in the corner of the sturdy balcony, read a bit in her chosen book, and occasionally dip into some poems by Cowper from a volume that was shelved nearby. After that, she usually met the family for a light repast of soup or fruit and nuts, chat awhile—usually about the baby—and return to the library until time to meet Elizabeth for needlework before early dinner. If at that hour the high round east window did not lend sufficient light on a dull November afternoon, she made use of the candle sconce near the chair. There, she gloried in the education she planned to give herself in the magnificent library. Occasionally she drew out a small pad of paper from her pinafore pocket so that, with the pen from the writing desk in the corner, she could jot down a pithy sentence to memorise for some future conversation. She was grateful to have learned this custom from the vicar of Hunsford, whom she, alone of the Bennets, admired.

One afternoon, the squeak of the door below her on the main floor of the library alerted her to someone's entrance. She supposed that Darcy or Bingley had entered, but if both had come in to talk, she must leave or make her presence known. She stood and peered over the great mahogany rail only to see a man alone. He was tall, apparently young, and when she caught his profile, she saw that he had a moustache. She could not identify him nor did she recognize his gait as he strode purposefully to the leather-bound books near the fireplace. The gentleman looked up, book in hand, and acknowledged her with a smile and a bow. She refused to acknowledge the brazen smile, but she nodded stiffly. He settled at a table with his selection, and suddenly Mary realized that she was alone in a room with a strange man. Quickly she shelved her two books, pocketed her papers, replaced the pen in the inkwell desk in the corner, and left through the hall.

Mary found her mother in the nursery telling Callie to "be sure to hold his head" and saw Callie, who had been doing just that, frown at Mrs. Bennet, glaring silently, as if holding her anger in check.

"Mama! There is a strange man in the library!"

"Oh dear. Cannot Darcy prevent the public use of his own library? What would Mr. Bennet think? But perhaps Darcy does not know." Mrs. Bennet wiped her hands and stepped into the hall with Mary. Nurse Callie's face registered relief as Mrs. Bennet reached to close the door. "We must prevent draughts."

Before they found Darcy, however, a hubbub at the foyer drew them to the grand staircase. Elizabeth joined them and they watched Mrs. Reynolds welcome Mr. Bennet and Kitty, who had come early for the holidays. As Mrs. Reynolds told the footman where to take the arrivals' luggage, Elizabeth and the Bennets descended to greet them. Mr. Bennet, uneasy about being on the scene during Elizabeth's lying-in, now hurried to tell her how glad he was that "Little Charlie" had come and that Elizabeth looked well. Catherine rushed to Mary to tell her how bored she had grown at Otherfield. "That Miss Bingley kept gathering Beth into her arms, saying, 'Come to your favourite aunt, honey,' and she treated me like an intruder. I don't suppose you will be calling yourself Charlie's favourite aunt?"

"No indeed, Kitty. I hardly see the baby for thirty minutes a day, and so far what he favours is being fed, as far as I can detect." Mary gladly showed Catherine to her room while Elizabeth stayed to visit their parents. They helped the obliging Polly unpack Kitty's frocks and hang them in the wardrobe. While they worked, Mary told Kitty of the wonderful library, but Kitty barely took notice. Then Mary mentioned the strange man in the library—"tall, with light brown hair and a stride like Wickham's"—and Mary made a face at this, indicating her annoyance at the man.

Kitty, however, looked up with interest. "He wasn't in uniform, was he?"

Mary gave her a look of disgust. "Of course not. And he has a ridiculous little moustache."

Kitty's eyes sparkled. "What a mystery! But how much nicer if he were in regimentals."

"For shame, Kitty. I thought you had stopped being enamoured with officers. Surely after…" Mary stopped short. She had almost mentioned Lydia! She merely shook her head and frowned, hoping that one day Kitty would get redcoats out of her head. Perhaps her unhappy stay at Otherfield had set Catherine back, rather than helping her. "Come on; let me show you my private entrance to the library. We'll be very quiet, in case the man is still there."

Kitty was glad to follow her through the impressive ballroom. She looked around in awe at the high-ceilinged room that stretched over nearly the whole front half of the mansion. "Without Christmas decorations, this room is enormous! I hardly recognized it! Is the library in here?"

"No, but the door is." Mary walked with her through the hall to the unobtrusive small door leading to the balcony, and she opened it noiselessly. Catherine peeked over the polished mahogany railing and saw the gentleman sitting near the fire and chuckling softly while reading his book. Mary, standing behind her, heard the snort followed by a low-pitched laugh, and she looked too. Kitty watched intently, as if willing the man to look up, while Mary whispered, "Come along, Kitty. We must go." Mary turned, expecting her sister to follow.

Instead, Kitty leaned over the ornate railing and said, "Good afternoon, sir."

Mary fled through the door, embarrassed to be seen there and ashamed for Kitty's boldness. Just before the door closed, she heard a pleasant "Afternoon, miss," from below.

In the corridor near her own room, Mary spied Elizabeth pulling her pelisse around her shoulders. Lizzy smiled invitingly. "Mary, if you are not otherwise engaged, would you walk out with me? Papa is tired, and Mama is arranging things in his room. The sun is so invitingly warm for this time of year, I simply must go out. But I may need an arm to lean on."

Mary was not loath to humour her sister, especially the one who had sacrificed so greatly as to marry such a man in order to provide for her sisters. She slipped into her room to don her spencer and came right out, calling, "I cannot read this afternoon at any rate. A strange man came into the library."

Elizabeth laughed, and when Mary joined her near the large stairway, she said, "The 'strange man' is Mr. Oliver, who is soon to be the vicar of Kympton. He means to read the whole of Saint Augustine's works, but Reverend Wynters keeps him busy most days. He is free to come here only on Tuesdays."

Though glad of that, Mary sniffed. "Well, he could not have been reading anything by Saint Augustine just now, Lizzy. He was laughing!"

Elizabeth regarded her quizzically as they descended to approach the side door. "And saints are not funny, I suppose?"

"Certainly not!" Mary could not even imagine such a thing.

They crossed the garden to enjoy the autumn wood and dying witch hazel near the trout stream. Elizabeth pointed out a favourite tree, now a graceful fan of limbs with twigs stark against the pale blue sky. "In summer it spreads like a perfect green umbrella, shading the hillside." She did not add that it was the very tree under which Darcy had surprised her when she and the Gardiners first visited Pemberley. It seemed long ago now, but the tree remained precious to her, though she had been heartily embarrassed at the time. She inhaled the sharp air appreciatively. "How I have missed the woods and hills these last weeks!" She strolled ahead and almost burst into a run as she used to do, but bethought herself and waited to take Mary's arm. "I forget I am no longer a carefree girl. Imagine my being a mother! Will I ever become used to it?"

"Oh, I imagine you will." Mary skirted a briar that reached out over the path. "And just think, Mama and Papa once had to grow accustomed to us. We think of them always as parents, but once they were young and carefree. And now…" Mary paused, not wishing to think them old.

"Grandparents!" Elizabeth finished for her. "And Papa rests after a short ride. He never used to nap in the afternoon. One doesn't like to think of them actually growing old…" Her voice trailed off, as if the thought also saddened her.

Mary looked off in the direction of the stables, where she noted one tree shaped differently from all the others. "Look, Lizzy! All the oaks and maples fan outward, but that tree stretches all its limbs upward, like many hands in prayer!"

Elizabeth smiled. "You have spotted Darcy's precious linden tree. And in summer you would like it even better, when its heart-shaped leaves and delicate yellow blossoms appear. You must spend a summer with us sometime."

A rustle behind them warned of Catherine's approach just before she called, "Lizzy! Mary!" As she caught up, she confronted Mary. "Why did you not stay with me? I talked to him."

Mary rolled her eyes. "Indeed."

"And he said I must apologise to you. He thought he frightened you." Catherine inhaled deeply, happy to slow to her pace.

"He did not frighten me; I simply could not stay alone in a room with a man to whom I have not been introduced."

"La, Mary, don't be such a stick. He is rather nice, even if he is a clergyman, and I think his moustache quite becomes him. He is

61

not so exciting as an officer, but I liked him." Catherine pulled at the cloak she had grabbed hurriedly.

"Then I am surprised that you did not stay there." Mary, who considered a moustache to be a dandyish affectation in a clergyman, tried to meet Elizabeth's eyes to see whether Catherine's boldness had outraged her as well.

"Oh, he said I must excuse him while he returned to Saint Augustine. I asked him what was so funny about Saint Augustine, and he said, 'Another time I will tell you.'"

Elizabeth spoke her motherliness. "Kitty, you mustn't disturb Mr. Oliver. He is serious about his reading, and you know you have not been properly introduced."

Kitty stamped her foot. "You are just like Jane; you want me to be a fine lady like you, I'll warrant." Petulance coloured her voice.

Elizabeth laughed then and took Catherine's arm playfully. "I am no fine lady at all, Kitty, just a tired one. Let's try that bench, and you can tell me about dear Jane." She pointed across the stream.

Mary felt certain that Lizzy could have instructed Kitty more pointedly. But she swallowed her distaste and crossed the footbridge with them to the bank above the stream, where they sat on a weathered but clean wooden bench. Catherine, her spirits revived, gave the Nottingham news and even refrained from complaining about the overweening Caroline Bingley, except to say that she acted of late as if she were Jane's truest sister. For a pleasant interval, they might have been back at Longbourn, recapturing maidenly pursuits. But soon the creeping autumn chill sent them back to Pemberley's fireplaces and a fine tea with the refreshed older Bennets. At dinner that evening, Elizabeth asked Darcy, "Do you suppose Mr. Oliver would come for tea some day? I have been remiss. My sisters and yours have not been introduced to him, and if he is to frequent our library, perhaps he ought to be acquainted with all of us."

Georgiana put in, "Indeed, I have never yet set eyes on him, and Kitty says he is very nice."

Darcy spoke teasingly to Elizabeth, "If he has not been introduced, how is it that Kitty knows he is very nice?"

Kitty coloured at his teasing. "I happened upon him in the library, sir."

Darcy smiled and returned his attention to the succulent pork loin on his plate. "You are in the right, Lizzy. We cannot allow Kitty so great an advantage over her elders. I will ask him to tea on Sunday."

Though the elder Bennets spent Sunday at Otherfield with the Bingleys, the rest of the family enjoyed tea with Mr. Oliver. A somewhat nervous-looking Mr. Oliver acknowledged Elizabeth's introductions with a stiff bow to Mary, to Georgiana, and less solemnly to Kitty, while the girls curtsied formally. When they seated themselves, he hesitantly folded his tall, thin body into the proffered chair. "Miss Catherine was so kind as to introduce herself to me in the library."

Elizabeth smiled. "I have asked the girls to let you pursue your studies undisturbed. Have you made a good start?" She poured his tea and offered the tray of raspberry scones.

He gingerly balanced his cup and saucer with his left hand and reached out his right for a scone, then looked around for a place to put it. Delia placed a large napkin on the polished table next to his chair and he smiled his relief as he set it down. "I wondered how to drink tea without a third hand." Then he responded to Elizabeth. "I have made a start, but there is so much! I have never seen so complete and magnificent a collection." He turned to Darcy. "You have excellent taste in books, sir."

Darcy thanked him. "The library was my father's treasure. I have tried to finish the sets he started, more to honour his memory than to indulge in my own taste, which might run to more historical or fictional works."

Catherine, who had opened her mouth several times to address the guest, finally found an opening. "Tell me all about Saint Augustine, Mr. Oliver! Why do you want to read all his works?"

Oliver laughed. "Oh, I do not expect to live long enough for a project like that! I merely hope to study enough to keep my preaching orthodox."

Kitty squirmed gleefully. "Mary told me that Saint Augustine once had a vision of the child Jesus at the seashore. He was digging a hole in the sand, and…"

Oliver laughed, putting up a hand to stop her. "A medieval tale, I am afraid. Those medievals liked their saints floating above the earth in all manner of miracles."

Elizabeth turned to Mary. "What story is that?"

Mary felt her face warm at the unwanted attention, but his cavalier dismissal of the tale gave her courage born of indignation. "He walked the shore trying to understand the Trinity. He asked what the child was doing, and the child said, 'Digging a hole to put the ocean in.' Augustine said, 'You cannot do that; it is impossible.' And the child said, 'It is easier for me to put the whole ocean into this hole than for you to understand the Trinity.' Then the child vanished, and Augustine knew it was Jesus." She raised her chin high and stated firmly, "I read that in a book." She felt sure that any clergyman who scoffed at beautifully devotional legends would give dry sermons.

Oliver brushed some crumbs from his mustache with the large napkin. "Oh, there is *some* truth behind it, I am sure. I fancy it was meant to convey to simple souls much of what the saint wrote in his treatise on the Trinity."

Darcy looked up in interest. "What was that?"

"He prayed for his readers, and he begged them to correct him if he went wrong because he knew he tackled a subject beyond him. Great men are that humble." Oliver gratefully relinquished his cup and saucer to the attentive Delia even as he reached for another scone. To Darcy he added, "It is one of my favourite parts of Augustine's work, because as I read it I am assured that a great saint has prayed for me. That is comfort in trying times."

Mary's eyes widened at that. She forgot her embarrassment and her resentment. She determined to find that book some day and take that solace for herself. Catherine showed her discontent with the turn of the conversation by asking, "Mr. Oliver, do you like to dance?"

He smiled at her. "As long as it is not as they say angels do, on the head of a pin." His smile made his moustache crook unevenly, and he seemed to know this, because he soon stopped smiling. "Or in a sedate parlour, such as this."

Georgiana exchanged a nod with Kitty, seeming to agree—though she said nothing—that Mr. Oliver was indeed a nice man. Mary just cocked her head. She was not so sure.

## Chapter 8

BY EARLY DECEMBER, ELIZABETH FELT STRONG ENOUGH TO PLAN the dinner at which Darcy wished to entertain the Reverend and Mrs. Wynters before they left for their London apartments. Catherine immediately requested a seat near Mr. Oliver, and Elizabeth complied good-naturedly. Mary cared little for such formal affairs and would just as soon forgo the event, but since Lizzy would certainly wish all to be there, she raised no objection. As it happened, she found herself seated comfortably between Georgiana and Mrs. Wynters, and she tried to lean a bit forward and smile her thanks to Elizabeth, who was seated at the foot of the table next to Mrs. Wynters. Georgiana began speaking of their Christmas music, and Mrs. Wynters showed much interest, telling them that she played the church organ at Kympton. This captured Mary's full attention. "Is the organ like enough to the pianoforte that I might learn? I should dearly love to play an organ one day."

"Really?" Mrs. Wynters set her wine glass down and looked straight at Mary. "I should be delighted to help you try it out any Saturday afternoon before we leave. Would this Saturday suit you?"

"Indeed, yes. When may I meet you at Kympton's church?"

"I look over Sunday's music right after breakfast. Come as soon as you like."

"Indeed, if Elizabeth will but give me directions, I shall be there as soon as possible." Mary reckoned this one fancy dinner as time well spent. She smiled around the table at the other guests and noted that Catherine chatted gaily with Mr. Oliver, while Mrs. Bennet, next to her, told Reverend Wynters more than he needed or cared to know about the birth of Elizabeth's son. Darcy, at the head of the table, with Wynters at his right and a quiet Mr. Bennet at his left, tried often to convey his gratitude for the reverend's faithful service these many years. However, as Mrs. Bennet wished to provide Kitty free rein to converse with the young, unmarried Mr. Oliver, she kept up a steady stream of patter with Reverend Wynters. For her part, Elizabeth was prevented from anything more than an occasional word with Mrs. Wynters to her right and Oliver on her left, so she actually found herself committing a social atrocity: chatting with her husband across the table—a pleasure she rarely indulged in at these dinners.

Mary urged Georgiana to accompany her for her organ lesson, but Georgiana had already promised to help Mrs. Darcy prepare for the children's Christmas party on that Saturday. Hearing this, Mrs. Wynters made Mary promise to come, even alone. "You will get on faster, at any rate, and by the end of the session I will wager you will have the feel of the instrument."

"That is uncommonly good of you, Mrs. Wynters. I shall be there, of course."

Mrs. Wynters leaned close to Mary and lowered her voice. "You know, the Darcys have been so generous in reviving all the Christmas traditions for their tenants and the nearby villagers. I hate to find any discrepancy in their most wonderful arrangements, but my heart goes out to those young people too old for the children's party and too young for the ball. I often wish they could be involved too."

Mary could not help but agree. "Could they not join in the ball? It is such a shame to have to wait until a certain age in order to come out socially." She wondered much at the difference between Derbyshire and Hertfordshire. Meryton's balls welcomed all who wished to attend. "But I suppose they can anticipate attending the ball when they will be of age."

"Yes, they do, but so often young men who will not inherit must move to town to find some employment. Many of the girls may still be near enough to enjoy it, and some country boys find work on the farms. Still, I remember my own awkward years between childhood and coming out, and I am afraid I wasted too much time envying others."

"Are there groups of carollers they might join?" Mary thought of Meryton assemblies when she played and young folks sang noels.

Mrs. Wynters thought about that. "Not such as you find in town. But I have a small group of girls who sing in church. Perhaps I will check with Mr. Wynters to see if a waggon could be got to take them around the village and to farmhouses. It is a lovely thought, Miss Bennet."

Elizabeth rose, and the women departed to the parlour for coffee. Mary touched Georgiana's hand. "Miss Darcy, would you join a group of carollers if you were free? Or is that something fine ladies do not do?"

Georgiana thought awhile and then giggled. "I believe the answer is yes—to both! Fine ladies probably do not do it, but I would."

"Then let us try." She found Mrs. Wynters talking to Elizabeth near the silver urn from which Elizabeth filled coffee bowls. Mary spoke to her confidentially. "If you make up that group of carollers, Miss Darcy and I would like to join them. And perhaps Kitty might come also." She hoped to ask Kitty about it whenever Kitty finished telling Mrs. Bennet all about her dinner conversation with Mr. Oliver.

Mrs. Wynters squeezed Mary's hand. "Bless you, Miss Bennet. We shall be honoured to have you." The gentlemen joined them in the parlour, and Mrs. Wynters signaled her husband to join her in a corner where she could propose to him their projected excursion. Mary managed to apprise Kitty of the plan, and seeing Oliver alone, Kitty ran to tell him of it—rather loudly Mary thought, scowling.

Mr. Oliver commented that such involvement of the young people in festivities of the holy season impressed him favourably. "Reverend Wynters tells me that the young men of the parish work each year on a stable scene in the church yard. It seems they add figures to it each year, though he says he wishes they would improve the principal figures instead of adding figures of townspeople like the French do. And when the scene is up for viewing, they like to celebrate with wassail." Kitty laughed at that. "But still, they have their part, so I'm glad the girls will have theirs." Mary noticed that Kitty's exuberance made Mr. Oliver raise his voice too. She wished for more decorum in the handsome parlour. She had no desire to hear the man's pulpit voice.

Her father approached her and asked, "What is the matter, Mary? Are we growing too boisterous for your refined taste?"

Mary realized that she must have been frowning, and she shook her head. "Oh Papa, Kitty seems to want to shout out all our plans before they are even settled. She thinks her precious Mr. Oliver should be interested in all she does."

"Well, Mary, Kitty could do worse." Bennet took his daughter's arm and steered her to a chair. "Darcy speaks well of the young man. I never pictured Kitty marrying a clergyman, but if she does, it won't bother you or me. Let the church elders and the pious dowagers of the parish worry about it. They might be loath to accept a flibbertigibbet for their parson's wife!"

On Saturday Mary, provided with Elizabeth's simple directions, set out early to walk to Kympton, there being no servant available at so busy a time to take her by carriage. She knew she had the right path when she passed the cottage with its sentinels of sculptured yews at the front door. Reaching the church and finding the door open, she ventured in and looked around. She walked up the aisle and savoured the lingering beeswax-and-linseed oil smell of the small country church, so like Longbourn's church and yet somehow even more comfortable. Perhaps its emptiness encouraged her to feel she belonged to these pews, this pulpit, and this polished wood altar with its plain white covering. She was admiring the oval window above the altar when she heard a noise behind her like a cough, but when she turned, she saw no one.

"Up here," Mrs. Wynters said, and Mary raised her eyes to a loft in the rear of the church.

"How do I reach you?"

"The stairway is below, opposite the door you came through."

She made her way back to a door marked "Choir," which opened onto a well-worn stairway. It circled around as it rose, and its old wood steps creaked as she ascended, some noisier than others. She found herself at last in an open loft with a low banister rail that reminded her of her library balcony. Her eyes beheld the small organ and Mrs. Wynters standing next to it, pumping a bellows. The kind organist pointed to the organ bench. "Take a seat. I'll work the bellows."

Mary thought the organ just the right size to learn on. She tried a few keys but no sound came out. Mrs. Wynters leaned over and pulled out some stops. She also pointed out the foot pedals. "Try those first."

As Mrs. Wynters pumped, Mary played tentatively at the foot pedals, and then tried the lower keyboard, and finally the upper. By the time she had managed to play one hymn completely through, the light streaming through the east clerestory window had paled, and she knew she must start for Pemberley.

"You will make an organist, I believe, Miss Bennet. Come next Saturday if you like."

"Oh, thank you. I shall!" Mary thanked her again and again as they descended the creaking old stairway.

"And the following Saturday evening, prepare to join the carollers. I will give you the music next week, and I am certain you and Miss Darcy will know the noels. We have obtained the much-used, Langley-farm waggon, so wear your warmest and oldest gown and pelisse."

Mary delighted Georgiana with her news, and Miss Darcy joined her the following week. The two young ladies took turns playing the organ and working the bellows, and Mrs. Wynters, though at first she teased that they had left her nothing to do, overlooked them, suggesting stops and techniques.

Georgiana, who had studied organ with a music master at Lambton, had little need of the lesson, but she protested she was glad of it. "It has been so long since I have played one, I had almost forgotten."

The next week, with helping at the children's party on Tuesday and carolling on Saturday, Mary and Catherine fully entered into the season and had grown to think of Miss Darcy as another sister. But despite the holiday spirit, Mary remained eager to steal some hours in that wonderful library whose balcony so often beckoned to her when she passed the ballroom door. How fortunate that

Polly had shown her the entrance which made stealth easy for her. Whenever possible, she slipped across the polished dance floor and through the small door to enjoy the many works of poetry and religion shelved so conveniently right at the balcony. One day she ran her hands longingly over Fordyce's sermons, a much better edition than the one at Longbourn, but she returned to the Bunyan, which had become a favourite. She felt most at home there and in the music room, and daily she came to love Pemberley, though its grandness still awed her. No less did she remain in awe of Mr. Darcy, whom she could hardly address without a trembling at her knees. She would be glad to return to Longbourn, but her time in Derbyshire passed comfortably enough.

A few days after her carolling excursion, having helped Lizzy and Georgiana wrap presents to be given the servants on Boxing Day, Mary again sought her favourite corner on the balcony and read of Christian the pilgrim, now relieved of his load of guilt but confronting the giant Despair. Suddenly an inadvertent sound of both guilt and despair escaped her lips as several pages fell from the book in her hands. She quickly retrieved the pages, glancing over the balcony to assure herself she was alone. She placed them carefully back in the book, closed it tightly, and re-shelved it. Regretting it deeply, she would read no more in *Pilgrim's Progress*. She looked once more to the main library floor, still glad to see no one below. Then she reached for the Cowper volume, examined its binding, and finding it secure, settled down with it, sadly missing the Bunyan work, but resolved to search out only newer, well-bound books in future. She cast her eye on a volume of Blake that looked hardy enough and noted it for her next selection.

As it happened, Mary failed to fully acquaint herself with the Blake, because preparations for the holiday ball had her mother so excited, and consequently the servants so flustered, that Elizabeth encouraged Mary to spend more time with their mother. Mary's deliberate temperament, Elizabeth found, counteracted, to some extent, Mrs. Bennet's more excitable outbursts. Thus, Mary helped her mother watch the transformation of the grand ballroom as the floor was thrice covered with wax and polished, the walls were festooned, sconces filled and fresh candles or oil put in all the lanterns, and candelabra were brought in for all the tables. A platform was erected for a small orchestra, but its placement so near the L-shaped hall where cards would be played became a matter of consternation for Mrs. Bennet. While Mrs. Reynolds announced the places on the refreshment table for punch, tisane, fruit, currant cakes, and pastries, Mrs. Bennet as quickly objected, being certain that more suitable arrangements could be found. Mary, whose two days helping Lizzy wrap presents for Boxing Day had been serenity itself in comparison, now endeavoured to bring calm to Mrs. Bennet when her suggestions went for naught. "Mama, might not the music cover the occasional outbursts from card games?" and "Perhaps Mrs. Reynolds wishes the punch bowl so near the table edge so that no drips may soil the cloth when guests refill their glasses." And in this manner, the Pemberley ball came to fruition as it had done for many years, even when deprived of the bustling assistance of Mrs. Bennet.

Christmas found the manor teeming with so many guests that every carriage was needed to take them to Lambton's church for the early service in a parade of coaches that resulted in an empty carriage house and an overfilled church. Mary sat with Mr. and Mrs. Bennet, just behind Jane and her family, and Mary found the service both solemn and sweet. Mr. Bennet said it was ample, and Mrs. Bennet pronounced it terribly long. In Darcy's pew across the aisle, Lady Catherine slept silently through it, sitting erect the whole time. From time to time Mary glanced at her, marvelling at that talent, which she supposed all fine ladies must cultivate.

On Boxing Day, Elizabeth asked Mary to help distribute gifts, first to the servants and then to the farm hands and some other tenants. Not that they actually bestowed the gifts, but they had to sort them for the proper recipient, while Darcy personally presented them. The children, who had received their gifts earlier at the party, remained near to enjoy watching their parents.

The following day all the guests were allowed to enter the transformed ballroom to behold a feast for the eyes. It was all much grander than Mary could have imagined during the preparations. She recalled Netherfield's ball of some years ago, grand on a lesser scale, when Elizabeth first danced with Darcy. From the assured way that Elizabeth smiled and welcomed her guests, Mary surmised that Elizabeth would be happy to dance at this one, even with Mr. Darcy. From a chair near the small pianoforte, Mary watched the noble Lady Catherine across the room as she directed servants to place cushions and a lap robe in a chair next to her for her daughter Anne. Miss de Bourgh had seemed out of sorts since her arrival before Christmas, and Mary wondered what could ail her. Perhaps the arduous journey had overtaxed her delicate health. Mr. Collins had spoken of her as a wondrous, sweet girl, and of Lady Catherine as noble indeed. Mary searched in vain to discern these qualities. She had seen Lady Catherine once before, at Longbourn, but never had she seen Miss de Bourgh until she arrived at Pemberley. Mary studied the two of them, strongly tempted to think that, had she met them as strangers, she might have deemed them insolent. But she knew they must be grandly noble ladies because Mr. Collins had said so.

Some of the arrivals from the villages nearby placed themselves near her, and Mary smiled at the one of the group that she recognized, Miss Alicia Johnstone. Mary had once helped Mrs. Reynolds keep watch on the wandering Miss Johnstone during a morning visit. Now that lady of prodigious proportions regaled her friends with authoritative information about the Pemberley household. "You would think, from this splendid array, that Mrs. Darcy always entertains perfectly. You should see her at-homes! Why, she does not even pour tea from the table near the hearth, as the former Mrs. Darcy used to do. There is one of her sisters." She pointed to Mary. "And that is Mrs. Reynolds, chief of the household staff, watching me as usual." Indeed, Mary noted, Mrs. Reynolds's alert eyes were full on that lady. "And that most beautiful lady before the fireplace is Mrs. Bingley, another of Mrs. Darcy's sisters. Her husband attends her adoringly, as always. They purchased Ilkestone Park, you know, between Eastwood and Newstead Abbey in Nottingham." Miss Johnstone certainly revelled in her superior knowledge, and indeed Mary herself was enlightened by her speech. Though she and Mrs. Bennet had stayed there last year for the holidays, she knew Bingley's estate only as Otherfield.

Miss Johnstone chattered on, her wide, red face aglow, her chins quivering as she spoke, reminding Mary of a Gillray cartoon. "There is the widow Heatherton, also of Nottingham. Her husband used to work on the grounds here. He once captured a throstle for her, and she still keeps it in a cage."

A thin lady in her party objected. "And does the poor bird never get out?"

"Oh, sometimes on fine days she takes the cage outside."

Mary's sympathy, like the thin woman's, was all for the bird. She strained to discern the woman spoken of, and she supposed it to be the stately, silver-haired woman near Elizabeth, wearing grey muslin with long sleeves. Admiring her good taste, Mary wandered closer to her. Just then, the starched looking lady in purple next to the regal one complained, "Yes, it is hard to find servants of integrity. Just last month I had to dismiss a scullery maid for drying used tea leaves and selling them to the greengrocer. But I blame the grocer even more. He certainly knew that they were not fresh tea."

The lady in grey muslin concurred. "It is unfortunate that one must go to London for genuine tea at Twinings."

The orchestra tuned up, and Mary turned her attention to the set beginning to form. The Darcys and the Bingleys led the way, followed by Colonel Fitzwilliam and Miss Bingley. Catherine Bennet placed herself in the way of Mr. Oliver as he passed, and he bowed politely and took her to the dance.

Mary now felt a kinship with Miss de Bourgh, as the set grew down the length of the hall and neither she nor Anne danced or seemed to desire to do so. Mary rose and edged toward her, meaning to engage Miss de Bourgh in conversation. She stopped at the refreshment table and watched as a servant brought a tray to Lady Catherine, who accepted a cup of punch, nodding stiffly. Anne, however, refused even to acknowledge the servant's offer, but fixed her stony gaze above the heads of the dancers. Mary bethought herself and moved no nearer.

When the music stopped, Elizabeth and Jane sat down to visit, while Bingley went, as if on cue, to bow before Miss de Bourgh. She rose woodenly to join him in the next dance. Darcy drew near Lady Catherine, who had beckoned, but she remained seated as on a throne, hoarsely intoning, "Lord David did not come this year?"

Darcy shook his head. "No, Lord Exbridge remains in mourning, inconsolable still, though all his friends have urged him otherwise."

"I am sorry for it. So few my age are here, and none who remember Lewis de Bourgh as he would. But I mean to consult with you." Lady Catherine stood grandly and took Darcy's hastily-offered arm. Mary turned toward a general hubbub from the L-corner, near the cards. There among folk from Kympton and Lambton stood Lydia! The effrontery of it! Surely Wickham had not insinuated himself here as well. She looked over the whole room as best she could, and decided he had not. Kitty, with Mr. Oliver in tow, wended her way over to Lydia, who had laughingly detained a young, red-faced gentleman. He seemed rather bent on rejoining an elegant-looking young lady waiting nearby. Lydia, saucy as ever, boldly teased as if she thought nothing remiss in her behaviour. Mary felt the whole affair had turned to a scene of dissipation and corruption.

She found the warm ballroom stifling. She tried to catch the eye of Mrs. Gardiner, who, she imagined, must share her disgust. Perhaps Lydia had seen her and read her reaction. Indeed, she hoped so, for how else would Lydia ever bethink herself and repent her misdeeds unless someone reminded her how reprehensible they were? Still, Mary would not approach Lydia. She adhered to the dictum of First Corinthians: "In respect to evil, be like infants, but in your thinking be mature." She would avoid as much as possible even knowing the frivolities of her erring sister, as Mr. Collins had so often adjured. She knew Lydia prided herself on being first in the family to have caught a husband, with never a thought to how sinfully she had done so, and Mary would never condone such behaviour.

Mary moved to the familiar corner, now quiet and relatively empty, and slipped through the door to her refuge, the library balcony. She no longer cared for festivity, and though the balcony was dark, she would light no candle. Obscurity suited her, and soon she could grope her way to her wonted chair to ponder the distressing situation. Had Elizabeth known that Lydia would be there? Had she come with the Bingleys? Was she actually staying in the house? Mary did not recall any room being readied for her. Certainly she had not been at the Christmas service or breakfast, nor had she been at last year's ball or the first one. But had she grown so brazen as to attend this one? No doubt Mama would be pleased to see her frivolous favourite. Mama did not mind the infamous way Lydia had run off with Wickham, no matter how tardy their marriage was. To Mama, a husband was a husband, and the sooner got the better.

Slowly the muted music from the dance soothed her ruffled dander, and a musing solitude engulfed her. She started from near somnolence when the library door opened below, sending a wide beam of light from the hall through the room. She crept noiselessly from the chair to the door, but shadows under the door and voices from the ballroom warned her that slipping in unnoticed was impossible just then, and light from the ballroom might reveal her presence to those who had entered below.

Light flickered as one candle flame rose and then another. She could make out Mr. Darcy as he stoked the fire in the grate and added a small log. Lady Catherine's voice, never timid, burst through the silence. "Darcy, you must save her. She is so timid, so spiritless. Witherspoon is but an opportunist, a cringing sycophant now, but when I am gone he will rise up, and she hasn't the strength of will to refuse him. Of course, now he appears docile, bowing to Mr. Collins and me, and so courtly and smiling to Anne. I insist that you come to Kent and see for yourself."

Darcy had made a few grunts of understanding while she spoke, and Mary gave up trying to escape. She slipped back into the chair, where she tried to block out the voices to no avail. Darcy finally said, "Have you learned anything about him?"

"Only what he tells Mr. Collins. He has not taken orders. He is a mere verger who rings bells and tidies vestments and altar vessels. I am certain, however, that he is not the simpleton he pretends to be. Anne smirks and simpers and calls him Howard and in every way encourages his cloying attention. Nobody we can find in Kent knows his family or even where he lives. He presented himself to Mr. Collins one day some months ago and offered to work around the church on weekends, saying he 'just wants to be near such a holy man.' Any fool can see there is something suspicious about the fellow. Mr. Collins may have earned a reputation for something or other, but anyone knows it is not for holiness."

"Does Witherspoon gamble?"

"Oh, I do not know. He has not been seen in Kent to do anything but follow Collins to the church door and sidle up to Anne as soon as Collins engages me in conversation. His gamble, no doubt, is to get his hands on the de Bourgh property."

"Can you read his intent so clearly?" Darcy did not seem, by his tone, so anxious as Lady Catherine might wish him to be.

"It is worse since my illness. During that time, Anne went to every Sunday service with Mrs. Jenkinson and, by Mrs. Jenkinson's account, left that lady conversing with Collins while she walked a bit with Witherspoon. When they returned, Mrs. Jenkinson had to report that she could not observe them after they walked off into the woods, and Anne returned glowing—or gloating. She is smitten, Darcy, and you must talk her out of that nonsense."

"But if she likes him, and you know no real harm of him, why not relax and let her choose as she will? Do not suppose I will mind losing any claim to the property. Surely you would wish, above all, for your daughter to find happiness?"

Up in her balcony, Mary frowned, remembering the proud Darcy of former days. She remarked his calm and the almost romantic turn of his views. Had he changed so completely?

Lady Catherine exploded in new fury. "Oh that Anne! Her health is poor, her mind too easily influenced, and her will is as porridge. Any firm resolve is beyond her powers. She is defenceless against that conniving flatterer. I alerted Colonel Fitzwilliam to the danger to Rosings, but he played deliberately obtuse. Tonight he fawns over the Bingley woman, so I perceive that avenue soon to be lost. Promise me that after I am gone you will look after her affairs."

"Of course, Aunt, as much as may be. But I will be neither inclined nor able to turn her mind from anyone she truly loves. And pray, do not imagine that you will be so soon gone." Darcy's tone remained calm, soothing, as to a child. "And you could do as you wish with the property now. Engage your attorney and attach an entailment so that only Anne or her children may inherit. You might even leave it to Hunsford, should Anne die without issue."

Lady Catherine snorted. "Without issue indeed! Do you think such a sickly mite could survive childbirth? She would die and leave that good-for-nothing Witherspoon to bring up any heir she would have."

"Please, Aunt. Anne is not yet married, and you may be all wrong about his intentions or hers." After a pause, in which Lady Catherine only grunted, Darcy went on, "And I believe the music has stopped. I must lead my guests to supper."

"Wait! Before you go, promise to visit in the spring as you used to do. You may bring Mrs. Darcy and my grandnephew, if you will. See the situation for yourself, and I know you will agree with me. I am never wrong about such things."

Darcy extinguished one candle. "Aunt, I will promise to look into the Kent situation as soon as I can—by proxy if not in person. I will not rush Elizabeth into any arduous journey, and Charles is much too young." The other candle went out, the door opened, their voices died out below, and only the crackling of the dying fire sounded through the library. Mary made her way to the door and watched the outline of light beneath it until no moving shadows darkened it. Then she slipped back into the bright hall, blinking against the glare, and mingled with guests moving toward the staircase to the supper room.

Once downstairs, Mary was accosted by a frowning Mr. Oliver. Bowing, he greeted her solemnly. "I saw you briefly when dancing began but not afterward. Are you so invisible in a crowd, Miss Mary Bennet, or do you so disapprove of dancing?"

Fortunately, Mary had time only to respond, "No sir," before Darcy and Lady Catherine passed and she could excuse herself to join her sisters, trusting that Lydia would not choose to be one of the party. Lydia had never cared to be among those who might frown upon her lack of decorum. Jane and Catherine sat at a table with Bingley, and Mary joined them. Elizabeth, with Miss de Bourgh and Mrs. Jenkinson, looked around for Lady Catherine. Elizabeth smiled as Darcy escorted the dowager to her table and then turned to care for their other guests. After the meal—which had progressed amid praise for the sumptuous banquet, the Bristol glass, and the new Spode china—Elizabeth became free to join her sisters and parents, just as Jane explained to Kitty, "Lydia visited us a fortnight ago, and I mentioned this ball. The poor thing had not been to any festive gathering for so long, I did not think it improper for her to join her sisters. She and Wickham are staying at the inn at Lambton, as the Gardiners always do. Naturally, Wickham does not dare to show his face at Pemberley, but that need not prevent Lydia from her enjoyment."

Kitty nodded as she said, "Lydia stayed upstairs in the card room. They just began a round of piquet when supper was announced. She said she had eaten enough from the refreshment table and would forgo supper. Perhaps I should do that." Elizabeth arrived and sat next to Mary, across from Jane and Kitty. Bingley stood behind Jane, searching for Darcy. Kitty made to rise, saying, "If there is sufficient room at the card table, I can watch them play." Jane put a hand over hers and whispered to her, and she sat down again. Mary rejoiced that Kitty showed no resentment at being curbed. Across the supper room, Mr. Oliver joined Reverend and Mrs. Wynters, and Mary relaxed, preparing to listen to Jane and Elizabeth, as she usually did, allowing herself a comfortable, unobtrusive reverie. But soon Elizabeth turned to her. "Why did you not play for the group this evening? Georgiana looked for you in vain and finally had to play alone. And you practised so often with her."

Mary wanted to say they might have asked Caroline Bingley, who always spoke enviously of Georgiana's Broadwood grand, but she simply said, "I am sorry to have missed it. But surely the noels are still to come?" Then she applied herself to the delicious curry.

Elizabeth persisted. "Georgiana wanted to share the honours with you, as she played only the folk dances you had done as duets. She thought them thin without your part." She looked sternly at Mary. "Did you slip into the library to continue *Pilgrim's Progress*?"

Mary spoke almost before she swallowed. "Oh no, Lizzy. I haven't looked at that book for many days now." She coloured a little, fearing she had spoken untruly, at least in part, and choking back what she thought of adding—that she only devoted herself to sturdier books now. Happily, Georgiana led Lady Elliott to their table, and Darcy arrived to sit with Elizabeth as Bingley sat down with Jane. Mary became, for a while, the listener she had intended to be. Supper progressed with no further embarrassment, save only Mrs. Bennet's overly loud comment to the assembled group: "Mary, look at that Colonel Fitzwilliam, simpering over Caroline Bingley. What a pity he has forgot how pleased he was with you at the Meryton Assembly. You should have placed yourself in his way and smiled at him. Why must you neglect your social duties? He might just as well be squiring you, you know."

Mary shrugged. "I am sorry, Mama. I have just now noticed him." She smiled inwardly to think that his attentions to Miss Bingley might well be the result of her own advice to him at that very ball.

Mrs. Bennet, showing dissatisfaction at Mary's indifference, kept after her about her "bounden duty" to marry. "And you know, Mr. Grantley showed a remarkable attention to you. Have you read the essays he gave you?" Mary nodded absently. "Well, you be sure to thank him and show a lively interest. He may be a bit peculiar, but he is not so bad, really. You could do much worse."

Mary was saved from answering by Georgiana's beckoning her to the pianoforte. Together they played noels while many country folk sang. Once, when she looked up from the keyboard, she saw Mr. Oliver eyeing her with a puzzled frown. She avoided his eyes, as he had no call to be questioning her earlier disappearance. She concentrated instead on her embarrassment at having overheard the conversation of the awesome Mr. Darcy and his even more awesome aunt. She reflected long on the unhappy complications of even unintended eavesdropping.

## Chapter 9

B Y THE WEEK FOLLOWING THE GREAT CHRISTMAS BALL AT Pemberley, the announced engagement of Colonel Fitzwilliam and Miss Bingley captured the common interest. Elizabeth pointed out to Mary that Jane and Charles Bingley smiled every bit as much as did the happy couple. Lady Catherine, abandoning her sedate silence whenever the subject arose, disapproved in the most stentorian tones. Mrs. Bennet, only slightly more temperate, reserved her petulance for Mary. "That might just as well have been you, Mary. The Colonel was right fond of you at Meryton's Assembly, and if you would learn to smile and look admiringly at a man and cultivate a few flattering ways, I would not have to despair of you ever finding a husband. You certainly could have done as well as Miss Bingley if you had only tried. When a man is ready to marry, he is often not too particular about the lady."

Lady Catherine, overhearing this, sniffed. "Indeed yes; and I could tell you the exact moment when the Colonel became ready to marry." But she did not do so. Mary held her peace, though she could well have seconded her mother's view that the Colonel's choice was indeed just to be married, though he seemed to have been more particular as to his choice than Mrs. Bennet gave him credit for.

The happy couple, chaperoned by the Hursts, left for Norfolk to solicit the Earl's approval. The Bingleys, promising to return for the christening of their godchild, retired to Otherfield Park. The Bennets made arrangements to leave after the christening, Mr. Bennet declaring that never again would he stray so long from his own library at Longbourn. Mary looked forward to the departure eagerly. She did not ache for either the travel or for Hertfordshire but desired only to quit the environs of the accident that spoiled *Pilgrim's Progress* and of her unintentional eavesdropping, both embarrassments should they come to light. With luck she could forget them before summer visits came due, and she may even be able to avoid that, saying her mother needed company. At any rate, it was Catherine's turn to visit Pemberley, and at worst, she would be safely at Nottingham. Bingley was not half so daunting as Mr. Darcy.

After the christening, when all the other guests had departed, Elizabeth approached Mary in the music room where she was playing duets with Georgiana. "Mary, I wonder if I could ask you to stay on for a while."

Mary hoped her horror at the suggestion did not register too violently with Elizabeth. "Oh no, I do not think so."

Kitty, embroidering a towel as she listened to the music, looked up. "Why ever not? Surely you are not needed at home!"

Elizabeth explained, "Reverend and Mrs. Wynters have gone to their London retirement apartments, and Kympton's church is without an organist. I thought, since you enjoyed playing the organ, you would not object."

Mary did object. "Oh, no, that is much too great a responsibility for me." She considered the subject closed.

Elizabeth went on, "Mr. Oliver asked Darcy if you could possibly be prevailed upon to fill the post for a short time. He feels that having no music for Easter is simply unthinkable, and Mrs. Wynters had trained a small but faithful young choir that he does not wish to discourage."

Mary grasped at any alternative. "Perhaps one of the choir members…"

Annoyingly, Elizabeth persisted. "Of course, he acknowledged his reluctance to impose upon the sister of his patron, but he felt you had the strength and musicianship to succeed. Mr. Darcy and I would be greatly obliged if you would at least attempt it."

All the burden of her guilty secrets settled heavily on her, coupled with her instinctive distaste for a task that involved leading young people, even those as genial as the carollers she had met. Of course, she had wanted to play organ, but not for a constancy and not there. "I really could not, Lizzy; I am sorry. I have barely learned the organ, and I am clumsy with the stops. Perhaps Mr. Oliver should follow Reverend Wynters's lead and marry an organist himself."

Elizabeth smiled broadly—and teasingly sweet, Mary thought. "He most particularly requested you. In time, he may find that some parishioner is able to do it. But for now, and to please us, do consider it."

At that moment, Darcy entered, effectively crushing the categorical denial Mary meant to make. He smiled at Georgiana and complimented her artistry, causing her fingers to falter. The piano fell silent as she murmured her thanks. Then he turned full on Mary. "Miss Bennet, we look forward to your staying on with us." But he gave her no chance to say she could not. Taking his wife's hand, he pulled her to the door of the music room. "Come to the library and see the beautiful work Mr. Oliver has done."

As soon as they left the room, Catherine dropped her needlework and cried, "Oh, Mary, how could you give up a chance to stay here where the sheets are so soft and silky, and you get hot and cold water every morning in your room and excellent curry and ginger beer at tea and everything is so nice?"

"Such luxuries are not necessary to my contentment, Kitty. They are only the consequence of money, and that is the root of all evil."

"You puzzle me exceedingly. Imagine doing the music for *him*! La, if I had learned to play as well as you, it could be me. Oh, do get to know him, Mary. Find out if he likes me."

Mary remained indifferent to such a plan and abhorrent to remaining at Pemberley. "Kitty, with all my heart I wish that it were your offer and not mine. I hate to refuse, but I look forward to relaxing at Longbourn." Mary realized that she would enjoy being an accomplice in Kitty's romance no more than she enjoyed being privy to Anne de Bourgh's. She felt caged; she had to get away. She noted Georgiana's silence, and to Kitty she whispered, "I can understand his hesitancy in asking for Miss Darcy, but she plays ever so much better than I do, and if no one else is available, she well might offer; she is that good. Besides," she spoke aloud, "Mama needs me at home. Who can she exhort to sociability when you are so willing to oblige?" On that, Mary sought her room to finish packing and make her imminent departure obvious to the Darcys, though a faint twinge of conscience told her how ill she answered their cordial hospitality. On the way to her room, she reflected that, while soft sheets and other luxuries did not entice her, she really would miss the luxury of that library. She determined to stay out of sight until the carriage came for them next day.

Mary found her trunk packed and ready to close, and only a few things set out for the morrow. She smiled, and in her heart she blessed Polly for her foresight. All was as good as accomplished. She hurried across the corridor to the grand ballroom, so silent now, and with only four great wreaths adorning the walls as a reminder of its recent gaiety. She made her way to the balcony she loved, but when she reached it, she heard the Darcys in the lower library. She turned to leave, lest any new secrets reach her ears.

Elizabeth exclaimed in approval, and Darcy said, "Good as new."

Mary hesitated at the door.

"He noticed the problem when he opened it to record Charles's christening, and he whispered, 'I'll fix this for you.' All the early pages had come loose, with all our family's history threatening to fall out. But they are secure now, and look how easily the pages turn."

Elizabeth agreed. "Why, it is almost better than new."

"He said he learned to repair books from necessity at Ramsgate— such a poor parish even the altar ritual books were falling apart."

Mary turned from the door and listened intently. Elizabeth was saying, "It is not as if you have neglected your fine collection."

"Our fine collection," Darcy corrected. "No, the Bible itself was readable, except at these first pages. Oliver said both the glue and the threads of binding need refreshing from time to time, especially where there is a fireplace."

"And he offered to look at all these books?" Elizabeth's tone emphasised the immensity of the task.

"Yes. He loves books and appreciates using the library. I almost hate to accept the tithes he pays me for the living. This kind of work is invaluable." His voice trailed off as he and Elizabeth left the library, and Mary looked longingly at *Pilgrim's Progress*, neglected there in its familiar place on the shelf. If she left as planned the next day, would he even think of examining books so far from the fireplace? If she did not leave, perhaps she could hint that it too needed rebinding. Perhaps she could manage to stay a short while, just until a regular organist could be found. If she took the post as requested, Mr. Oliver might feel obliged to fix the book. She would talk to Elizabeth, perhaps unpack the top layer of her trunk, and stay a short while.

MRS. BENNET INSISTED THAT THE WHOLE FAMILY STAY ANOTHER day when she learned of Mary's plan to stay on. "If she should find it abhorrent when she first tries it, how could she return to Longbourn without us?" She followed this with her more pressing reason. "Mr. Grantley surely looks for Mary to be at the February assembly in Meryton. She really should not miss such an opportunity to cultivate a valuable acquaintance." Mr. Bennet, eager for home but loath to leave Elizabeth, made but faint objection, and so Kitty enjoyed another night in her soft sheets.

When Mary returned from her first practise, Mr. Bennet, ensconced in the foyer with a good book and a decanter of wine, greeted her. "And how did you enjoy leading the choir?"

Mary shrugged. "I can probably endure it for a short while, until a regular organist can be found. The choir girls have fine voices, though some are but twelve years old."

"And they know the music?"

"Well, yes, in a manner they do. But if I sing with the altos, the sopranos falter, and if I try to help the sopranos, they all go flat."

Mr. Bennet nodded, smiling. "If I were you, Mary, I would merely threaten to sing with them when they are out of tune. They will work hard to get it right."

Mary knew well that her family could abide her playing with far greater aplomb than they did her singing, and his advice did not surprise—or amuse—her. After the Bennets left for Longbourn, the advice rang in her mind during subsequent practises, and she was far less inclined to join the singing. For services she never did, and usually they went well enough.

Mary grew to enjoy the comfort of leisure time in the library as well as her walks or rides with Elizabeth on errands to Darcy's tenants and other townsfolk. When she relaxed in the morning room now, Mary took up needlework on her own, as she had learned to enjoy it, while Elizabeth nursed her child. Mary even became familiar enough with Mr. Darcy to relax a degree when he dropped in, as he so often did between his tasks in late morning. He treated her as his own sister, not hesitating to discuss business of the manor with Elizabeth in her presence. Usually Mary rose to leave when he opened such a subject, but Darcy always bade her remain.

One morning in late February, Darcy gestured her as usual to remain at her pursuit when he came upon them quietly at their tasks, Georgiana's songs wafting in from the music room. "Please, Miss Bennet, I never mean to disturb the peace of your occupation." He turned to Elizabeth. "My dear, Lady Elliott asks Georgiana for an early visit in London, which suits my sister, who likes to avoid the height of the social season and wishes to return home for Easter. I would like for us both to convey her there and then to approach Lord Exbridge about his unhealthy isolation. What think you?"

Mary sincerely hoped Lizzy would not feel she must stay home to keep her company, and she wanted to give her that assurance, but since she had not been consulted, she hesitated to say anything. She could see that Lizzy frowned and delayed her answer. Finally, Elizabeth said, "Of course Georgiana must go, as Lady Elliott is such a good friend for her and we do not wish Georgiana to miss the amenities of London society." She looked at her husband with pleading eyes. "But Charles and I have become so used to this tranquil hour. Would you be very angry with me if I stayed here?"

"No, indeed. I perceive that you have grown rather necessary to your son, despite the wet nurse. But you do see that I must go?"

"Oh, yes. Though my preference is to be with you always, that is my selfishness. Charles has come to need me for this hour, as he also needs Callie and the stability of the nursery, so I must sacrifice my need of you. Please hold me excused this year. Can you look upon it as welcome time alone with your sister? I do not like to think I have come between you two in any way."

Darcy sighed. "I had feared that would be your choice." He leaned over and kissed her cheek, brushing the baby tenderly with his fingers as he did so. "Georgiana says she is ready to leave on the morrow. Lady Elliott will see to her return, so I do not mean to stay away more than a se'ennight. I will miss you."

"And I you. I will pray for your success with Lord Exbridge. Will you visit in Kent as well?"

"I mean to spend one night there, as Lady Catherine has requested. I cannot spare more than that so near to planting time. The weather bids fair, and I leave you in good hands." He smiled on Mary. "We will both be alone with our musical sisters."

Mary did not know whether to be glad for the greater ease she would feel at his going or sorry for the loss of Georgiana who had lately been a true sister to her. Still, she had apparently not been part of Lizzy's decision, and for that she was grateful.

The next day, Mary bid a polite farewell to Mr. Darcy and a warm one to Georgiana, while Elizabeth held Darcy ever so long in embrace and fondly kissed Georgiana, sending her off with a store of the winter's remaining currant and cherry jams for Lady Elliott. With Darcy, she sent damson wine for Lord Exbridge.

A large and empty silence ensued after the carriage rolled away, though Mary anticipated an increasing ease of life. She would concentrate on the choir and her organ work, and hours with Lizzy in the morning room would be as sweet as their times at Longbourn. However, Elizabeth was, if anything, more silent, and when Mary looked for her next morning after breakfast Delia explained, "Mrs. Darcy had breakfast in her sitting room, and desires that you join her there with your embroidery." Mary gathered her threads and pillow slips and made her way upstairs to the sitting room. There Lizzy smiled her welcome and tended to the suckling child. No music could have reached them, even if Georgiana was home to play and sing. If Mary tried to remind Lizzy of some homely joy of Longbourn, the reply she got was a nod or a murmur. Mary wondered much at the diminution of her sister's witty spirit, and she almost began to look eagerly for Darcy's return.

At the church, things went much as usual, with practises improving in both antics and music. The girls became relaxed with Mary on Wednesdays, and their chatting and larks increased, while on Sundays they showed that they could be serious and that their singing had spirit. In particular, a tall, willowy sixteen-year-old girl named Emmaline Langley, a lively brunette with sparkling blue eyes, liked to entertain her friends with moues and sallies, and she often held the final note of a motet long enough to make her friends giggle. This happened only at practises, when Mr. Oliver operated the organ bellows, and Emmaline kept her eyes on him rather than on Mary. On Sundays, for morning services, young Tom Hooks worked the bellows, but he would not be able to perform that office for practises until late spring when it would be light out. Emmaline kept turning adoring eyes on Mr. Oliver, never noticing the sign to cut off the last note, even after Mary's reminders.

"Miss Langley," Mary often reproached her, "you must watch and stop singing when I nod, as the other girls do."

"I am sorry, Miss Bennet. I was distracted. I will do it right on Sunday, I promise." And she invariably did so, because then her view of Mr. Oliver leading the service below could comprise Mary as well, and she could follow directions as well as anyone. Nor did she care to call attention to herself in that manner when her parents were present in the congregation. Mary eagerly awaited the day when young Tom could be present for practises and she could command the attention of the older girls, who all seemed infatuated with the new vicar.

Mary spoke to Miss Langley after the third practise in a manner she hoped would bring results. "You have a lovely voice, Miss Langley, but no one voice should be heard in choir. Your continuing inattention is a frivolity that shows lack of respect for the other singers."

Emmaline reddened, but she did not improve. She seemed determined to make Mr. Oliver notice her and appreciate her fine voice. After a while, Mary resigned herself to the nonsense, having reluctantly agreed to keep the choir until Easter as Mr. Oliver requested. After that, Emmaline could intrude herself on the vicar's notice however she pleased, and good luck to her. How unfortunate that Catherine had not stayed behind and joined the choir. She could have offered Emmaline some competition, perhaps to more effect, since Catherine was closer to Oliver's age. And, to Mary's way of thinking, he really ought to marry; then not only would choir girls be more attentive, but also he would not so often intrude himself in Pemberley's library. She reproached herself for her possessive attitude toward the library, but she could not conquer it. And now, Oliver set up supplies for repairing books on a table in the corner farthest from the fireplace. He regularly appeared not just on Tuesdays to read, but also on Fridays to examine book after book from the shelves. Occasionally, he took one to his corner table, where with ruler, stylus, paste-pot, and threads he plied his new trade. Sometimes he even hummed as he worked. Mary found it hard to keep her mind on what she read whenever those sounds invaded her quietude. When she could no longer stand it, she sighed, shelved her book, and headed for the door. Usually Oliver called as she left, "Sorry, Miss Bennet, if I have disturbed your study." She waved to him then, hoping that her impatience did not show, but she could not, in truth, declare that he had not disturbed her.

Darcy returned, as promised, before ten days had elapsed, though now daytime cares took him to the fields when he was not consulting with his steward. In evenings, at dinner and after, he admitted little by little his small success with Lord Exbridge. "He did agree to see me at least and was pleased with the wine you sent." And another evening, when Elizabeth asked him about his trip: "Lord Exbridge remarked that the taste of the wine reminded him of his own fields nearby, which he has not visited these two years or more." And at another time: "Even when I was about to leave, he could not promise to ask Martha and young David to live with him. At the door he hemmed and hawed and said only, 'Perhaps, one day.'"

"Oh, dear. Being so much alone cannot be good." Elizabeth's sympathetic tone gained hope. "But you did at least see him. Perhaps, as with Lady Catherine, time will bring him to relent. And I promise to accompany you next spring."

Mary felt she should say something, though her awe kept her a listener most of the time. "Did Miss Darcy bear the journey well?"

"Yes, thank you, Miss Bennet. But after I had left her with Miss Elliott, I kept wondering whether I should not have asked her to come with me first to Lord Exbridge. Only my fear that he would refuse to see me made me defer to her shyness and save her that supposed rebuff. I am sorry now that she did not come." He turned a rueful gaze on Elizabeth. "She may have been more successful with him."

"Perhaps, but you must not discount the success you did have. And next year, she must accompany us there." Elizabeth's bright eyes sought his, and Mary noted a sparkle in them she had missed of late. "And what of Lady Catherine? Does she continue well?"

"Indeed yes. She talks of joining us again next Christmas. Unfortunately, I arrived on a Monday and could not stay to observe Sunday service as she had requested. I must make other arrangements for that, perhaps after Easter, when Mary and Lady Elliott will be returning south." He turned to Mary. "Will you be greatly relieved when your stint at the organ is over?"

Mary felt that the organ playing was the least of her concerns; the lively choir members were a handful she might well wish to relinquish, but all she did was nod to Mr. Darcy's question.

One early spring practise finished with a truly stirring version of Neander's "He Is Risen." Mary complimented the girls, wished them good evening, and slipped from the organ bench quickly. Just as quickly, Oliver dropped the bellows and moved before her to the loft staircase. "Miss Bennet, I would like to talk to you. May I walk you home?"

Mary noted the stricken face of Emmaline and actually pitied the child. She firmly declined such an offer, hoping Emmaline heard that too. "Mr. Darcy's steward, Mr. Shepard, waits in the churchyard with a carriage."

She was annoyed to find that Oliver, preceding her as usual, looked back, smiling. "Good. I need to talk to you. If I may ride with you, I will walk back."

Mary hoped her tired feeling of annoyance did not show too greatly. How she looked forward to Easter and her return to Longbourn! Let Catherine visit Pemberley. She would be welcome to it. Mary realized she would actually enjoy being Mrs. Bennet's excuse for summer visits and assembly attendance. Inconveniences she could predict displeased her far less than did surprising ones. She descended the narrow stairs with the vicar still looking back occasionally as if he feared she would fall. Well, if she must have his company in the carriage, perhaps she might approach him about repairing the volume she had ruined so long ago. She had not found an opportunity to do so as yet.

As they reached the lower church, Oliver said, "Don't be hard on Emmaline Langley, Miss Bennet. She tries, I believe."

Mary smiled. If only the young girl could have heard! "Oh, yes. And she sings well, but she lacks concentration. How distressing to see such capable girls grow careless about praising God in song!" Mentally she urged him to defend the girl further, because she now saw the child lingering at the foot of the stairwell.

Instead, Oliver opened the church door for her, followed after, and offered his arm as Mary stepped over a muddy patch in the churchyard. He lowered his voice. "I think you might find a special patience for Miss Langley. She puts me in mind of your younger sister."

"Oh Kitty is not that bad!" Mary rushed to her sister's defense.

"I referred to your other sister—Mrs. Wickham."

"Kitty is my younger sister." Mary spoke firmly, as to close the subject.

Mr. Oliver, perplexed, frowned at her. "But Miss Catherine introduced me to *her* younger sister at the Christmas ball. And, if I am not mistaken, you avoided Mrs. Wickham on that occasion." He latched the churchyard gate with a decisive twist and regarded her sternly.

Mary resented the implied reproach. What right had he to question her behaviour on that or any occasion? "Our cousin, the Reverend Mr. Collins, advised us to consider that girl as one dead, and I have done so."

"Good Lord! Why do such a ghastly thing? She seemed lively enough to me."

Mary declined to respond, feeling that Lydia's scandalous elopement was no business to bruit abroad. She kept to herself the memory of how Lydia had shocked all the family while acting as if she had done a clever thing. If now the family all choose to forget about it and act as if her subsequent marriage fixed everything, how will Lydia ever see the error of her ways? Surely Mr. Collins had the right idea. Not knowing just how to explain herself, Mary gave no answer.

Oliver stood by the carriage and handed her in. Inside, he commented, "I sincerely hope that Christ does not, when we behave badly, consider us as dead, though we may well deserve such treatment." Again receiving no response, he continued, "But seriously, Miss Bennet, you do not consider that your sister has harmed you in any way? As Catherine observed, since you are Mrs. Darcy's sister, you are well received in any society."

Mr. Shepard, who had raised his eyebrows at the vicar's entering the carriage, looked in after Mary and asked, "Home to Pemberley, miss?"

"Yes, of course, Mr. Shepard. Mr. Oliver has some business to discuss, and he will walk back afterward."

Oliver would not be put off. "Can you not forgive your own sister, who has not really harmed you in any way?"

Mary set her jaw, wishing to drop the subject he would not let go. "Forgiveness is not the question. As you pointed out, she has done me no wrong, nor do I imagine that she has. I am sure Mr. Collins only means for us to act in such a way that will help her to repent before God, which she cannot do as long as she does not acknowledge the transgression."

"And do you not know, Miss Bennet, that your appearing to bear such a grudge will do more harm than any repentance of hers can do good? Why, as Catherine boasted, Mrs. Darcy's marrying so very well puts the rest of her sisters in a position to marry very well indeed."

"More fool Kitty. I much prefer to think that Lizzy's sacrifice in marrying as she did frees us from the necessity of marrying at all." Mary rejoiced to find Oliver silenced at last. Perhaps he had never before realized the plight of dependent single women. She could tell him of sacrifices greater even than Lizzy's and for less fortune. Charlotte Lucas, for instance, had married Mr. Collins without loving him, though she well knew that Elizabeth had been his first choice. That was sacrifice indeed.

At length, Oliver sat back in the swaying carriage and murmured, almost to himself, "Your youngest sister's marriage harmed her more than it did her family, and life will bring her to repentance. Another sister's marriage helped the family more than it did herself? I think not. I do not accept 'sacrifice' as Mrs. Darcy's lot." His narrowed dark eyes fixed coldly on Mary. "Observe Mrs. Darcy more closely. I believe she deeply loves her husband. Ask her."

Mary let him rattle on. What does this gangly stranger know of the matter? Though the rigid hauteur of Mr. Darcy at Hertfordshire was not in evidence here, and Elizabeth did indeed relax in his presence, still Mama had told her often enough how Lizzy had accepted the proud and rigid Mr. Darcy to save the family, knowing Longbourn was entailed away from them to Mr. Collins. Elizabeth was atoning for her refusal of Mr. Collins. Surely Mama knew more about it than this nosy clergyman did. Mary could not forget her first impressions of Darcy, and she remained wary of crossing him. She particularly feared his discovery of the book she had mishandled. In a burst of bravado, she blurted, "Sir, could you examine a book with loose pages on the library balcony? Elizabeth so highly praised your work on their family bible, and once I dropped some pages…"

"The Bunyan work?" Oliver smiled. "I rebound that some weeks ago. You did not notice?"

"I have not dared to touch it for fear of worsening its condition."

"It was the first book I worked on, and Mr. Darcy never knew. I had heard, from beneath the balcony where I examined some fine Italian volumes, the rustle of paper and your dismayed exclamation. After you left, I searched out the work that Mr. Darcy told me you were reading and spirited it off to work on it, returning it the next day. You did not even miss it?" Oliver's teasing smile, again crooking his ridiculous mustache, irritated her.

"No, sir. For a whole week I could not even look at it on the shelf." Then Mary sat back, relaxed. She would never have to confess that to the formidable Mr. Darcy.

Mr. Oliver looked away and coughed a bit nervously. "I have begun ill, Miss Bennet. My real thought this evening was to ask if you knew that Mr. Darcy had requested that I accompany you and Lady Elliott when you return after Easter—Lady Elliott to London and you to Hertfordshire."

Mary had not known. Still, Elizabeth had promised to send someone, but Mary had assumed it might be Mr. Shepard or one of the servants. "No, sir. It is a very long journey."

"For me, it will be even longer, as he sends me into my native Kent on a summer errand. Reverend Wynters will return to the country then, and he will preside at summer services."

Mary shrugged. It mattered little to her, but she thought he might have sounded more sorrowful at leaving his parish so soon.

Oliver regarded her solemnly. "I hope this will not interfere with your plans or lessen your comfort."

She remarked the concern in his voice. "Oh no, sir; Mrs. Darcy told me she would send someone with me, and I believe Lady Elliott is very nice." Kent… the county name finally reached her consciousness, and she felt she knew the errand. He would be checking on Miss de Bourgh's romantic alliance. Fortunately his primary attentions must go to Lady Elliott, and she need not join much in conversation, or she might find it hard to conceal her guilty knowledge all the way to Longbourn. The carriage slowed in the Pemberley drive, and she realized she may have spoken curtly. "Thank you for the escort—tonight and on the journey to Longbourn. Good night, Mr. Oliver."

He stepped out, handed her down, and looked at her archly. As he bowed, he intoned, "'Let truth be free/To make her sallies upon thee and me which way it pleases God.'"

How strange, she thought, as he started off. Then she recognized the quote from *Pilgrim's Progress*, just at the place where the pages came out. She called after him, "And I thank you for mending Mr. Darcy's book too!" She watched him bow to Mr. Shepard, who drove past him to the stables, and then Oliver strode off.

## Chapter 11

THE VERY NEXT WEDNESDAY, MARY HAD CAUSE TO RECALL Mr. Oliver's assessment of Emmaline Langley. Practise over, Mary removed her spectacles to address the girls and commend their work. She also reminded them of the times of services during holy week, so that they could make plans to be present. Then she complimented Tom for his work on the bellows, being most happy that he could now attend practises. She was truly relieved that their most difficult motet went well enough that she could be sure of it for Easter. She assembled music to take home for practise and hurried to the staircase. Halfway down, she realized she had left her spectacles on the side of the organ. She sighed, and turned to move back up against the girls coming down. Reaching the top, she saw Emmaline seated at the organ, the spectacles on her nose and her fingers brushing the mute keys deftly. Emmaline removed one hand from the keys, shook her finger at Lucy Ostrom, who, with Dorothy Baker, watched entranced. Her pinched nose gave her voice a nasal tone as she admonished mockingly, "Miss Langley, pay attention there!" Lucy and Dorothy doubled over, laughing.

Mary watched awhile in some amusement from the dark well of the stairway, and suddenly she realized the scene could well have been Lydia displaying the same high spirits, and the resemblance came clear to her. She stepped forward, they noticed her, and a sudden silence grasped the girls. Mary shook her head at the foolishness, and at that moment, it dawned on her that Emmaline's pattern of fingering had had method to it. She exclaimed, "Why, Miss Langley, you really can play the organ!"

Emmaline reddened and jumped off the bench, handing the spectacles out to Mary. "No, Miss Bennet—I play only the pianoforte."

Mary retrieved her property and put them in her reticule. "If you and Tom both come early next week, I could acquaint you with the stops and pedals, and I dare say you could learn the organ readily enough. Or I could work the bellows while you learn." What a fine thing if she could train up a successor, one who might relish the position.

Emmaline, still flustered and embarrassed, nodded her agreement. Mary flipped on some stops, went to the bellows, and said, "Let's try. Play what you were playing." After twenty minutes, Mary determined that Miss Langley would indeed make an organist with a little practise. Knowing that Mr. Shepard awaited her, she excused herself, saying she would come early the next week. She rode home amazed at this "Lydia" who had learned at least the discipline of music.

A fortnight later, the Wednesday before Easter, Mary walked to Kympton thinking of Emmaline, who had progressed nicely. The day at Pemberley had been busy, with grooms and carriages much in demand even late into the afternoon. Darcy distributed Easter gifts to his tenants, Elizabeth visited Jane, and Mrs. Reynolds had sent Shepard on several shopping trips to Lambton. Mary, no horsewoman, happily undertook the walk on such a fine late afternoon. The route had become as familiar to her as the path from Longbourn to Meryton, and it was not a whit longer. Mrs. Reynolds assured her that Mr. Shepard would be there for the return trip as usual, though Mary said she could walk back as well if need be.

The girls and Tom were assembled in the loft when she arrived, and she hurriedly apologised to Miss Langley for not meeting her earlier. While they practised, Mr. Oliver was busy in the church below, walking from workroom to sanctuary, preparing the church for the next day's ceremonies. This kept Emmaline's eyes, if not on Mary, at least in the right direction. Practise went well, possibly because the girls preserved a kind of Sunday decorum or possibly because they enjoyed singing music they now knew well. Even difficult harmonies presented few problems that required their going over it again. Mary did not sing nor had she threatened to do so, though she smiled now, remembering her father's advice. Their Maundy Thursday hymn and ritual music, as well as the more glorious motets for Easter, were refined and polished as fitting for the high holy days.

After asking the group to be on time for the morrow, Mary followed Tom down the creaking spiral of the stairs only to discover that not only was it raining, but no carriage awaited her. Mary shrugged, turned back for the umbrella she kept in the loft, and stamped heavily up the stairs. She did not wish to surprise any more impromptu frivolities. As the girls filed past her, she warned them of the rain. "Be sure to change your boots as soon as you reach home. We want no hoarse voices for Easter!"

Umbrella in hand, Mary ventured out into an evening that was still somewhat light but overcast and dripping. She hoped for clearing, though the aid of the full moon would surely come too late to help her, so she resolutely set out along the road Shepard always used.

Unfortunately, Shepard did not come nor did the rain subside. Instead, the dripping increased to a soaking downpour. Though she was able to hover beneath one of the ample bow windows of the cottage during a particularly heavy spate, Mary arrived at Pemberley a sorry, sodden clump, dripping pools in the foyer. With Polly's ready help, she changed completely for a late supper, but her throat ached and scratched its warning that she, at least, would be hoarse indeed. How fortunate it was that her voice was not needed.

Chapter 12

Thursday dawned bright, but Mary found she could not leave her bed. Fever, dizziness, a stuffy head, and muscle aches all attacked at once, and when she tried to stand, she fell back onto the bed. She tried to tell Polly that she must be up and dressed, but no sound came. Polly, though interpreting correctly Mary's intentions, shook her head and left. She returned shortly with Mrs. Darcy, followed by Mrs. Reynolds, who exhorted Mrs. Darcy to leave the sick room, lest she endanger her baby.

Elizabeth did return later, however, and found Mary leaning comfortably on her pillows in half-sleep, having downed the dose of honey, lemon, and spirits that Mrs. Reynolds had ordered. "Mary, Georgiana has agreed to play the organ today for you. She will be up to check with you about what you planned for Maundy Thursday. Here is a pad and pen for a list." She placed pad, pen, and inkwell on the stand next to her bed. "How fortunate it is that she and Lady Elliott returned so soon from London!" Elizabeth also handed her a small grocer's bag. "Mr. Shepard sent you some mint suck-upons to soothe your scratchy throat, and he begs me to add his abject apology. You just stay here and get well."

Mrs. Reynolds again shooed Elizabeth from the sick room and sat down beside the bed, the very picture of remorse. "Oh, Miss Bennet, if only I had not sent again to the greengrocer for the additional condiments cook requested for the Easter feast, none of this would have happened. Can you ever forgive me?"

Mary tried to tell her not to worry, but finally just touched her hand. Soon Miss Darcy came to sympathize and to make sure of the day's music, and Mary scribbled out a list. Miss Darcy took it, examined it, and asked, "Is the music here?"

Mary shook her head.

"Is it at the church?"

Mary nodded.

"And I will not need to sing?"

Mary smiled and shook her head, then fell back on the pillows. Lady Elliott came in to add her condolences, and she soon left with Georgiana, who wished to go early to Kympton to see and arrange the music.

Mary slept most of that day and Friday, only partially awake for the onion soup that Mrs. Reynolds fed her every few hours. "Mrs. Darcy wanted to tend you herself, but I insist that she not expose her baby to any possible infection. Besides, your illness is my fault, you poor dear." Mary smiled wanly, finally growing used to her inability to speak. When even Mr. Darcy came to commiserate, Mary, shocked at his brotherly attentions, actually appreciated her lack of speech, as she did not know what to say to him.

Saturday found her no better. She was vaguely aware of a note and a lovely lily that appeared in her room, and it was only later that she learned they had come from Mr. Oliver at Kympton Saint Giles. Mrs. Reynolds remarked on her red nose and swollen throat, while her continued stuffy head and forced silence warned Mary that she would not be up on Sunday. When it appeared that the Easter music must proceed without Mary, Georgiana came with pen and paper to volunteer timidly for the sunrise service. Mary managed to list the music, but her head was so fuzzy that she could not be sure the order was right. She added at the bottom: "Miss Langley knows. She can help."

As she looked at the uncertain scrawl before her, Georgiana said, "Would it not be wonderful if you wake tomorrow feeling well enough to go?" Mary smiled and closed her heavy eyelids. That was a resurrection she did not expect, and she did not think Georgiana expected it either.

Mary remained stubbornly ill despite chicken soup from the kitchen, rose-petal syrup and carpenters' herb from Mrs. Reynolds, and reed rhizomes and herbal tisanes ordered by the apothecary. She grew no worse, but her listlessness and other symptoms persisted. Miss Darcy played at both Easter services, and she returned in the afternoon smiling with relief. "It was lovely! Miss Langley helped a great deal, and the sermon moved me deeply. If I had not been nervous, I might have enjoyed the whole morning. Lady Elliott appreciated Saint Giles too and said Mr. Oliver is an uncommonly good preacher." She looked pityingly into Mary's pale face and disheveled brown hair framed in the immense pillows. "Are you no better today, Mary? The sun is so bright."

Mary squeaked feebly from her propped-up position. "Perhaps." A barely audible sound emerged, and she smiled, hoping for some improvement soon.

"Mr. Oliver sent you this, in gratitude for your work in preparing the choir so well." Georgiana held out a package in plain wrap as for the post. Mary frowned intently, and she elbowed herself higher in the bed. She slipped off the loose wrapping to find a fine bound volume and a note.

She read: "I asked young Tom to copy this music for you to keep. He fancies himself a composer, so it was good practise for him. I hope our choices were happy ones. Steven Oliver."

Mary turned the pages slowly, reverently. Damon's "Have Mercy, Lord, on Us"; Cruger's "In the Cross of Christ I Glory"; Bach's "Jesu, Joy of Man's Desiring"; hymns by Herbst, organ pieces by Bach, Hassler, Gardiner, Wesley, Hodges; and some lively folk tunes at the end. It was truly a magnificent collection and all in one book. "What a treasure!" Mary exclaimed, and it came out in a frog-like whisper, but audible. "How can I ever thank them?"

"You can get well. That would please us all."

Mary did indeed feel some sign of improvement—enough to wish she could move to the music room with her new folio. And in a few days she did just that, delighting in the firmness of the binding, the easily-turned pages, the sure way each page remained flat and open on the stand at the pianoforte. She had seen no such book before, and she wondered if it was a binding of Mr. Oliver's original invention. She sent a note in praise of his and his pupil's work.

## Chapter 13

MARY, ENJOYING HERSELF ALONE IN THE MUSIC ROOM WHILE Georgiana entertained Lady Elliott in the morning room, began to play some of the folk tunes in the back of her precious book. She skipped over ones that she already knew well—though she noted that these had new and interesting-looking harmonies—and she concentrated on the new ones, attempting them one after the other. One particularly sprightly tune caught her fancy, and she stayed with it until her playing grew easy and loud, at last giving quite a lusty rendition. Georgiana burst into the room, followed by a perplexed-looking Lady Elliott.

"Mary! What are you playing?" Georgiana looked flushed and excited.

Mary turned back two pages to the title. "It is called 'Mansion of Peace.' Do you know it?" Almost at once she recognized one passage as the tune Georgiana reverted to so often in her melancholy. "Oh, is this your remembered piece? I did not at first recognize it; I must have played it at the wrong tempo."

"Not at all. I am sure you have it right. Oh, please, may I try it?"

Mary rose from the bench immediately. "But of course. I did not mean to secure your instrument for myself."

"Oh I want you to feel free, as you well know. It is I who may wish to secure your treasure-book for my pleasure. I swear I will copy every note for myself, only humour me just now." Georgiana turned back to the beginning and studied it awhile before playing. "Oh! There are words too." And unselfconsciously, Georgiana did what she rarely did in front of anyone: she sang as she played, and she adopted the livelier tempo as indicated. When she finished, she said, "Oh, Mary, it is like finding a lost childhood friend. How can I ever thank you?"

Mary flushed with pleasure, and she would have torn out the pages for her, but Georgiana shielded the book as the treasure it was, and she reached for pen and the staff paper which Darcy had carefully lined for her use. Soon she was thoroughly absorbed with her copying, and Mary tiptoed over to Lady Elliott to explain to her in a whisper about Georgiana's obsession with the tune. Then she excused herself to pay a last visit to her other treasure, the library, for a delightful hour with Bunyan and Cowper.

Her energy almost back to normal, Mary helped Polly collect her belongings for the journey home to Hertfordshire. Her palpable yearning for the plainer comforts of Longbourn surprised her. Oh, she might miss the large soft beds, ginger beer at tea time, and Sunday suppers of vegetable pie, and she would certainly miss the library, but she could even look forward to the frivolity of the Meryton assemblies. Those folksy social gatherings had never appealed to Mary before, but she found herself pleased at the prospect of a society where she knew everybody. Her months at Pemberley had stretched to a much longer sojourn than she had reckoned. While she had grown comfortable enough at Pemberley, she felt assured that life back at Longbourn, even after being the guest of her sister, would still suit her just fine.

In these last few days, Darcy had been much at Kympton, and one day Elizabeth confided to Mary that Mr. Oliver's errand in Kent would involve his meeting Lady Catherine and Miss Anne. Mary nodded. "That is kind of Mr. Darcy. He is a devoted nephew." Mary, relieved to know legitimately at least that much, still hoped she could manage the long ride without any conversation on the subject. Overhearing her host and his aunt stuck in Mary's consciousness "like burrs," as Bunyan had noted of fancies. Mary, not much given to fancies, let guilty knowledge haunt her in much the same way. She preferred to ignore whatever she did not need to know, and she endeavoured to push unwanted words from her mind, "like sparks that from the coals of fire do fly." She thought then of Oliver's words about Elizabeth, and she wondered greatly about Lizzy's quiet mood during Darcy's absence. After a lull, she ventured to ask, "Lizzy, Mama says you married Mr. Darcy to atone for refusing Mr. Collins and losing Longbourn for us. Was that true, or did you really love Mr. Darcy, as you seem to now?"

Elizabeth, completely unprepared for such a query, looked at Mary as if wondering what thoughts had prompted such a question. "I loved him then deeply, immensely, though perhaps not as much as I love him today because there are always new reasons to love. How could you ever think otherwise?"

"Well, Mama accounted for your changing opinion of Darcy by her own constant scolding you for refusing Mr. Collins. She thought you were providing for us, and I was truly grateful. But it did seem, seeing you here with him, that you loved him very much, and I was confused."

Elizabeth studied Mary for a while, noting her serious, open expression. "I see. No, I never could convince Mama that I truly loved Darcy, possibly because it was only Papa and Jane who knew the whole truth about him. Now I will tell you. It was Darcy who found Lydia in London, Mary, and who paid Wickham's debts, and who purchased his commission in a second regiment, and he did it for love of me. When I learned that, I was completely in love, though my dislike of him had long since melted away."

Mary was dumfounded. "It was not Uncle Gardiner?"

"No. Of course, he could not take the patrimony of his own children for any such thing. But I know I may trust you to say nothing of this. I do not believe either Kitty or Mama could keep from embarrassing Darcy if they knew it. Lydia is bad enough. She feels somehow that it entitles her to ask him for even more on account of his generosity to them once. I knew by that gesture the fine man Darcy was, and when he asked me again to marry him, I accepted gladly."

"*Again?*"

"Yes, that is the wonder of it. He did all that even after I had rudely refused him, thinking him the world's proudest man. I was even worse to Darcy on that occasion than I was to Mr. Collins on refusing him. Oh, you can imagine my love and gratitude when he swallowed his justifiable pride and asked me again. I thank God for it daily."

Mary, amazed at this discovery and happy for Elizabeth, promised solemnly to keep her secret, only sorry to have yet another secret to harbour. "I see now why you seemed so quiet and sad when Darcy went to London. I fully expected you to be more relaxed, yet it seemed you were much less so."

"That is true. I feel complete only when I know he is nearby."

Mary respected her greatly for her revelation, and as much as she had appreciated what she had seen as Lizzy's sacrifice, she was delighted to know it was never made.

The journey in Lady Elliott's magnificent carriage did not discomfit Mary as her travel north had done. The carriage, with its decorative stripes of silver and red, impressed her even before she viewed the cosy interior. And whenever they passed someone on the road, the Elliott arms on the side of the coach drew interested glances to see who travelled within.

Mr. Oliver, as eager for his native Kent as Mary was for Longbourn and Lady Elliott for London, made even meal stops brief. Then, he kindly returned to the carriage with boiled eggs or biscuits, or cheese and fruit whenever the inn offered such foods, fearing the ladies had been rushed. Mary felt no lack along the way except for, as Lady Elliott pointed out, a decent wash-up. Darcy had provided generously, and when they stopped, Oliver always enquired after the best that the inn offered.

Once, when Lady Elliott slept, Oliver stared thoughtfully at Mary from his perch across from her. Finally he said in low tone, "Have you accepted your youngest sister yet?"

Mary looked at the carriage floor. "I believe I must. You may be right about Lydia, for you knew about Lizzy."

"You asked her?"

"Yes, sir. Soon, I may see Lydia at Longbourn to observe her more carefully as well. Perhaps when you are in Kent, you may meet Mr. Collins and learn why he advised us as he did."

"Mr. Collins?"

"He is the vicar of Hunsford and my father's cousin. If Lydia does repent, he may change his mind too."

Oliver laughed softly, glancing at the sleeping Lady Elliott. "Mrs. Wickham may well have repented her choice many times over already. Mr. Darcy led me to believe that the wife of a man like Mr. Wickham would have many reasons for sorrow."

Mary frowned. "Still, she has always acted as if she did a clever thing in catching him. It is a pity he was so celebrated in Meryton as a handsome prize to be won."

"Of course, I saw her but once, and my impression may be inaccurate, but she appeared as a waif desperate for fun to forget the miseries of her lot. Did you not see it in her eyes at the ball?"

Mary struggled to recall her fleeting glance at Lydia on that occasion. "No, sir. I had not looked at her closely, and I am not good at forming conclusions at any rate. I only heard her empty laughter."

"Ah, you heard, then, the forced quality of her gaiety. Did that not speak to you of her misery?"

Mary puzzled about that. "I cannot say I have ever been so astute as to see what any person would wish to conceal. I have not the gift." Pretence, so foreign to her own habit, escaped her notice in others. She resolved to accept Oliver's assessment, and in future, she would look more carefully at Lydia's bravado. She sighed deeply.

Oliver smiled. "Perhaps that is only because you would not think of putting on a false impression for the benefit of others."

She wondered how he could know that. "Mr. Oliver, when I was very young, I heard a prayer in church begin, 'Jesus, our internal Shepherd...' Up to that point, I had lied as much as anyone, mainly to avoid the discomfort of Mama's displeasure. But from that day on, I imagined Jesus shepherding my inner thoughts, and I have tried to live without disguise. When I said it one day to Lizzy, she laughed and said the prayer was to 'Jesus, our *eternal* Shepherd,' but I held to my version because I want Him there. But I try so hard to be forthright that I am blind to others' deceits. However, in Lydia's case, I will try in future to see it your way."

"And forgive her?"

"Oh please, Mr. Oliver. To forgive is to accept such a lordly role. People do not offend me. My sister Jane always said most injuries are mere fancies not at all intended by the so-called offender. I try to avoid fancies. How can I be so bold as to forgive?"

Lady Elliott, who had been awake some little time, remarked, "How beautifully bizarre!"

Mary's face warmed, and she was not sure that Mr. Oliver had not reddened, finding the Lady awake. He spoke in more normal tones of his youth in Kent, and he seemed in good spirits, Mary thought. He referred to games played with his two older brothers behind inns and butcher shops. He said his brothers were robust boys who called him "Bookworm" or "Preacher" from his earliest remembrance. Mary could relate to that, but when she tried to compare the Kent he described to Elizabeth's description of the country parsonage at Hunsford with its surrounding woods and hills, she deduced Kent must be a most varied county. She told him so.

"Oh, we visited the country too. Once, when we were exploring the woods, Richard and Martin forged on ahead, pushing brush and twigs aside, but I could not keep up, and every hefty twig snapped back into my face. They found that hilarious. A particularly sharp withy cut my lip so deeply they had to take me home to be bandaged, staunching the blood as we went. The scar is still there, but at least I can cover it now with a moustache." He fingered it, smiling.

Mary, ashamed at having found the moustache a dandyish pretension, yet teased, "And did you forgive them?"

Oliver sat up straight, frowned, then erupted in laughter. "Why, you have me there! I believe I never looked upon it as injury so much as my own awkwardness. I think I probably felt guilty for making them take me home."

## Chapter 14

AFTER EXHAUSTING HIMSELF IN ENTERTAINING THE LADIES FOR several miles, Mr. Oliver lapsed into lulls of quiet and finally nodded off, leaving Mary to amuse her hostess in the Elliott carriage. "Perhaps it is my turn to sleep soon, Lady Elliott, but I do not think I could fully relax in so grand a carriage; I might drool on the plush bolsters or fine silk hangings."

"I pray you, do not worry about such trivialities." Lady Elliott laughed, revealing dimples in her pale cheeks. "Are you impatient to be home, Miss Bennet?"

"I believe so, though not so much as to make me anxious. I have been away longer than I intended, and certainly longer than ever before from Longbourn." Mary looked out of the spacious window on to the rolling hillsides. Her mind went back to Pemberley with its lovely rolling park. "Lady Elliott, have you known Miss Darcy for a very long time?"

Lady Elliott paused to think. "About seven years. Actually, I knew her companion, Mrs. Annesley, and it was when I encountered Mrs. Annesley in Bath that she introduced me to Miss Darcy. They had gone there to see if Mrs. Annesley could benefit from the waters."

"And did she?"

"Not that I noticed. Nor did Lord Elliott, who had hoped the waters could cure his apoplexy. In fact, he died there."

"Oh, I am sorry." She was indeed sorry to have started such a subject but searched in vain for another. "It is sad that people go there only in their extremity, when it sounds such a romantic place for a vacation. I suppose the experience discouraged you from ever returning?"

Lady Elliott smiled. "My experience did discourage me, but it was not merely my husband's death that did so. Bath itself is all vapor, shouting, smoke, and confusion. If that is romantic, I will have none of it. Has not Miss Darcy given you a similar impression?" She adjusted her pillows so as to have a more comfortable view of her companion.

Mary thought awhile. "No. Miss Darcy has been wonderful to me, but I believe she speaks less about herself and her experiences than does anyone else I know. When I asked about her recent stay in London, she said only that she always enjoys being with you. She did not mention a single museum, theater, or park. She said only that you went somewhere everyday, and that she was well entertained. She might have been anywhere from her account of it. She certainly never mentioned Bath to me."

"Well, as to that, I say intelligent girl! The less said about Bath, the better." Lady Elliott smiled and shook her head, causing grey curls to bob beneath her bonnet. "But I know what you mean. Miss Darcy notices everything, tries to please whomever she is with, and dwells little upon her own concerns. The most I ever saw of her spontaneous enthusiasm was upon hearing you play her song. Then nothing would keep her from finding out about it. And your hint about her striving to find a part of her lost childhood is the closest I have heard to an explanation of her shyness. You must be a very observant young lady."

Mary hastened to assure her that this was not so. "I only hear what others say. It was Elizabeth—Mrs. Darcy—who told me about that tune she plays. And as often as I had heard it, I was so dull that I did not so much as recognize it when first I played it. Georgiana did that herself." Mary leaned back and thought of Georgiana, wondering if she was happy. How strange if she should not be, as rich and as loved as she was. "I do hope she finished copying it, for I have my copy with me to enjoy at Longbourn."

"I believe we can be sure she has it. Every clue to that past must be precious to her. I now recall that she perks up on some London streets, and once she even asked me to slow the carriage while she peered carefully at some of the large houses. I believe it was near Regent Street. Do you happen to know anyone who lives there?"

Mary shook her head. "Not unless the Darcy town home is near there. The only persons I know in London are my aunt and uncle, and they live in Gracechurch Street. I do not think they could possibly have known Georgiana as a child."

"I suppose not." Lady Elliott refrained from pointing out the unlikelihood of Georgiana's ever having visited so unfashionable a district as Cheapside. "I would love to help her find herself; she is such a dear soul. Perhaps when next she visits, we will keep going to the area she is curious about, until she may see something that brings back a memory." Lady Elliott then leaned back, engrossed in her thoughts.

Some time later, Lady Elliott left her two passengers at a London post where Mary had to await a carriage to Hertfordshire and, Mary assumed, Mr. Oliver to Kent. Mary reluctantly bade farewell to the elegant lady, happy to have come to know her a little better.

When Mary turned to say farewell to Mr. Oliver, she found him bent on escorting her to Hertfordshire before going to Kent. When she looked at him quizzically, he shrugged, "Mr. Darcy instructed me to see you safely to your family. You do not mind?" Mary actually found herself relaxing, and until then she did not know how reluctant she had been to travel post by herself. Fortunately, their wait was short, as was the distance to Meryton, where the postillion pointed out a carriage waiting at the Dragon Inn. Mary recognized it as her father's, and she looked around for Wilkins. She thanked Mr. Oliver for his kind attentions. "I'll not detain you, sir, and I bid you good journey into Kent." Mr. Oliver alighted from the carriage then to hire a carriage back to London, and when he waved and smiled to someone behind her, Mary saw with surprise that her father and Kitty waited by the carriage. When Wilkins transferred her trunk to the Longbourn carriage, she again said farewell to Mr. Oliver and joined Kitty in the carriage.

Mr. Bennet greeted her warmly. "Ah, Mary, we have missed your pithy remarks. You have stayed away too long; we are all in danger of sinking into frivolity. And while Kitty and your mother do not think it such a perilous state, I have suffered great anxiety." He grabbed her bandboxes and put them on the highboard with Wilkins.

Mary ignored his wry humour, just happy to be back. On the ride from Meryton, she listened patiently to Catherine's excitement over glimpsing again "that tall, handsome Mr. Oliver—who smiled at me!"

Mary immediately felt sorry that Catherine's visit to Pemberley would likely take place during Oliver's whole summer stay in Kent. And what a pity that the vicar could not entertain Kitty's attentions, which should certainly have been more welcome to him than those of the silly young choir girls. Then Mary sat back in the coach, marshalling her thoughts and affirming her resolve to enjoy visits with her mother. Having accompanied Elizabeth on errands to townsfolk she did not know at all, she would welcome visiting familiar neighbours. She would study people with the attention that she had heretofore reserved for books and music. Lacking lively effusions of wit and humour to add joy to her world, Mary resolved to imitate Georgiana in the way she served others' wishes in all that is good. She had enjoyed full acceptance at Pemberley while doing Lizzy's bidding, and she would be an agreeable sister to Lizzy when living there permanently.

*Volume Two*

# Chapter 1

IN THE DAYS THAT FOLLOWED, MARY FOUND CATHERINE LESS giggly and less tearful than formerly, when Lydia had been her favoured companion. While Kitty remained at Longbourn preparing for her journey north, Mrs. Bennet concerned herself with those preparations as well. Though Mary wished to do anything which would further Kitty's desire to wed well, she often found herself at a loss. Thus, she pursued her own interests, devoting herself to books and music as she used to do, while yet deliberately keeping alert to the others, even helping Kitty from time to time with suggestions for which gowns she may wish to have at Pemberley. Catherine was blossoming into a winsome and gracious young lady who may well profit from lengthy visits to sisters whose judicious marriages enhanced Kitty's prospects for a good marriage.

Mary spent some hours with her fine music book that Tom and Mr. Oliver had made for her, and she set about memorising the motets and most of the lively diversion pieces included in it. She often found herself turning to the much-fingered pages of "Mansion of Peace," and she wondered whether Georgiana's influence or her own preference drew her.

After Kitty and Mr. Bennet departed for Derbyshire, Mary's days followed her mother's schedule more often than her own, and reading and music both suffered. She resolved not to mind this, telling herself that her new study of people around her must be increased. The first day without Kitty found Mary accompanying her mother to see Lady Lucas. "She is tiresome enough, I know, Mary, but she will want to know all about how Lizzy's baby is progressing, and you are just the one who can tell her." Mrs. Bennet handed Mary her bonnet, making Mary wonder at such haste. She tried to recall incidents when she had noticed Charles and his progress, but the only one that came to mind she felt was unmentionable. She wondered at Lizzy's telling even her that the baby had bit her while nursing. Well, she might at least report that he was teething.

In the event, Lady Lucas found more obvious pleasure in recounting, when Mrs. Bennet allowed her the time, all the exploits of Lucas and Louisa Collins, who, as Lady Lucas said "were of much more interesting ages" than the Darcy baby. At the Lucas home, Maria Lucas was summoned to entertain them at the pianoforte, giving a creditable performance. Other than congratulating her, Mary found little time or opportunity to speak at all.

Another day they had to visit Mrs. Philips for a lively exchange of Meryton and Longbourn news. There, after listening for a while and finding it a repeat of the news recited at Lucas Lodge, Mary politely requested of Mrs. Philips to try her pianoforte, as it was in another room and would not disturb her mother and aunt. Happy for the surprise practise session, she discovered—when she found it irksome to flatten the music constantly while playing—that already no book but her own pleased her.

Most evenings, however, Mary could pursue a shorter form of her chosen regimen, especially as the days lengthened. And she resumed her needlework also, since Lizzy had pressed upon her some fine linen to cut, hem, and embroider so she may have linens like Pemberley's. Certainly Mary, considering her chosen future, had no need for such things, but she enjoyed some satisfaction in the accomplishment. Perhaps she may offer them as a gift on the occasion of Kitty's wedding, should that take place soon. Fingers that played organ and pianoforte were now as educated in plying the needle, and Mary gloried in her new achievement, which she hoped always to use to benefit her hostesses.

One June morning shortly after Mr. Bennet returned from Pemberley and the daily routine settled in, Mary looked for a welcome stay-home day, as most of the country families would be deep in preparation for the Meryton midsummer assembly. She worked the edging on a pillow cover in a pattern Lizzy had taught her and found, as she smoothed the embroidery, that she quite liked it. She reached for its mate as Mrs. Bennet bustled into the morning room carrying Mary's Sunday bonnet. "Mrs. Philips has brought the most wonderful news! Put your things away, Mary. We must visit Mrs. Long."

"But, Mama, I have this pillow sham to finish, and we hardly ever visit Mrs. Long except at church." Even as she said it, Mary realized she was going against her resolve to please, even if her hostess was her mother.

"To be sure, child, but this is a special case. You can do your work another day. Come, come."

Mary feared that the next day's free time was in doubt, though as yet her mother had not mentioned the assembly. She reluctantly put her things away, already feeling the loss of her plan for the morrow, which was to copy notes on Blake and Cowper, and work on a new étude. Mary knew her regret went against her deeper resolve to interest herself in people around her, but her old ways bid fair to return.

Mrs. Bennet would not be put off. "Come, hurry! You cannot find a husband by staying at home with all your planned work."

Mary smiled. "I cannot find a husband at Mrs. Long's house either." But that she did not regret, as she finished putting her sewing things away in her reticule. "Why is Mrs. Long so important today?" She fixed her bonnet on her head.

"Why, because she has a *nephew* to visit—such a welcome change! Mrs. Philips says he is a fine, fashionable young man of about twenty, with four thousand a year from a nice little property in Nottingham." Mrs. Bennet grinned smugly.

"What a pity Catherine is not here to meet him!" As she carefully tied the ribbons of her bonnet, Mary groaned inwardly. How tiresome that her mother could not relinquish her urge to marry off her daughters! "Mama, could you not wait until Kitty returns? She wishes to marry."

"Of course she does. It is the duty of every girl to wish to marry. And mind you, do not own to your full twenty-two years before young Mr. Stilton. If you smile more, you will look quite as marriageable as either of Mrs. Long's nieces, and they both have fiancés."

Mary felt herself enlightened as to Mrs. Long's sudden desirability. Having found someone for the nieces, does Mrs. Long now mean to service the nephew? It would be a strange nephew indeed who allows that. Mary glanced wistfully at her unfinished work and dutifully accompanied her mother out the door. On the walk to Mrs. Long's house, she firmly resolved to discourage any interest the poor, unsuspecting young man might muster for her. She knew she could not convince her mother that unmarried girls could indeed thrive as well as their married sisters, but Mary would not change her mind for all her mother's pleading.

Chapter 2

M RS. LONG SMILED BRIGHTLY AS MARY AND MRS. BENNET entered her parlour, and her welcome for Mary was if anything even more warm than that for Mrs. Bennet. "My dear, we began to despair of your return to Hertfordshire after comforts such as your mother described at Pemberley." Her teeth clicked in a way Mary always found so distracting.

"Oh, Mrs. Long, you must know that luxuries are never so comfortable as are the familiar, ordinary things of home." Mary curtsied and sat in the chair indicated by Mrs. Long's knobby outstretched finger.

"You hear that, Mrs. Bennet? That is just the kind of good sense Mary is known for, and that is the very reason I am so glad to see her."

Mrs. Bennet, who had remained standing while she examined the room to see if any additions had been made since last she saw it, nodded with satisfaction. Not only had no changes been made in the plain room, but her daughter had pleased this loving aunt, so perhaps she would also please the nephew. She sat down comfortably in a straight chair, her back erect. "Such a lovely room this is, so warm and bright."

Mary frowned as she looked at the faded walls and frayed curtains. What could her mother mean?

Mrs. Bennet went on. "You do well to keep it just as it is. How I envy you these spacious windows."

Mrs. Long dipped her head slightly. "And in high summer, I am grateful for the larches which shade them." She cast a knowing look at Mrs. Bennet. "You heard, I trust, that my nieces from Devonshire have engaged to marry their neighbours, the Davis brothers. They often visited me in hopes of meeting someone more exciting, but perhaps, like Mary, they learned that home comforts are best."

"Why yes, Nellie, your sister did tell me your news, and I am delighted for them. Their mother is fortunate to find them settling so near home. I am forever telling Mr. Bennet that sad was the day when Jane and Bingley moved from Netherfield. What fine visits we had when they were so close. Not that I resent Mr. Grantley's coming here, mind you, especially as he has shown such favours to Mary. But to have my daughters settling so far from Hertfordshire is a great inconvenience to me."

"Of course, though my sister would not dislike a bit of a journey to visit them now and again." The click of her teeth made it sound as if she disapproved of something, but Mary was unsure what it was. "But now my brother," went on Mrs. Long, "sends me his son from Nottingham, a dear boy, James Stilton. I am at a loss to know what he means to do here or how I am to entertain him. He talks of hunting and horses, and I can offer him little enough of either. Of course, he has his own horse on which he made the journey. And he speaks of returning to Nottingham in plenty of time for the goose fair in early autumn."

Mrs. Bennet looked a trifle alarmed. "But surely he means to attend the midsummer assembly at Meryton?"

"I do not know. He may enjoy cards, and for all I know he dances." Mrs. Long touched the gnarly fingers of her two hands together. "Of course, he does play the pianoforte—a strange thing in a young man—so possibly he also dances." She sounded unsure, or else it may have been her manner of speech which again reflected disfavour. She turned to Mary. "I have asked my Lottie to send him in here. Perhaps you would request to see the pianoforte. You know so much about music, and you could tell if he plays well or not."

As if on cue, the young man himself appeared at the door. Mary wondered in fact if he had not been listening some time in the hall, waiting to make a splendid appearance at the opportune time. Splendour marked his attire, certainly. He was dressed in a white linen shirt, grey vest and tights, and tall boots; and his wide smile beneath sharp blue sparkling eyes lighted first on his aunt, then on Mrs. Bennet, and finally on Mary, who did not return the smile.

"Good morning, Aunt. You wished to see me?"

"Yes, James," she said, clicking. "Meet my neighbours, the Bennets. Mrs. Bennet has kindly brought us her musical daughter, Mary. Perhaps you will demonstrate for her the fine tone of my old pianoforte."

Mary looked sharply at Mrs. Long, uncertain as to what that lady desired of her now that she had made the overture herself. So she turned her solemn glance to the young dandy, his lingering, impish smile pasted on his face as if covering some secret joke. After an awkward silence, Mary felt she had stared long enough on the silent boy and she rose in dutiful response to his aunt's offer. She warily followed Mr. Stilton to the pianoforte in the sitting room adjoining the parlour. He played a lively tune not at all badly, and then he pulled another stool up to the instrument and asked her to play the bass portion of some four-hand arrangements of folk songs. "I usually play these with my friend in Nottingham who likes to copy and transpose all kinds of music. He thinks one day to compose music himself, but I have seen nothing of his. I believe that, like many young men, he overestimates his talent." Mary noted that he seemed not to include himself among those young men. She attempted the bass part which, somewhat repetitious, presented no problems, and she easily kept his sprightly pace for "The Highland Laddie." Much of the interlude in the music room went well, despite the lingering odour of dying roses in the close parlour. James had obviously been told something of Mary's ability, and he kept up his tight smile—*Encouragement?* she wondered—as they played. When they reached the last of the duet arrangements, "The Irishman," he sang in a thin but accurate tenor, ending with "Nobody loves like an Irishman." She did not recognize that line, and she turned to frown at his leering smile and his arched eyebrows. "Of course, I have a good deal of Irish in me. Can you tell?" The too-familiar gleam affronted Mary, who found all his smiles more teasing than pleasant, and saying nothing, she turned away.

Mary rose from the stool. She hoped to discourage his forward manner. "I know few Irishmen, though I believe my brother-in-law, Mr. Darcy, is Irish on his mother's side." At the same time, Mary suddenly realized that Darcy's aunt, Lady Catherine, must also be Irish, and the thought did little to dispose her happily toward that nationality. This young Stilton was certainly not at all to her taste, though his proficiency at the instrument impressed her. "I do not know any other young men who play the pianoforte."

As if ashamed of his prowess, he said through his smile, "People do not often think of music for a sporting man. When I was but eight, I asked my father to let me drive his four-in-hand, and he handed me the reins. The horses ran away with us, and Papa grabbed back the reins as the horses wrenched them from me. He told me my fingers needed exercise, and he recommended the pianoforte. I attacked the exercise with a will, meaning to become a better horseman. By the time I could handle that carriage, I also enjoyed the music, and I am sure that is what Papa wanted." Again he turned his suggestive grin on Mary. "Papa has a sly way of trying to change my behaviours. In fact, I suspect he sent me to Hertfordshire as part of a plan to reduce my gaming. He greatly objects to paying my debts." He looked off, thoughtfully stroking his sharp chin. "I must find a way to run up a few while I am here, just to thwart him." He turned again to the instrument and took up a piece that Mary particularly liked. It was so lovely that the thought of his shocking habits and of his defiance toward his father flew from her mind.

She glanced at the title over the notes, but the hand-copied page simply read, "Transcription." He noted her interest, and he rose, bowed with a flourish, and offered to let her try it. She played it over a few times, until she could play it at the tempo she had heard.

At that point, Mrs. Bennet, weary of old stale gossip in an old stale room, came to summon Mary to walk home. "That is pretty, Mary. What is it?"

Since Mary did not know, Stilton told her. "My friend from Nottingham transcribed part of a harpsichord piece for pianoforte. The whole of the original is a second concerto of those called 'Brandenburg' by Bach." He turned as Mary rose to join her mother. "If you plan to attend tomorrow evening's assembly, I shall bring my music and we might play for the guests. You are planning to attend, I trust?" His grin irritated the daughter and charmed the mother.

Mrs. Bennet quickly answered, "Of course we will be there. It is our social duty to join our neighbours." Mary had not so planned, but she knew she must go to please her mother.

When they left, Stilton's ceremonial bow annoyed Mary even as his everlasting smile ingratiated Mrs. Bennet. All along the path, Mrs. Bennet ignored the lovely white birch wood on the crystal afternoon as she pressed upon Mary the importance of cultivating "that charming young man who is to inherit a decent property in Nottingham. What a fine thing for you! You could live near Jane and Bingley!"

Only relieved that James had not repeated any words or gestures of unseemly intimacy, Mary said, "Mama," hoping by her tone to discourage her mother's visions of such a bleak future. She could perfectly well live near Jane and Bingley one day, maybe even with them for a time each year. She did not need Mr. James Stilton for that.

## Chapter 3

THE MIDSUMMER ASSEMBLY SURPRISED MARY, WHO RATHER enjoyed it. She wondered if indeed she resembled her younger sisters in the days of their frivolity. Mrs. Bennet and Mrs. Long watched fondly as young Mr. Stilton took Mary's hand and led her near the top of the set, just behind Miss King and Jeremy Lucas. Stilton's dancing rivaled the high fashion of his watch chain—much hung with seals—and his clear blue eyes glistened, somewhat wildly to Mary's mind. But the clinking of his watch chain so amused her that Mary actually smiled while dancing. Mr. Grantley claimed her for the next two dances, surprising Mary and her ever-watchful mother, to say nothing of the many other mothers who had never before seen that man forsake his cronies and join the dance. And when he commented on how she seemed to enjoy her first dances, she thought again of the ridiculous clinking, and the word "rattle" came to mind. She smiled again because the word applied so fittingly to Stilton.

"This is midsummer madness indeed," said Lady Lucas to Mrs. Bennet when she came to enquire about Mr. Stilton. That young man had introduced himself to Lady Lucas prior to asking Maria Lucas to dance, exactly as his aunt had primed him to do. Afterward,

Maria introduced him to Miss King, while Mary Bennet danced with Jeremy Lucas, and then with his brother Richard. Stilton, quite the beau of the ball, showed his aunt that he could indeed dance, and what's more could enjoy it, and Mary shared in his popularity, as he returned to dance with her twice more.

On the way home, Mrs. Bennet did not seem overly pleased with Mary's smiles. "You must smile at a man, not as if you find him amusing, but as if you find him irresistible. Then he will find you irresistible too." Mary only smiled again, deciding that she wanted neither to find a man irresistible nor to be found so by any man, least of all Stilton.

Back at Longbourn, Mrs. Bennet happily recounted Mary's triumph to Mr. Bennet, who took it calmly enough to enrage Mrs. Bennet. "How fortunate that I directed Mary to wear her blue muslin tonight, for she made such a fine picture with young James Stilton in his finery! Of course, she added a tucker of lace, which vexed me. She has as nice a figure as any girl there and could show it to greater advantage, but Mary will be so tiresomely modest. Oh, but that fashionable young Stilton set her off though—why, I believe she danced every dance."

"Oh no, Mama," Mary corrected. "During one set I answered Maria Lucas's questions about Mr. Stilton, and another time I stopped for refreshments with Mr. Grantley." Still, to herself, Mary had to admit a certain pleasure in not pursuing her usual course of watching others and reflecting on the good Christian lesson of being overlooked.

Mr. Bennet, eyebrows raised, regarded Mary solemnly. "And your legs did not stiffen or fall off?"

Mary took him seriously, as usual. "Oh no, Papa. If anything, they became more limber."

"I am glad to hear it."

Mrs. Bennet, hearing Mary so matter-of-fact about her evening, hastened to take the account back into her own hands. "And she danced *three* times with Mr. Stilton. Such a fine, elegant young man in a linen shirt of the latest cut, dark blue tights, and a prodigiously handsome watch chain! Mrs. Long herself said the two of them might have been made to stand up together. What a delightful neighbour she is!"

"I perceive, Mrs. Bennet, that Mrs. Long with a nephew is far superior to Mrs. Long with nieces," Mr. Bennet said, leaning back in his leather chair.

Undaunted, she went on. "Indeed yes. And then, you know, after supper Mary and Mr. Stilton played a duet that delighted the whole company!"

"You mean the whole company actually listened? How singular!" Mr. Bennet's tone registered his just doubts. "And who is this paragon, pray, who sweeps our Mary off her feet?"

"Why, a nephew to Nellie Long, of course, as I told you—you know, her brother's son who will inherit a fine property of his own in Nottingham of *five* thousand a year."

Mary frowned at hearing the property's estimate growing at her mother's every recital. Why, at any rate, did she try to impress her own husband?

Mr. Bennet turned to Mary who was still frowning at the suggestion of being swept off her feet. "And Mary, did not Mr. Grantley take it ill that you found a stunning new friend?"

"Of course not, Papa. Why ever should he? I danced with Mr. Grantley as well—and do you know he did not even bring his walking stick? I do not believe he needs it at all, and he certainly seemed younger without it. He complimented us both on our duet after supper, and he did not seem out of sorts about it."

"And you took refreshments in his company. Did he not question you about the American essays?"

"Oh yes, Papa. He said I was to tell you 'It is a wise father who knows his own daughter.' I do not know what he meant by that."

Mr. Bennet smiled. "Why, I would say he meant that your interpretation of his book must be truly original. Did you enlighten him on the real meaning of American freedom?"

"Certainly not. I only told him he could have his book back at any time, as I would not read such drivel a second time. It is in your library, in case he should call for it, though he urged me to keep it. I do not care for such paradoxical sentiments."

"You found them so, did you?" Mr. Bennet looked his interest, encouraging her to go on, though Mrs. Bennet continued to make clucking sounds of disapproval. It was not her idea of a proper topic at a ball.

Mary went on, obliging her father. "Yes, Papa. Such fervour for liberty is itself a slavery, and to an idea that could so easily become a rage for doing exactly as one pleases. It fully explains why men would rebel against our sick king as if they had the right to do so. But I think that the contented man who accepts whatever God sends is freer by far."

Mr. Bennet laughed gleefully. "And did Mr. Grantley share your sentiments?"

Mary shrugged. "I do not know. He laughed just as you did now, and then he gave me your message."

Mr. Bennet, still smiling, sat back at ease. "So you had your triumph at a ball. Well, it is your turn, Mary. But mind you, do not lose your head and go running off to Gretna Green. I do not know how your mother and I would keep our composure without your sage words now and again."

Mary reassured him. "Of course not, Papa. I have no intention of marrying at all. It hardly seems necessary now, you know. Kitty may do so, as she is keen on it, but I would not wish you to be left with no daughter at all."

Mrs. Bennet immediately and vehemently objected to any such proposal, and Mr. Bennet calmly supported his wife. "Oh, if it comes to that," he said, "I have become quite a traveller of late. If your mother and I visit three, or even four, counties a year, that is fine with me. We need hardly stay home at all."

Mrs. Bennet did not look pleased at his response, and Mary sat silent, feeling sad. At length, Mr. Bennet asked, "Is something amiss?"

Mary sighed. "You did not say five counties, and it occurs to me that poor Lydia's improvident husband may keep her moving from county to county herself. How she must long for a home! It is a pity she was overeager for a husband and marriage."

Her father was silenced, and he looked at his daughter with rare genuine respect. Mary felt his wonder but also felt she did not deserve it. She knew that it was Mr. Oliver who had noted Lydia's disguised misery. But if Lydia were to visit Longbourn, Mary resolved to notice it for herself.

IN JULY, LYDIA WICKHAM DID VISIT LONGBOURN, AND SHE CAME alone. Her sullen pettishness relieved by bursts of wild laughter and her offhand remarks disparaging the homely pleasures of Longbourn rendered Mary's study almost unnecessary. That was fortunate, for it was a kind of study so foreign to Mary that she knew she would have botched it utterly. Rather, she accepted Mr. Oliver's word on the state of Lydia's misery, and she interpreted Lydia's every action as confirming it. This left her with an immense wonder that a stranger could, at a single meeting, assess a truth that Lydia obviously meant to hide. But it did not render Mary capable of equal discernment. Lacking his clue, Mary realized that she would certainly have believed every word Lydia said and would have been shocked by much of it.

Mary knew her lamentable record on that ability. Had she not, at Pemberley, marvelled at how the Darcys always managed to sit or stand close during an evening, seeming to want no other amusement? Had she not heard their giggles over the jealous antics of Darcy's hunting dog, Fitz, when he shoved his nose between them? Had she not witnessed their shared pride and awe over the perfect tiny fingers and toes of newborn Charles? Yet, she'd had to ask Elizabeth if she loved her husband! Mary resignedly felt that this was simply her nature. She regarded Mr. Oliver's insight as divine inspiration of Biblical proportions. Mrs. Bennet had told Mary, "Lizzy marries this stiff and odious man because she thinks of you and your future." As always, Mary took the words at face value. Any other knowledge of her sister came from what townspeople said of her, and if their views contradicted her mother's, she merely tried to puzzle out some solution or accept the enigma. Her study had always been for music and books. She heard and mentally recorded people's words in the same way she copied words she read. Could she ever hear what a person did not say? She resolved to try with Lydia.

During the three weeks of Lydia's visit, Mary had cause for compassion rather than censure. At the July assembly, Lydia's still-bold, still-childish teasing for dances too often bounced off mother-warned youths who withstood Lydia's advances. Could the whole tattered history of Lydia's elopement have been unfolded even to Stilton? Even he did not consent to partner Lydia until Mary prevailed upon him to do so, and she noticed that he went to his aunt immediately afterward as if he had to explain. Later, when the sisters met to talk of the dance, however, Lydia compared Stilton unfavourably to the dashing militia members no longer quartered in Meryton. In Mary's new view of Lydia, she saw this as wistful memories bringing back Lydia's carefree days. Could Lydia possibly have come to believe herself ill-suited to marriage or at least to marriage with Wickham? Certainly she did not act like a married woman.

Then abruptly, after a session in the library with Mr. Bennet, Lydia left Longbourn. Mary became again her mother's sole excuse to visit abroad or to stay home to welcome Stilton, whose habit it was to visit for an hour or so, usually in the music room. After that,

Mrs. Bennet invariably found some reason to go out, and Mary's plans for other summer accomplishments had to be curtailed. Still, Maria Lucas had taught her to cut silhouettes, and she had a passable profile of Mr. Stilton, cut in the music parlour, before he returned to Nottingham. She had done that only for something to do after he had examined her treasure book, admired its binding, and then dismissed the selections with extreme distaste—"So much church music!" It was then she recalled that Mrs. Long appeared at church alone during the whole of Stilton's visit. Her dissatisfaction with that silhouette began at that thought.

She preferred the more recognizable one she had cut of Mr. Grantley, who had graciously consented to sit for it after a visit with Mr. Bennet one evening. She also had a tolerable one of Mr. Bennet, much criticized by Mrs. Bennet as "entirely too roundish." She had never managed one of Mrs. Bennet, who could not sit long without talking or gesturing.

August arrived without Mary's memorising a single étude since June, without having read a whole book since early July, and with several linens hemmed but not embroidered. Then, in the second week of August, just when she was feeling rushed to complete some of her work before her Michaelmas visit to Jane, Sir William Lucas called to ask if she might accompany Maria to Kent for a visit with his older daughter Charlotte. It was to be short, a mere fortnight, during which he was required to be in London. He proposed to accompany the two girls to Hunsford, then leave again immediately, returning to escort them back. He explained that Maria required company while there, lest Lady Catherine concentrate too much on her when they must visit Rosings Park. Maria had never overcome her awe of that imposing dowager, and she wished for Mary because Mary seemed never flustered. Mrs. Bennet, having no

Stilton to require Mary's attention, urged her to go see for herself whether Lady Lucas had truthfully told of Charlotte's wonderfully comfortable life. Mary agreed and was ready to leave by the last week of August, though she hardly relished a journey south so close upon her journey north.

# Chapter 5

Sir William and Maria entertained Mary on the journey with tales of Hunsford: its splendid gardens, its comfortable rooms, its serviceable staircases. Much of the talk reminded Mary of Collins's own panegyric on his vicarage when he wished to make Elizabeth his wife. Later, they turned their praises to Rosings Park, and again Mary felt that Sir William did little but quote Collins on that grand estate of his noble patroness. Mary recalled that Elizabeth had told her the substance of his information without any elaborate commendations, and as mere riches did not excite her any more than they had Elizabeth, she directed her questions to news of Lucas and Louisa Collins, and away from Lady Catherine. Sir William was glad to boast of his grandchildren, and for much of the remaining journey, he regaled them with tales of their antics. Most of these Mary had heard from Lady Lucas, but she did not mind the repetition. Finally, she remembered the name of Harold Witherspoon and asked about him, but Sir William knew little. "Mr. Collins praises him as a humble and industrious verger." He did not even know what that young man looked like, never having visited on the Lord's day. As they neared Hunsford, Maria pointed out landmarks familiar to her in the beautiful countryside, while

Mary kept thinking about the verger, glad that she would soon be able to make up her own mind about him.

They arrived at Hunsford on Monday afternoon, and Charlotte welcomed them warmly. Mr. Collins, whose surprisingly expanded girth suggested vast prosperity indeed, bowed less and boasted more than Mary had remembered. He showed her around the ground floor of the vicarage, insisting that she admire any addition suggested by Lady Catherine. In the morning room, she had to exclaim over "the new draperies that hang like silk" and at the stairway observe "the genuine mahogany newel post." Mary only nodded at this. To her mind, finery of any kind amounted to mere vanity, nor could he show her anything she had not seen at Pemberley, where it was regarded as ordinary. As he spoke, she grew more conscious of his apoplectic mien, his puffing, and his halting speech. She worried about his health and became overly conscious of his size. Try as she might, the saying "The bigger they are, the harder they fall" stuck in her mind. It occurred to her that it may be young Lucas who would inherit Longbourn, or even Charles Darcy! Not knowing the full provisions of the entailment, she could only conjecture as to what would happen if Collins should die before Mr. Bennet. But truly, Mr. Collins did not look well.

Mr. Collins had stopped at the staircase, and Mrs. Collins approached. "Observe my dear wife," he said, as if she were part of the tour, "she keeps to modest apparel. She does not braid her hair nor adorn herself with gold or pearls or costly array. Lady Catherine praises her in all things, though she sometimes scolds her for feeding me too handsomely." He patted his stomach. "Lady Catherine would approve your plain apparel as well, Miss Bennet. And Mrs. Collins tells me you made yourself useful in a Derbyshire parish with your good works. That is a fine thing in a woman." Mary idly puzzled over his praise of embellishments in furnishings while he decried them in women.

Sir William approached to take his leave, telling them duty called him to Saint James Court, and Collins walked out to the carriage with him.

Charlotte did the honours above stairs, much to Mary's relief. She did not think she wanted to see what climbing stairs would do to Mr. Collins. Charlotte merely showed Mary to her room and made sure she would again find the way. She also said wryly, "It is at Rosings Park, where meats are many and sweetmeats rich that Mr. Collins is urged to eat his fill. Then he must—he says, out of politeness—praise each food, in thankfulness to his generous patroness."

Young Lucas, whom they encountered in the nursery, took to staring solemnly at Mary. A sturdy, quiet lad of about four, he surprised her by approaching to touch her gown as Charlotte pointed out educational reasons for the nursery decorations. Charlotte frowned at her son and directed him, "Lucas, you must bow to Miss Bennet, and say good day. You must not wrinkle her nice gown." As he obeyed his mother, she said to Mary, "He usually runs from strangers. I can not imagine why he did that."

Mary assured Charlotte that she was more honoured than disturbed by the attention, while Maria tried in vain to attract the child. "Lucas, come to Aunt Maria." But he stood his ground and bowed to her as well.

Although distracted by the solemn child's continuing stare, Mary saw only gentleness in Lucas, and she occasionally turned to smile at him while attending to Maria as she gave Charlotte news of Lucas Lodge.

By Tuesday, Mary had learned that the vicarage had no pianoforte and few books. Happy that she had improved her needlework skills, she offered to help Charlotte, who was sewing dresses for Louisa to grow into. Charlotte explained, "I found myself always a bit behind with Lucas, who grew faster than I had provided for. Lady Catherine frequently pointed out that his sleeves were too short for his arms. With this child, I mean to be prepared."

As they worked quietly, the companionable comfort recalled Mary to Longbourn with her sisters. Then Lucas, released from the nursery for a time, wandered in and watched attentively, gradually edging closer to Mary. He did not touch her, but kept his eyes on her hands as she worked. Mary, moved by his silent surveillance, smiled at him as she worked. Charlotte observed in amusement, "I believe he finds in you a kindred spirit, a person of deep quiet. Usually, he follows me around, though now he takes quite an interest in baby Louisa. He screws up his face and seems upset if she cries. But never have I seen him attach himself to a visitor as he does to you."

Later, when Lucas returned to the nursery presumably to nap, Maria joined them in their work. She had been walking the grounds to remember favourite haunts of her previous visits, and she reported on some changes. "The little glen surrounded by trees has been much used since last I was here. Was it you who put hassocks by the tree stump?"

Charlotte looked her surprise. "No, not at all. I would not touch that area, as it is part of the Rosings estate." She paused, considering Maria's information. "Perhaps we are wrong about Miss Anne never meeting Witherspoon in the woods."

Glad for the mention, Mary ventured to put her questions about Witherspoon to Charlotte, who laughed gently. "Oh, he just showed up here one Saturday last year and presented himself to Mr. Collins. He calls him 'Venerable sir,' which pleases Mr. Collins. And he offered to do odd jobs about the church, saying it would please him to work 'so near to God.' Now he arrives at every week's end, stays at the inn, and comes to polish the candelabra, bells, and thurible on Saturday. Then he brushes the pews, cleans the floor, changes flowers, makes himself a regular servant to the church. On Sundays, he rings the church bells, attends the service, and follows Mr. Collins out. I notice that when Mr. Collins engages Lady Catherine in conversation at the door, Witherspoon bows to Miss de Bourgh and endeavours to give attentions to the daughter as Mr. Collins does the mother. He used to bow to me also, but I ignored him, and he discontinued the habit, for which I am grateful."

"Surely you were not rude to him. I cannot think that." Mary had always respected Charlotte as Elizabeth's good friend.

"I hope not. I just try to be busy enough with the children to appear not to notice him. Something about the way he creeps about the place unnerves me. If I am not mistaken, Lady Catherine shares my sentiment. She once asked me privately if I thought that Witherspoon and Anne meet secretly in the park. At the time, I pointed out to her that Anne never goes out alone and surely is not strong enough to attempt it on foot. I felt that I reassured her, but now I do wonder." Charlotte held up the frock she was hemming and studied it as if measuring. "Mr. Collins gives the fellow a shilling each week for his services, and he bows and thanks my husband as if it were a half crown. There is something of the packman or thimblerigger in his manner, but I cannot imagine what he could be selling."

"But he comes only on Saturday? Where does he live?" Mary pressed the newly embroidered cloth between her hands as she had seen Elizabeth do.

Charlotte glanced approvingly at Mary's work. "I believe he said he lives with his ailing mother somewhere in town. And he must have some work there as well, for he does not lack money. However, he never talks of it, and while here he wears a kind of pinchbeck shovel hat and seems to emulate a clergyman. I admit that at times I see a touch of mockery in it, but despite my misgivings, he seems a harmless young man for all his strange ways." She set aside her finished work and thought awhile. "Still, Lucas runs from him." She said this slowly, solemnly, as if perhaps her remarkable son may have insight she might attend to.

Mary finished the small robe she had been decorating. "I rather look forward to seeing him; he sounds a fanciful character."

Charlotte praised her fine work, thanking her even as she wondered when such talent had been acquired. As far as she could remember, Mary had assiduously neglected needlework in the years when Charlotte was their Hertfordshire neighbour.

At dinner Maria, having become curious through Mary's questions, brought up the name of Witherspoon. Mr. Collins, rolling his eyes heavenward, called up an eloquence usually reserved for a Rosings Park meal. "Ah, such a splendid young man! He is so conscientious, so industrious. I wonder how we ever got on without him. After his week's work in London, you know, and caring for his ailing mother, he comes here to offer himself, just to embrace the church. Miss Bennet, you would appreciate him above all, as you too have offered yourself in service to a church in Derbyshire. Mr. Witherspoon is so honest, so forthright, and so eager to please. I daresay, when you meet him, you will see how much you two have in common. And each Sunday, you know, he presents a small gift to Miss de Bourgh—some sweetmeat or trifle brought from a London baker's shop. He once told me he fears that Miss Anne lacks nourishment. Can you imagine such kindness, when he cannot be a wealthy man, surely, and must work hard for every shilling. But, you know, I worry about him, living as he does in cheap rooms in London, where he may be exposed to typhus or worse. Indeed, last week I thought I heard him cough. You remember, Mrs. Collins; it was when Miss Anne mentioned his many arduous labours. What a shame the man has never taken orders! He has such respect for the clergy and takes on all of the verger's work here at Hunsford, saving me a great deal of labour, God bless him."

Charlotte offered Mary a second slice of roast, and as she declined, Collins helped himself to it and another dollop of potatoes with gravy. "There is just one strange habit Mr. Witherspoon has," he said and then paused, chewing slowly. "That is, when he greets little Lucas, he bows and calls him 'Master Lucas, future vicar of Hunsford.' And then he laughs as if there were some joke. I can make no sense of it."

Charlotte gently spoke up, while handing round the fruit bowl. "My dear, you observe how Lucas runs from strangers, and he usually runs from Mr. Witherspoon as well. Perhaps your verger simply attempts to take the rebuff in good humour."

Mr. Collins nodded as he chewed, and Mary found herself astonished at Charlotte's appearing to explain in so gentle a way the actions of one she had admittedly thought disagreeable. Here indeed was the dutiful wife, speaking as her husband would approve. As to Witherspoon, she eagerly awaited the Saturday arrival of this oily paragon. She would judge for herself, using her best attempt at discernment.

Chapter 6

WEDNESDAY MORNING, AS MRS. COLLINS AND HER TWO helpers added to Louisa's future wardrobe, Rose interrupted the intermittent, low hum of their homely chatting. "Excuse me, ma'am, but you and Miss Bennet have a caller in the parlour."

"Who is it, Rose?" asked Charlotte, as Mary looked up in puzzlement at hearing her name.

"Mr. Steven Oliver, ma'am."

Surprised at having forgotten that the vicar was in the area, Mary slowly laid aside her work, arranging it carefully.

"Thank you, Rose," Charlotte said as she stood. "Maria, do come along. I believe you will like Mr. Oliver."

Mary said, "I did not know you were acquainted with the vicar of Kympton."

"Oh yes. He has been living at the inn for many weeks, but I believe he said he would be returning to Derbyshire this week. Perhaps he has come to take his leave."

As they entered the parlour and greeted their visitor, Charlotte introduced her sister, and said to Maria, "Mr. Oliver has been consulting with Mr. Collins and Lady Catherine, as he holds a valuable living from her nephew, Mr. Darcy, near Pemberley."

Mary watched as Oliver bowed to Maria, endeavouring to notice what Kitty called his "kind brown eyes," but in the low parlour light, they looked to her merely frank, deep, and shaded.

Having greeted Maria, Oliver bowed to Mary. "Miss Bennet, I have met your cousin, as you supposed I would do, and have had many fine conversations with him and also with Lady Catherine. In fact, I reported to her this morning, as my work here is over. Perhaps I will leave for Derbyshire tomorrow. I do long to see the people of Kympton again."

"I hope you will speak with Mr. Collins again, Mr. Oliver," Charlotte remarked. "He has greatly enjoyed his talks with you."

"Thank you, Mrs. Collins, but I met Mr. Collins by the beehives just now, and I took leave of him. I could not go without saying farewell to you also, but I see I leave you in better company. Did Miss Bennet tell you what great assistance she offered my parish, Mrs. Collins?" Oliver's smile took in Mary as well as Mrs. Collins.

"No indeed. Mary is far quicker to help than to speak of it. But Lizzy kindly wrote to me of Mary's willingness to play the organ at Kympton." Charlotte took a seat and gestured the others to take their ease in the small but comfortable parlour. Mary saw that the few tasteful ornaments and the plain chairs exactly fit the modest manse. Only the silky drapery seemed too fine for the room, to Mary's thinking.

Mr. Oliver smiled again as he sat. "Oh more than that! Miss Bennet took on a dozen or more rather lively young girls and formed them into a fine choir. She has a talent for quiet management."

Charlotte readily agreed. "I believe even my young son has sensed it. She is the first stranger he has ever favoured."

"You have an astute lad, Mrs. Collins. Or perhaps you have raised him to a discriminating taste. I congratulate you."

Mary, embarrassed at such notice, turned and meant to speak quietly to Maria on some less personal topic, but Rose came in, and all turned to her. "I beg your pardon, ma'am, but an express just come for Miss Bennet, and the courier wishes to receive a reply." She offered Mary a short note.

"It is from Papa," she said after she opened it.

Charlotte showed her concern. "I pray all is well at Longbourn." Mr. Oliver expressed concern too, and Maria could hardly contain her agitation.

Mary finished the note and assured them. "All is well at home," and she turned to Maria, "but our family must leave for the North sooner than we had planned." She caught Charlotte's eye. "Mr. Darcy's cousin, whom I believe you have met, Charlotte, is to be married at the Cathedral of Norwich Mills, and Mama has a special invitation from the earl, which she says must be accepted." She turned again to Maria. "Oh Maria, Wilkins may come for me on Sunday. I am truly sorry that I cannot stay here longer with you." Mary took the pen and paper Rose had brought for her reply.

Mr. Oliver hastily broke in. "Miss Bennet, why put Mr. Wilkins to such a journey? As I mean to go so near, could I not accompany you to Longbourn? If I am not mistaken, your mother would take it ill to be sending out a servant when she must make hurried arrangements. I can readily put off my leaving until Friday, if you need time to prepare. You may even be at Longbourn by Sunday."

Mary saw the sense of it, and she wanted to be grateful. But to miss seeing Mr. Witherspoon now that her curiosity was so aroused disappointed her more than she could admit was proper.

Oliver noted her hesitation. "I assure you, Miss Bennet, I would consider it an honour to be of service to your family. Please allow me to do this."

Afraid she may have offended the gentleman, Mary turned quickly to Maria. "Now I must ask to abandon you even earlier. I am truly sorry."

Maria quickly assured her. "Do not worry about me. Charlotte promised me that if we are invited to Rosings, she will bring the children, and Lady Catherine always concentrates on them, so I will have little to fear."

Mr. Oliver laughed gently. "Yes, Lady Catherine is a formidable, majestic presence, is she not? But, I think, harmless."

When Mary saw that Maria too could laugh, she thanked Mr. Oliver, and wrote her note, with a message sure to please Mr. Bennet, who hated to part with Wilkins. She promised to be home by Monday or Tuesday, hoping to surprise them even earlier if possible. Oliver certainly read Mrs. Bennet accurately in assuming that she would want all servants at her ready call. How astute he was, even with so slight an acquaintance of Mrs. Bennet! She felt confirmed in taking his word on Lydia's true feelings.

As Mary handed the finished and sealed note to Rose, Oliver took his leave, promising to call for Mary early on Friday. As the three ladies returned to the morning room, Mary pondered the kind of discernment Oliver showed with Elizabeth, Lydia, and even Mrs. Bennet. Perhaps along the way, he might reveal his assessment of the paradoxical Witherspoon.

Chapter 7

Mary, not overly eager to attend the Norfolk wedding, but happy to save time and effort for her family, took leave of Hunsford early on Friday with a secret sigh of disappointment at never seeing for herself the storied Harold Witherspoon. Maria, in saying good-bye, whispered her promise of a full report on the young man. Oliver called for her in a hired carriage whose owner had business in London, and he sat aboveboard with the owner as far as the London post house. Mary, alone within the carriage, tried to collect her thoughts after the day of rushing to get ready, but instead she nodded off. She woke to a view of needlelike trunks of pines in a sea of mist, and she idly watched a bead of water run a trail down the carriage window. Only then was she aware of a steady light rain, and she feared for the health of the two exposed on the highboard.

Soon the whirring of the wheels changed to a clatter, and Mary looked out at a dim and foggy London. Inside the Bell, Oliver assured her that the two on the highboard had kept fairly dry beneath a heavy blanket. They bade farewell to the carriage-man and ordered supper. After a generous cut of a joint of beef, with tea and buns for Mary and ale for Oliver, they learned, to their dismay, that the mist had erupted into a deluge. The postillion announced that no post could leave for Hertfordshire until morning, and then not until the road was tested and found safe. Mr. Oliver apologised to Mary as if the delay were his fault, and he guaranteed her a proper room for the night, as Mr. Darcy had provided ample funds.

Mary, sorry that she could not reach Longbourn early, yet rejoiced in the consolation that she had not promised the early return, so her parents would not worry. And if rain made the Hertfordshire road impassable, they would understand any further delay. Evening at the common room of the inn found Mr. Oliver in apparently good spirits. When Mary mentioned her regret at being the reason for his not leaving on Thursday as he had planned, he dismissed her concern. "I have sent my report to Mr. Darcy days ago, and I am not needed at Kympton while the Reverend Wynters is there. I hurried my departure merely because of my wish to see Kympton and its people again. Mr. Wynters does not plan to return to London until Michaelmas." Mary silently approved this eagerness to return. Surely a clergyman must feel close to his parish.

"Did you meet a Mr. Witherspoon, sir, while you were in Kent? I have heard much of him, and I really wished to see him for myself. Unfortunately, I never did."

Oliver's moustache turned up with his wry smile. "Oh yes. He is a strange character, indeed, rather small of stature, and somewhat ill-favoured in appearance. Perhaps for that reason he multiplies his bows and scrapes, as if everyone else is of the nobility and he the lone underling. But I found him a rather simple, trivial fellow for all his obsequious gestures. Miss de Bourgh appears to enjoy him, in an amused way. But I believe only your cousin Mr. Collins is truly fond of him."

Mary nodded, again regretting that she had not seen the fellow but not wishing to show undue interest. "Thank you. Perhaps it is as well I did not meet him. It might be embarrassing to be so treated."

"It was for me, I assure you. Like Mrs. Collins, I curtailed my conversation with him."

As the number of travellers stranded by the weather grew to a large mass huddled around the fire, Mary and Mr. Oliver moved to a far corner. For a while, at that remove, they could converse easily. Mr. Oliver expressed again his thanks for her work at Kympton. "The fine selection of hymns you taught those girls will fill their minds with a wealth of devotion as they mature."

Mary expressed her doubts, knowing well that their minds at present were hardly so enhanced. "Once, when they were mocking me, Miss Langley fingered the organ and they sang a different version of a hymn. They had changed 'wash the stains of sin away' to 'Miss Bennet staying in the way.'" She relayed this, feeling he should be shocked at such irreverence.

Instead, he laughed heartily, saying only, "Oh, that Emmaline! She certainly is a handful. Did you mind her acting such a quiz?"

Mary had to admit that she did not, especially since he had pointed out her resemblance to Lydia. "I believe it is quite natural for young people to display high spirits." But a tinge of resentment at his lack of compassion for her wounded dignity gave her second thoughts about this favourite of Kitty's. Also, it seemed that Emmaline presented stronger competition for Kitty than she had before realized. How very inopportune that by the time Oliver reached Kympton, Catherine may very well be on her way to Norfolk for the wedding, in the company of the Darcys. She would be losing any occasion to further the acquaintance she so desired.

Oliver spoke next of Charlotte Collins, whose good sense he respected highly, and he praised young Lucas, so devoted to his calm, sensible mother. Of Mr. Collins, he said little. Mary ventured to ask how he got on with Lady Catherine. His initial response was a grin and "Very carefully," but then he turned serious and thoughtful. "I was distracted by her continuous straightening and stretching her back as she sat. I fear she was in great pain, but she said nothing of it. One can understand curt speech, and even petulance if pain is tormenting a person." Again, Mary marvelled at his keen observations.

After a brief silence, Mr. Oliver seemed to relax another degree, and he mentioned that he had found time to visit one of his brothers. "Richard is ostler now where my father once worked, on Lord Gibbon's estate. We sometimes used to play there when Papa let us ride on the waggon with him. Richard reminded me how he and Martin teased me, calling me a dreamer and 'Preacher.' Now he prides himself on being a prophet, announcing my calling before I knew it."

Mary well understood teasing. "My younger sisters used to call me 'Miss Conscience,' and they meant nothing good by it. They also called me clumsy because they learned to dance before I could even curtsy. But dear Jane—Mrs. Bingley—patiently taught me both to curtsy and to dance."

"You were fortunate in Mrs. Bingley. I had no such relieving kindness, having only brothers. They outstripped me in all physical feats, usually daring me to imitate them, often to disastrous results, which amused them no end. Even when I grew taller than either of them, they could climb our large elder tree by leaping to a branch and hoisting themselves up. I could reach that branch without leaping, but never could get up there with them. They would sit up in that tree and laugh uproariously."

By the fire, a raucous singing swelled, more lively than tuneful, and Oliver spoke louder and faster, as if trying to keep Mary from being exposed to unseemly ribaldry. "Miss Bennet, will you be visiting Pemberley after the wedding in Norfolk?"

Mary also had to raise her voice. "I believe I am to visit at Otherfield—that is, my sister Jane's home in Nottingham. But we may venture occasionally to visit Lizzy at Pemberley. My two older sisters are very close. And I hope occasionally to revisit that fine library."

"Did I not see Mrs. Bingley at the Christmas ball? She was, I believe, that beautiful woman with a smile as serene as any angel in heaven."

"Oh yes. Everyone notices Jane for her beauty and goodness, though people are sometimes easier with Lizzy, whose lively wit charms them."

Oliver nodded as if he understood. "And I observed at supper on that occasion that the Bennet sisters enjoyed one another's company for a long time. I felt a twinge of envy."

"Then I am glad you found time to visit your brother in Kent."

"Not quite the same, I'll warrant. Richard still teemed with memories of my greatest embarrassments." The singing near the bar grew bawdy indeed, and Oliver hurried on. "Until I was sixteen, I believed every word they said, and they pulled some wild tales on me. Once when I was about ten, I noticed that Papa had milked all the cows but one, and I asked why he did not milk that one. Papa said, 'Oh, she is dry.' And my brother Martin took me aside to explain that she was lying in the pasture that morning when a snake came up and milked her dry. He spoke so solemnly I believed it, even after hearing him and Richard snickering together shortly afterward. The next day I offered to go to the farm with Papa to watch the cows and chase snakes away from them, and those boys got another laugh."

Mary smiled as she asked, "And did you forgive them?" She stressed the word "forgive."

Oliver laughed. Mary thanked him for so entertaining an evening and asked to retire. He saw her safely upstairs to her room and pointed out his, in case she should need anything. Mary could only surmise that his mission at Hunsford must have satisfied him greatly, to put him in such fine spirits. Perhaps Lady Catherine's fear for Anne had proved groundless.

Chapter 8

ON SATURDAY, MARY AWOKE EARLY, FINDING THAT THE FIRE in her room had died. The overworked inn servant being unavailable, she dressed quickly and ventured downstairs. The large room, strangely silent after the previous evening's revelry, exuded welcome warmth. Apparently many sleepers had been accommodated in the room, some of whom still slept on straw pallets by the door. Rain drummed steadily on the windows near the secluded table she chose, far from the sleeping travellers. The innkeeper came to her with rasher and eggs and coffee, which she begged him to exchange for tea. When he brought the tea, he gave her the unwelcome news that the Hertfordshire post was mired near Saint Albans. "The postillion rode in during the night for help, but no carriage can start that way until after the rain stops."

When Mr. Oliver joined her later, she broke the ill tidings, still fearful that he would greatly rue having delayed his departure to accommodate her ease. On the contrary, Oliver showed no discomfort or hurry. "We must thank God your man Wilkins was spared so perilous a journey." After breakfast, Oliver located a set of draughts and challenged Mary to a game. She had not played in years, and he claimed the same unfamiliarity, yet he won every game. At length, they passed the draughts on to two men who had been unobtrusively and unsuccessfully attempting to improve Mary's strategy. By then the inn again resounded with tales of upsets along the rutted and mud-softened roads, mishaps, delays, and near disasters. Toward evening, the flow of ale slowly turned an atmosphere of comradely misfortune into raucous hilarity alternating with angry shouts.

Mr. Oliver again contrived to shield Mary from the worst of the clamor. He found a relatively quiet corner, darker than they liked, but secluded. There, he coaxed her to describe her summer at Longbourn. She told him of Lydia's short visit and abrupt departure, of Mrs. Long's nephew and his music for duets, of Mr. Grantley and his just-for-appearances walking stick. Then she watched for his reaction as she added, "For the first week Kitty remained at home, and she told me of once walking Pemberley's grounds with you. You pointed out the snow-covered coppice wood as icing on a giant cake. She believes you have a poet's eye." Mary had hoped that the poet's eye, something she had not herself ever witnessed in the vicar, indicated some interest in Kitty. Surely Catherine would be superior to Emmaline Langley as suitable helpmate for a churchman. "It is unfortunate that you have been from Kympton in these weeks that she has been at Pemberley, else you may have come to know her better. And the great pity is that when you finally reach Kympton, Kitty will likely be at Norfolk with the Darcys."

"And will she not return there after the wedding?"

Mary found this question heartening. "Perhaps not. At least she will not be there long, as she returns to Longbourn with Papa and Mama."

Oliver was disappointingly unmoved by this answer. Even worse, he returned the subject to her first information. "May I assume that you did not meet your youngest sister with silence when she visited?"

Mary felt her face heat up. "No indeed." Should she tell him that she feared he had guessed correctly about her, that Lydia had laughed much, but only in sport? Had she learned to pity this sister tied to a ne'er-do-well for life? "Lydia seemed to have lost interest in former friends and neighbours. In some ways, I pitied her."

Oliver showed his gentle smile. "Of course, we will not talk of forgiveness. But pity… it is a start."

"Oh, as to forgiveness, I never fancied myself injured. And in general, my thoughtless inattention to others puts me more in need of forgiveness than of bestowing any." She looked off to the noisy end of the room and added softly, "In fact, on account of it, God may withhold forgiveness from me."

She had not thought Oliver would hear that, but he sat up straight, his eyes shadowed, yet with a piercing gleam. "Why should that be?"

"Do we not pray, 'Forgive us… as we forgive'? And I have not had reason to forgive, and to try to do so seems putting myself above some person who, as Jane always says, probably never intended to offend. Certainly thoughtless Lydia never did."

"What a singular notion!" Mr. Oliver paused, looking off into the distance. He returned his gaze to her, saying, "Consider rather that you forgive so readily that it happens before you even note any offence. Or because of your automatic forgiveness, you take no offence. In the same way, God's forgiveness can reach you even before you realize that you need it."

The intricate notion swam in her head, muddled with the stale air and damp mustiness of the inn. She knew not what to make of it, but it sounded vaguely hopeful, and she thanked him. She added, suddenly noting that rain no longer pelted the windows, "I do hope we may continue our travel tomorrow, though it is Sunday."

Mary, whose back was to the inn door, felt a fresh breeze as someone must have entered. At the same time, Oliver sat up, rigid and alert. Several loud voices hailed the late arrival curiously, asking about roads and rain. A man answered that the rain had stopped, and the wind being strong, guessed that roads may soon improve, though they were still soft. An order for ale all around greeted this welcome news, and shortly the newcomer, apparently desirous of privacy, came to a table just behind a coarse wooden pillar very near Mary and Oliver. She heard a chair scrape back and then another, and realized there must be two. Mr. Oliver, his eyes in their direction, shrunk back deeper into the shadows. Mary did not look around, thinking such curiosity improper for a lady. At any rate, the murky air and the thick post would likely prevent her seeing. But soon a placating voice quite familiar to Mary said, "Do not worry. You will have it soon. My wife did not succeed in Hertfordshire, but she will fare better in the North. Her sisters have not laid down rules as her father has."

Wickham, of all people! And in London, though Lydia said she had left him with his northern regiment. His speech certainly explained her sudden departure from Longbourn. Mary opened her mouth to speak, but Oliver raised his hand to silence her. He seemed to be looking around as if to make a quiet exit, but their corner was far from either stairs or door. He shrugged and mouthed the word "wait." The vicar seemed suddenly to have lost all his good humour, and his frown would have silenced her even without his impertinent gesture. Wait they did, while Mary formulated many warnings for Kitty about this volatile gentleman.

Meanwhile, the men behind her argued, though Mary heard little from the unknown man, whose voice, whining and low, only sporadically rose above the uproar over by the dying fire. He demanded money of Wickham, so likely he was one of the gamesters or tradesmen to whom Wickham owed money. Could Wickham be trying to escape from his regiment and this fellow followed him? She caught a bit of the stranger's plea. "... as good as done... keep up appearances... old one dies... money." They were strange words if money was owed, but the request for money was plain enough.

Wickham, closer to her, sighed—a long, not-quite-patient groan. "I can give you no more than a guinea at present, but more is coming. Be patient."

The other man muttered some more, then asked, during a lull at the fire, "Have you taken orders yet?"

"No. That takes money too, you know, and once you are married will be soon enough for that." He spoke as with authority, as if he were somehow in charge. That puzzled Mary.

The other man grew excited, and he shouted some parts of his response. "... sooner than you think... collapsed last night... surgeon not sanguine... Why do you think I contacted you?... need serious money... ready... dismiss the fat idiot..." The whole transaction began to sound more like one of Wickham's harebrained schemes than a debt of any kind. Mary pitied Lydia indeed now, since it seemed that she must somehow fund it. Still, if he means to take orders, perhaps Wickham intends to stabilize his life, and Lydia must benefit from that. It could do Wickham no harm to come closer to the church.

Wickham, speaking more seriously but still commanding, said, "No gifts are needed. You were certain of her last week, and you have no rival, surely." At this, he laughed sneeringly, and the other man joined in.

The other voice replied, "No, no one… fine lady… ready… take your place soon."

Wickham must have left the regiment and was to take a new place soon. As a clergyman? What a fine thing for Lydia if it should be permanent! But so much of this talk was unintelligible to her that Mary resolved to dismiss it all from her mind. If his situation improved, Lydia would boast of it in time.

Meanwhile, Mr. Oliver, his fists against his forehead, seemed to be in pain. At the sight of his knuckles white in flickering candlelight from the table, Mary tried to remember what she had heard of apoplectic fits, and she whispered, "Are you ill, Mr. Oliver?" He shook his head and again put out a hand to silence her.

Wickham was promising to send an order express to his wife to approach her brother for money for his schooling, since he had a ready position. Mary wondered why he could expect Bingley or Darcy to support him in some career, but his speech to the other man was full of assurance about it. The two, more companionable now, chuckled over some expected good fortune. Again Mary took heart for Lydia's sake if it were so. Mary heard one chair scrape back, then the other, and the candle went out. "Not so good as the living I should have got, but it will do." With that, Wickham led his companion back to where the ale flowed. They ordered more, then dropped their mugs on the table noisily and strode out into the night.

Mr. Oliver arose then and guided Mary to the stairs, where she asked him what he made of that extraordinary conversation. "Surely it reflected no credit on either gentleman. Did not you think so?"

They reached the upper floor before he replied. "As your friend Bunyan says, 'I wish I could speak truth in speaking better of them.'" Mary, hoping that his sombre feelings had lifted, laughed. But Oliver merely added sadly, "Nor can I now speak or think well of myself."

Mary's bewilderment showed in her puzzled expression. "But you said nothing whatever."

Oliver's smile lacked cheer. "In that forced eavesdropping, I was obliged to learn that I am an unspeakable fool to think I can judge character, and how I will suffer for my ignorant presumption!" Then he bade her to prepare to leave very early on the morrow.

Mary remained perplexed, and since she could not sleep, she tried to make sense of all she had heard. She too took herself for a fool in supposing she had known the vicar's errand at Kent. Surely it must have concerned Wickham in some way. But why would Darcy not have disclosed Wickham's erratic character to him? If he had done so, Oliver could not now be blaming himself for misconstruing it. Then she recalled how artfully Wickham had insinuated himself into society at Hertfordshire, earning a reputation superior to Mr. Darcy's over a short time. She finally dropped off to sleep after arriving at some dim sense of it all.

## Chapter 9

THE NEXT MORNING'S RIDE IN STRAINED SILENCE INCREASED Mary's conviction of the vicar's moodiness. She glanced out the window, saw many muddy patches alongside and ahead of the carriage, and she ventured a guess at his worry. "Do you think the liveryman will be able to avoid miring us? Perhaps we may be required to push the carriage out of a mud hole."

Oliver started from his brooding. "No, Miss Bennet. I believe we are safe." The vicar resumed his look of tense preoccupation. Mary left him to his misery, whatever it was, and directed her gaze out the window again. When they reached an inn where the horses were changed, Oliver handed her out, still in silence.

She glanced at his drawn face and guessed he had not slept. Perhaps he had gallantly offered her the only comfortable room at last evening's inn. "Mr. Oliver, I thank you for providing so well for me. I was able to sleep well indeed."

Oliver nodded absently. "I am glad, Miss Bennet. I cannot say the same for myself, though the bed was fine."

She congratulated herself on guessing at his lack of sleep, but she had apparently mistaken the cause. Her thoughts went to the conversation they had witnessed and to Oliver's blaming himself afterward for misinterpretation of the wily Wickham. That had seemed to bother him, and she hoped to restore his ease. "It is hard indeed to understand the machinations of a mind bent on deception, is it not, sir?"

His eyes opened wide. "How right you are, miss. And worse when one's only duty was to uncover that very deception and the attempt was bungled." He lapsed again into dullness, and she despaired of trying to lighten his mood again. Again she puzzled over Darcy's strange request. Surely he knew Wickham better than anyone else. Why send a stranger to report on him? She gave it up. She did not understand Darcy, and the ways of men were far beyond her ken. In fact, she hardly understood women! Fortunately they were not far from Meryton, and she could walk home from there if she had to.

In the end, she did not have to. Not only the rest of the Bennets, but Mary herself was surprised to arrive at Longbourn on Sunday afternoon. Mr. Oliver, anxious over something and eager for Derbyshire, hired a private carriage at Saint Albans to take them immediately to Longbourn, where he stayed only long enough to be sure that all Mary's things were carried into the house. There he apologised for allowing little time for rest or breakfast, excused himself, and went off. Mary firmly resolved to warn Catherine to forget that volatile man. Such a changeable man must be more suitable to the young and frivolous Emmaline after all than he was to Kitty.

At Longbourn, Mrs. Bennet proudly showed her the elegant invitation. "Just look at the embossed coat of arms! The Earl himself must have given the invitation though you see the note inside is in Bingley's hand. Such an amiable man! See how fine the sentiment is? Oh, the envelope too has the embossed insignia! And they are to be married in Norwich Cathedral. Caroline Bingley must be proud indeed. Just look Mary—we are to stay at the Earl's estate at Norwich Mills! We are to be guests of the Earl himself!"

"And the happy couple will be staying there too? And Jane and Lizzy?"

"Oh, yes. Happy couple indeed! Don't you know that you could have been the bride yourself? Why did you not work harder to please him after he was so impressed with you at the assembly?" Mary did not reply, but soon Mrs. Bennet again gloried in the prospect of actually staying under the roof of the earl. "I don't believe even Sir William Lucas has stayed at an earl's estate! Mrs. Philips is quite put out that she has not been invited, but I dare say even a castle could not accommodate all the relations of the Bingleys and the Fitzwilliams. I understand Mr. Darcy is to attend the groom, so in a way, we are related to both bride and groom. How fortunately our dear girls have married!" Mrs. Bennet's high spirits abruptly changed again, and she frowned a bit and added petulantly, "However, neither of my daughters has a title. I suppose Miss Bingley counts herself clever indeed to have carried off the son of an earl. A pity it is, as long as she was to have him, that Miss Bingley did not marry him years ago. Then my dear Jane and Bingley would not have left Netherfield. I am certain it was she who goaded Bingley into moving near Pemberley. What a disobliging, arrogant woman she is! The Colonel could surely have done better. And such airs she puts on—I wonder how she will bid us address her now."

Mary moved to calm her. "Mama, she will be Mrs. Fitzwilliam, no matter how she wishes to be addressed. It is the Colonel's brother who is viscount, and Mr. Darcy often says the Colonel neither possesses nor desires a title. But he does have a nice little property near Castlebury, and Miss Bingley may enjoy being thought a great lady in Castle Park. Still, Pemberley is much greater, Mama. You may be assured that Lizzy fares much better." Mary admitted to some curiosity about the earl's Norfolk estate, but she felt no real eagerness. It was unlikely she would get to explore the Norwich Mills library.

Mary, according to Mr. Bennet's plan, would return from the wedding with the Bingleys to begin her visit in Nottingham. Catherine, who was attending the wedding with Elizabeth, would take Mary's place in the Bennet carriage and return to Longbourn. As the time to leave approached, Mary found herself eager for the journey, and she wondered if her penchant for quietly staying at home had given way to a need for excitement, like her mother's. She did not think she was eager for the pomp of the wedding, nor did she relish a visit from James Stilton, who had promised to visit at Nottingham. For whatever reason, Mary enjoyed packing again for a visit of some months, supposing she would not return to Longbourn until after the Bennets visited Pemberley for Christmas. A bit guiltily, she even packed her best gowns.

# Chapter 10

T HE FAMILY REACHED NORWICH MILLS—A FINE SETTLEMENT IN gently rolling countryside—in good time for the fashionable autumn wedding. The earl's mansion—a large, comfortable-looking edifice with a white-pillared entrance at the end of an elm-shaded sweep—heralded a happy visit. They were met by Caroline Bingley, who spoke and acted as if she were hostess, and never had she been more ingratiating. Jane and Mrs. Hurst were present also, as was the Earl's daughter-in-law, the amiable Lady Helena. When the shooting party returned for tea, Colonel Fitzwilliam introduced his portly father and his handsome brother Henry. Then the young Lady Helena, though still quiet, modest, and respectful, livened in her manner as she gravitated to her husband. She let Viscount Henry do all the talking, but her face plainly showed an interest in all around her, which had been absent while he was not there. Though not strikingly beautiful, Helena flashed a pleasing smile frequently at her husband, and Mary noted that her dress, though fine, was not ostentatious. Caroline's jewelry bespoke more grandeur than did Lady Helena's.

Darcy and Bingley, who had come early for the rehearsal, entered the room and enquired about the Bennets' journey, and

Mr. Hurst followed, saying nothing as usual. Mr. Bennet allowed that the trip was less tedious than arduous, which he supposed every journey ought to be. Mrs. Bennet complained of the wind whistling incessantly through the coach, affecting her nerves most disastrously. Mary stated that the countryside was lovely and the weather dry, if blustery.

Elizabeth, Catherine, and Georgiana were expected next day, the morning of the wedding. That evening, however, just as the whole party gathered in the drawing room after supper, a sound of voices at the grand entrance alerted the company to their earlier-than-expected arrival. Georgiana hurried to embrace her brother, offer her good wishes to Caroline and Fitzwilliam, and greet the others. Elizabeth, having greeted the Bingleys and the Fitzwilliams, threw Darcy a look that bade him follow her to a secluded corner where, with hushed whispering, she handed him a letter. Mary noted Darcy's surprise at whatever news Lizzy brought, as he tore open the letter with a puzzled look. Just then Catherine, having embraced her parents and greeted the others, came over to Mary.

"Guess who came to Pemberley two days ago! Mr. Oliver! He said he had seen you. What were you doing in Kent?"

Mary, pleased that Oliver had hurried to Pemberley to see Kitty after all, explained her short stay with Maria at Hunsford. She would have added tales of her adventures on the road, as well as the cautions she meant to give Catherine about the strange man's changing moods, but servants came with tea, scones, and fruit for the new arrivals, and Catherine left her for the refreshments, excusing herself with, "I am famished." Mary quietly observed the company that had now grown quite large but had quickly separated into knots of quiet conversations. Henry Fitzwilliam detached himself from Helena, Georgiana, Caroline, and the Colonel, and approached the Earl with a look of concern on his face. Because he raised his voice to the older man, Mary heard him announce his worry about Darcy.

She turned to see Darcy holding his opened letter, his expression serious, even fretful, in contrast to the high spirits of the augmented party. Then Darcy seemed to fight off his distress and escort Elizabeth to the refreshments. As they passed Mary, she heard him saying he must not dampen the festivities, but he must leave for Kent immediately after the wedding. Henry approached him as Elizabeth took tea, and Mary thought she heard some reference to Lady Catherine's health. Mary immediately felt she must be mistaken, as Lady Catherine had been well when she left Kent not long ago. Then Catherine beckoned her, and she joined her sisters.

The wedding, most delicately grand to the obvious satisfaction of Caroline and Mrs. Hurst, was a ceremony fitting an earl's son, though that earl's son seemed only just tolerant of the pomp. It took place on a sparkling crisp autumn day which later added to the festive send off of the happy couple. They headed to Castle Park and were followed by Mr. and Mrs. Hurst, who wished to see where Caroline would live. Mr. Bennet turned from the avenue to the stables to check on the readiness of his horses and carriage for the next day's journey south. Mary, to enjoy the fine day, accompanied him. There they observed Darcy already mounted on his fine black steed. Henry Fitzwilliam stood at his side. "If Lady Catherine should die, send express to me, so the Fitzwilliams may be represented at the funeral. I adjure you: do not bother my brother at such a time."

Darcy frowned down at him. "Of course. But I pray it does not come to that."

"We all do." Henry watched Darcy ride off, looking after him long and pensively before going back to the manor.

The following morning at the breakfast board, Elizabeth sat apart from the still-jubilant guests, and Mary noticed that she ate little. If the difficulty concerned Lady Catherine, Mary could not but wonder at Elizabeth's sorrow over so disagreeable a lady. Surely there had been little enough love between those two to lose. Or, remembering how Elizabeth missed Darcy on a previous occasion, it could possibly be Darcy's loss she felt. She must have expected to return to Pemberley in his company.

Breakfast over, Mary thanked her bounteous host the Earl and spoke also to Lady Helena and Viscount Henry before setting off to assemble her things to be put into Bingley's carriage. Elizabeth followed, and when they reached the top of the staircase, Elizabeth took her hand. "Mary, please come to Pemberley for a few weeks. Mama and Papa have agreed to stay awhile, and you have seen little of Kitty lately." Then she lowered her voice. "Besides, Jane and Bingley have been giddy as newlyweds themselves, and no wonder! They have been little enough alone since they married. Would you greatly mind staying with me at least until Darcy returns? I mentioned the plan to Jane, but she had some notion that you wish to be in Nottingham for reasons of your own."

Mary examined her feelings and decided that was not actually the case. Just then Jane joined them. "Oh, Mary, you have already had a visitor at Otherfield, and most disappointed indeed was Mr. Stilton that you were not with us a week ago."

Warmth crept up Mary's face, and she worked to school her voice to indifference. "Oh, we played some duets at Longbourn when he visited his aunt, Mrs. Long. He is very musical—an unusual thing in a man."

"So I understood. And immediately I made plans to start Beth at the instrument, lest I be remiss as a mother. One never knows when music may attract a beau. Perhaps when you visit, you may introduce Beth to a gentler handling of the pianoforte than she now displays."

Elizabeth broke in laughingly. "Good heavens, Jane. Have you so much of Mama in you that you begin already to think of Beth's beaux?" The two laughed together, carefree as young girls, and Mary realized that Jane truly had welcomed this wedding.

Mary assured Jane that she would be glad to oblige, though she doubted the efficacy of the instrument as an attraction to men, most of whom take little interest in it. Then Elizabeth pled her case. "Dear Jane, please lend me your visitor at least until Darcy's return. Once Kitty leaves for Longbourn I shall be forlorn indeed. Besides, I have a fine pattern and some lovely blue muslin. I should dearly love to send Mary to you in a new gown."

Mary did not need a new gown, being more comfortable in her old ones, but she did not mind staying at Pemberley long enough to explore that Blake book she had not had time for. If Catherine too stayed awhile, she may even have time to warn her of the strange Mr. Oliver, so that she may open her eyes and judge for herself if she wished to pursue the acquaintance. He might, after all, be again visiting the Pemberley library, and if Kitty refused to be discouraged, Mary could be philosophical about it and hope to see three sisters well married and in the vicinity. In such a case, she might not have to depend too long on any one of them. She could explore three libraries, play on their instruments, and walk their varied grounds—a bright prospect indeed. She let Jane know that she would gladly accept Lizzy's offer.

After they had seen the Bingleys off, Elizabeth took Mary's arm. "Thank you for agreeing, for Georgiana's sake as well as for mine and Jane's. When you are here to play duets with her, she seems livelier somehow. Otherwise, she so often plays and sings 'The Mansion of Peace,' and I fear she reverts to the doleful tempo she used to play before she knew the whole piece."

Mary said, "Perhaps there is more to her childhood past that she wishes to recall. Can Darcy not help her?"

"I fear not. He says he was at school during her earliest years. He did think that Lady Catherine might be able to help her, as he guesses that their father sent her to their aunt to be cared for during his long mourning for their mother. But if Lady Catherine is really dying, that avenue too may be lost. Please try to bring Georgiana out of the dreamlike melancholy that so worries me." Lizzy squeezed Mary's hand. Mary told her that of course she was glad to oblige Elizabeth, whether it was to benefit Georgiana or Jane. Still, she puzzled over Lady Catherine. Charlotte must have sent word of some sudden reversal in that lady's health.

Elizabeth smiled sweetly. "Did you see the Bingleys' smiles? One could easily take them for the wedding couple. But of course, they must have thought Caroline would be with them always, and to find her so well situated and the Hursts so taken with Norfolk must delight their good hearts."

Mary nodded her agreement, but it bid fair to tarnish the shining future she had just planned for herself. It was all very well to depend on sisters for a visit, but for a lifetime? Would they be hoping all the while to see her marry, and if it happened, would they rejoice in it as Jane did to see Caroline married? Her thoughts turned to young Stilton. True, he was no reader, he boasted that he never so much as darkened a church door, and his moderate estate would provide scant occupation for him. What kind of life would that be? Could she endure so empty an existence? Even to please her family, she did not think she could, but she hoped it would not come to that. She trusted that the ridiculous young man's interest did not even come near to the prospect, despite Jane's sallies. She determined to pray over it, accept whatever future God sent, and attempt to remain easy at heart. At present, it did not seem that her sisters minded her presence, and Pemberley was not only the most comfortable place for her, but the safest. Stilton would certainly not venture thirty miles to seek her. She entered Elizabeth's carriage with Georgiana, still content with her own lot and philosophically indifferent to Kitty's.

THE NEXT FEW WEEKS SHOWED MARY A PEMBERLEY NEW TO her. Fall still bloomed like summer, and the gardens beckoned. Her linden tree still wore some heart-shaped leaves, and she imagined in them love stretched up to God. Sometimes with Elizabeth she gathered flowers to be dried or witch hazel and herbs to be stored for healing; sometimes she strolled the walk between the coppice and the stream and enjoyed the rippling water and the echoes of woodmen's axes preparing for winter fires. Though she meant to investigate the Blake work, she returned instead to *Pilgrim's Progress*, even taking it with her past the oaks and chestnuts on the north lawn and up wooded hills to where a stone bench overlooked the great house. There she read or worked for a time, watched as the men went out to fish—if Mr. Gardiner visited—or out to hunt, which Mr. Bennet preferred. In Mr. Darcy's absence, Mr. Shepard provided guidance to the well-stocked stream, and Elizabeth entertained Mrs. Bennet and Catherine and, for a short visit, Mrs. Gardiner. Mary never neglected her morning hour of music with Georgiana, and sometimes Georgiana even accepted her invitation to go out and explore the gardens. Once, on a particularly fine day, the two of them shared the stone bench in companionable silence, when Elizabeth and Catherine called them down for a picnic on the lawn. Charles, released from nursery and pram, rolled on the lawn under Callie's watchful eye, and Georgiana produced a ball and played with the lively child, leaving the sisters to converse of Longbourn days.

Catherine spoke of her longing to see Lydia. "Papa never lets me go, though Lydia often invites me. But lately he says he would not even know where to send me if he wished to. Wickham has left the regulars, you know, and they move around so much now."

Elizabeth nodded. "Yes indeed. Lydia told me as much when she came this summer, unhappily, that was just at the time when you went with Jane to London to help her shop for Caroline's wedding." Elizabeth turned to Mary. "I believe she had been at Longbourn as well."

"Yes." Mary did not wish to discuss Lydia's desire to see Kitty, as she might well have been no fit influence for her pliable sister. "She just missed you there too, Kitty. But she did not stay long." Should she say that Lydia seemed unhappy, as Oliver thought? But then, Oliver had put his own discernment into some doubt. She added only, "She did not confide in me." Callie brought Charles, again in his pram, over to his mother, and Kitty and Georgiana went for a walk by the stream. As an afterthought, Mary added, "From what Mr. Oliver and I heard at the post inn, Wickham had sent Lydia to beg money from the family. He spoke as if he had some scheme to take a living as a clergyman."

Elizabeth jumped up, and then grabbed the pram which had almost overturned. "Do you mean that it was Wickham plotting with Witherspoon to take over Rosings and Hunsford?" She plopped down again next to Mary. "Why did you not tell me?"

Mary could only think: Witherspoon! The very man she had wanted to meet, and she never looked at him! "But I understood that Oliver had rushed to tell you about Wickham…" Suddenly it dawned on Mary that Oliver had recognized not Wickham but Witherspoon. "Oh, Lizzy, I have been so stupid. First, I thought Oliver went to Kent to learn about Miss de Bourgh and some verger at Hunsford, because I had overheard Lady Catherine and Mr. Darcy in the library at Christmastime. But I felt so guilty overhearing it that I never mentioned it to Mr. Oliver, and he never told me his errand. Then, when he seemed so upset at seeing and hearing Mr. Wickham, I thought rather that Wickham was the real point of his errand." Close to tears, Mary blurted out, "Oh Lord! It must mean Wickham will replace Mr. Collins at Hunsford. What will our cousin and Charlotte do?"

Elizabeth put her arm around Mary. "No. It means only that he is up to another scheme, which may prove as fruitless as his previous ones—just another folly that comes to naught." Lizzy picked up Charles, who was fussing since his near upset. "There, there, little Charles. You are going to be fine." She looked at Mary. "And let us hope little Lucas may be fortunate also."

"Do you think it may come out all right?" Mary dearly hoped her reticence did not cost Charlotte any difficulty.

Elizabeth shook her head slowly. "We can only wait and see. Darcy and Lady Catherine mean to entail the de Bourgh estate so that Witherspoon can never have the legal power he now takes for granted. We must pray that all goes well in Kent."

Catherine and Georgiana returned, and Elizabeth, Callie, and the baby returned to the house with them. Elizabeth told Mary she had a letter to write, and Mary guessed that it must be to Charlotte or Darcy. Mary tried to resume her reading, but the words swam before her eyes meaninglessly, her mind on Darcy's endeavours. Elizabeth's voice had rung with worry but never despair. Her faith in

Darcy, palpable as her love for him, confirmed Oliver's judgement on their marriage, no matter how he belittled his own discernment. His self-reproach on that very trait must have been founded on his observation of Witherspoon alone, without any knowledge of Wickham's influence. He had missed Witherspoon's treachery, and he blamed himself for it. Was his real fault that he, like Jane, thought too well of people and failed to recognize a scoundrel? Perhaps this was the warning Catherine needed. She had to smile at herself as she reckoned that she had been too much with her mother: she already considered Catherine and Mr. Oliver a match!

Sunday, though a steady rain dulled the morning, the Bennets and Georgiana went to Lambton with Elizabeth for divine service. At the church, they met Jane, Bingley, and Beth, who had stayed at Lambton's inn that Saturday night. The Bingleys returned with them to Pemberley. Then the older Bennets took advantage of the rain's cessation to tour the park in Darcy's phaeton, purchased for just such excursions. Jane teased Mary that she came to visit her "tardy guest." Mary saw that Jane sparkled despite the grey weather, and her heart blessed Elizabeth's thoughtfulness that had promoted this renewal of the Bingleys' bliss. Mary and Georgiana took Beth to the small parlour for fruit and sandwiches, and then, as was their custom, on to the music room for duets. After a short time, Beth slid off the chair where Mary had enthroned her as audience, leaving her soft doll in the chair. She ducked under the piano bench and climbed up between the musicians. In the midst of one of the lively dances Stilton had given Mary, the toddler added a note or two occasionally. The additions did not appreciably diminish the effect, and once or twice seemed actually to enhance the music. When that happened, Georgiana giggled and Mary smirked, praising Beth for her fine musician's ear. Because they laughed, so did Beth, but she did not thereby increase her contributions. She seemed as content to listen as to join in. Jane, Bingley, Catherine, and Elizabeth joined them, and all marvelled at the child's quiet appreciation.

"And has she never pounded the keys or run around the instrument?" asked Jane as the dance ended.

Georgiana assured her that Beth was "either a musician or a critic—she adds a note only when we falter." Then she invited Kitty to the nursery to "play aunt," as she called it, and they went out smiling.

Elizabeth complimented Mary on having done wonders for Georgiana's humour, while Bingley complimented his lovely daughter and told Mary she would be welcome at Otherfield as soon as possible. "With your example, she may learn to respect the instrument instead of attacking it as she flies by."

As if knowing she was the center of attention, Beth touched a few keys tenderly, and then slid from the bench and under Mary's skirts to join her parents. "I play too!"

Bingley swung his bubbly daughter to his lap, just as a servant arrived with an express letter.

Elizabeth tore it open. "It is from Darcy." After she read a little she groaned. "Lady Catherine has died. Darcy has sent for Henry Fitzwilliam to represent his father and brother at the funeral." Elizabeth caught Mary's anxious eyes on her. "He says he was not in time to fix the inheritance, but he was glad to be able to attend her in her last days. He adds that the future of Rosings is up to Miss de Bourgh now."

Mary looked down, ashamed. "And if Wickham succeeds to Hunsford, I wonder how well and how long he will tend his flock." She searched her mind for any relieving comfort. "At least Lydia may have a real home. I think she did not like moving so often." As she spoke Lydia's name, she thought of the many times she had avoided doing that, and wondered if Elizabeth noticed the change. It did not seem so. The Bingleys listened and stared, wondering. Beth looked at her sombre parents, and her face puckered as if to cry. Jane soothed the child with one hand and a ready smile, while Elizabeth acquainted them with the scheme Darcy had intended to foil, had he arrived in time. Bingley, understanding aglow in his face, exclaimed, "That was the problem on Darcy's mind in Norfolk! It was not just Lady Catherine's failing health. No wonder he left so precipitately. I trust he does not blame his tardiness? He did what he could."

Elizabeth examined the letter again. "It does not appear that he feels remorse. He says 'Whatever comes of Anne's marriage, perhaps it may be for the best.' Oh, but he had not yet received my letter. He did not know Wickham's part in it." She sat back, dangling the letter from pinched fingers. "Oh, Mary, if I had been more open with you about our fears, he might then have known all from the first."

Mary, deeply moved by her sister's assuming blame for secretiveness, the very fault she knew to be her own, prayed fervently that all would turn out well.

Jane handed her daughter to Bingley and sat beside Elizabeth. "I wonder. Miss de Bourgh thought ill enough of Wickham. Pride alone may prevent her falling in with any scheme of his. And she certainly will not marry so soon upon her mother's death that she will not learn of it by then."

Elizabeth sighed. "Perhaps it is as you say, though if she is in love, nothing may change things now. We must hope for the best. And, as Mary observed, even if the worst occurs, at least Lydia may benefit."

Chapter 12

Sunshine brightened the following Sunday, and Catherine pressed Elizabeth to walk to Kympton Saint Giles for services, but Elizabeth declined. Catherine's pouting had been little in evidence at Pemberley, but shades of her petulance followed this denial. "Why is it always Lambton? It is farther."

"Darcy prefers a parish whose pastor is not beholden to him. He wishes neither to be tempted to critique the preacher nor to be judged as if doing so. He says he wants to keep his mind on God." Elizabeth left no doubt that Darcy's way was hers as well.

"Then how does he find out? As patron, he ought to know." Catherine was not to be satisfied, and her father frowned at her boldness.

Elizabeth laughed good-naturedly. "Oh, people who are upset waste no time letting him hear it. Darcy has had many complaints concerning Mr. Oliver, and they serve only to confirm him in his choice of vicar."

Catherine stared, wide-eyed. "They do not *like* Mr. Oliver?"

"At first he heard the new vicar was too loud by half. Singing or preaching, his exuberance filled the little church so as to drown out any birdsong or lowing of cattle outside. For a while, Darcy sent carriages for any church members who wished to try Lambton instead, and there were takers for some weeks. Then the discontent died down, and by six weeks' time, the last carriage remained empty. When Mr. Darcy enquired, the same people told him services elsewhere were 'sleepy' by comparison. They became content to stay awake during services. Now, he only hears that the vicar lavishes his attention on the very young, the very old, and the very poor. And the complainants"—she patted Kitty's hand—"are often young ladies like you who would wish to attract his attention to themselves."

Seeing Catherine blush, and sorry to hear her come so close to whining, Mary offered to walk to Kympton with her. "Kitty is right. It is a lovely morning for a stroll."

It was settled that the others would attend Lambton's later service in a single carriage, and Mary and Catherine set off. Mary enjoyed the walk through the pine woods on so fine a day, and Catherine's spirits revived as they walked.

At the service, Mary frowned to see Emmaline Langley in a pew ahead of them, apparently with her parents, though the choir sang. Afterward, Catherine hurried to greet Mr. Oliver, and Mary intercepted Emmaline, who introduced her to Mrs. Langley. She recognized Mr. Langley as the driver of the team that had pulled the carollers around to several farms the previous Christmas. Mary questioned Emmaline's deserting the choir.

Emmaline, crestfallen, explained, "Mrs. Clifford says I cannot behave well enough."

"Nonsense, you can behave well enough. You just save that behaviour for Sundays." Mary smiled. "If I remember rightly, it was only practise that brought out your foolery."

"Yes, and I told her I would be better at service, but she dismissed me before she ever found that out."

"Then she weakened the choir by one very fine voice, and I am sorry for it."

"Three voices; Lucy and Dorothy had to leave too, and it was my fault." Emmaline looked and sounded as if she might cry, and Mary again saw a fleeting glimpse of Lydia in her.

"I did find today's choir number a bit thin, even faltering. Surely Mrs. Clifford would not wish so thin a sound for Christmas. If I were you, I would apply for readmittance in a week or two." Mary noticed Catherine looking around for her and so took leave of the Langleys to join her sister. "Kitty, how did you think the choir sounded?"

"I hardly noticed. Mr. Oliver sounded wonderful. Did not you think so?"

Mary smiled. "I hardly noticed." But as they walked home admiring the crisp, bright day, Mary found she could indeed recall the lesson on the good shepherd who approaches his flock sometimes to feed them, sometimes to shelter them from harm, and sometimes just to talk to and pet them. She tried to imagine Christ taking such special care of her. Yes, Mr. Oliver could preach from—and to—the heart.

Reaching Pemberley before the Lambton worshipers returned, Mary left Catherine to await them while she went to her room to try on the gown Letty had finished. She took it off again immediately and quickly put on an old pinner instead, returning the gown to Letty's workroom with a note.

In the parlour, Catherine greeted the returning party, now enhanced by the Bingleys and a dapper stranger. Elizabeth asked Polly to summon Miss Mary to the parlour while Jane introduced James Stilton to Catherine. "Mrs. Long's nephew, you know, but he lives just five miles from us. It seems he brings an invitation for us all, to the harvest ball at Nottingham Castle."

Stilton bowed stiffly, coughed, and surveyed his grand surroundings with misgivings approaching awe. He murmured, "A general invitation... posted. Just a few miles from Long Eaton... all gentry included."

Catherine, all delight at the prospect, beamed at this fine fellow. "Oh! I love a ball! And at Nottingham Castle! What could be greater? Is it to be soon, sir?"

Stilton accepted the high back chair indicated by Elizabeth but sat rigidly at the end of it, both hands gripping a fashionable walking stick with a burnished lion head. "Next Tuesday, miss, when the moon is full."

Mr. Bennet, amused at the young man's discomfort, chided him. "You were never so in awe at Longbourn. Should I be offended?"

"Oh no, sir." But he did not unbend. Elizabeth bade him relax, and he shook his head. "I fully expected to be impressed, but this"—he gestured timidly at his surroundings—"why, it could be Sudbury or Chatham. I did not know another so grand even existed!"

Elizabeth recalled her own introductory tour with Aunt and Uncle Gardiner. As she spied Mary coming she teased, "Perhaps one day you will become immune to Pemberley's power to intimidate, as I begin to do." Observing Mary's plain attire, she voiced her disappointment. "Did you not try on your new gown as I suggested? I hoped you would let us see you in it."

Mary blushed and whispered to her, "I mean to beg Letty to raise the neckline. I wish to be less fashionably and less nakedly dressed. Else I would have to wear my spencer indoors as well as out." She turned to greet Stilton, and Catherine broke the exciting news he brought.

"And you are sure to go, while Papa says if Mr. Darcy returns, we may be on our way to Longbourn before that." She sighed. "And you even have a new gown for it." Elizabeth reminded her of the lovely ice blue gown Letty had made for her at midsummer. "But I wore that twice already." Mary, sorry to hear Catherine again lapse into ways she had all but conquered, assured her she had looked like an angel in her lovely gown at the Norwich wedding.

Stilton returned to the object of his visit. "Then I can expect to see you at the ball, Miss Bennet?"

Mary hesitated. "If Mama and Papa and Kitty attend, I would go of course. Or if I am at Otherfield and Jane and Bingley wish to go, I shall accompany them. But I do not like such lavish entertainments in general.'

Stilton forgot his awe of Pemberley in a flash. "But Miss Bennet, we had such a fine time at the Hertfordshire assemblies! Surely the notables of Ilkestone and Long Eaton can be no different." His sharp blue eyes sought hers, but she looked down as she sat near Jane.

"At Meryton and at Lucas Lodge, of course, all was friendly, and all the folks familiar. But even last year's Christmas ball here was no temptation for me to dance. I am not so keen on dancing as Kitty is."

Mr. Bennet addressed the young man about to urge Mary further, "And will your parents be at this ball?"

"Oh yes, sir. They mean to be. They always are."

"Then perhaps Lizzy will allow us to stay until then, even if Mr. Darcy returns. Then Kitty and Mrs. Bennet will enjoy a ball, and the event will serve to delight at least two. And I would like to meet your parents."

Elizabeth readily agreed to this, Kitty was ecstatic, Stilton satisfied, and Mary resigned. But she feared that her father attached more importance to Stilton's interest in her than a casual invitation to a strange castle indicated.

After refreshments that Elizabeth ordered and Stilton picked at, Mary undertook to show him around Pemberley. The library impressed him not at all. "It's just books." The small oratory on the ground floor with its lovely stained glass window made him shudder with distaste. "A church in one's home! Bizarre." His grimace reflected his disgust. She thought the music room with Georgiana's Broadwood grand would elicit some enthusiasm, but he merely nodded from the doorway. None of her own favourite rooms pleased him, so they ventured outside, where she meant to show him her bower on the hill, her favourite tree, and the gardens. However, his eyes sought the far buildings beyond the park, and he pointed enthusiastically. "Oh! Show me the stables!"

Never had she been there before, but he led her straight to where Mr. Watts attended the large carriage house and the horse barns where they saw many clean stalls, all in a row, a name above each. "Do you ride, Miss Bennet?"

"No, not at all."

"But you must indeed. The exercise is beneficial, and you would find it as delightful as a dance once you are comfortable on a horse."

Watts enthusiastically agreed, though Mary knew no expression so contradictory as "comfortable on a horse." Watts led them to the stall of a grey mare, the only stall with no name above it. "She's gentle as a kitten. I could saddle her up now, and the gentleman and I could help you mount. The sooner you learn, the better, I say."

Mary, who had picked her way carefully over the stable yard, disagreed. She rarely had found dancing delightful, and she wondered if climbing upon such a monstrous animal could ever be found so. They prevailed upon her then in concert, offering to lead the animal so slowly that she would have nothing to fear. She looked down at her old pinafore and realized she could not use preservation of her clothing as excuse, and at length, she relented. Once seated gingerly on the gentle mare, she was led around the paddock. After what seemed ten minutes but was actually thirty, Mary was able to direct the creature around the paddock unaided. She had to agree that the experience suited her far more than she had anticipated. As she slid unceremoniously off the horse, braced by the helpful arms of Stilton and Watts, she pleaded, "Please do not tell Mr. Darcy."

"Why ever not, miss? He bought that mare for you at the Lambton fair apurpose. He was planning to teach you, same as the missus, so's you'd feel free to ride with Mrs. Darcy or Mrs. Bingley."

Mary, astonished that Mr. Darcy could have thought of such a thing, pounced upon a likelier explanation. "He must have meant my sister Kitty. She is the lively one."

"Oh no, miss. Miss Mary Bennet, he says. I don't doubt Mr. Darcy feared as Miss Kitty would be unsafe on any horse." He lowered his tone, speaking confidentially. "She's a bit of a tear, that one. No, he said 'Miss Mary will name her and ride her,' and he will be well pleased as it's begun."

All wonderment, Mary thanked him, and she took Stilton's arm because her legs felt too rubbery to walk without it. They made their way back to the great house, Stilton with his puckish smile painted on his face. "What a fine horsewoman you will be. And I will ride over some day on my great bay Willie. Then you can show me all around Ilkestone Park on horseback!"

Slowly Mary regained the feeling in her legs, and she let go Stilton's arm. She looked around for field workers, but it was Sunday so none were nearby. Stilton took to overturning stones in the path with the tip of his walking stick. They passed a neat row of beehives, the pride of Mr. Shepard. Stilton paused. "Watch this!" He grinned. With his walking stick, he prodded a small green inchworm until it clung to the tip of the stick. Then he shook the worm free just at the opening of one hive.

Mary was aghast. "No! Mr. Shepard would hate his hive to be contaminated!" All her hostess-like politeness fell from her, and her obligation as guest of Pemberley fired her anger.

"Oh, you need have no fear of that." Stilton's eager eyes were on the worm. Even as he spoke, Mary watched with revulsion as bees swarmed from the hive, all stinging the hapless worm as they carried it from the hive. The worm, now a puffy white mass two or three times its former width, dropped lifeless to the grass from which it had come. Stilton laughed uproariously. "You see? Bees know how to protect their hives."

Mary leaned against a tree trunk, not recognizing her linden at first. A line from Psalm 118 came to her with a new image: "They compassed me about like bees." She felt again a sick weakness, much worse than her wobbly legs. Disgusted with Stilton's fascinated amusement and ashamed at having witnessed a torturous death, she turned eyes wide with horror on the thoughtless mirth of her companion. She had no words to speak her disapproval, but she felt that if any came to her, they would only increase his derision. Dulled by the incident and distanced by Stilton's unfeeling response, she clung to the linden—something she could still admire. James urged her on and even walked back to offer his arm, but she could not touch him. "Thou hast thrust sore at me that I might fall: but the Lord helped me." The further line from her favourite psalm encouraged her. She felt strength enough to return to the house but not to speak another word to her companion.

## Chapter 13

Darcy returned on Monday while the family assembled at tea. He embraced Elizabeth and Georgiana, declared he was tired but not discouraged, and fell into a chair. "Once I received your letter, Lizzy, I knew how my errand had failed, and I did what seemed best. Anne could not be disturbed at her time of mourning, so I spoke rather with Mrs. Collins about Wickham's involvement. She must decide whether, how, or when to open it to Anne, to Collins, or directly to Witherspoon. What happens at Hunsford is in their hands now."

As he greeted the others, Mrs. Bennet asked, "Was Lady Catherine in great pain? Were you with her at the end?"

Darcy moved nearer to Elizabeth but spoke to the whole group. "My aunt faced death like Shakespeare's thane of Cawdor: nothing in her life became her like the leaving it. After two days' watch with her, I remarked that I had not seen her attending physician. She said, 'Oh, he pops in daily to see if I'm dead yet.' A little after that, we heard him speaking to Anne in the next room, and she said, 'A long illness wearies the doctor. Anne's complaints are his bread and butter now.' The day before she died, her left eye remained closed. I asked if it pained her. She said, 'No. Like my feet, it has died on ahead of me.' And I must give my aunt her due"—he leaned over and put his arm around Elizabeth—"she praised my lively Lizzy as a better choice than hers for my wife. She called Anne a 'languid soul without will, who lets herself be a dead weight, bridling her spirit as she does.'"

Elizabeth wiped away a tear. "No languid soul she! Forthright to the end. She will be much missed, even by her inattentive physician."

Mrs. Bennet interposed sternly, "It was not a very motherly description of poor Miss de Bourgh."

"But fairly accurate, I daresay." Elizabeth, eyes on Darcy, had gained in spirit with the arrival of her husband.

Darcy added that he had asked Lady Catherine if she wished him to urge against Anne's marrying Witherspoon, but she turned her face from him, saying, "I wish for nothing but death."

The fresh hot tea, apple tart, and grapes put before him by Mrs. Reynolds took his attention, and he revived a bit after partaking of it liberally. Soon all were in better spirits. Elizabeth took Mary by the hand and drew her over to him. "You may commend the spirit of our dear Mary, who has named her mare Grey Dawn and has taken three lessons on her."

"Good work, Miss Bennet. Did Watts take you out?"

"Yes, sir. Thanks to you, sir." Mary, always in awe of her brother-in-law, went no further.

Elizabeth smiled meaningfully. "Watts had assistance." She said no more, nor did Mary.

But at the veiled reference to Stilton, Catherine perked up. "And we are all to go to a ball tomorrow at Nottingham Castle."

Darcy groaned. "Of course." He closed his eyes as if calculating. "Harvest moon."

Elizabeth sensed his reluctance. "Oh, we do not have to go. Mama and Papa can take the girls. You are tired, and like Mary, I have grown beyond the degrading thirst after outrageous stimulation." Then she grinned. "However, after so long without you, a quiet evening together may be outrageous stimulation indeed!"

Mary blushed and Darcy laughed, pulling Elizabeth closer. "Dearest Lizzy, we will talk of this tomorrow."

Chapter 14

THE BENNETS ATTENDED THE BALL WITHOUT THE DARCYS, AND they met the Bingleys and the Stiltons at the newly built inn attached to Nottingham Castle. During the evening, Mr. Bennet stayed close to Mr. Stilton, seeing that his wine glass remained full and speaking to him in low tones. After the flow of much wine, Mr. Bennet did more listening than speaking. Mrs. Bennet, charmed by the gracious and lively Mrs. Stilton, complimented that lady of high fashion on her splendid gown, with its long sleeves and low neckline. The two of them, over dinner and punch, discussed that lady of unparalleled nobility, Mrs. Long. "Nellie is such a fine lady of right good sense. No wonder her brother sends his son to her for instruction in country ways. And her cottage is so nicely furnished, you know, with good solid furnishings that have stood the test of time."

Mrs. Stilton could not agree more completely. "Young people, you know, are hot to change everything. That is such a mistake."

Mrs. Bennet saw the Bingleys come near in the dance and nodded wisely. "Oh yes. My own daughter stayed but one year in Hertfordshire after her marriage, and then moved clear to Nottingham. Not that I disapprove of Nottingham, mind you. But they had a fine house in Hertfordshire that we could visit daily. However, it is perhaps providential that now they live close to you because Mary is soon to spend some time with them."

"Really? I believe James did say something of the sort. What a fine, steady girl she is reported to be, and James is quite fond of her already, you know. Would they not make a fine match?" Mrs. Stilton smiled shyly, and Mrs. Bennet beamed upon her. No conjecture in the world could have pleased her more completely. Mrs. Bennet believed in the match because of her firm conviction that marriage was every woman's proper business and Mrs. Stilton for reasons of her own. Mrs. Bennet told the boy's mother that his fastidious style in dress could open Mary's eyes and make her more willing to adopt the latest fashions, and Mrs. Stilton praised Mary's fine, steady, bookish temperament, sure it would somehow make James similarly disposed. The Bingleys danced and chatted on a cloud all their own. Catherine spotted some officers and soon learned which ones loved to dance.

Mary agreed to dance the first set with James Stilton, once she learned that she would not have to touch him very much nor speak often. Indeed, Stilton expected her only to listen as he regaled her with idle assertions and impudent falsehoods that his vanity spawned. Then she spent the evening talking to the Langleys, whom she had noticed during the second dance. This couple introduced her to parents of other choir members at Kympton, and they all pleaded with her to return as organist, but Mary offered them no encouragement. She said merely that Mr. Oliver was competent to assign duties in his parish. Mrs. Langley thanked Mary for her kind advice to Emmaline. "But if Mrs. Clifford does not immediately relent, I don't know if the child will ever try again. She finds it so hard to be humble."

Mary nodded—wisely, she hoped. "That is a rather universal failing, I believe."

By the time Stilton returned to lead her to the last dance, Mary reflected that she had indeed grown beyond a thirst for dancing, and the whole rhythmic movement passed for beneficial exercise. On the whole, she preferred riding Grey Dawn, because that was not done in a crowded, stifling room.

In the return coach to Pemberley, Mary listened tiredly to Catherine's delight in the officers and Mrs. Bennet's delight in the Stiltons, while Mr. Bennet, like Mary, suffered their effusions in silence. Upon arriving at Pemberley, however, Mr. Bennet took Mary's hand and detained her in the foyer while the exuberant two entered the parlour to regale the Darcys with their respective triumphs over wine, cheese, and ginger beer set out for them. As Mr. Bennet led Mary to a bench, Catherine could be heard from the parlour saying, "La, you should have been there, Lizzy!"

Mr. Bennet, all seriousness, drew her attention from the other room. "Mary, I have in the past teased you, too often perhaps. Your solemn quotations, your reading while walking, and your original scruples have all amused me at times, I must admit. But I ask you to forgive me that and to believe me seriously when I say I have always loved you and wished only the best for you."

His serious words and tone moved and alarmed her. "Of course, Papa. I know."

"Now I want you to promise me that when this Stilton fellow proposes marriage to you, you will refuse him."

Mary was astonished beyond words. Finally she blurted out, "Oh Papa, it is not gone that far, I assure you. He doesn't mean—"

"He means to ask you, though I agree he does not act the lover," Mr. Bennet interrupted. "He has already convinced his parents that you will be his bride. Yet, like you, I do not believe he loves you. His smiles mock and his eyes want softness. But even if he came to love you, and more absurdly, if you came to love him, you must refuse him. You would be utterly miserable with him."

Mary could believe that. "But, Papa, this is absurd indeed. We barely spoke a dozen words together this evening."

Mr. Bennet shifted on the hard bench. "Yes, I observed that he danced much, while you were otherwise occupied for much of the evening. Did he offer you any refreshments?"

"No, sir. Mr. Langley took care of that."

"Did he tell you how fine you look in your new gown?"

"No, but Mrs. Langley complimented me sweetly."

"Did he, tonight or at any other time, show more interest in the things you value than in himself and his own interests?"

Mary thought about that. "No, not that I can recall." Some of his interests, indeed, aroused her severe distaste.

"Precisely. You see, I had been warned before we ever came north that something about Stilton's interest in you was suspect. For that I am indebted to Mr. Grantley, who took it upon himself to check the boy's background and reputation. He learned that the claim to property from his grandfather is genuine enough, but that his actual moment of possession depends upon his father. This is due, in large part, to the son's careless prodigality. He has lost considerable amounts in wagering, chiefly on horse races, but he indulges in other frivolous pursuits. His neighbours say he is the sort who wishes to carve up the world like a great roast, keeping the biggest part for himself."

"He never mentions such things to me," said Mary, astonished at these revelations.

"After plying his father with much wine, I extracted from him the terms on which Stilton may claim his inheritance. At first, his father meant him to receive it on his twenty-first birthday."

"Yes, so he told me."

"Did he also tell you," Mr. Bennet paused and shifted his weight on the uncomfortable bench before continuing, "that his father delays his inheritance by six months for every hundred pounds the boy loses or spends frivolously?"

"No indeed. And has he ever done so?"

"So much that his inheritance is now due on his twenty-fifth birthday, and it recedes apace. It is a classic case of 'the father gathers, the son squanders,' but in this case the grandfather gathered, and the father only tries to preserve it. But the son is bursting to get his hands on it that he may squander it."

Mary's eyes widened. After some thought, she said, "I did notice that his only enthusiasm at Pemberley was for the stables." And for the hives, she thought, with a shudder.

"His mother pleads for him, and she has got her husband to agree that when he marries you, he will receive his inheritance."

"But what an absurd proposal, Papa. What can they mean by it?"

"Mrs. Long has conveyed to them your good and steady character, recommending the match as if it could communicate such a character to him as well."

"Impossible. Do they think temperaments are contagious? I have no influence over him."

"My dear, I do not know what they think, but I know they have no right to use you in this ungallant manner, and I suspect Mr. Stilton thinks the same or no amount of wine would have led him to warn me. Promise me faithfully and solemnly, my child, that you will refuse him."

Mary, deeply touched and yet puzzled by his insistence on so unlikely an occurrence, hoped for some assurance that her mother might not prevail. "But will not Mama tell me to accept any offer from a man of property?"

"That well may be, but we must face the certainty that this particular young man and his property will soon be parted." Mr. Bennet stood and placed a hand on Mary's shoulder. "Promise me, Mary."

"Of course, Papa. I will refuse James Stilton if he asks."

"Promise. And he *will* ask, probably often and as soon as we leave for Longbourn."

"I promise. But I do hope you are wrong. And his parents are most unjust to propose such a thing. Mr. Stilton wields all the influence; in fact, he calls me the most biddable young lady he knows."

"Then you see what danger you are in. He will needle you, pester you, and try every means to make you feel guilty for refusing him. And yet, if you were to accept, you would both be penniless within a year. Do not forget your promise."

"Of course not, Papa. I will do as you say. Thank you." And on that, they entered the parlour to mingle with the others.

Kitty was pirouetting around the large parlour as if to prolong the dance or recreate it for Darcy and Elizabeth. Mrs. Bennet, on seeing Mary at last, exclaimed over her magnificent conquest. "Such a fine, fashionable young man, and his mother already fond of you, though you have hardly met her! What a sweet couple you make— and you will be living close to your sister."

"Mama, do not imagine that I mean to marry Mr. Stilton, even if he asks me. He is not so fine a match as you may believe, and he certainly is not fond of me." Mary wondered much at her parents' differing impressions.

"He most certainly *is* a fine enough match for you, Mary! His property is considerable, his eye for fashion could improve yours, and he is even musical! What more could you ask?"

"Mama, did not his mother tell you that he ridicules anyone who goes to church, including his own parents? He is a freethinker, Mama. Do not wish that on me."

"La, child! You cannot expect to have everything in a man."

"Mama, if I must marry, at least I must marry a Christian."

"What do you mean *if?* Of course you must marry. And if you wait and wait for a perfect man, you will find that he is waiting for a perfect woman."

Mary laughed. "Well, that would suit me, Mama. Let Kitty be quick to marry. I do not look for it."

"Of course Kitty must marry. But so must you. How ungrateful to let a chance slip by, just because he does not suit you in everything."

Mary's eyes went to Mr. Bennet, who was frowning, and Elizabeth, catching the exchange, turned the subject. "Mama, how did you like Nottingham Castle? And the new inn attached to it?" At that, Mrs. Bennet proved she had truly examined her surroundings, and she praised the sconces, the mirrors, the draperies, the staircases, giving each its due. Mary gave her sister a grateful smile.

## Chapter 15

M ARY LEFT PEMBERLEY THE DAY AFTER THE NOTTINGHAM BALL, waiting only to bid the Bennets Godspeed to Longbourn. Jane and Bingley had come to say farewell to them also, and they meant to transport Mary with her trunk to Nottingham. Then on Thursday, the Darcys visited Otherfield, bringing Grey Dawn to Bingley's stables for Mary, who marvelled at the great man's generous spirit. "And you must not leave her behind again. She is yours, you know." Darcy took her hand gallantly as he bade her farewell. Mary reflected gratefully that Elizabeth had indeed softened him. Or perhaps, as Lizzy had explained, she found him so and only then loved him enough to marry him.

For three weeks Mary, dreading to respond with the rejection that would mortify her mother, successfully contrived never to be alone with James Stilton. He rode over most mornings on Willie, and if it was early enough, they went riding with Bingley. If Mary had already had her ride, they played duets in the music room, usually with Jane as audience and Beth assisting at the instrument. If he came even later—which often occurred, causing Mary to deduce that he was no early riser—Jane or a servant accompanied them on a walk in the gardens or a chat in the morning room.

Jane, who had been apprised of Mr. Bennet's information, most diligently provided a chaperone. On Jane's at-home days, Elizabeth often came, and she also understood Mary's dilemma and did her part when necessary. On the day before some of Elizabeth's at-home days, Mary accompanied Jane in the pony cart to Lambton's inn, and they visited Pemberley in the morning. Mary knew Stilton cared not to follow there, and Jane could visit Elizabeth while Mary aided Mrs. Reynolds in watching Miss Johnstone, whom Darcy had dubbed "the overstuffed wanderer." Once in the small parlour where Mary followed alone, Miss Johnstone addressed her, to Mary's great surprise. "Are you staying here with your sister again?"

Mary's slight hesitation and her quick look around to see if the lady might have been speaking to someone else betrayed her amazement. "No indeed. I am guest of the Bingleys at Nottingham, but Jane likes company on her ride here to see Lizzy."

"You are fortunate indeed to visit in such society." Miss Johnstone fingered a damask chair cover lovingly. "Like your sister, you were not born to it."

"Yes. I am grateful." Mary frowned, wondering to what this conversation led.

"Tell me, does your sister always tease Mr. Darcy as boldly as she usually does when he joins the guests for refreshments?" Mary shrugged and nodded. The broad-faced lady continued. "I wonder that he tolerates her impertinence so good-naturedly. Perhaps you might advise her"—she lowered her voice confidentially—"that in a few years, when she has lost her good looks, he may tire of such countrified treatment. Then she may lose her place to one who esteems him, as is proper." Her look of happy contempt at this thought annoyed Mary, who recoiled at such boldness.

Astonished, Mary could think of no reply but to echo what Jane and Bingley often said. "Mr. Darcy admires Lizzy for her wit. And I believe Lizzy truly esteems her husband. I am convinced that he knows it."

Miss Johnstone smiled in a superior manner, making Mary aware for the first time of the gap between her front teeth. "As her sister, I supposed you would defend her. But mark my words: her impudence will cost her dearly one day."

Mary was so taken aback by her attitude that she almost failed to note the souvenir of the day slipping into Miss Johnstone's reticule: a miniature beaker of German forest glass that had adorned the mantel shelf. Mary fought the urge to mention impudence as she held out her hand and said calmly, "Mr. Darcy would miss his sample of Waldglas. He speaks highly of it."

Miss Johnstone had the grace to blush as she gave her usual excuse. "It might have been mine, you know. I knew him long before your sister did."

Mary thought, but did not say, "But he married my sister." Just as Mary replaced the beaker, Mrs. Reynolds arrived to let her know Jane had summoned the pony cart and to remain with Miss Johnstone. She nodded as Mary went out and Jane reached the door of the parlour. On the long way home, Mary wondered aloud, "Why on earth does Lizzy allow that Miss Alicia Johnstone to visit if she requires such guarding?"

Jane, contriving as always to say something good, offered, "The lady appears to be a most loyal admirer of Mr. Darcy. Elizabeth understands and pities her."

The next morning Jane, tired after her day abroad, declined to accompany Mary when she rode out with Stilton, but Bingley did so, holding Beth before him on the saddle. Stilton, who ignored

Bingley and his daughter, kept urging Mary to greater speed, a request which Mary chose to ignore. When they reached a downed tree crossing the forest path, Stilton spurred Willie to leap over it, and he called to Mary to do the same. She shook her head and calmly followed Bingley, who guided his horse carefully around the tree and back to the path. Mr. Stilton raced further up the path and then back to chide them. "Why did you keep an old lady's pace?" Again he spoke to her as if Bingley and Beth were absent.

"Mr. Stilton, we are merely out for relaxing exercise. I have no thought to risk the horse's legs and my neck for a thrill of speed. The air is fine, and Beth enjoys the pace we have set. You, of course, may do as you please."

He continued to gallop ahead through the woods, coming back intermittently to boast of Willie's pace. Whenever he left again, Mary relaxed, as she and Bingley pointed out to Beth the pretty birds and the lush groundcover. Once she pulled up her horse as Bingley did the same to enjoy the song of a sparrow bold enough to remain close. "Listen to the bird, little Beth." Mary whispered, "Hear that clear whistle, then a kind of chirp, and finally a throaty purring!"

Beth whispered back in awe. "He purrs like a kitten." Before starting off again, they inhaled the sweet woody smell of rotting leaves and dank undergrowth. When at last they turned for home, Mr. Stilton had been long out of sight. Back in Otherfield's near orchard, almost to the stable, Stilton pulled up behind them at a sensible pace, and Mary greeted him politely. She was amused to see a twig with a brown leaf in his usually well-tended hair. Then she also noted a scratch on his cheek, with dried blood and a smear of dirt, and she guessed that he had sustained a fall. She became convinced of a mishap when she noted that he, who prided himself on impeccable dress, now sported a blotchy mud stain on his doublet. Perhaps he would not urge her to greater speed in the future. He appeared out of sorts, and his voice was accusing as he addressed her. "I don't know why you chose to stay behind! You are not so young that you must ride like a baby! You might have accompanied me."

Mary, whether she rode like an old lady or like a baby, did not respond to his affront. She refused to believe that whatever had happened to him had been her fault. He took leave of them abruptly as they reached the stables where Ben waited to take Beth from Bingley.

"How did you like your ride today, little one?" he asked.

"We saw a brown bird!" Beth told Ben excitedly. "And he made three songs!"

Bingley dismounted and helped Mary off, and Ben took the horses, commenting on the state of their shining coats. "Not frothy like that young man's horse." He watched Stilton ride off as he raced for home. "I believe he will kill that creature riding like that."

Bingley, smiling as if he too had noted Stilton's disarray, remarked, "Or vice versa." Mary felt sorry for whatever woman would one day marry that rash young man. She rejoiced in her chosen life, sure that her contentment would lie in being of service to the sisters with whom she would one day live, and only sorry that she could be of so little service to them now.

# Volume Three

Settled

## Chapter 1

O N A FROSTY, LATE OCTOBER MORNING, MR. DARCY RODE over to Otherfield with Mr. Oliver, and they requested to see Mary Bennet. She had repaired to Otherfield's small library after a brisk ride in the park and was just opening a strange-looking novel, *The Mysteries of Udolpho*, when Sarah summoned her. Only sorry she had chosen her comfortable pinafore instead of a more presentable gown, she hurried down. In the parlour, Darcy greeted her warmly, but then quickly grew serious. "Miss Mary, we bring a proposal which I hope will elicit your full consideration. Mr. Oliver has expressed his fear that Kympton may well have a quiet and somewhat cheerless Christmas service unless you undertake to play the organ again. It seems that many of your faithful choir girls have been turned away and the few remaining are losing heart."

Mr. Oliver echoed Darcy's briskly businesslike tone. "Miss Bennet, I have been commissioned by the churchwardens and by Mr. Darcy to make the position of organist an official one with benefice. If you would be so good as to accept it, the gratitude of the whole parish would be yours. Unfortunately, Mrs. Clifford has resolutely refused to reinstate the girls and indeed has ousted others who voiced support when they petitioned." At this point he paused, gazed briefly at the chocolate-coloured carpet, then met her eyes and spoke more familiarly. "Were you not bothered occasionally by their antics at a Wednesday evening practise?" Mary nodded and shrugged. "How is it that you never dismissed a chorister, Miss Bennet?"

Mary, bewildered, reflected awhile. "Why, Mr. Oliver, I never once considered them mine to dismiss. I mean to say, if they elected to praise God in song, how should I discourage them?"

Oliver looked at her intensely. "Indeed! My dear Miss Bennet, I pray you will agree to help save the Lord's choir. The church elders and Mr. Darcy allow me to offer a stipend of fifty pounds per annum for our organist and to provide a residence. I do not like to presume to ask you to take on such a chore, since you are a gentleman's daughter, yet I beseech you to do so."

Mary hesitated. Could she accept such a task for a constancy? She had not noticed his offer of a residence, and the pittance he mentioned was hardly a sufficiency, but while her father supplied her pocket allowance and she could reside with her sisters, she calculated that it would do quite well. She required little. But still she was puzzled. She fingered the flowered pattern of the chair tidy. "Mr. Oliver, why are you so eager to preserve the choir? With your robust encouragement, your congregation sings very well."

"Yes, and I continue to exhort them to it. However, the young girls need their special status in the church, and they have a natural devotion that I wish to foster. I hope you also wish it." His earnest gaze caught her eyes.

Mary did rather wish it, yet the responsibility daunted her. "Perhaps I could accept the post until Christmas, and return to Longbourn afterward with my parents. I cannot expect to be forever an inconvenience to my married sisters." In her mind, she heard again the sigh of relief when Jane was spared her lifelong guest. At that time, Mary had wavered in her own plans for a placid future.

Mr. Darcy broke in. "You are certainly no inconvenience! But of course, you need a place of your own. The church at Kympton will be renting the vacant gardener's cottage at Pemberley. And though I would gladly offer it just to have it occupied, Mr. Oliver contracts for fifty pounds yearly, so that the cottage may remain available to the church as residence for the organist. My dear sister, you are to consider it your own."

Oliver added, "Once Mr. Darcy is fully recompensed for the living at Saint Giles, I will become full rector, and at that time I am prepared to add fifty pounds to the organist's benefice." He leaned forward, earnestly searching her countenance.

From his chair Darcy twisted toward her as well. "Added to your inheritance, you may well find it an independency, since I perceive your wants—chiefly books and music—are simple. You may look over the cottage at any time, and if you wish any changes, I will arrange for them. And of course, you may frequent our library and music room at your leisure." He too seemed to be pleading.

Mary, truly overwhelmed, found her mind abuzz with her new future. She tried to remember the cottage from passing it on the way from Pemberley to Kympton. She did remember the rainy evening she had stooped for cover beneath one bow window during a stinging downpour. All she knew was that it seemed a comfortable and clean place, and large for a cottage. "You are surely too generous, Mr. Darcy."

"Not at all. Mr. Oliver has reminded me of the precarious situation of unmarried ladies who might be constrained to marry against their wishes, and we hope to forestall that in your case." He sat back, relaxing as Mary seemed to convey agreement in her smile.

Mary, pleasantly bewildered by this turn of events, mentally tallied the problems and benefits of her changing status. "May I remain here awhile, riding to Kympton until the heavy snow comes?" She thought of Beth's progress at the pianoforte, two keys used unerringly and another inserted with less accuracy. Why, she might even be training a future organist for Kympton! Darcy saw Bingley with his hunting dog from the parlour window, and he hurriedly took Mary's hand, thanked her, and excused himself to join Bingley and Mr. Hurst.

Mary felt a momentary awkwardness with Mr. Oliver, and then smiled at her own embarrassment. After all, she had already travelled with him. It was not like being alone with Stilton.

Oliver took her hand in a similar gesture of gratitude. "I cannot tell you how pleased I am that you accept the post. I know that, with two sisters well married, you have no need to earn your living." He looked down and assumed an apologetic tone. "I did not like urging you into a place so unthinkable for a gentleman's daughter."

Mary smiled wryly, again recalling Jane's liberation moment. "Oh, I have discovered certain disadvantages to being always a guest—for me as well as for my sisters. I felt truly comfortable only at Longbourn. I welcome the cottage, and I may even grow to like the responsibility of the post, I assure you."

"You have had your ride today already? I would like to show you the road to Kympton."

"Oh, but Mr. Bingley showed it to me some days ago. Still, sometime next month I will return to Pemberley. Will you want me before then?"

"Right away, please. Come Sunday, if you will. Then I may announce that all are welcome in the choir. Will Wednesday evenings be convenient again for practise?"

Mary thought about that. "I do not take Grey Dawn out in the dark. Could a carriage be sent for me until I remove to the cottage?"

"Of course." Oliver made it sound as if no trouble at all would occur with the transport. Mary knew otherwise, and she mentally pushed forward her move to Pemberley and the cottage.

Suddenly she wondered if she, an interloper in the parish, should accept such a fine post. "Mr. Oliver, will not Mrs. Clifford desire the position? I do not like to interfere…"

"I understand. However, Mrs. Clifford has agreed to work with many ladies of Kympton who clean and decorate the Church, and she asks only to be relieved of the organist's duties."

Mary thanked him then, and her mind turned to an insistent two notes dinging from the music room. "Would you excuse me? I believe my niece calls me."

Mr. Oliver smiled and nodded. "May I await Mr. Darcy in the music room, or do you prefer to play without audience?"

"You are most welcome. Jane is usually there to observe her daughter. She will be glad for company."

By the time they reached the music room, Beth had slipped from the bench to squat on the carpet and play with the foot pedals. On seeing Mary, she scrambled back up. Mr. Oliver greeted Mrs. Bingley, accepted the chair she indicated, and prepared to listen.

Beth tested her two keys. Mary placed her little finger on a third. Then she put her left arm behind the child to command the bass notes, and started their familiar dances—tunes she could play without much thought while her mind teemed with notions of a future all new to her. She did not direct the child's fingers, yet as far as she could notice, they seldom missed. Mr. Oliver added an appreciative note to the audience, loud in applause and fulsome in compliments.

As they finished, Jane remarked, "Beth has three notes to play now, because she is three years old. Just think," she laughed, "she will command almost four octaves when she is thirty."

Oliver joined her in laughter. "At that rate, I do not expect to be present to hear her use the full keyboard!"

The little one skipped off holding Annie's hand, bound for the nursery where nuncheon and a nap awaited. After tea and buns provided by Sarah, Mr. Oliver pointed to the hedgerow in the distance and asked Mary to show him the grounds. She led him to the reading bench in the small meadow by the larches, which was her favoured warm-weather place, and they wandered the footpath. Oliver started off with a healthy stride, and then slowed his pace. "How is your reading coming, now that you are away from Pemberley's library?"

Mary smiled ruefully. "I must admit that Mr. Bingley's books are less to my taste. I try to enjoy Mrs. Radcliffe's novels as so many claim to do, but I find no joy in terrors for excitement that in the end come to nothing."

"You would prefer real terrors?" He feigned shock.

Mary shrugged. "One supposes that real terrors would threaten loss of life or soul and may at least cause me to amend my behaviour."

He laughed as if he found that funny, but she had been quite serious. He shook his head thoughtfully. "Did you ever complete your study of the works on the balcony at Pemberley?"

"No. I read *Pilgrim's Progress* and the books of poems by Blake and Cowper. But poems require many readings, and I would hardly call my reading of those complete. There are many other books that I have not even opened."

"When you do, I hope you will apprise me of any that need rebinding. I have still two sides of the main stacks to examine, and I do not know when I may get to the balcony."

"But that means you have covered half of them!" Mary was impressed. "It is good of you to take such pains with them."

He stared off toward the gardens. "I owe the Darcys a great deal more than I could ever repay. And I do enjoy the work almost as much as I enjoy use of the books." The path ended at the orchard, now almost denuded of leaves but with some fruit still to be gleaned. With interest, Oliver touched some carefully protected grafts on three of the young trees. "Sometimes the best apple trees are not the sturdiest, and when the strain can be improved on these poorer quality but sturdier trees, the finest orchard results." He tenderly turned the supple branch of one and examined the graft. "Your brother has an exceptional gardener. He has a surgeon's touch."

"I shall relay your approval to Mr. Webster. You seem to know gardening."

Mary looked at the branch he held and knew she would never have recognized what looked to her like a bandage.

Mr. Oliver pointed out several more such grafts. "My father did a bit of this on our fruit trees, but I never learned the art myself." Off in the distance, they could see Bingley, Darcy, and Mr. Hurst crossing a field. They were carrying guns, and Ben followed, carrying a number of birds.

Mary pointed to the hunters. "Do you not hunt, sir?"

Oliver showed his crooked half-smile. "About as well as I climb trees. The birds are safe from me, but God help the other hunters if I had a gun in my hands." He remarked on the large number of birds. "These fields are well stocked. You will not lack for game pies."

"Mr. Oliver, when I am here or at Pemberley I lack for nothing." But suddenly Mary saw what she would willingly lack: James Stilton strode toward them from the stable.

As he neared, he exclaimed loudly, and with some consternation, "Miss Bennet, I perceive you do indeed walk out alone with a gentleman when the fancy takes you."

Mary introduced Mr. Oliver as her pastor and employer, seeming to deny his being a gentleman, which startled both young men. Stilton she called a neighbour of Jane's. Oliver excused himself then to join the returning hunters. The other two stood quietly as Darcy and Oliver took leave of Bingley and Hurst. Then Mary begged to return to the house, explaining that she had already had her ride, her reading, her music, and her walk, and she was tired. She did not mean to be reprimanding Stilton for tardiness, as she had been glad of that; however, his reply indicated that he took it so, and he promised to come earlier on the morrow. She was not glad of that.

*Chapter 2*

THE FOLLOWING MORNING MARY WOKE EARLY TO THE UNUSUAL sound of excited voices below stairs. She dressed hurriedly for her ride around the park, hoping that it was not Stilton causing a stir. Upon descending the broad, east stairway, she heard from the breakfast room the unmistakable voice of Caroline Bingley, now Fitzwilliam. "But my brother told me that the east room would always be considered mine."

Mary retreated quietly back up the stairs, noting that Caroline's voice rang with heightened self-importance, and she wished for no confrontation over anything as trivial as a room. She did not hear Jane's soft reply. She found Sarah entering her room to tidy up, and she begged her, "Help me change linens, please, and move these with my things to the small guest room. Miss—rather, Mrs. Fitzwilliam desires this room."

Sarah tried to object, but Mary swiftly collected her things, and so Sarah reluctantly helped her. To Sarah's continued objections, Mary only replied, "It means nothing to me, you know, and I may be moving soon at any rate. I have committed myself to Kympton." They moved her spare belongings quickly, and Mary refused to let Sarah talk her into fresh sheets. She may decide to move to the cottage even sooner than she had planned. Then Mary went down again to the breakfast room, kissed Jane, and whispered to her. Jane looked both sorry and relieved.

"But this is so like you, Mary." To Caroline she said, "Mary defers to you. The room is yours."

Strangely, this did not sweeten Caroline's tone, and Mary wondered if some great strain was on her. Had she left her husband? Why? While Caroline supervised the disposition of her considerable number of boxes and a trunk, Jane told Mary the shocking news. "Viscount Henry Fitzwilliam never returned from Lady Catherine's funeral. Yesterday, his horse reached Norwich Mills, bearing a full wallet, an empty pannier, and no blanket. The Colonel and a servant set out immediately to search for Sir Henry. Caroline did not wish to remain in a home not yet familiar to her without her husband, and she chose rather to come here."

It now occurred to Mary that Caroline wore severe black. "Oh dear. How the family must worry." She thought of that sweet Lady Helena who seemed to depend greatly on her husband. "Poor Lady Fitzwilliam! How frantic she must be." She saw the pity in Jane's gentle eyes. Then she thought of another wife who diminished when her husband left her. "Will they ask Darcy's help?" She dearly hoped Lizzy would not have to part with Darcy again so soon.

"The Colonel means to ask where Darcy last saw Henry, and he believes Darcy will go along at least to point that out. Mr. Bingley offered to accompany them as well, but Fitzwilliam begged him to stay, knowing Caroline would wish it. I understand the Colonel and his servant will scour the Duxford road and every other route to Norwich Mills. Darcy may choose to help them."

Caroline returned, stiffly smiling. "Please order a fire in my room. The grate is cold."

Mary took upon herself the obvious rebuke. "I am sorry. I sleep best in a cool room, and my morning ride warms me." She fingered her crop and glanced out the window, spying Bingley setting Beth before him on his large bay.

Mrs. Fitzwilliam surveyed Mary in her riding habit and shuddered. "Horseback riding may be suitable for men and hoydens."

This puzzled Mary, who wondered why, in that case, saddles were made expressly for ladies. She knew that Jane, the most ladylike person she knew, had long been accustomed to ride, even on Nellie at Longbourn. Surely Caroline must be mistaken. She excused herself and reached the door as Jane said firmly, "Ben will be in to make a fire after he has saddled Grey Dawn."

At the stables, Mary told Ben as she mounted that Mrs. Fitzwilliam had need of him in the house. "Mr. Bingley and Beth will join me, and we will ride the Ilkestone Park path today."

Inside, Caroline looked beyond the breakfast room to the small parlour. Her eyes grew wide. "Where is Charles? Did he go with the others to Duxford?"

Jane placed her empty plate on the oak sideboard for the scullery maid. "No. He offered, but the Colonel would not have it so, saying he left his wife in her brother's protective care."

Caroline's stance relaxed, but her rejoinder retained her bristly tone: "My husband, the *Honourable* Darcy Fitzwilliam, is all thoughtfulness." Her tight smile warned Jane, who in future refrained from referring to Fitzwilliam as the Colonel.

Jane approached the window and drew aside the curtain. "Bingley and Beth are riding this morning. You can observe them from here." Across the garden, Mary rode Grey Dawn to meet Bingley and Beth on Shadow. "Beth likes to do whatever Aunt Mary does."

Jane smiled proudly, totally unaware that her observation further ruffled Mrs. Fitzwilliam.

Caroline pointedly repeated that riding horses did not become a lady, muttering, as if to herself, "But then, Miss Bennet will not become a lady."

Jane heard the strange remark, along with an accompanying simper, and she wondered much but did not enquire, as she did not feel she had been addressed. Soon she told Caroline that a cosy fire warmed her room, hoping this stately, black-clad woman could unbend as she had sometimes done formerly. "Please do not worry so. I am sure they will find the Viscount. Darcy may well know the exact road he meant to take."

Caroline seemed little heartened by this, and Jane searched her mind in vain for some comforting word. In a while, Bingley came in smiling, his daughter on his shoulders. "Beth likes to ride high." Caroline sat down again to breakfast, ignoring her room with its newly built fire, and Bingley set Beth before her to greet her aunt. She did this with the semblance of a curtsy, which almost upended her. Bingley kissed his sister. "Mary will be in from the stables soon for breakfast," he told Jane. "After that, the duets may begin in the music room."

Beth reached for a roll from the table, and Jane took it from her, broke and buttered it, and gave it to her piecemeal. Caroline put one arm around the child. "So Beth still plays whenever the pianoforte is open?" She leaned over and cooed, "Do you help Aunt Mary make music?"

Beth nodded wisely, her mouth opening for more of the roll. "And Tilton, too." She bit the piece and giggled. Mary arrived, greeted them, and helped herself from the plentiful sideboard offerings. Beth continued to giggle as she finished her roll.

"What is so funny, little Beth?" Mary asked, attacking her food with a will.

"Tilton."

Mary chuckled. "He is, rather." She finished quickly and retired to change to her homely pinafore.

Mrs. Fitzwilliam, after trying to overcome her curiosity, finally asked, "What is 'tilton'?"

Sarah entered at that moment and announced, "Mr. Stilton," and he followed her in, his ever-present grin fading at the sight of a stranger. Bingley introduced him to his sister with a look that made her understand that he was "tilton." To Stilton he said, "Miss Bennet rode a little late today and just went to change. Have some ham or sausage?"

Stilton, appearing nervous, politely declined. "If I may, sir, I will wait in the music room." Bingley nodded, and Stilton left, followed by Beth.

Caroline smiled. "A music master already? Are you not over eager, Charles? Beth is barely three."

"Oh, he is not here for Beth. He appears to be courting Miss Bennet, who attempts to ignore the fact. They are rather amusing to observe."

Caroline rose, her spirits revived. "Wonderful! I am prepared to be amused. I will join the audience." She attained the music room, found a chair at a remove from the pianoforte but facing it, and sat comfortably just as Mary arrived, followed by Jane, who joined Caroline. With little prelude, the two played their usual duets and included the four-hand arrangement of "Highland Laddie," which Stilton had brought with him. The child sat between them, her fingers searching her notes, alertly prepared to sound them when one or the other of the performers touched her. At the end of each piece, they thanked Beth handsomely, Stilton for her careful performance and Mary for sitting between them, though she did not say as much. After a musical half-hour, Stilton asked Mary to walk with him in the garden.

Mary turned Beth over to Annie as she said, "Of course. Mrs. Fitzwilliam, would you care to take a turn with us?"

Smiling secretively, Caroline promptly agreed, and Stilton's face tightened as she did so. The three of them strolled to the apple orchard, which began with trees as yet too small to bear much fruit, and proceeded slowly toward the larger trees still bearing the scant remains of the autumn harvest. Mary, who had talked with the gardener since her last visit, explained that the first trees would provide fine eating, while the far orchard would be set aside for cider. When they reached the far section, she pointed out grafts designed to improve the cider strain and provide stronger trees which would eventually bear eating apples. "Mr. Oliver says Webster is an excellent gardener, Mrs. Fitzwilliam…" She turned, only to find that Caroline was nowhere to be seen. "Oh, Mr. Stilton, we had best turn back. We must have tired Mrs. Fitzwilliam."

Stilton would not agree to it. "Mrs. Fitzwilliam surely knows her brother's park well enough to find her own way."

Mary started off. "Really, I must return to the house."

Stilton grabbed her hand and prevented her walking further. "Miss Bennet, Mary, surely you and all your family know that I mean to marry you."

He seemed to find this bald statement a sufficient proposal, because he said no more. Mary replied, "I am sorry to hear it." With her free hand, she reached for a bruised apple on the ground.

He extended his arm to allow her to stoop but frowned. "Surely you must have expected it."

"I expected nothing of the kind. I am sorry you ever thought an acquaintance such as ours tended toward any more than neighbourly amity. Please do not mention it again." She wrested her hand free. "Good day, sir." She hurried back through the orchard, rubbing the apple to a burnished gleam. Stilton stared after her, more angry than perplexed. Then he stalked to the stable for Willie and rode off at a punishing pace.

Mary composed herself before entering the house. She congratulated herself that at least the unpleasant confrontation was over. She need not again be plagued with searching out a third party to defuse Stilton's feigned ardour. In fact, she may have seen the last of him, neighbour or not. She bit into her apple, reflecting. Caroline had unwittingly done her a singular favour, God bless her.

# Chapter 3

NEXT MORNING AFTER BREAKFAST, MRS. FITZWILLIAM, ROBED IN another elegant black gown, drifted into the music room and, finding it deserted, sat down to play. As Mary passed the room, she noted the slow and mournful rendition of "Peaty's Mill," and she thought sadly of Georgiana's tune. She wondered if Caroline longed to be again at Norwich Mills. She made her way to what Bingley called his "unread library," intending to try again the Radcliffe novel so many seemed to enjoy. As far as she had gotten, she found it only dark and unrealistic. She took the book to the window, intending to sit there and read, when she saw Jane leading Beth outside, with Annie attending to her small charge. Deciding that the day must be unseasonably fine, she found her shawl, took her book to the garden, and headed through the larches to her comfortable bench. She would leave the pianoforte to Caroline, to provide whatever solace it could bring her.

Mary's reading was pleasantly interrupted after a short time when Jane strolled up with Elizabeth, just come from Pemberley. "With Darcy away and Georgiana gone to town with her maid, the comforts of home draw me less and the company of my sisters more," said Elizabeth, as she sat by Mary. "In fact, I came to urge you to join me or at least occupy your nearby cottage."

Mary allowed that she had been considering the move but had not yet opened the subject to Mr. and Mrs. Bingley. Jane put her hand on Mary's as she too sat down. "Of course, you must do what is convenient for you, now that you have an important post in Kympton."

"I would feel better with such a fine neighbour to visit often," said Elizabeth. "The irony is that Georgiana planned her London visit just at this time so that Darcy, on finishing the harvest, could spend more time with me! Instead, this morning when the nurse came for little Charles, I wondered what to do for the day. I came here looking for you only to find a dour Caroline Fitzwilliam, seemingly bent on solitary mourning. I prefer to think along more hopeful lines for her lost brother. Jane supports my view."

Mary closed the book, whose pleasure still escaped her, as they sat one on either side of her. She looked up thoughtfully. "Indeed, if the horse returned with money intact and the food and blanket missing, that does not suggest foul play. Does it not say that Sir Henry kept what he needed and sent the horse for help? And, as they say, no news is good news."

"Let us hope so," said Elizabeth, "for I have had no news from Darcy and Watts since they left."

Jane looked up. "Did Watts go with them?"

"Yes. He has a brother living near Duxford, on the farm where they grew up. Mr. Darcy thought Watts might prevail upon his brother to help Fitzwilliam, since he knows the surroundings so well." Elizabeth smoothed her gown, which a gentle wind had billowed. "Darcy said he planned only to take the others to Cambridge, where he had parted with Viscount Fitzwilliam, but he probably decided to help them search. I expected to see him home this morning. For their sakes, I rejoice, much as I miss him. An extra pair of eyes in the wooded areas must be welcomed."

"Do not say so to Bingley, I pray you," said Jane. "How he wanted to join them! But the Colonel declared Bingley must stay with Caroline, as he had entrusted her to him."

Elizabeth gave her a knowing smile. "It is fortunate that you have so fine a reason to welcome her!"

Jane started as if to chide Elizabeth, paused, and simply returned her smile. Then she pointed out the currant vines at the edge of the circle of larches that surrounded them. "Does this put you in mind of our little hermitage at Longbourn?"

Elizabeth looked all around her and nodded. "Do you plan to build a similar, small pavilion here?"

Mary also examined her surroundings and only then realized why she had come to feel the place so like home. In response to Elizabeth, Jane shrugged. "Mr. Bingley makes many plans, but I wait to see. From week to week this small, tree-ringed meadow changes from bower to cluster of benches to artificial pond to pagoda. When he finally decides, construction and planting will proceed apace, but I fear that until everyone he respects agrees on one plan, nothing will happen." She leaned across Mary to face Elizabeth. "You of all people ought to understand, Lizzy. Is that not the way you have gowns made for yourself?"

Elizabeth laughed. "True, too true. I prefer having them made for my sisters. And sometimes"—she fixed a teasing scowl on Mary—"the gown is redesigned so that it is no longer fit to wear at court."

Mary squirmed. "Oh, Lizzy, you know I will never have to appear at court, and bare shoulders do not suit me." Lizzy begged to differ, proclaiming Mary too modest.

Jane pointed through the thin line of larches to the house where Caroline had come out to enjoy the sun, carrying a ball and leading Beth by the hand. "Beth's nursemaid has many helpers. I sometimes wonder why we need Annie."

Mary watched idly as Caroline stooped over the little girl and whispered to her. They began to roll the ball back and forth between them. The two mothers exchanged experiences with nursemaids, and Elizabeth added, "Darcy tells me Charles needs a young nursemaid who will learn to love him and grow in loyalty as he grows. Then when he takes his place as master, she will become head housekeeper and look after his interests as her own. He expects Callie to become another Mrs. Reynolds." She reached over Mary to take Jane's hand. "Let me warn you: if you have a boy, Darcy may advise Bingley the same. But like you, I prefer to keep my hand in this child-rearing business."

"As Mama did with us," Jane agreed. "Perhaps we will learn a greater appreciation of her lively interest in us as we watch our children grow."

"If you are to follow her lead, you will soon be looking for a beau for your little one." Lizzy turned her head toward Beth playing with Caroline.

Jane laughed heartily. "No, indeed I will not. At least, not at present."

Mary discerned through the trees a bright finch that flew from a larch to a bush near the bow window where Beth ran after the ball. Suddenly the bird rose from the bush, thudded against the pane of the window, and dropped to the ground. The child forsook the ball beneath the window and scooted over to the fallen bird, stooping and reaching out. Caroline fairly screamed, "No, Beth! Do not touch! The bird is dead!" She reached Beth and pulled her away, retrieving the ball as well. "It is dirty too. Poor dead bird. Do not touch."

Mary left her sisters and walked toward the bird, thinking it must need either help or burial. As she stood near the circle of trees, she was close enough to the two playing ball to hear Caroline appear to be coaching the child as they played, but she could hardly credit her own ears. What was Caroline telling Beth to say? Again ashamed at overhearing what was surely not meant for her ears, she resolved to forget. She stood hesitating, unwilling to make herself known to Caroline. Her eyes sought the bird she had come to help. That dazed finch fluttered, flew a zigzag pattern to the bush it had vacated, and rested on an outstretched twig. Beth saw and pointed. "Dead bird! Dead bird!"

"Well, not so dead after all," said Caroline, laughing.

Bingley came from the carriage house, saw Jane, and strode through trees to her. At the sound of his voice, Beth spied the little group and ran to them. "Mama! Papa! I saw the dead bird fly!" Mary followed the child back and retrieved the book she had left on the bench, making room for Bingley, but he declined to sit, as he picked up his daughter.

Elizabeth sighed. "When will little Charles become so chatty? He is almost a year now. Shouldn't he be saying more than 'Mama,' 'Papa,' and 'no'? He walks, runs, and frightens me at his wish to clamber up stairs alone, but he remains a little man of few words."

"Beth started talking at about ten months I believe," Bingley boasted.

Jane hastened to add, "But she did not walk until a full fourteen months. I believe girls are often faster at talking than boys are."

Bingley put in, "They continue to out talk us all their lives."

Jane moved next to Lizzy and put a hand on her arm. "You

know we have no experience with little boys. You must be our patient guide in raising them."

Beth squirmed out of Bingley's grasp and ran to Jane, who took her hand and cued her to greet her aunts. She dutifully curtsied to Elizabeth, deftly, since one hand was steadied by an attentive Jane, and she said, "Aunt 'Liza"; she repeated the performance to Mary, who listened carefully to her greeting and answered her, smiling. Beth pointed toward the house where Caroline still sat observing the finch flitting from branch to branch. "Dead bird," Beth pointed.

Bingley, amused, said, "Not so dead, Beth. He can fly; he is not dead."

Beth repeated, "Not dead," and asked, "then what?" She raised her chin importantly.

Bingley again picked her up. "Why, the bird is alive, like we are." Beth turned to Jane, who carefully formed the word "alive." Bingley looked over at his sister and frowned as he remarked to Jane, "Caroline has yet another black gown. I do not remember her having even one."

Jane nodded. "Her attire of mourning bodes the worst. Did you find Colonel Fitzwilliam talking so fearfully of his brother?"

"No indeed. He said that the way of the great stallion's return suggested that Henry had sent Gallant for help. He was beginning to regret starting out at once, without the aid of the horse, which was spent. But he spoke as if sure of finding him alive."

"Alive," echoed Beth.

Elizabeth rose from the bench in acceptance of Jane's offer of a light repast before preparing to leave for Pemberley. "Then let us hope that Caroline may catch her husband's optimism. I pity any wife who cannot share her husband's feelings." Mary too had compassion for Caroline, and she had greater reason.

Chapter 4

Mary sent some of her things in Elizabeth's carriage as her pledge toward moving to the cottage as soon as may be. She readied a few parcels to send with Shepard when he came for her on Wednesday, and then she spent two days assembling the rest of her things and setting Jane's guest room in order with Sarah's help. Early on Saturday, she took leave of Bingley, Jane, and Beth; and when she spoke to Caroline, the worried wife graciously said she understood Elizabeth's need for a family member with her husband away. Mary, sure of the familiar way to Pemberley, refused Jane's kind offer to send Sarah with her. Then Mary loaded Grey Dawn with what she could reasonably carry, leaving her trunk with Jane, who would transport it to Pemberley after Sunday service at Lambton.

On the rather lengthy ride to Lambton, Mary already missed gentle Jane, amiable Bingley, and amusing Beth. Consequently, she reviewed all her reasons for moving. She hoped that Caroline could settle in better with no other guest in the way. She also knew that, with Watts gone to help Darcy and the Colonel, it would fall to Mr. Shepard to come for her every Wednesday afternoon, and this she was glad to avoid. Elizabeth must rely on him greatly in Darcy's absence, especially if harvest was not completed. And of course, Caroline spoke truly that Elizabeth may need a family presence other than baby Charles, who could distract her from her worries but could not converse or sympathize.

At Lambton, the ostler took her horse while she entered the inn for refreshment. She was served a plate of an egg dish left from breakfast and found it most satisfying. She asked the innkeeper what was in it, thinking to prepare herself for life on her own, never dreaming that the cottage would come with servants. He replied that the concoction was simplicity itself: "Just a few eggs, salt and pepper, some fried bacon, and a dollop of cream." After asking him to repeat it slowly with directions, she felt sure that she could manage it herself, and she thanked him.

Elizabeth welcomed her warmly at Pemberley, begging her to stay in her former room, but Mary hesitated. "I do not wish to unpack twice, but if I may, I will stay the night and assemble my things in the morning."

"But Tom and Betsy may not return for weeks. They worked so hard readying the cottage that I hadn't the heart to refuse their request to visit their former neighbours in Devonshire. With no servants at all you cannot possibly stay there!" Elizabeth directed Polly to take Mary's small pack of her night's needs to her room, and they followed the maid to Mary's familiar room across from the ballroom.

Mary, amazed that she would have such capable help, still wished to try out her new independence, and she assured Elizabeth that she would enter the cottage on the morrow but would visit everyday after breakfast. She did not mind being alone, and she promised to bolt the cottage door at night, lest any animals should wander in from the woods. Elizabeth sighed and accepted the arrangements.

Next morning, Mary rode over to Kympton to play for the service, and as soon as she returned, she took what possessions she could carry on Grey Dawn to her cottage while Elizabeth and her maid attended the Lambton service. Mr. Watts's boy Bill took the horse to the stable and Mary stood before the handsome cottage, admiring two sculptured yews that stood on both sides of the entrance, almost as sentinels. Entering, she relaxed completely in its homelike, plain loveliness. She glanced into the large parlours on each side of the small entryway, one bright with sun and the westerly one dimmer. On the first floor, she quickly chose one of the two bedchambers, both of which gave a splendid view of the gardens. Once settled, she went down to find the kitchen. After all, she had a recipe to try, and Elizabeth had given her eggs and a rasher when she had requested them. She found wood ready in the stove, and with a little difficulty and the assistance of several matches and twigs, she lit it, sure that the principal task was now done. She spent a time searching for knives, tongs, and a griddle. She replaced the grate over the fire and sliced a few bacon pieces from the rasher. Though she judged them thicker than slices she had seen, she did manage to fry them on the grill to her satisfaction. With a towel over the iron handle, she pulled the griddle from the fire, and with tongs, she removed the bacon slices onto the hard and scratched surface of the clean wooden table. She cut them in pieces as small as those she remembered from the inn and breathed a sigh of relief. Cooking involved more work than she had imagined, but the innkeeper had told her the first steps would be the hard part. She looked again at the fire, still burning steadily, and took the short walk to the dairy house where a maid happily supplied her with cream in a pitcher. She returned with a strong sense of adventure about making her very first meal. She found a bowl in the scullery, cracked two eggs into it with the bacon pieces and some of the cream, and mixed them all well. Then, she remembered the salt and pepper. She found some salt near the stove but no pepper mill. Not knowing the amount, she sprinkled what she considered a small amount into the mixture and stirred again. She added more in place of the missing pepper, and stirred it up again. Then she took a pan from where it hung on the wall, poured into it all the contents of the bowl, and put the pan on the grill. At this point, something went awry. Perhaps the stove fire had risen in heat, but quite soon, she removed the pan again and viewed the concoction. She scooped the top of it onto her plate and then tried to scrape the browned part from the bottom of the pan. She did not succeed as well as she would like, but finally judged it satisfactory, thinking she could at least use it again sometime as it was. Then she remembered to close the draft so the fire would die in the stove, and she sat down to sample what she had saved of her meal. She found it much saltier than what she had tasted at the inn. Next time, she would not be so liberal with the salt. She ate it, proclaimed it just edible, and prepared to hurry to Pemberley. But first, she had to down two glasses of water as antidote for the salt she had consumed. She noted that, when she returned, she would have to replenish the kitchen's supply of water. Perhaps Lizzy could let her have some from the well-house near Pemberley's kitchen. On the whole, Mary decided that she had never sufficiently appreciated the cook.

At the cottage door, she found Jane and Bingley, and saw Mr. Webster hefting her trunk from the ledge behind the carriage. He and Bingley insisted on putting it inside for her, wherever she wanted it. As they went upstairs to follow her directions, she turned to hug Jane, who whispered, "Let us visit here awhile, Mary. Darcy is home and planning to leave again. Let us allow Elizabeth some time with him."

Mary readily complied, even as she apologised for the nasty odour from her kitchen. When she explained her experience at cooking, Jane understood. "Perhaps Mama should not have prided herself on keeping us from kitchen duties, since she could not have foreseen that we would all be blessed with a cook. But I am certain you will succeed in time."

Bingley returned to them, and Mr. Webster took the carriage to Pemberley's carriage house, while Jane and Bingley toured the cottage and visited awhile in Mary's sunny parlour. "It seems a fine house for you," Bingley observed, "but where is the library?"

Mary laughed. "I am afraid that is at Pemberley for now, though I dream of finding a circulating library. Imagine, me being a renter of books! Someday, I must also learn from Betsy how to cook." And she revealed to Bingley her first disaster which he could, of course, smell even from the parlour. As they laughed together about that difficulty, Mary found herself wondering how Lydia fared and whether Wickham furnished help to supply for her inadequacies. She worried about young Lydia, even as she appreciated the lesson on avoiding improvident husbands, such as Stilton.

When the three of them went to Pemberley for dinner, Elizabeth smiled her gratitude at Jane for allowing her the morning. Darcy told them his news, or lack of it, concerning his quest. "We rode with Fitzwilliam the whole likely route from Cambridge to Norwich Mills but saw no sign of Sir Henry. The Colonel exchanged his horse for Sir Henry's there, bade his servant stay and rest, and loaded up with food and a packet of healing herbs such as he had used in battle. We hope the horse may lead him to his master."

Bingley registered some doubt of that. "A dog may be more helpful. I have never known a horse that willingly returns to an area of disaster. But Gallant may indicate being near it by a display of skittishness." Worry showed in Bingley's usually happy countenance. "I expect this news will not greatly please Caroline. She already seems to fear the worst."

Mary could not help seeing how tired Darcy looked. "I am sorry your task proves to be greater than you anticipated, Mr. Darcy. I pray you are not terribly discouraged."

"No, not at all. But we must find him soon because whatever supplies he had must have given out. You are probably right about horses in general, Bingley. If only this one may be an exception. It is our best hope."

Jane also remarked Darcy's tired look. "Will you stay awhile and rest, Mr. Darcy?"

"Watts asked for a day with his wife and son, as he means to give young Bill some directions about work around the stables. At any rate, our horses must rest tonight. We leave tomorrow early. With Fitzwilliam's servant not returning, we will be needed to provide some help. The Colonel, who seems to know that his horse and his servant must rest, gives no thought to his own rest. I fear he may come to harm or perish of fatigue." Darcy smiled at Lizzy, who regarded him as if she thought he too might perish of fatigue. He tried to hearten her. "We established a kind of outpost at George Watts's farm, in the barn, and he agreed to be there at sundown tomorrow. Even if he finds Sir Henry, how can he move him without help? We may even need a waggon if the Viscount is injured. Watts will bring an extra horse for his brother George, whose plough horses do not manage the wood paths well. We are convinced that the forest area and fens must be explored, since the roads showed no trace of him." Darcy put one arm around Elizabeth, who could hardly take her eyes from him.

Elizabeth spoke one of her many worries. "If the horse cannot lead you to him, what else can you do?"

"Explore every wooded area between Cambridge and Norfolk, unless you can suggest a better plan."

Elizabeth could not. Mary helped herself to yet another glass of water from the table pitcher, and when Darcy turned to ask if she had any suggestions, Mary spoke the one thing on her mind since her salty breakfast. "He would need water even more than food, I imagine. If there are fens, will there not be running water in those woods?"

Darcy frowned, trying to remember. Elizabeth only then noticed Mary's extraordinary thirst and asked what had got into her. Mary admitted her folly in thinking she could cook for herself, telling her what had happened when she tried out her one recipe. "I have much to learn." Elizabeth firmly ordered her to take all her meals at Pemberley. Mary meekly submitted, saying, "Else there may be neither pans nor supplies when Betsy and Tom return!" She had at least made the worried couple laugh over her stupidity, which heartened her. She wished her ignorance might always spawn some relieving virtue.

Darcy even agreed to keep her suggestion in mind. "I will stop and listen for running water. It may well be that Sir Henry looked for water, even if he had to crawl to it."

Mary reminded him, "Mr. Bingley seems to know about hunting dogs. Could yours not help?"

"Perhaps he could, if we were hunting the Colonel. But Fitz has never seen or smelled the Viscount, and we have no vestige of his clothing. It is a shame we did not think of it at Norwich Mills, but I fear Fitz would be at a loss just as we are."

When the Bingleys took their leave, Mary asked to adjourn to the music room, recalling Georgiana's kindness in contriving to leave the much-parted couple alone. She played the liveliest tunes she knew, hoping to hearten Darcy in his difficulty, but as she played, she thought the music less lively than formerly, somewhat thin without Georgiana's part, and a bit depressing. She hoped it was only her own flagging spirits that made the music seem less sprightly. Mary spent some time on her Christmas music for church, and then she sought the library for a half-hour at Blake's poems. Finally, she repaired to the small parlour, lit a candle, and took out her sewing, conscious that, as a householder, she needed linens. Her glance rested on a particularly fine painting Georgiana had made for her, a copy of one of the Gainsborough paintings Darcy had purchased. Mary had declared it too beautiful for one who had no place to put it, but Georgiana, saying that she wished Mary to remember her, pressed it on her. Mary would now have a place for it. That loveliness would call Georgiana to mind whenever Mary entered her parlour. She did not work long and returned to the cottage in the gathering dusk, bearing the precious painting in the plain frame Mr. Shepard had fashioned for it. She felt blessed and grateful for all the good people she had come to know through her sisters.

Mr. Darcy and Watts left the next day early, taking blankets, a waggon, and an extra horse. As soon as he left, Elizabeth took on the quieter, more thoughtful mien which Mary had noted before. Still, Mary wished to hearten her. "Do not worry, Lizzy. I am sure Mr. Darcy will find the Viscount; he is so determined."

Elizabeth sighed. "With all my heart I hope it is so, for he feels it most deeply. Yesterday he blamed himself cruelly for having hurried home after the funeral. I assured him that Sir Henry would not have allowed an escort at any rate, but he would not be consoled."

Mary asked to spend time in Pemberley's chapel to pray for his and Colonel Fitzwilliam's success, and Elizabeth gladly joined her. "It is a capital idea, Mary. Perhaps I will not feel so helpless."

On Wednesday, after her practise with the choir girls, Mary returned to Pemberley for a late dinner and was surprised to find Mr. Darcy at table. Elated at first, thinking his quest must be over, she looked again at his crestfallen demeanor as he picked at his food, and she knew it was not so. She wanted desperately to ask what was wrong, but at the same time, she feared the worst and did not wish to hear it or to make him say it. Elizabeth, who looked no less stricken, answered her question as if it had been written on her face. "Oh, Mary, Colonel Fitzwilliam did not return to the farm as planned; neither Monday nor Tuesday at sundown did he come. They have scoured the forest paths fruitlessly, and now they have two to search for." Elizabeth sounded as if she might cry, but she swallowed and went on in a firmer voice. "Darcy asks me to inform Bingley, so that Caroline may know the state of things. And since now Fitz may be of some help, he will return tomorrow with the dog." She turned then to Darcy. "Have you hope still?"

"Of course." But he shook his head sadly. "I hate to count on it, because there are no sureties in life, but Watts reasons that Fitzwilliam may have found his brother in a condition that required care and so would not leave him. We must believe that and renew the search vigorously because even the Colonel's additional supplies cannot last much longer." Darcy reached for Elizabeth's hand, whether to strengthen her or to glean strength from her Mary could not guess. "Fitzwilliam's greatcoat is still in the loft where he left it, and that may help the dog lead us to him." He looked at Mary then and smiled. "If that does not suffice, I am bringing my hunting boots to wade every stream I find. I believe you may be right about their need for water." He looked tenderly on his wife, a kind of pleading in his eyes. "I hate to leave you such a task, as it will be a delicate one. Try to find Bingley alone; he is the right one to tell his sister the unsettling news. Perhaps Mary will agree to accompany you to Otherfield?"

Mary most readily agreed. She wished to be with Elizabeth and to give any service that she could.

Chapter 5

THE NEXT MORNING, MARY CAME EARLY TO PEMBERLEY, but Darcy had already left. She hurried through breakfast because Elizabeth had ordered the carriage that would take them to Nottingham, and she knew Mr. Shepard would be prompt. During the ride, Mary was vaguely aware of the route now growing familiar to her, but she worried about Elizabeth, whose silence possibly meant that she feared delivering her message. Toward the end, Mary noted not a single landmark, overcome as she was with apprehension for Lizzy and with concern as to how Bingley and his sister would take this startling news. The journey was slow, and yet Mary found herself surprised when they slowed to enter Otherfield's avenue. She whispered to Elizabeth, "Do you wish me to come with you when you see Bingley or should I visit Jane and Beth then?"

"You are kind, Mary. I shall try to see Mr. Bingley alone, but perhaps you can tell Jane if Caroline is not by. But if she is with Caroline, you must keep it from her. Oh, Mary, Darcy is so worried that the Colonel overspent himself and is in dire need somewhere. We must keep praying that at least *he* may be found." Elizabeth stepped out of the carriage after Mary, and Mary nodded her agreement.

Jane and Bingley, clad for the brisk weather, came around the house as for a morning walk, surprising Mary and Elizabeth at the avenue. Mary suspected that the Bingleys were surprised also, but a warm welcome showed them pleased. Mary took Jane's hand and asked her to walk out to the familiar bower with her, while Elizabeth asked Bingley to take her inside. When Mary relayed to Jane the dreadful news which Darcy had sent to Bingley, Jane nodded, concern in her face. "I knew by her look that Elizabeth feared something, but this is disaster indeed. Caroline has been remarkably strong until now, considering that she keeps to mourning dress, but I know not how this will affect her. We must go in. Bingley is not one to keep it from her long, and she may need me when she hears this. I have some tincture of gillyflower and mint I must prepare, should she faint. At times I believe her nerves are very like Mama's."

Inside they learned that Caroline had just returned Beth to the nursery, and Bingley emerged from the parlour, his face white. He turned to Elizabeth, just behind him. "Darcy is right; I had best tell her and soon, but I fear her reaction." Seeing Jane, he searched her face for the intelligence he soon knew was hers, and asked her to be close by.

Jane settled Mary and Elizabeth in the morning room, saying she would have some refreshments prepared for them, and excused herself to go for the restorative. Mary found Elizabeth relieved of one burden but still apprehensive.

"My heart goes out to Caroline, Mary. I do not know if I could handle such news of Darcy." Elizabeth took Mary's hand and held it tightly. No sooner had she done this than a shriek from upstairs and a thud as of someone falling brought the sound of Sarah's hastened footsteps. Mary and Elizabeth followed up to the east room, where

Jane rushed in just ahead of them. Bingley knelt over his sister on the floor while Sarah grabbed the fire screen and fanned her.

"Her pulse is thready, Jane. What shall we do?" Bingley asked, looking up at her helplessly. Jane applied the smelling salts and gave Bingley a cloth dipped in hartshorn, which he put to the prostrate woman's forehead.

Slowly Mrs. Fitzwilliam sat up, shaking off the salts Jane held beneath her nose. Caroline moaned brokenheartedly, "This cannot be. How could he have gone back alone? What can have happened to him?" Her eyes lit on Elizabeth, and she grew furious. "I blame Mr. Darcy for this! He knew the route; he should have stayed close by my honourable husband." Elizabeth tried to assure her that everything was done that could be and that Mrs. Fitzwilliam must hope for the best and be brave. But then Caroline lashed out anew. "This was your doing! You kept your husband home with you when he should have gone with the Colonel!" Her piercing scream sent Mary back a few steps. She wished to be elsewhere even as she pitied poor Caroline, who must indeed be beside herself to call her husband the Colonel.

Jane gently moved to Mary and Elizabeth and whispered, "Please go to the breakfast room. I asked the cook to put out fruit and biscuits. We will care for Caroline." Caroline was screaming something about Darcy's gross negligence as Jane spoke. "Then do not stand on ceremony, but you had best leave soon. Thank you for coming. I know it was not easy since you knew not what to expect. Caroline is really not herself, though she has been remarkably strong until now. Perhaps she has been holding in her fears too tightly." Jane embraced her sisters quickly and returned to Caroline, weeping bitterly in her brother's arms as if all hope were lost.

Elizabeth led Mary to what seemed a second breakfast—one just as fast as the first—and then they summoned the carriage. The ride home, only a bit more companionable than the ride there, showed Elizabeth worried about the Bingleys. "I am thankful that she has the news, but, oh Mary, just think how Jane's life with Bingley will change if Caroline loses her husband so soon. It might be far better if she had never married, because before it she had learned to be content. She might now spend her days ruing what she has lost."

Mary would not give in to such gloomy thoughts. "We must not think it, Lizzy. Darcy will find them both. He must." She surprised herself by showing more faith in Mr. Darcy than even Elizabeth herself could admit to.

Two anxious days elapsed, during which Mary and Elizabeth engaged in desultory conversations over their meals, always coming back to their fading hopes for the Fitzwilliam brothers. The first day, over their needlework, Elizabeth had asked, "Should we not have heard something by now?"

Mary had calmed her by saying, "Duxford is far, is it not? And they must search in all directions from there. I do not think they could return so quickly. Please, Lizzy, let us keep our prayers hopeful."

On the second day, at what felt like their aimless work, Elizabeth sighed. "What can be keeping Mr. Darcy? All the night I dreamt there was a dreadful beast in the woods, devouring the men one by one. The idea of those fens and marshes haunts me. This wait is unbearable!"

Mary caught her dread but cautioned, "Lizzy, this is not Italy. The terrors of Mrs. Radcliffe's books do not happen in present day England. And does not Mr. Watts's brother know the safe paths? You must keep up your spirits." But truly, Mary grew dejected herself. If Caroline's fate should become Lizzy's as well, Mary realized that, all her life, she too would mourn the brother whose strength and kindness she had come to depend on. At dinner Mary forced herself to say to her quiet sister, "Please keep hoping, Lizzy. Mr. Darcy is so great a man. He will find a way."

"Oh Mary, let us pray so. Darcy is much more than a great man. He is a *good* man. He must come back to me. I cannot now learn to live without him." She had to leave the table then, and Mary too felt like crying. Instead, she made her way to the quiet oratory and poured out her pleading heart all night instead of returning to her cottage.

On the next day, as they doggedly pursued their work in Elizabeth's sitting room, they heard Darcy's voice below. Elizabeth raced to the stairway, while Mary stood in the hall, the linen still in her hand, and rejoiced that he had returned. She prayed that his news of the others would be as good. Darcy reached Elizabeth quickly, and they mounted the last few steps still joined in their embrace. Mary noted that his hunting boots were a bit soil smudged and watermarked. She returned to the sitting room, picked up Elizabeth's embroidery from the floor where she had dropped it, and placed it carefully on the small table near Lizzy's chair. As the two entered the room, Elizabeth's lively face raised Mary's hopes.

Darcy sank to a chair and unfolded his tidings of cautious optimism. "Colonel Fitzwilliam had indeed found Lord Henry. They are now headed to Norfolk on the waggon. Sir Henry had met with some kind of accident and fallen from his horse. Apparently the frightened horse stepped on his ankle, and the Viscount had sustained a head injury as well. Fitzwilliam said when he returned to the site of the accident, the horse became skittish and impossible to ride. He pulled his supplies from the horse, losing the reins, and the horse ran off a second time. They expect to find him again back at the stable. But at that point, the Colonel heard lapping water from beyond the marsh and carefully made his way over spongy ground to a drainage ditch because he was thirsty." Darcy looked at Mary and smiled tiredly. "And in doing so, he found his brother, who had made his way down the steep bank for the same necessity."

Lizzy glanced at Mary. "It was as you said: water must be found." Mary, recalling the experience that had occasioned her observation, looked down, her face warm, and Elizabeth quickly asked Darcy, "How did *you* find them?"

"Fitz led us right to the place of the accident and led us over safe ground to the ditch. We walked along the water until we found them. The problem was getting the two of them out of there. Of course the Colonel, having rested a bit, could have climbed it, but he would not move from his brother."

"Was Sir Henry so weak," Mary asked, "or was his ankle broken?"

"He had probably been without food for some time, and when we reached him, he was feverish and his ankle much swollen. The Colonel had given Henry all the supplies he brought, so by then he also suffered some weakness. But we gave them what food we had while Watts and his brother went back for strong blankets and rope. We made a kind of sling for Sir Henry, and we managed to pull him up to where we could carry him over soft earth to the waggon waiting on solid ground."

Elizabeth rang for some tea for Darcy, whose red-rimmed eyes and sprouting whiskers accented his weariness. "Was Sir Henry able to tell his story?"

"He must have told his brother, as Colonel Fitzwilliam seemed to know what to do for him. He had placed a poultice on Henry's wounded head. When we found them, Henry still had it wrapped around his head with the Colonel's scarf. He could sit up, and he declared he was much better, thanks to what Henry called his brother's 'battlefield skills'; but I can't say we have the full story yet. We fed them, gave supplies, and they left immediately for Norwich Mills. Lady Helena has been long enough concerned and undoubtedly wishes to nurse him, even in her present condition."

Mary did not like to ask about that, but Elizabeth, who seemed to know what Darcy meant, asked, "But her lying-in is not soon, is it?"

"I know not for sure, but I think a few months at least."

Elizabeth's mood, considerably lighter now, shone in her eyes. "And what did the Colonel say when first he saw you?"

"'I am hungry.' But his grin told all."

"That is so like the Colonel! He has a truly buoyant spirit. Does Caroline know her good news?"

Darcy nodded. "She will soon know. I asked Watts to go directly to Nottingham. The Colonel will be gone for a few more days as the waggon trip will be slow. When Lady Helena takes over, Fitzwilliam will rush to reclaim his bride."

"Thank God for that!" Elizabeth exclaimed, and Mary thought she spoke relief for Jane, but then Elizabeth added, "Caroline was beside herself with fear for the Colonel."

Mary suddenly realized that she was still idly holding the curtain she had been working on when Darcy had arrived. Now as Darcy took his tea, she took up her needle. "It is fortunate that you had an extra horse, since Sir Henry's had abandoned the Colonel!" Then, as Darcy began pulling at the laces of his boot, Elizabeth stooped to help him, teasing that she would be his valet. Mary took her unfinished work and discreetly excused herself to the library.

Sometime after supper, Watts arrived with the happy report that the relief at Nottingham had been palpable, even celebratory. And the following Sunday, when the Darcys returned from the Lambton service, they relayed an invitation from the Bingleys for Sunday dinner at Otherfield. Fitzwilliam had arrived there, news of Sir Henry was hopeful, and they wished to celebrate with the Hursts and Darcys, and Mary also must attend.

Mary had some misgivings about facing Caroline after her outburst on their last meeting, but she need not have done so. A smiling Caroline sought her out, saying with a meaningful smile, "Miss Mary Bennet, you are wanted in the parlour." Puzzled at this but obliging, Mary went to the parlour where she found herself facing Mr. Stilton, attired as for a dinner party. She had the instant foreboding that he too had been invited. Fortunately, such was not the case, but she once again had to listen to his awkward urgings. He bent one knee to the floor as he pleaded, "Miss Mary Bennet, please ease my mind and say you will marry me!" Mary remained standing at the parlour door, and she bade him rise at once.

"Mr. Stilton, I have no intention of marrying you. You must seek your fortune elsewhere." Stilton stood and looked at her in surprise; he had never told Mary his parents' stipulations concerning his inheritance. She went on. "You must understand that my situation has been stabilized. I am a cottage dweller in no need of marriage. I am sorry for you, but I must beg you to importune me no further in this matter." Then she turned and left the room.

Later at the dinner table, Mrs. Hurst asked about the angry young man she saw leaving at a reckless pace as she and her husband arrived. "Why, he fairly growled at me as I left our carriage." Jane and Elizabeth exchanged knowing glance, while Mary, relieved that Stilton had been angry rather than sad, said nothing to enlighten her. She devoted her attention to her plate, taking her cue from Mr. Hurst, who refilled his plate as soon as it showed through. She could not keep up his pace, but her concentration matched his.

Caroline, who might have explained to her sister, did not, being busy at her assumed role of benevolent duchess. Throughout the dinner and afterward, she could not have been prouder if she herself had found her husband—and had done that most cleverly. She fairly crowed her graciousness to Mary and Elizabeth, while she thanked Mr. Darcy profusely as if he had done all just for her. At the dinner, Bingley requested all the details, for which Mary was grateful. Colonel Fitzwilliam, rested and in fine spirits, happily told them as much as he knew about the accident. "Henry must have reached the thickest woods after evening had fallen, and a low branch he did not see in time caught his head and bent him back. He grabbed for his blanket and supplies just as I had done, and the horse jerked his head, pulling the reins free. Then Henry fell, and the horse somehow kicked his ankle, making him unable to catch the horse again."

Bingley let the Colonel finish his wine before asking him to go on. "So, did you find him where he fell?"

"No. Actually, he said he lay there for a day, until his water gave out, and he knew he must find some. By then he had heard water lapping against rocks, and he carefully crawled over spongy turf and rolled down the bank, feeling intense pain in his head and ankle. Already feverish when he reached the stream, he at first just put his head in it to cool the fever. This did not help much, of course. By the time I found him lying beside the river, he did not respond to my call, and I feared the worst. But when I lifted his head and put brandy on his tongue, he opened his eyes. Then I went to work in earnest to revive him. I washed his wounds with an alkanet solution and rubbed some pine resin on them. I applied the dead nettle, sorrel, and broad bean poultice I had prepared earlier on his head. I gave him some rose hip tea and put beech leaves on his swollen ankle. It reminded me of finding my good friend Sir Michael on the battlefield with a great head wound. The treatment was the same."

Darcy looked at him in surprise. "Surely you do not mean Michael Williams, the apothecary who followed you to war?"

"The very one."

"Was he knighted? I saw him not long ago, and he said nothing of it."

Fitzwilliam laughed. "No. But our regiment always called him Sir Michael, because after every battle he boasted of his exploits and used to say, 'If I were only rich enough, the Regent would have knighted me.' We agreed, because it is best to agree with him, and he has been Sir Michael to us ever since."

Bingley urged him back to his story. "By the time Darcy found you, had you made progress with Sir Henry?"

"His fever had gone down, until we ran out of herbs and food. And he had been able to tell me what happened to him, but by the time Darcy found us, his head was again on fire and he began to talk as if Papa was with him. I was worried, I tell you." He turned to Darcy then. "Lady Helena relieved his fever with some blackthorn bark tea, and he is quite himself again. His horse had reached the stables again—before us—but Henry refuses my suggestion to rename him, from 'Gallant' to 'Dastard.'"

Darcy laughed heartily and interposed, "I am glad for one thing out of all this. I was able to see my cousin's remarkable gift for military leadership. He knew exactly what we must do to raise his injured brother: he ordered blankets and ropes, directed us to lash the blankets to thick poles, and secure the ropes to the makeshift sling. Once Henry was on this battlefield pallet, he told us to string the long ropes taut over sturdy branches on top of the bank. Then, from the river edge, he and George pulled one side, and Watts and I the other until the pallet reached the upper bank. Watts and I had a hard time keeping up with the farmer and the soldier, I can tell you. It is a miracle poor Henry was not dipped in the water again."

Elizabeth said, "And I am glad for another reason: Georgiana was saved from the tension of these days. By the time she learns of it, she will know the happy ending." Darcy seconded her feelings, knowing Georgiana's fondness for Fitzwilliam.

Bingley asked only how Lady Helena received Sir Henry's return, learned of her tears of joy, and then permitted other conversation. Festivity lasted late into the evening, and the whole party stayed the night. In early morning, Elizabeth, Darcy, and Mary bade farewell to the Fitzwilliams and the Hursts, who set off for the North. After sampling the breakfast board, they thanked the Bingleys for a grand celebration and a restful night. They returned to Pemberley happy in the thought that Jane and Charles could resume their calm existence. On the way home Darcy asked Elizabeth, "Were you as worried about me as your welcome implied?"

"For that you must apply to Mary. She accused me of inventing a Gothic novel about your exploits. You must never provoke me to it again!" Elizabeth then turned the conversation to Georgiana's expected return from London and how surprised she would be at all their news.

Chapter 6

By mid-November, Mary found her cottage to be home indeed. Betsy and Tom resided in the rooms behind the kitchen and provided the great comfort of meals, washing, and whatever she could require. Even as she admired the sculptured yews that stood watch at her door, she now loved even the tawny leaves on the path and the hedges, now mere tufts of twigs along the footpath to Pemberley. She also grew fond of the bridle path through the pine woods, past the lovely trellised porch of Kympton rectory—which reminded her of Netherfield—to the simple two-chambered old church of Saint Giles. On her twice-weekly brisk ride, she could often glimpse the tall, stone steeple all the way, and she wanted to tell Grey Dawn, "There. That's where we are going!"

When the Bennet family arrived from Longbourn for the long winter visit, Kitty surprised her by asking to stay at the cottage in her guest room. Mary was happy for the company, and even happier that Catherine could forgo the luxuries she had praised at Pemberley. She suspected that her sister meant to accompany her to Kympton in order to see Mr. Oliver, and she immediately resolved to walk to church on Sundays so that Kitty could do so.

On her first evening at the cottage, Catherine showed her a letter from Lydia revealing that Wickham had found a kind sponsor, would study and take orders, and now awaited a "very fine living" where they may settle—"one that may well surprise the whole family!" Mary doubted the surprise, but she held her peace. She thought it strange that Lydia could sound so assured, whereas no word of an intended marriage had come from Miss de Bourgh. Kitty invited her to guess about the living, but Mary said only that any provision for a stable home would be a fine thing for Lydia. She knew she could not guess with any but complete accuracy, as Hunsford was the only name that swam in her head. She feared Kitty was disappointed in what must have seemed like Mary's lack of interest, and for that she was sorry.

One Sunday, as Mary prepared to play for the advent service, Tom Hooks whispered shyly to her before going to the bellows. He held out a sheaf of papers. "Please, Miss Bennet, would you read this before I show it to Mr. Oliver? It is an assignment."

"Of course. May I take it home and return it to you next Sunday?" He nodded assent, so she took the loose papers from him and tried to keep them reasonably straight as she placed them in her reticule. She wondered briefly about this assignment for his teacher and why she should be any judge of it. Perhaps it contained a musical composition, she thought idly as the girls took their places and she arranged her music in order at the organ.

After the service, she gave Tom's request little thought until, arriving back at the cottage with Kitty, she felt the bulk in her reticule. She sent Catherine to the breakfast room while she sat in her comfortable parlour and read the pages, keeping them carefully in order, as he had not numbered them. She saw with surprise that it was a short dramatic work, perhaps a Christmas pageant, and really quite charming, she thought. As she read, she imagined choir members as the angels, and Tom as the shepherd about whom he wrote. She took it along to Pemberley when she and Kitty went there for Sunday dinner. After the meal, when they gathered in the drawing room she read it to Catherine, Elizabeth, and Miss Darcy. As she finished, Elizabeth remarked, "What a charming little piece! I always fancied that Mr. Oliver tutors him to return the favour his own pastor did for him. Now I believe he must see this boy's great promise and wishes to further his education for that reason."

Georgiana asked to see the script. "I could almost picture the little shepherd refusing to go visit a child in a cave, thinking his duty was to stay with his sheep! How did he ever think of such a thing?"

Kitty also seemed to enjoy it. "Mary, will your choir present this as a play?"

Georgiana, more lively than Mary had seen her for some time, caught the idea. "Yes, what will you do with it?"

"I hadn't thought of that. I thought to return it and tell him how I like it. Do you suppose he may have wished it to be presented?"

Elizabeth said, a bit sadly, "But it is so late for that. How could we ever assemble costumes, even if the girls could learn the simple lines?"

Catherine's enthusiasm bubbled up. "But look at how he has made a main character of one boy and many angels for the group of girls! Do not you suppose he had them in mind?"

Georgiana enthusiastically spoke of old costumes used for Christmas pageants when she came home from school as a child. "We had theatricals then, and do you know, even Miss Anne de Bourgh took part once! I am sure my brother remembers." Georgiana led them to an upper room full of trunks and old furniture where she extracted from one large trunk many relics of old Christmas pageants. She held up a long white gown. "Won't this be long enough even for Miss Langley?" She pulled out yet another. "This is about right for Dorothy Dixon, do you not agree?" Mary nodded her agreement as Georgiana held it against herself. "I wore this one when I was ten."

By the time their candles burned to stubs and the hems of their gowns had swept up trails of dust from the floor of the little-used room, they had assembled simple costumes for several shepherds and as many angels, and they folded each again carefully and put it into a box for servants to bring down later for brushing and airing. As they returned, laughing over their soiled gowns and still excited about their project, Mary said, "We have a lovely 'Glory be to God' which the angels could sing as they enter. The girls love that one."

Elizabeth smiled, brushing the bottom of her skirt. "And who shall be the audience?"

Mary frowned, taken aback. "I had not thought of that. We could not do it in church." Reality attacked their rosy scenario, and doubts assailed her. "I am not even sure the girls would wish to do it."

Georgiana thought that it would be a fine entertainment for the children's Christmas party, provided the girls wished to perform it.

Elizabeth, obviously delighted to see Georgiana's exuberance, smiled broadly. "Good! I wish to see this production if it is to be."

Catherine, who had never been part of a home theatrical, began to have misgivings. "Much as I do not wish to dampen our enthusiasm, Mary was right to question whether the girls may wish to learn this as much as we wish them to. After all, we are not proposing to don those old costumes ourselves and learn the parts."

Mary decided to approach the girls on Wednesday. "Georgiana, please do nothing about costumes unless I can be sure that Tom and the girls agree." Mary dearly hoped that if the production took place, the Reverend and Mrs. Wynters could be present to see the young folks involved again in Yuletide festivities.

After practise Mary had a few words with the girls about their practise until Mr. Oliver left, so as not to spoil Tom's surprise for his teacher. Then she read the script to the girls. The girls all showed an immediate desire to participate, and Bella Hooks assured her of Tom's approval. "He even said he could bring his friends to play some of the other shepherds!" Mary saw that Tom had fully anticipated her. The girls chose parts for themselves before even thinking about costumes and offered to come on Saturday to practise. When Mary told them she would bring costumes, they were doubly eager. They came to look at the manuscript to read their lines and say them over before leaving for the evening. Mary had to shoo them out, lest Mr. Oliver worry that they were walking home too late. Most of them left reciting lines as if they meant to learn them that very night.

On Saturday, it appeared they had done much of their memorising. Tom appeared with some friends who took great interest in the shepherd costumes. Mary imagined that Tom had actually coached the eager young people. Mary realized that this must have been the boy's desire all along. The costumes created much glee for the impromptu cast there assembled, and each shepherd and angel chose a fitting robe. The hubbub in the loft must have reached the ears of Mr. Oliver working below to prepare the sanctuary for Sunday, and Tom grew nervous lest his teacher grow curious. He begged Mary not to tell the vicar, who had not yet seen the lesson. He said quietly that he truly hoped Mr. Oliver could judge the production by seeing it played rather than reading it. This started a chain of requests.

"May my parents come?" "Oh, my mother would love this above all!" "Oh, please may my father hear it? He is a shepherd!" Mary had to say she could not promise such a thing.

"I must ask Mrs. Darcy about this. The coach house cannot hold such a crowd as you wish to impress! We must wait."

"Oh, please," begged Tom, "do ask good Mrs. Darcy!"

Mary feared that Elizabeth would regret her kind offer. She would speak to her sister, but she warned the youngsters not to count on having so great an audience.

When Elizabeth heard the problem, she said immediately, "Why that is quite simple: the young people must give two performances. On the feast of Saint John, if they come to the ball with their parents, they can perform for the adults. Our guests will enjoy it, and it will add greatly to the noel singing." Mary was doubly delighted at this, knowing that Mrs. Wynters would indeed see the young folks having their very own part in the Christmas celebration.

Back at the cottage after the Christmas ball, Catherine sat in the parlour, declaring herself too exhausted to ascend the stairs. Then, she proceeded to go over all her delight in the evening, not the least of which included two dances with Mr. Oliver. She also complimented the cast of Tom's little play, which everyone had enjoyed greatly. "And you know, the last scene, where the angel comes in dressed as a shepherd to offer to tend the sheep was best of all! It was a grand idea to let the angel costume show under the shepherd's robe, so anyone would know it was really an angel."

Mary laughed. "That was the invention of necessity. There was an angel dress long enough for Miss Langley, but no shepherd one, and she had no time to take one off before putting another on."

"It came out perfect," said Kitty, "and they certainly learned their parts well in so short a time. I told Tom what a fine work he had written, and I heard Mr. Oliver tell him so too." Kitty sprawled on her chair, her legs extended. "Do you know what his assignment was?"

"No, Tom never told me." Mary took the tray Betsy brought for them, thanked her, and said she would not be needed further.

"Mr. Oliver told him to illustrate Saint Luke 21:34. Tom said he chose the part about 'worldly cares' because they involve everyone and people even think of those distractions as virtues, since they see it as their duty. Mr. Oliver declared it splendid, and so did I." Mary had to agree, and she went to bed feeling that for once she had thoroughly enjoyed a Christmas ball at Pemberley. Part of her pleasure had consisted in Stilton's absence, as she had feared the Bingleys might have invited him. But mainly she felt she really belonged to Pemberley now, and she knew some of the local folks, especially those of Kympton. She had danced with some of them as well as with her brothers, and she had been pleased to see Mr. Oliver dance with Kitty, and even with Lydia, whose attendance did not affront Mary this year. Rather, since she learned that Lydia had travelled without Wickham, she feared her sister may be on another begging tour, and she pitied her. Mrs. Wynters had found Mary and told her, "The angels and shepherds were such a grand addition to the festivities this year. I told young Tom how fine I thought it."

Surprisingly, Miss de Bourgh had attended with Mrs. Jenkinson, commandeering all the comforts formerly accorded Lady Catherine. She spoke more often and more forcefully than Mary had ever heard her before, and she had long converse with Mr. Darcy, causing Mary to wonder about an announced wedding in the offing. Miss de Bourgh did not dance, however, and wore only mourning dress throughout her stay.

At supper Elizabeth had noted that Wickham's pretension in trying to become a preacher had no more genuineness than Blaise Castle's pretension to historical value. Jane chided her gently, saying she had always hoped for Wickham's desire to turn from immature things. Mary saw that her sisters accepted the turn of events in Kent and seemed to do so with no regrets that Anne had not been warned in time, so she relaxed also in the prospect of

Lydia's possible advancement. She knew that Mr. and Mrs. Collins had declined attending Pemberley's ball, and she hoped it was only because Collins did not wish to be away at Christmas from his post at Hunsford. She truly wished them the best, even as she desired so fine a place for Lydia and her husband, especially if he had, as Jane hoped, cast off his immature ways. They had also mentioned the absence of Colonel and Mrs. Fitzwilliam, Elizabeth opining that Mrs. Fitzwilliam probably preferred to celebrate at Norwich Mills with the Earl.

The following day Mary came down late and found Kitty in the breakfast room ahead of her, humming to herself. Catherine, with a knowing smirk, asked, "Have you heard anything of late from Mr. or Mrs. Collins?"

"Not at all, except that they could not come for the Christmas ball. Surely Mr. Collins does not leave his parish at the holy season." Mary refused to ask for the intelligence that Kitty apparently wished to have teased from her, though Kitty resumed her humming and appeared ready to burst with it. No doubt Lydia had revealed Wickham's whole plan to her. Mary wondered more about what Darcy had learned from Miss de Bourgh, but of course, she would not ask him.

Only after the Christmas visitors had embarked for Nottingham, Kent, and Longbourn, did Mary find time to try the cottage pianoforte her sisters and brothers had presented her for Christmas. As she played a quiet and dreamy andante, she reflected on the stirring music of the Christmas service, realizing that the choir girls had been far easier to handle since they had undergone the rigorous treatment by Mrs. Clifford. She hardly knew that lady, but she conceived a gratitude for her. Oh, Emmaline still flirted with Mr. Oliver at practise, but she did not have to endure further mockery of herself, and their parents had expressed such pride in the girls' performance that Mary felt a new contentment in her situation. Though her sisters were still too bountiful—she caressed the keys of her spinnette—she would not in the future be forced upon their hospitality. She would find contentment in her different kind of world, and she looked ahead to the promise of tranquil days.

## Chapter 8

B Y LADY DAY, MARY COULD LOOK BACK ON A COSY WINTER IN her cottage. All things about it pleased her except for its not being far enough from James Stilton. By then, he had found her and proposed to her more times than she had bothered to count. These proposals had come at times off-handedly, at times pleadingly, at times with simulated passion (love), at times with genuine passion (anger), at times grovelling in desperation, and once in a manner honestly. On that occasion, he openly acknowledged that she alone held the key to his inheritance, and he inadvertently mentioned having to wait until his thirtieth year unless she relented. She advised him to avoid gaming events, find employment, and repay his father for his losses. This left him speechless because he had never been so open as all that.

Besides Stilton's regular proposals, she had received two letters from her mother on the subject. The first advised her that an offer from a landed gentleman was not to be refused, and if Mary was the prudent and dutiful daughter that she should be, she would accept Mr. Stilton. This letter ended, "If you will not, I will count you no daughter of mine, and I will never address you again." Mary replied, as her father had counselled, that Mr. Stilton's claims to land were too tenuous and too distant to credit. Mrs. Bennet's second letter began with her intense shame at her daughter's obstinacy, rendering her so embarrassed that never again could she face Mrs. Long. It went on to chronicle her many visits to that lady, quoting Mrs. Long's continued amazement at Mary's obdurate refusals. At the end of that letter was a note in Mr. Bennet's hand: "My dearest Mary, keep up the good work." Mary laughed when she read it, wondering what her mother had made of it or if she had even seen it. Even Mrs. Long had written once, declaring her surprise and sorrow at Mary's "unnatural willfulness." Mary returned a short note thanking that lady for her Christian kindness in concerning herself over Mary's future wellbeing.

A week or so before Easter, Elizabeth, Georgiana, and Mary worked quietly on some baby clothes for the second Darcy baby, expected in August. Jane's lying-in would precede Elizabeth's by a few months, bringing to Mary's mind those days of Jane's bliss after Caroline's wedding and Elizabeth's similar happiness when Darcy returned from Lady Catherine's funeral. Mr. Darcy entered the morning room where they worked, a letter in his hand and a puzzled frown on his face. "Lizzy, Colonel Fitzwilliam seeks my advice 'as a happily married man.'" Darcy smiled at his wife. "He is correct about that at any rate."

Elizabeth looked up. "Does he ask you to teach him contentment?"

"I think not. He declares himself to be satisfied with his state, but he fears that his wife may not be so. He says she had been adjusting beautifully and smoothly to married life and the society of the village, until her sojourn in Nottingham during his trouble. He had brought her there at her own request, and he thought he had done the right thing, but on their return, he felt she never again took the same pleasure in her surroundings. She does not even seem able to rejoice with them over the birth last month of a son to Henry and Helena. Her low spirits have him puzzled. He has even recommended to her some of the healing remedies he learned from French women who followed the troops during the war. She tried them all: dittany, oil of jasmine, and boiled primrose. All were to no avail, and he seems to think I can help him. I confess I am at a loss to do so. I have not myself known Caroline to be pettish nor depressed; if anything, she has always been quite the opposite. And I hesitate to say anything to Bingley. Lizzy, do you suppose she regrets her marriage?"

Elizabeth shook her head. "At the wedding and after, and even during her stay with the Bingleys, I detected a satisfaction, even at times a radiance, perhaps a smugness, that positively oozed contentment. I cannot believe she acted a part."

"Then you think Fitzwilliam is mistaken?"

"I might say so," she began thoughtfully, "but he had so accurate an assessment of your friendship with Bingley on my earliest acquaintance with him that I hesitate to question his judgement." She put down the little garment she had been holding and looked up, frowning. "Perhaps... the birth of a son to her sister-in-law... and Louisa Hurst's childlessness... do you suppose she wishes for a child or fears she may be childless like her sister?"

Darcy accepted the surmise as most likely, and he turned to take up pen to reply to his letter when he heard Mary's little cough and slight murmur. He turned to meet her gaze and asked, "You do not agree, Miss Bennet?"

Mary looked down, hesitant. "Perhaps. But something I once heard... but surely it is nothing."

Elizabeth immediately said, "Tell us, Mary. What did you hear?"

"Yes, what?" Darcy was all attention, and Georgiana, usually silent, echoed him.

Mary started softly, "Once at the piano, Beth called me 'Lady Mary.' I corrected her, and she shook her head, saying 'Aunt Mary, Lady Caroline.' I did not think it any more than a childish thing, like playing princess. But outside, that day you visited us, Elizabeth, do you remember, when the men were off to find the Viscount? I had gotten up and gone to look at a fallen bird, and from the edge of the trees I heard Caroline coaching her. She said, 'Practise, Beth: say Lady Caroline.' I fear she expected that the Viscount was lost forever, or would be found… not alive. I prayed it was not so."

Elizabeth's eyes registered full understanding. "That does explain her persistence in wearing mourning dress, though the Colonel had not been so despairing. And it possibly explains her dire reaction on hearing that the Colonel had disappeared. Her hopes for advancement must have been dashed at that time."

Darcy took it in slowly. "You mean she may have expected her husband to succeed to the earldom? If that is so, then the son born to Lady Helena would add no joy for her." He resisted believing it of her but finally seemed to do so. "How can I tell Fitzwilliam such a thing? He could not possibly make her what she aspires to now."

They were quiet and sombre for a time until Georgiana meekly spoke. "If it is only a matter of a title, could you not appeal to Lord Exbridge to recommend Colonel Fitzwilliam to a knighthood?"

Elizabeth took up the idea enthusiastically. "Of course! You could mention his valour and perseverance in saving his brother. If he agrees, I am sure the regent will consent to his request. Then Caroline could have the title she desires."

Georgiana joined Elizabeth in her optimism. "Oh, I am sure he will do it!"

Darcy nodded, but he did not smile. "Perhaps he might. But I could never tell the Colonel that!"

Mary, who rather liked the idea, spoke up. "But you could tell him what you planned to do—Lizzy's idea about a child—and beg him to be patient. Then, if he should happen to be offered a knighthood, we must hope that he does not refuse it."

Darcy now caught the idea with full spirit. "Hope nothing! I will tell him not to refuse." And he started off to write his letter but turned once more. "Lizzy, could you manage to travel this early summer? It might be well to leave Charles in the care of his nursemaid more, to prepare him for sharing the nursery and your time." Elizabeth nodded. She did not want to think herself ill because of pregnancy. Darcy smiled. "I believe we should visit Exbridge, and Georgiana should come too. I do not believe Lord Exbridge could refuse you and Georgiana anything."

## Chapter 9

Soon after Easter, the Darcys stopped at the cottage, Charles running at his father's heels. They invited Mary to accompany them to London and Hertfordshire. "We are only three; there is certainly room in the carriage. Elizabeth is not so large yet!" He looked at his blushing wife with tender care and loving pride.

Elizabeth beamed becomingly. "Miss de Bourgh has kindly invited us to enjoy springtime in Kent as Darcy used to do. We thought you may wish to visit at Longbourn while we are there. And it would please Georgiana to have your company to London, I am sure. We will return to Derbyshire in early June or midsummer at the latest. I will wish to be near Jane for her lying-in, and I shall be quite ready for some rest myself by then."

Mary surprised herself at how readily and with few regrets she declined their generous offer. She invited them in to see how her parlour had been arranged around her cottage pianoforte. Elizabeth looked around the fine room devoid of frills, and she dared to set Charles down. He ran from chair to chair until he climbed onto the piano bench. "What a comfortable arrangement! Even my wild child shows his joy in it. Why, you already have him yearning for lessons. You can make a veritable James Stilton of him in time."

"Please," Mary groaned, "you would never welcome that, indeed." Darcy expressed his approval as well, recognizing some of Georgiana's work adorning the wall and admiring the spare furnishings as both tasteful and sufficient. He asked if her two servants were adequate to her needs. Mary hurriedly replied, "Oh yes, quite. All the comforts I could wish for are before me. I have even become a borrower of books from Lambton's circulating library, as well as from yours."

"And you must feel free to use our library as often as you like in our absence. Are you quite certain you will not accompany us?" Darcy urged her.

"Oh yes, Mr. Darcy. The choristers begged to continue until Whitsun, and they are doing so well already with Simon Browne's 'Come, Gracious Spirit' that I could not disappoint them. After that I will read more, and while you are away, I may occasionally visit Jane." Mary rang for Betsy and asked for some refreshments for her guests.

Elizabeth reached out to capture Charles as he hopped by and thanked her for offering to visit Jane. "The Gardiners will come in June, and if they should precede us, do not feel obliged to be hostess to them. They will stay at Pemberley and are aware that we may be away."

Darcy laughed. "Mr. Gardiner and Shepard are great fishing companions, and Mrs. Reynolds is so grateful to them for bringing Elizabeth to me that she treats the Gardiners like royalty."

Betsy came in unobtrusively to deposit tea, fruit, and sandwiches, and Mary, while pouring tea, asked Mr. Darcy, "When you heard from Miss de Bourgh, did she say her health remains robust? I had always thought her frail."

"She does not say," Darcy replied taking his cup. "But she mentioned visiting some families in the parish to discourage gossip and to caution peacekeeping. If she so eagerly takes over Lady Catherine's parish concerns, she must feel healthy indeed." He helped himself to a sandwich.

Knowing that at Christmas Anne did not appear to be the "languid soul without will" that Lady Catherine had deplored, Mary supposed there was more of her mother's spirit in her than Anne had previously displayed. Elizabeth voiced a similar view. "Perhaps, no longer intimidated by her mother's domination, she discovers a will of her own. Let us hope it does not mean she will become a poker before whom all quake in fear."

Mary ventured then to ask the question foremost in her mind since Kitty's revelation of Wickham's plans. "And does she mention the verger Witherspoon?"

Darcy shrugged and took the wriggling Charles from his mother. "Not a word. But she may be saving her wedding plans to tell us in person when we visit. Still, if she commands him as regally as she did Mrs. Reynolds at Pemberley, I may actually pity the man." They finished most of the fruit and sandwiches as Betsy brought a fresh pot of hot water and Mary again poured tea. Charles displayed fine manners with the food before him. His eyes did all: he looked at a sandwich or a strawberry, then at his mother. If she nodded, he took it and made sure to finish it before looking again. Such curbing of exuberant spirits must have cost Elizabeth and Callie many trials; Elizabeth, for all her lack of previous experience with little boys, had done well indeed. The guests rose to leave, and the attentive Betsy came to collect plates and tea things.

At the door, Darcy said, "If you change your mind, let us know by Sunday. We would be happy to include you."

"Thank you, no. But if in your kindness you could carry a letter to Papa and Mama, I would be grateful. I will bring it before then."

Just in front of the cottage, the Darcys met Mr. Oliver returning from Pemberley's library. Mary lingered in the doorway to hear their hearty greetings and Darcy's subsequent banter with the vicar. "We leave for Kent soon, Mr. Oliver, to learn the truth concerning Miss de Bourgh and the verger. And who knows, all may work out well for them… And you, Mr. Oliver, when may we expect you to take a wife?"

Hearing no reply, Mary watched the vicar shrug and smile as Darcy continued. "Ah, you avoid marriage as death, do you?"

To this, Oliver rejoined, "Perhaps there are parallels, sir. To die well, one must attain to a love that breaks all lesser bonds. To marry well demands a similar love, I hear."

Echoing his mock-serious tone, Darcy asked, "And are you as ready for one as for the other?"

"Whichever God wills," Oliver said with a slight bow.

Darcy frowned at that. "Seriously, Oliver, you do not deplore the state, I trust?"

"On the contrary," Oliver's equally serious reply came, "I believe matrimony presents the truest taste of God's life that this created world provides. But as it is the state in which the two become one, I must find one I wish to become." He returned to his teasing tone. "I believe that you yourself did not find such a one at my age, twenty-six?"

Darcy laughed and drew Elizabeth closer. "No, I must admit it took a few years longer. Then you have not yet met such a one?"

Oliver hesitated. "Unfortunately, the selection requires a certain mutuality." His cryptic reply quieted Darcy, who perhaps recalled his own difficulties.

Elizabeth again transferred her squirming offspring to Darcy. "You remind me of my mother's caution against a too-nice discrimination. She used to tell us that if we waited for the perfect gentleman, we might find that he is waiting for the perfect lady. Yet God is so good that, with time, our ignorant prejudices may be overcome, and just such a commingling of aspirations may occur." She gazed lovingly at her husband now lifting Charles high enough to delight and quiet the boy.

Mary recognized her mother's dictum regarding husbands and watched Lizzy fascinated, wondering how she could ever have doubted Lizzy's love for her husband.

Oliver bowed and took a step toward Kympton. "And His goodness overflows to others too. I have been happily pursuing Augustine again in your superb library. Thank you." As he passed, he waved to Mary in the doorway, surprising her, and then causing her to laugh at herself. Did she think she had been invisible to them?

## Chapter 10

AFTER WHITSUN, MARY OBSERVED HER REGIMEN CAREFULLY, AS she had done in her days at Otherfield. She spent some time riding or walking, had a light breakfast of whatever Betsy put out (she had given up trying to learn to cook); she played some music, did some reading, and worked on some sewing, an occupation Elizabeth would be happy to know she had come to value. She had also sought out the formidable Mrs. Clifford to beg for lessons in the art of transposition. Some hymns presented so difficult a range for the young, untrained voices that she had long regretted her inability to adapt the music to suit them. Surprisingly, Mrs. Clifford graciously offered an afternoon a week for these sessions at Kympton's organ, and Mary resolved to show her gratitude with gifts of produce from Pemberley gardens and orchards to which she had full access.

One misty morning after her ride, she found a letter from Elizabeth, which Betsy had laid on the hallway table for her. Surprised that her sister had thought of her at all, the bulk of it astounded her. She opened it eagerly and sat in the parlour, still in her riding coat, to learn the prodigious news.

Dear Mary,

How exciting and how fortunate it was to visit Lord Exbridge, for ever so many reasons! Now when I think we may not have done so but for your information about Lady Caroline (for so she is to be), I am so unspeakably grateful to you. While there, we met Lord Exbridge's daughter-in-law Martha and his grandson and namesake David. We learned that Darcy's letter requesting our visit prompted the lord to do what his family had been urging for over two years: he asked his son's widow and her son and daughter to come live with him. Martha Exbridge played hostess charmingly. She no doubt provided exactly what the lord needed in his home after living so long in bleak loneliness.

Now here is the real surprise of our visit: Georgiana thanks you more than any of us for your suggestion because the visit opened her closed past to her! As soon as she entered the mansion, she exclaimed and began to wander the rooms as in a dream. She explained that it exactly matched a vague childhood impression, and she declared that she knew every inch of the place. Darcy could only guess at the connection, but Lord Exbridge confirmed that Lady Catherine had often visited, many years ago, with her teenage daughter and much younger niece. When Darcy was at school, his father, in deep mourning for his wife, had asked Lady Catherine to care for his little daughter, who was sent to her with her nursemaid until about her sixth year. Exbridge confirmed that Lady Catherine and Lord Lewis had brought the girls frequently for long holiday visits when his son's family also visited. Georgiana stared at young David, who also studied her, and together they remembered games, toys, and places they had known when very young.

By evening, Lord Exbridge grew lively, sharing their joy in remembered pleasures and filling in details that they only half recalled. Martha Exbridge played country dances, and we danced—even in my condition—along with the young couple. Never have I seen Miss Darcy so lighthearted, and she declared that when she had played "Mansion of Peace," it was this house she thought of sadly, thinking it lost to her forever. I have come to believe it was this loss that gave birth to her shyness, and Darcy and I beheld her grow whole again. If my eyes did not deceive me, young David felt the same. He who had been shy and awkward on first greeting us, became warm and smiling at Georgiana's delight, and his gaze rested most comfortably on his childhood playmate. When I tired of dancing, I sat down to play the boulangerie and Darcy took Martha's hand for the dance. Afterward, young Susan showed her prowess at the instrument.

Later still, Darcy sat down with a renewed Lord Exbridge and told the story of Henry Fitzwilliam and his brother's valiant search for the Viscount. At learning the details of the care Fitzwilliam provided, Lord Exbridge himself suggested knighthood for the Colonel, and he vowed to write the request to the Prince Regent himself! That fortnight could not have transpired more favourably than it did. We are

all indebted for your information concerning Lady
Caroline. (You observe how I practise the title, lest
in the future I should make an unforgivable lapse!)
We had found Lord Exbridge still half alive, but we left
him a man of purpose dictating a full commendation
of Colonel Fitzwilliam and planning to restore his own
country residence to the splendour it had when Capability
Brown had landscaped it. He also insisted that he,
Martha, David, and Susan would convey Georgiana
to Lady Elliott in Saint James Court, where Georgiana
will visit for the summer. I suspect that she will visit as
much with the future Lord Exbridge as she does with
Lady Elliott, but as that serves only to enliven her, I
am sure Lady Elliott will approve.

Darcy and I came directly to Longbourn only to
find a disappointed Lewis Grantley, M.P. Having
heard that a daughter was expected to visit, he came
looking for you! He informed us that some singular
interpretation of essays he had given you caused him to
reread them, effecting a change in both his mind and
his manner. Our Netherfield neighbour now declares
that such extreme devotion to personal liberty might
break a nation into individualism, could destroy all civil
discourse, and could fracture community. He devotes
himself to his own country with renewed appreciation, no longer trying to uphold the ideals of revolu-
tion. Mama relates how he appears now in church
and mixes readily with country folk. Talk of him has
grown kinder, and many of our neighbours, including
the Lucases, comment that, as with Mr. Darcy, they

may have been all wrong about Mr. Grantley. What a civilising effect you have had upon him! He begs to be remembered to you, even as he appears to pay some court to Kitty, who tolerates his attentions quietly. Papa and Darcy agree that he has a good influence on her, as she neither pouts in his absence nor flirts in his presence. Papa sends his love, as does Darcy. Mama sends her exhortations to you-know-what! We leave soon for Kent and whatever revelation Miss de Bourgh has for us. The rest of our tour has been so delightful that we are resolved to accept graciously what Kent holds for us. Give our love to the Gardiners, who may soon be at Pemberley.

Yours, Lizzy

Mary, all wonderment at Elizabeth's revelations, went upstairs to change for breakfast humming and reciting to herself, "To everything there is a season, a time for every purpose under heaven." After breakfast, a full rain set in and Mary resigned herself to staying indoors, but no sooner had she settled down to needlework than Aunt Gardiner arrived in her carriage to ask Mary to accompany her to Nottingham to see Jane.

On the way to Otherfield, she shared much of Elizabeth's news about Georgiana, omitting only what concerned Lady Caroline, as she did not think Elizabeth would wish her part in that to be known. At Otherfield, Mary and little Beth entertained Jane and Aunt Gardiner for a short time at the pianoforte. Then Beth repaired to the nursery with Annie while Aunt Gardiner spoke of London fashions, registering her criticisms of them and quoting Mr. Gardiner's ridicule of most. "He says the young ladies talk of spotted muslin, tamboured muslin, and sprigged muslin endlessly, as if the whole world revolved around choosing the most fashionable muslin! I remind him that young men boast of their fast steeds, of horses bought for a trifle and sold for a king's ransom, of racing matches they always guessed right, and of killing more birds than anyone else."

Jane was well entertained, and Mary enjoyed their aunt equally. They did not stay long, as Jane grew tired, and the persistent rain forbade any walking outdoors. Mary returned with her aunt to Pemberley and one of Mrs. Reynolds's fine teas. Surprisingly, Mr. Gardiner and Shepard had gone fishing as usual, paying scant notice to the rain until Mr. Gardiner found he must change his wet clothes before venturing to join them for tea.

In the day's last light the rain stopped, and Mary picked up a favourite volume of Cowper's poems and walked the half mile to her cottage reading it.

<br />

J UNE DAYS SLIPPED BY WITH FREQUENT VISITS FROM AUNT
Gardiner and rides to Otherfield to attend Jane, who was now
confined to her sitting room. Mary's progress in transposition
satisfied her teacher, and Mrs. Clifford, whose respect for discipline was great, encouraged Mary in the effort. Each day Mary
enjoyed returning to her cottage with its comfortable solitude,
and she reflected often on her great good fortune. One evening
she lingered over the substantial cold supper set out by Betsy
before retiring, and her heart filled with grateful wonder at the
circumstance in which she found herself with no contriving of
her own. She blessed Elizabeth for loving so consequential a man
as Mr. Darcy, whose thoughtfulness and generosity constantly
amazed her. Sometimes Mary felt overflowing with wellbeing,
and sometimes she had the uneasy thought that such bounty
could not last. She tried to imagine a time when, if it did last, she
might tire of so long and uneventful a residence in one country
circle. She pictured herself old and wrinkled, pursuing needlework and music with gnarled hands, still enjoying books, the
countryside, and her neighbours. Somewhere along the way, she
reasoned, she would have to relinquish the pleasure of riding

on horseback. She did not mind the picture at all; she counted herself fortunate indeed.

A noise at the cottage door distracted her. The bell sounded, and Mary moved to the parlour where the swish of Betsy's skirts could be heard in the front hall. Then Betsy, attired in nightcap and robe, announced, "Mrs. Wickham."

Mary bade Betsy return to bed. "I will care for my sister, thank you, Betsy. Please do not disturb yourself further." Mary greeted Lydia warmly, but how weak and poor she looked! Her frayed and smudged travel robe hung in an uneven cascade of wrinkled fabric, and her face drooped in exhaustion. "My dear Lydia, what has happened?"

"Hide me, Mary, please. Wickham will not think to look for me here. You let Kitty stay with you at Christmas. Can you not let me stay in the nice room she told me of?"

"You are most welcome to stay here. That is a matter of course. But why?"

"Wickham might enquire at Pemberley or Nottingham, but he does not know this place. And Papa and Mama must not see me like this, or they would never let me go back to him." She broke down in bitter sobs, and Mary held her close, marvelling at the thinness of her body.

The whole puzzle left her wondering. Did Lydia want Wickham or not? "Where is your trunk?" Lydia could not make herself understood. She talked and cried together. Mary stroked her head. "Please calm yourself, dear. Betsy and Tom will hear you. Your screeching would frighten a wild beast."

Lydia gulped, found her kerchief, and blew her nose. "If I am a wild beast, I am driven to it. Wickham will be happy enough to see me when I have money. I only hope I can look better by then."

"We will forget your trunk. Tom can put it in your room tomorrow." She led Lydia upstairs to the guest room.

"I… I sold all my things to get post fare to Lambton, and I walked from there. There is no trunk." Lydia brushed her face with her sleeve. "If Wickham looks for me at all, it will only be for money. All he wants me to do is beg, and I am sick of pestering Jane and Lizzy and Mama for money. I am sick of his schemes. Can I stay here until January? That is when Papa gives me money. Wickham will want me back then." She stumbled over to the large curtained bed and fell onto it.

Mary did not comprehend why Lydia both wished to hide from Wickham and yet to return to him with money. What a strange bond marriage was after all! But how terribly thin Lydia looked! "You may stay as long as you wish, of course. Come, I will find some clean things of my own for you, though they may be short." But they found that Mary's nightgown, draped around Lydia's taller but thinner frame, reached a suitable length. "But you have grown so thin!" Suddenly Mary felt her delinquent hospitality. "Oh, Lydia, are you hungry?"

"Yes, but I am more tired." She fell back again onto the bed. "I must sleep or die."

"Of course. I will find something nourishing to leave for you when you wake." She gathered rolls and plums from the remains of her supper, then went to the kitchen, filled a pitcher with water, and put it on a tray with a cup of damson wine. She added some oat cakes and two apples to the supper things, and carefully balanced the full tray up the stairs and placed it on the table next to the stoneware basin for washing up. She looked with pity on her sleeping sister whose very existence she had once tried to deny. She shuddered at her unforgivable ignorance.

The following day after breakfast, Lydia recovered a bit of her spark, but Mary still saw how marriage had aged her youngest sister far more than it had done her older sisters. Lydia looked around the comfortable morning room and recognized a floral arrangement Jane had made years ago with pressed petals, now framed and hanging over the small fireplace. "Oh, Mary, how fortunate you are to be living in a place all your own with no husband to spend your money!"

Mary recalled reaching the same conclusion even before contrasting her situation with Lydia's. Still, she had enough reverence for matrimony to recognize her guilt in hiding a wife from her husband. "Are you sure you do not wish to return to your husband? You once loved him very much."

Lydia sighed. "And I will again if ever he loves me." Lydia looked off blankly and sighed again, muttering, "Why would any man choose to run off with a girl he did not love?" Mary could not answer her. "Now he seems to like any girl who smiles at him if she has money. And now Darcy," she spat out the name, "supports his schooling at Oxford, but gives nothing to provide for me!"

"And Wickham accepted such an arrangement? How selfish!"

Lydia shrugged. "Well, he is free now to accept any moneyed woman he likes. And because he likes money, I never have any. He really sent me back to Longbourn, but Papa would either send me back to him or keep me from Wickham forever. I do not wish Papa to know where I am. You must keep it from everyone, Mary."

Mary did not like to see Lydia so bereft, but what could she do? She rose from the table in the morning room that served as her breakfast room and everyday dining parlour as well. She spoke as heartily as she could. "Let us see what can be done with your travel gown. And we may find something of mine to fit you as well.

Indeed, with a few tucks, my things may well fit you, as you are grown so thin." They went upstairs and found a pinafore dress that fit fairly well on the taller-but-thinner sister.

Lydia laughed mirthlessly. "I never thought I would be glad to wear a grey pinner that fairly hugs my chin. Being a beggar alters my taste."

Mary searched through her bureau. "You will need a pelisse, a few under things, and boots. If it rains, I can find some pattens for you too."

"La, those noisy things? Better to just get my boots muddy." If Lydia's taste was altered, it was not transformed.

"Then you must often need new boots." Mary frowned at such lack of economy and would have resolved to offer nothing more had not she recalled the previous Sunday's sermon. No, she would not sort the deserving from the undeserving poor and let others regulate the measure of her charity. From the armoire, she brought out her new gown. "Here, Lydia, try this blue muslin. I am no wearer of fashion. It makes me feel like a window in draperies. You must have something to go out in, unless you mean to stay caged in the cottage." Then the consequences of Lydia's strictures on secrecy dawned on her. "You know, Lydia, as soon as the Darcys return, we must tell them that you have moved in here. Lizzy will find some nice things for you, I daresay."

Lydia looked up, alarm in her eyes. "But Wickham must not know. They must agree to that." She sat on Mary's bed, fingering the lovely gown. "Oh, Mary, may I go to church with you Sunday? I have not gone in ever so long, and Kitty says that Mr. Oliver is well worth hearing."

Mary smiled. "Kitty is greatly partial to Mr. Oliver. But come, by all means." Mary held up Lydia's lamentable travel gown and decided to take it out to the garden to brush off the dried mud and shake it well before washing. She picked up the matching bonnet from the corner chest as well, though she was at a loss as to how to restore its shape.

While she worked on Lydia's outfit, Betsy fairly ran to her from the kitchen door. "You must not trouble yourself with that, miss. Allow me to repair it." She took the gown from Mary. "Mr. Darcy would blame me for sure." She grabbed the bonnet as well. "I can clean and block this too." Mary gladly relinquished the task she had tackled with more will than ability. As she went to tell Lydia that Betsy would restore her things, Mary caught sight of Pemberley's phaeton approaching. She scrambled up to Lydia, explaining that she would be expected to go with Mrs. Gardiner to Nottingham. Lydia entreated her secrecy with such solemnity that Mary could not refuse.

"Especially at Nottingham, no one must know," Lydia explained, "because Wickham goes there more freely than to Pemberley."

Mary hurried down to join Mrs. Gardiner, determined to say nothing of Lydia. Indeed, as they neared Otherfield, with Mrs. Gardiner chatting pleasantly of Jane's healthy good looks yesterday and of her sanguine hopes for an easy birth soon to come, the burden of her secret lifted from Mary, and she turned her thoughts to Jane.

Chapter 12

Mary and Aunt Gardiner were shown to Jane's sitting room where Bingley and Jane quickly finished their conversation. Bingley rose and bowed to the visitors, took tender leave of Jane, and added, "I leave you in pleasanter company." And indeed, it appeared to Mary that their converse had been serious.

Mrs. Gardiner kissed Jane, saying, "I trust nothing is amiss, my dear. Such a heavy subject I fear we interrupted."

Jane laughed pleasantly. "Oh heavy indeed! My dear husband tells me that when Beth has a brother or sister, the two children must spend much of their day in the nursery. They, and any future children, will be company for one another, and Annie will have charge of them, though of course under my direction. It is to relieve me, he says." She looked at Mary. "We grew up differently, but perhaps he is right. And I can always visit the nursery."

Mrs. Gardiner heartily approved. "Yes, dear. We do our children no favour by keeping them near, coddling them, or showing them off to adult visitors. Not that a nursemaid does not sometimes spoil them. But the greatest favour we can do our children is to give visible example of love and esteem to our spouse. As they grow up, they may then look forward to maturity so they too can find such love. When they see how you and Mr. Bingley enjoy each other, they will long to enter adult society, and we can hope they will look for love and respect like yours. How I pity a child who has not that happiness to anticipate!"

Jane sighed and sat back, stiffening. Mary looked around. "May I bring you an extra cushion?" She took an ornamental one from the nearby settee and placed it behind Jane's arched back. Jane smiled her thanks as she quietly pondered her aunt's words.

Mary also thought about it. "I suppose a child cannot look forward to a good marriage if he sees parents ignore each other or quarrel." She did not add her next thought: or if one parent does not take the other seriously. She began to examine her own preference for the single life, thinking it possibly had roots in her father's rather open enjoyment of her mother's more foolish outbursts. And could that also be the stimulus for her own search for wisdom in the wise words of others to adopt as her own?

Jane sighed again. "Oh when one is in love, how simple it all seems, with marriage as the end of a road instead of a lifework to be learned and passed on." She brightened and turned to Mary. "Do you never mean to marry?—I do not mean Stilton; I mean anybody."

Mary hesitated, as her aunt, curious about the reference, teased, "Stilton?"

Happy to turn to a topic she could explain, she replied, "He is a neighbour of Jane's who proposes marriage every so often. Either he wants practise—a need I can attest to—or he mocks me. At any rate, he does not love me, and by now he must count on my refusal."

"And has he profession, pursuit, business…?" Mrs. Gardiner spoke as if she wished to establish in him something that would render him suitable.

"Hardly, unless you consider betting on horses a businesslike pursuit. He is a mere boy, due to inherit property in some distant future if he ever grows up. He is a nephew of Mrs. Long of Hertfordshire."

Sarah interrupted them with a large tray of sandwiches and tea things. Annie followed with a bowl of fruit and a steaming urn. When they had enjoyed some fruit rolls and tea, Jane returned to her first question, which Mary hesitated to answer, since Jane might consider it a reflection on her own marriage. "But really, Mary, do you not look to marry one day?"

The burden of her knowledge concerning Lydia returned to her. "At present, two of my sisters present an attractive model of the state, while one presents nothing if not warning against it. Perhaps, when Kitty marries, there may be a preponderance of evidence on the side of marital bliss. Or else the enterprise may look like a gamble, with the balance even. But in either case, since I do not feel constrained by circumstances, I believe I choose to live like the angels in solitary bliss."

Mrs. Gardiner interposed. "And have you none but your sisters to look to?"

"But it comes to the same thing," said Mary. "You and Uncle Gardiner present a fine model, Uncle and Aunt Philips another picture entirely, and of Mama and Papa I remain in doubt."

Jane smiled. "You know, Mary, Kitty and I guessed that a few years ago, when Mr. Collins chose Elizabeth, he might rather have settled on you. We thought you might have accepted him."

Mary acknowledged it was so. "But that would have been only to save Longbourn for my sisters. I never loved him, though I believed in him then more than I do now."

Jane and Mrs. Gardiner spoke together. "Thank God he did not ask you!"

Mrs. Gardiner looked about the sitting room, adorned with works of embroidery and pressed flowers like the one Mary had in her cottage. "But where is the chimney-board you decorated? Elizabeth quite raved about it in her last letter. Is it in the nursery?"

Jane reddened. "She should not have done so. It is a mere first attempt, which I would not have tried without Caroline's prompting and help, and my own knowledge that Beth was too young to criticize. Of course, I forgot that she will grow up to find it a clumsy effort."

Mrs. Gardiner would not be put off, and Jane admitted that it was in the nursery. "Just go through the adjoining empty room, which will be a schoolroom." As they went that way, Jane called, "I pray you, do not look for competence. Elizabeth is my least severe critic. In fact, she is no critic at all. Even Beth frowns upon it as an interloper in her territory."

Mrs. Gardiner, not to be put off, led Mary through the bare schoolroom to the nursery fairly bursting with colour, where Beth napped in the large crib. They silently examined the delicate board screening the cold fireplace. Also behind it were toys to be used when the child was older, which may explain Beth's annoyance. By now Beth may well wish to play with the hobby horse, the doll house, or the building blocks with painted letters instead of the stuffed toys near her crib, Mary thought. The two women exchanged looks of approval, even admiration, for the work on the screen. The whole presented a happy composition sure to instill memories of beauty. The lower border of roses and the upper one of stars set off an apple orchard in the foreground and elms in the distance where stylized figures of horses, rabbits, and children roamed a field of bluebells under the trees. They returned to Jane exclaiming their delight and congratulations. "You have given it Otherfield's apple orchard,

Netherfield's bluebells, and Longbourn's elms! How sweet it was to blend your own childhood with Beth's!" Mary could not place the roses and supposed they were added for colour.

"And the screen must follow them to the schoolroom, where they may need such a distraction when lessons become dull. Lizzy has nothing over me; I quite rave about it myself. And canvas on wood—was that not difficult to do?" Aunt Gardiner took Jane's hand in a congratulatory gesture.

"Oh no. Sarah helped me to stretch and glue the canvas." Jane looked down, embarrassed at their praise. "We stretched one for Lizzy too. She said she hopes to brighten her nursery if Georgiana can find time to teach her."

"You have set her a fine model and a challenge. I shall be eager to see her work." Mrs. Gardiner reached for her gloves and stooped to kiss Jane. "Mrs. Reynolds will expect us to tea."

In the carriage, Mary asked her aunt if it would be proper to add to a servant's pay if she takes on a particularly difficult cleaning task. "I tried to do it myself, but I perceived my certain failure almost as soon as she offered to take it on."

"Yes, a few extra shillings are always welcome. By all means, show your appreciation. And pretty gifts on special occasions are in order besides." Mrs. Gardiner sat back and studied her intensely serious niece. "You are learning to be a householder on your own now! No wonder you consider matrimony unnecessary."

"Perhaps," Mary said. "However, the more I live independently, the more my ignorance shows, and the more dependent I become on helpful advisors like you."

Her aunt smiled approval on the niece so many had underrated as rigid and plain. She touched Mary's arm. "I am afraid most of us learn more about our ignorance daily. When we are very old, we hope, wisdom may arrive. The good God waits patiently for us to grow into it."

Mary, surprised anew at her lovely and wise aunt, listened with an attention she did not remember according her on her visits to Longbourn. Even so, when they neared Pemberley, she made an excuse to take leave of her at the cottage rather than join her for tea, and she hurried to Lydia in her upstairs room. Lydia was engaged in putting careful darts in the muslin gown so as to preserve the lovely Spitalfields brocade, and without looking up from her tiny stitching, she remarked pensively, "You know, Mary, Lizzy tells Jane everything." She looked up then. "You must not let either of them know where I am." The top of the gown fell from her lap, and Mary noted that the extra material had been removed from the neck and shoulders. Mary thought ruefully that Lydia remained Lydia, even reduced to poverty.

"But we are on Pemberley grounds. Darcy *must* be told. At any rate, you are sure to be seen, and people tell Mr. Darcy everything."

"Oh no. Your lovely fenced garden at the side door can afford my exercise. The high fence with its climbing vines provides privacy, and I can watch for the gardener or your servants before using it. Mr. Darcy keeps nothing from Lizzy, so he must not know. It must be kept from both."

Mary did not care for the idea. "Mr. Darcy has been so good to me, and Betsy and Tom serve me only at his request. To keep so heavy a secret from him is unthinkable—and likely impossible."

"Please, Mary. They are all so open, the Bingleys as well as the Darcys. I do not think any of them could lie for me, even if they wished to. They must not know at all."

Mary promised only that she would say nothing, feeling sure that Betsy or Tom would reveal it to Mr. Darcy. But Lydia proved her slyness when, three days later, Mr. and Mrs. Darcy returned and Betsy enquired as to whether Mrs. Wickham had departed. Mary responded only what was truth at the time: that she did not know where Lydia was.

## Chapter 13

SOME DAYS LATER, MARY JOINED ELIZABETH AND AUNT Gardiner in the carriage to Nottingham for a long day with Jane. Bingley had engaged the surgeon and a midwife the previous day, as Jane had experienced the first real discomfort of her confinement. They found that the surgeon and the midwife were in Jane's room with Sarah, and the three women joined Bingley in the sitting room, where he had been banished, he said, for fidgeting. Soon the efficient-looking midwife bustled through for more towels and hot water, and returned to the forbidden room with them. It seemed hours later that a healthy squalling indicated the birth, and Bingley, who had been sitting with his head down in seeming agony, leapt to his feet. Dr. Pierce almost ran into Bingley as he came out of the room wiping his hands on a small towel. He pronounced Bingley the father of "a fine young hunter, his little fingers itching for a gun." Jane groaned a low denial from within the room as if she hoped not, while Bingley smiled proudly.

Beth sent up a yowl from the nursery, and Annie ran through the room to tend to her. The midwife handed the wrapped bundle to Bingley to hold until the wet nurse arrived. When she did, nurse and baby went through to the nursery, and Mary heard Beth cry in wonder, "Baby, baby."

Mary had fleetingly observed the red-faced newcomer wrapped in white as he was borne past them, and she watched with Mrs. Gardiner and Elizabeth as Jane and Bingley whispered together, and then Jane, exhausted, smiled at her visitors, who turned to let her sleep. Mrs. Gardiner took Elizabeth's hand as they returned to the sitting room, Mary following, while Bingley remained at his wife's bedside.

Mrs. Gardiner said, "Now, Lizzy, we transfer our vigilant attention to you. Have you kept up your exercises and got enough sleep these past weeks?"

Elizabeth grinned and begged her aunt to cease worrying. Mary wondered much at these sisters, her models throughout her youth now going through so much for children of their own, yet to her they seemed girls still. She counted on Elizabeth's ready wit as always, and on Jane's delicate tact, even as they now belonged to different families. Life's changes raised a touch of resentment in her, not aimed at anyone; but the orderly march of days, constant and predictable, was eluding her grasp. Inwardly she grieved, even as a new compassion for her mother formed within her. In spite of a thirst for gossip and excitement, Mrs. Bennet had been the chief engineer of the orderly youth Mary knew. What kind of mother would Lydia be, so like as she was to her mother? And, married a full six months longer than Jane or Elizabeth, why was she not a mother by now? Lydia's thinness now struck Mary as a possible sign of ill health, and she feared her care for Lydia had lacked the nurturing she should have provided. Yet the very persons she always turned to for advice and help in such ways were forbidden to her by her promise to Lydia. Every new day added, to Mary's dismay, more vagaries of that fickle monster known as Life.

With Darcy home and Bingley satisfied that Jane's health and strength were returning, the fishing party doubled. Shepard and Mr. Gardiner displayed their superior knowledge of fertile spots and effective bait, and Darcy vowed that he would regain mastery of his own stream. Mr. Hurst joined them for half a morning but soon dismissed the sport as uneventful and went to Lambton in search of card players.

Each day Mary, although grateful that the men kept busy so far from her cottage, fretted over Lydia, both wishing for and fearful of her discovery. She well knew that she would be blamed by Lydia for revealing her and blamed by Darcy for concealing her. She had requested more eggs and milk for the cottage provisions, hoping to improve Lydia's health and colour, but still she worried. She knew too little how to nurse, and Lydia knew less. Visits to Nottingham with Elizabeth and Mrs. Gardiner found Mary withdrawing more and more from the conversations, fearful of saying what she should not. But she enjoyed listening, and once in Otherfield's nursery, she smiled upon Beth's protective care of her brother William. (Darcy had forbidden Bingley's naming the child Fitzwilliam as both inappropriate and a name he abhorred; still he acquiesced to his godson being William.) Jane mentioned Bingley's strictures concerning the nursery, and Elizabeth laughed. "Darcy continues his prodigious care of your husband. It is the very rule he has given me, but I must say I agree with him. Callie, for all her youth, has more experience with little boys than I ever had, and I suppose we must bear the ills connected with having married above our station, Jane. We suffered enough in the getting of our husbands; we really must take time to enjoy them, however charming our children are."

Jane smiled her agreement. "And we can always repair to the nursery like this when our husbands go hunting or fishing."

Mary took it all in, remembering how much her mother had overseen their childhood. She could not recall ever having been confined to a nursery, and she did not think Lydia could ever have been contained in one. Except for library, kitchen, and laundry, they had the run of Longbourn. Should she pity her sisters' children for lacking such freedom? Mrs. Gardiner supported Darcy's view, and she should know; but Mrs. Bennet's concerns had always centered on her girls, and they seemed to still be so. By the time they had grown up, they had questioned their own parents' compatibility, or at least Elizabeth had done so. Might Lydia have fared better if she had learned her manners in a nursery? Mary did not know. Once again, she exulted in her own station in life; rearing children would not be a problem she would have to face.

In early July, Lydia again held forth on the wonderful state of the cottage for Mary, saying wistfully that if she could have such a charming place for herself, would not her life be beautiful? Mary had not time to reply before the bell sounded and Betsy could be heard going to the door. Lydia slipped quickly upstairs, whispering, "Remember, I am not here!"

It was not a family member, however, but James Stilton, sporting tufts of chin hair and streaky side whiskers. Mary wondered if it was the newest mode of being trifling and silly. She regretted his coming just at this time more than ever. He stood before her smiling assuredly as if conscious of cutting a dash, and when he spoke it was in a deliberately low tone. "Miss Bennet, I come to report having followed your advice. I abjured race tracks and have begun to repay my father."

"I am glad to hear it," said Mary indifferently. "And what paying position did you undertake?"

It was Stilton's turn to adopt indifference. "That does not matter. I have become what you entreated me to be. Do you not think it unspeakably harsh to refuse me still?"

"Not at all," answered Mary. "If you have indeed prospered, you no longer have use for me. Continue on that course and the inheritance is yours without burden of marriage."

Stilton exploded in anger, completely destroying his pose of maturity. "This is preposterous! You are being stubborn and selfish, and you enjoy tormenting me!"

Mary searched for words to make her refusal unmistakable, but the accusation of selfishness, coming as it did right after Lydia's hints of envy, caused her to pause. Supposing she were to go live with Stilton in Nottingham, might Darcy actually allow Lydia to remain in the situation she had come to enjoy? Perhaps the generosity that he had granted to one would extend to a second sister. But could she abide living with Stilton? In many ways, he was even more unsuited to her than Wickham was to Lydia. With some dismay, Mary noted Stilton's expression change to one of smugness, as if her hesitation was promised consent. She hurried to disabuse him of that notion. "Mr. Stilton, I could not possibly marry any man who scoffs at the rites of the church."

"Oh that," he spat out dismissively. "What difference does that make? We could be married in church if you like, and you would not be prevented from attending as often as you like. I can pray anywhere; God does not mind."

"I said nothing of that. It is I who mind. And if I am to attend church alone, it is better to do so here, where I am known and as I am."

"So it is your comfort alone that matters!"

Again his words dug into the rich soil of Mary's compassion for Lydia, as by habit, Mary applied criticism to herself as deserved. Her father's command came to her rescue. "If truth be told, Mr. Stilton, I cannot marry you even if I wished to."

Stilton's face tightened in an aggression born of a prize lost. "Why not? You are of age, certainly. And you live here as your own mistress."

"Still I must have my father's consent."

"Is that not for me to obtain? I will go to Hertfordshire immediately."

"No. There is reason for me to write to him first. And I can give you no better answer until I have heard from him. Give me…" She was about to say a fortnight when she recalled the desultory nature of her father's correspondence. "… A month or two. And I promise nothing."

A puzzled Mr. Stilton—rather than an angry one, for a change— rode back to Nottingham.

The following Sunday after service, Mary came down from the loft to join Lydia. She saw Mr. Oliver finish talking to the departing churchgoers and turn toward the vestry. Mary ventured to detain him to ask his opinion of folks who elect to pray to God alone, rather than in church. "Could such a one remain a Christian?"

Oliver frowned. "I trust this does not mean that you intend to adopt such a course, Miss Bennet?"

"Oh no, sir, never me. I like to attend church, and I seem to need to. But suppose some may feel constrained at services or bored. Might he not pray just as well on his own?" Mary had come to realize that she could not possibly marry Stilton if he was no Christian, not even to provide a home for her sister.

Oliver thought for a while, and Mary wondered if he found the suggestion bizarre.

"And is this someone who, in doing so, is rejecting his inheritance, a birthright of Christianity?"

"I believe his parents are indeed churchgoing Christians." Mary had only her father's word for this.

Oliver postponed removing his surplice and stole, turned from the vestry door, and directed Mary and Lydia to a bench in the vicarage garden. As he sat down with them, he began, "I would say that, as a theory, the program sounds much better than it turns out in practise. This someone is a friend of yours?"

She thought that over. "Yes, I suppose so."

"And do you observe him to pray a good deal?"

"No, sir, but I hardly observe him at all."

Oliver assumed a serious, even a sad, mien. "I know two such men myself, very well. And as with your friend, I do not observe any great tendency to address the God they acknowledge. Perhaps a hermit in a desert may commune with God without benefit of others, but a man of the world finds more and more occupations and fewer and fewer inclinations to think of God, let alone to pray. And if you were to ask what he believes of Jesus, he may well do as my brothers do, simply look uncomfortable and decline to answer. And upon further inquiry I find that this 'God' in which they believe is less Person than Idea."

Mary, perplexed and troubled, asked, "How does going to church help?"

Oliver shrugged. "I am not exactly sure. But perhaps any action towards God feeds faith and brings His help. And the presence of others may encourage us to accept grace and reduce our falling into lax habits. What do you think?"

"I suppose that I felt the church's help to my faith as a child at Longbourn, and I never thought to question the practise." She looked at Lydia for corroboration, but Lydia only paled and turned aside. "Is something the matter?" she whispered, but Lydia did not reply.

As if to avoid noticing, Oliver fixed his eyes on the top of a distant sycamore. "I trust Kympton Saint Giles has supplied some of this for you?"

"Oh yes," both ladies spoke as one, and Mary added thoughtfully, slowly, "It feeds my faith."

Oliver grinned. "And so it ought to do." He paused and gazed at the pine woods. "Worship grows in us secretly as God works. It is not the same as thinking about God, which can become the ridiculous vanity of trying to understand Him." He looked at them, more at ease. "Are you enjoying your sister's visit?"

Mary started at the word "visit," then replied, "Yes, very much." She could not help remembering his deep frown when she had disowned this very sister, and her face felt warm as she cast her eyes down. When she looked up again, she thought she detected silent laughter in his demeanor, and she hoped it contained no mockery. She tried to take Lydia's hand, but Lydia held back. "We must hurry to arrive before Mr. and Mrs. Darcy."

"Oh, Lambton Saint Mary's service starts later than ours. You should reach Pemberley before they do." Oliver stood with them and stepped toward the vestry.

Mary took leave of the vicar and hurried to the cottage, sincerely hoping that he understood Mr. Darcy's preference for Lambton. Lydia remained strangely silent during the walk, as indeed she had been with the vicar, though it was not like Lydia to be shy before any young man. Mary tried to interest her in the wildflowers dotting the ground under the pines, but nothing drew her out.

However, as soon as they entered the cottage, Lydia burst out angrily, "How did you know Wickham said that?"

Mary, dumbfounded, asked, "What are you talking about?"

"You know, what you said to the vicar about not going to church." Lydia's face and tone indicated the hurt of betrayal.

Mary sat down hard on the straight chair in the entry way. "But I never had Wickham in mind at all. Nor did I know aught of his practises. I spoke of a neighbour of Jane's who came here a few days ago. Does Wickham truly feel the same?"

"Yes." Lydia melted into tears. "Every time I wanted to go to church, he said I must go alone. The only time we ever were together in church was at Saint Clement's in London, when we were married. And I stopped going too."

Mary stood and put her arm on Lydia's shoulder. "Oh, Liddy. I had no idea." In her mind the words returned: "The two become one."

Lydia's sniffles subsided. "Kitty told me how nice it was to go to Kympton with you, sometimes in the loft and sometimes in the congregation. Our Sundays in Hertfordshire came back to me. I had not been to church in ever so long... My faith is even thinner than I was. What can I do?"

She tried to hide her head, but Mary took her face in gentle hands. "But you are doing it. Do not cry. Keep on coming and your Longbourn Sundays will come back to you." Mary stood back as Lydia dried her face. "They will be back at Pemberley soon, probably with Bingley, and they will look for me. Could you not reveal yourself and come along?"

Lydia shook her head and started for the stairway. "I will be all right."

Mary called after her, "Betsy and Tom will be gone all day. Whatever they left out for meals, you are welcome to take whenever you wish." She set off for Pemberley, still unsure whether or not to write to her father the question that burned her conscience.

Chapter 15

MARY WALKED TO PEMBERLEY PITYING LYDIA, ALWAYS FEARFUL
of revealing her whereabouts lest Wickham pursue her, and
yet she claimed he did not abuse her. She must soon write her father
about Stilton if she hoped to have an answer by messenger. She
did not wish to face Mr. Bennet with explanations when he came
in August. Yet she harboured misgivings about Stilton above and
beyond his strange faith. Was she, as Stilton said, only thinking of
her own comfort? She had hated hinting to Stilton that she might
relent, but how could Lydia gain the cottage she so praised unless
Mary went elsewhere? Already she had come to feel her situation as
an occasion of Lydia's envy, a circumstance that could easily lead to
quarrels. And much as sisterly compassion urged her to help Lydia,
she could not feel they were well suited as lifelong companions. No,
she must write to her father tonight, and according to his response,
she would cast her lot, even with no guarantee that Lydia would be
given the cottage if she left it.

To her surprise, she found that Jane had accompanied Bingley
to Pemberley. She looked pale, but her serene smile put Mary at
ease. They were all to have a farewell meal with the Gardiners, who
were soon leaving for London. Mr. Gardiner said he already missed

his fishing, and he vowed to return with the primroses in spring. Mrs. Gardiner admitted that she eagerly looked forward to seeing her children again, and she ate little in her haste for departure. Up Pemberley's impressive, broad, ash-lined avenue came the Gardiner carriage, and Mary exclaimed over its beautiful high polish. "Why, it looks brand new!"

Aunt Gardiner told her Shepard and Mr. Gardiner had spent part of two days sanding and refinishing the wood. "They meant to surprise me, but I came upon them behind the carriage house when I went to pick berries. Now it faces the dusty journey home, and I fear its newness will not survive the ordeal." Mrs. Gardiner waited for Mr. Gardiner to hand her up, which he did after the many good-byes. Darcy pressed such an abundance of gifts and provisions upon them that their carriage was filled to capacity, though they were but two. They rolled off behind two sturdy horses while the Pemberley party, always loath to see them go, returned to the parlour somewhat quieted. Elizabeth rendered a spirited "Highland Laddie" on the pianoforte and begged Mary to play some lively dances, but the attempt only pointed out the missing Georgiana, who remained another se'nnight in London. They spoke of her then, conjecturing as to the outcome of her new friendship with young David Exbridge. Darcy even allowed that he might be able to part with her to so congenial a young man.

Bingley asked Darcy about the young couple at Kent. "Pray, how did you like the verger of Hunsford? Will you get on well with your cousin-in-law?"

Darcy made a face. "In time, I may get used to him, which is all I can hope for at present." He touched the tips of his fingers together, bouncing them in mock humility, and he feigned the voice of the sycophantic Witherspoon. "Yes, Reverend Collins, venerable sir.

I will attend to it, venerable sir. Oh my, here is the lovely Mrs. Collins, and young Master Lucas, the future vicar of Hunsford, heh, heh." He went on in his own voice when Elizabeth finally stopped laughing. "And he bows like a bobber on Gardiner's fishing line. But Anne apparently likes him or finds him amusing. I am not sure which."

"Did she mention marriage?" Jane asked.

"Not even when I teased her," Elizabeth answered. "She took it good-naturedly, but effectively parried every remark on the subject. I believe our speculation only increased her private amusement."

Darcy nodded thoughtfully. "Lizzy, what did you make of Anne's recommendation that Mrs. Collins feed her son goose livers? How strange that she, whose health worried all the family, should take to prescribing a diet for a strapping boy like Lucas!"

Elizabeth directed her eyes to the chattering birds outside the window and paused before answering. "You know, at times I felt I was hearing Lady Catherine herself. Perhaps in her childhood her mother had made her eat them."

"I believe she did. I seem to recall having to eat them myself when I visited Rosings as a child." Darcy made a grimace of distaste. "I must ask Georgiana if she remembers a similar diet." Darcy smiled and reached over to rub Lizzy's shoulder.

Elizabeth turned to face him. "That convinces me that my whimsical guess about Anne may not be so far off the mark. What if she lived all those years quietly studying Lady Catherine as if the Lady represented a role that Anne intended to step into one day? Why, she even reminded Mr. Collins of the sixty-four windows in the mansion and of the prodigious fireplace in the upper parlour. Those had to be lines straight from Lady Catherine's repertory, because Collins often quoted them as if it was clever of him to remember."

Jane broke in gently, observing, "People are such great mysteries. Just when we think we have understood them, a wonderful new aspect shows in them."

Elizabeth scowled as if "wonderful" did not quite describe the case at hand. She amended her sister's observation by replying, "To be wondered at, perhaps."

No sooner were the Gardiners back in London than preparations began for the arrival at Pemberley of Kitty and Mrs. Bennet, who meant to be with Elizabeth in August. Georgiana returned from London and took upon herself frequent visits to Otherfield, bringing their family news to Jane and returning to give Elizabeth tidings of Jane's new baby. Darcy, pleased at his sister's new exuberance, learned a great deal about her stay in London for a change. As was to be expected, she had visited much with the Exbridge family, especially young David. Elizabeth remained restfully confined at home, less from necessity than from her wish to placate Darcy. Mary, though she usually did her needlework with Lizzy, sometimes accompanied Georgiana to Otherfield, learning much more about London than she had ever heard before. Georgiana reported not only her visits to Exeter Exchange, Bond Street, and Sackville, but also gaily recalled art pieces and what David had said about them; ducks and how David fed them; and specific meals, along with some of David's witty sayings during them. Jane also heard Georgiana's amusing tales of London. Often they found Jane in the nursery, and once Beth sang for them a new song she had learned. Georgiana told her she had never heard such a fine concert.

She supported this by regaling them with the tale that, while in London, she, Lady Elliott, and David had been so disappointed in the music at a concert, they had left early to watch hangers-on outside a theatre instead. On one occasion, Bingley joined them in the nursery, where he proudly displayed his son, and they saw how tenderly Beth touched "my baby."

On returning, Mary always stopped at her cottage, saying she wished not to interrupt Georgiana's report to Elizabeth. Mainly she meant to attend to her own concealed guest, though Lydia daily became more comfortable in a routine all her own. Mary had been invited to glean any remaining cherries from Pemberley's orchard, and this she did on several early mornings, as Lydia was particularly fond of cherries for breakfast. As cherries became difficult to find, Mary explored the wilder plots behind the carriage house as Mrs. Gardiner had done. She discovered raspberries to add to the breakfast board. Not used to such activities, Mary had not thought to use gloves, and she soon found her hands dirty and her arms scratched almost as badly as when she had once, as a child at Longbourn, caught hold of a squirrel. However, she felt rewarded for her berry picking as Lydia's spare form filled out. Indeed, by late July, Lydia appeared less drawn and even younger. Mary, however, when she examined herself in the glass, saw that she looked older. Soon she would be twenty-four, older than Jane or Lizzy when they married, and old indeed compared to the barely twenty-year-old Lydia. Each fine morning, Mary placed her basket of fruit inside the kitchen door for Betsy to wash and put out with a pot of cream, which she said was for Mary's return after riding. Grey Dawn was always saddled and held ready for her by the kind Mr. Watts, who had come to be quite friendly since his return from Duxford.

On one morning's ride, Mary determined to search for wild strawberries, and finding none, she rode a more daring path, ducking her way through thin groves to find dense undergrowth. She knew that her father had received her letter by then, and she started to wonder about his reaction, sometimes sorry she had written it. This fine life might be lost to her forever; and if her father had guessed correctly about Stilton, soon she would be poor, even destitute. She came out of her reverie only to discover that she had entered a small sheltered lea she had not previously discovered. She spied an artist at his easel at the far end of the grass, and she meant to skirt the area, leaving him undisturbed, but he turned at the sound of the horse and waved to her. She reined in suddenly when she recognized Mr. Oliver. "I did not realize that you painted!" she called to him. She glanced at the canvas, which she supposed would be a landscape of the pleasant area, but the work appeared rather to be a sea of faces. She tried to keep her eyes off it, tried to concentrate on Oliver's greeting, but she missed much of that.

Noting her interest, Oliver took the canvas from the easel and held it up to her. "It is just my early Tuesday hobby, keeping me from intruding too soon on Pemberley's library. I think this one is almost finished. What do you think?"

Mary, perched on Grey Dawn, studied the faces while the horse bent to the tufts of grass. The mix of men, women, and children in differing attitudes seemed somehow united in a shared tranquility. Fascinated, she asked, "Are they in heaven?"

Oliver frowned, turned it to his own gaze, and countered, "In heaven? Why?"

Sure she had got it all wrong, Mary apologised. "I thought of your sermon on prayer as the language of heaven. If prayer could show in a face, those faces…" She could not finish. Grey Dawn, searching for more grass, jogged her from the painting, and she looked to grab the reins and move away. At any rate, she could not express what she meant.

Oliver, looking pleased, moved ahead with the horse. "You flatter me. I call it 'The Blessing' because it represents my view of the congregation as I give the blessing. At least, that is how I recall it."

Mary found an excuse for her blunder. "Oh, I never see the people from that angle. From the loft, I see shapes of bonnet crowns, heads of hair, bald heads with fringes of hair, little girls pulling at bonnet strings, occasional noses, but no faces unless a baby looks up from a father's shoulder."

Oliver laughed. "But how well you expressed the feeling I intended, even so. Every time I give the blessing I feel bathed in peace, and I count myself the more blessed." He studied the canvas again. "Now I fear dabbing any more may destroy the effect. I will leave those corner faces as they are, undelineated."

Mary started at his word, thinking "undelineated" described her own future once again. She thought of something she had heard the vicar say. "Mr. Oliver, why did you say that married life presents the best picture of God on earth? Surely, as God is spiritual and good, one who attempts to live as angels do would present such a picture?"

Oliver turned his back to her as he set the painting back on the easel. Then he slowly faced her. "Yes, God is pure spirit, and the angels are that. But God is also One and fruitful. So an ideal marriage, where two spiritual persons become one, can be fruitful and good, and they certainly represent God's image as He meant us to do."

Mary let that thought hearten her, in the event that her father should choose to let her marry. She still half hoped he would refuse, and she meant to pray about it, hoping she could accept God's will no matter what the decision. Her restless horse bent to the grass again, and Oliver had turned to collect his brushes and paints, so she called good day to him and pulled Grey Dawn around to where they had entered these woods, picking her way back to the stables. Then she hurried to make sure Lydia needed nothing for the day.

## Chapter 17

HAVING URGED LYDIA TO ENJOY THE FINE DAY IN THE GARDEN, Mary went to Pemberley, visited a bit with Elizabeth in her sitting room, and made her way through the great hall to the library balcony. She had lately discovered a translation of *The Odyssey* that amazed her. Pagans of antiquity struck her as more religious in a superstitious sort of way than present-day Christians of the Stilton type. When she glanced down at the fireplace area, however, and saw no one below, it occurred to her to look into the books of Saint Augustine's works. She had long meant to find the treatise on the Trinity, hoping to become one of those readers for whom the great Saint Augustine prayed. She put aside *The Odyssey* until later and made her way down the ladder-like stairway at the end of the balcony. At least she might learn what was so amusing about that great saint. Reaching the floor, she hurried over to the matching set of leather-bound volumes and pulled one down. Opening it, she let out a small cry of dismay and disappointment, for it was not in English, nor even in French. She could not make out a word of it. Mr. Oliver, standing beneath the balcony and shadowed by it, said softly, "Is something amiss?"

"Oh, I did not see you." She hurriedly closed the large book. "I thought to learn somewhat of Saint Augustine, whose writings made you laugh, but I can make nothing of this. However did you read it?" She frowned and placed the book carefully back in its place.

Oliver slipped the work he had been studying onto a table and came nearer. "I do read some Latin. If you were curious, why did you never ask?"

"I did not wish to bother you, and it was Kitty you invited to ask about it."

"But it is no bother." His finger went to his face, brushing the moustache and flattening it. "Let me see, what did I find amusing? Certainly not all of it, and in fact, it may have been his utter seriousness that made me laugh at his lighter moments." After some thought, he told her of Augustine's letter to a pagan magistrate who had demanded that the Bishop restore a statue, which some Christians had destroyed, and for which they paid with their lives. Augustine's letter, all politeness, described in detail the enormous Hercules he would erect, using the finest materials and workmanship. Then Oliver paused. "The last line of his letter was 'Work will begin on it just as soon as you restore to life the sixty Christians you had slain.'"

Mary laughed. "I never thought of a great saint as humourous."

"A great saint is a great man. That includes some humour, I hope." He sat down at the table where Mary had taken a seat. "Once Augustine, his mother Monica, and some friends retreated to a house at Cassiacum, and Monica criticized one of his friends for singing hymns while using the latrine. Augustine teased her, saying, 'If he had been locked in there, could he not pray to be released?'"

Mary smiled politely at this, though she secretly sympathized with Monica, who knew what was fitting and proper.

Oliver gave Mary a few more instances, ending with the saint's insistence that all creation is good, but he admitted ignorance as to how demons could be so. "Finally, he concluded that demons could be good as sponges are, soaking up evil so that the worst of it will not soil us."

Mary listened, fascinated. "And you understood this even in Latin?"

The awe in her tone amused him. "But I am afraid my schooling in Latin helps very little in tackling that." He pointed to the large tome he had placed on the far table. "I was foolish enough to believe that Latin would enable me to struggle through Dante's Italian. I find myself getting only one word in three or four—a devilishly slow work. But then," he shrugged, "it is, after all, the *Inferno*. If I ever make it to *Paradiso,* the reading may be easier."

Mary could not help admiring such scholarship. "I learned a bit of French once, but I have forgotten most of it. How wonderful it must be to read many languages!"

"Thank you. Many persons I know regard it a useless enough accomplishment. It may well be, but I enjoy books in any language."

Mary excused herself then to return to the English language books on the balcony, but she had barely settled back into the world of Odysseus when Georgiana entered the library below looking for her. Mr. Oliver pointed to the balcony, and Georgiana climbed up as Mary, hearing her, left the harrowing adventure with Cyclops, closed and shelved the book, and joined Georgiana near the stairway. Georgiana, flushed with excitement, said as soon as she took breath, "Mary, I beg you to help me hostess Elizabeth's at-home today." Georgiana showed the easy smile she had seemed to learn recently in London. Lizzy had fitly described the new Georgiana as both bubbly and assured, and both younger and more mature than in her melancholy days. Her breathing now normal, Georgiana went on,

"I am expecting Lady Elliott and some others from London, and I fear Elizabeth's regular guests may be neglected."

Mary responded with a knowing smile. "You are, perhaps, expecting the Exbridges?"

Georgiana's eyes lowered even as her colour heightened. "Yes, David and his mother and sister come today with Lord Exbridge and Lady Elliott. The family returns to the lord's country estate, and Lady Elliott will pay a long visit with them."

They walked together through the large hall to a stairway they could descend together. Mary took her hand. "You have found your lost mansion of peace and your own peace as well, have you not?"

"I have indeed. And never again will I play that song so wistfully. If I had not seen the London home of Lord Exbridge, those childhood years spent with Lady Catherine would haunt me still. I hope you will come and meet them all. Lady Elliott tells me how she enjoyed travelling with you." Georgiana held the door to the parlour and let Mary precede her.

As she entered, Mary teased, "Some day, you must tell me your own opinion of Bath. Lady Elliott's view was not promising."

A number of Elizabeth's neighbours chatted with Mrs. Reynolds. There was indeed something of a Gillray cartoon in Miss Johnstone's profile, Mary realized anew. That ample lady sat calmly, and too smugly, near the sumptuous tea table. As Mary passed Mrs. Reynolds, a small folded paper glided unobtrusively from Mrs. Reynolds's hand to Mary's. While Georgiana greeted Miss Johnstone effusively, Mary glanced at the open paper and read "seal ring"—presumably the item of the day and the reason for the smug look. Delia announced, "Lady Elliott and party," but Mary knew that in the excitement she must watch carefully for Miss Johnstone's move to depart. She was able to greet Lady

Elliott with her eyes and briefly admire the stately Lord Exbridge looking hale and walking with lively step. Martha Exbridge, with shining smile and plump figure, was the very picture of Elizabeth's characterization as motherly. While Georgiana greeted each of the newcomers, Mary kept watch on Miss Johnstone, who sat quietly, looking very pink and showing no sign of leaving. Mary quickly acknowledged introductions, as Mrs. Reynolds assisted with the tea things. Martha and Lord Exbridge declined Georgiana's offer of a tour of Pemberley, but young David, smiling and handsome, urged his timid young sister to accept, and after tea, the two followed Georgiana out.

Darcy, having learned of his noble visitors, arrived to greet Lord Exbridge. "I see my sister has taken charge of your grandchildren."

Lord Exbridge chuckled. "I fear it is rather my grandson who wishes to take charge of your sister. Never have I seen two young persons so quickly smitten. Perhaps they have spent sixteen years searching for each other."

"It seems so," agreed Darcy. "Georgiana arrived home with a new sparkle, to be sure. We are indebted to you." His glance included Martha and Lady Elliott in his thanks. "You, sir, are looking amazingly fit after your journey. I trust my eyes do not deceive me."

Exbridge smiled. "Actually, we spent the night at the Lambton Inn. It was all I could manage to keep young David from a midnight visit to his lady love." He helped himself to a plum from the proffered basket. "I trust David may be pried away in an hour or two. We mean to spend the night at Foxbridge. The servants have prepared the manor for us."

"We are delighted to have you again in the neighbourhood, sir." Darcy's face showed his pleasure. "Please favour us often with your presence at Pemberley."

The lord examined with approval the plum he had sampled. "You have, I see, kept up your father's fine orchards."

"I hope I have neglected nothing of what my father built up."

A cloud settled momentarily on the old lord's countenance. "It is a fine thing when a son can show such deference to his father's memory."

Fearing the man's renewed melancholy, Darcy hastened to add, "Or a grandson."

Mary drew her gaze from the kindly, white-haired lord as Miss Johnstone slipped quietly to the door. She followed immediately, and Mrs. Reynolds again took over duties at the tea table, assisted by the alert Martha Exbridge. In the hallway, Mary overtook her departing neighbour who waited there for her carriage. "The signet ring, if you please, Miss Johnstone."

A brazen and angry expression flitted across the wide, flushed face of the compulsive guest. "She really should never have been mistress of Pemberley." Then she reached into her reticule and slowly extruded the large ring. "It might have been mine, you know."

"Of course, but as it is not, we must return it." Mary took it from her and saw the lady out with forced cordiality, knowing that Elizabeth's pity would demand it. Afterward, she stepped into the side parlour to replace the ring in Darcy's desk. When she again reached the large parlour, the young guests had returned and were being introduced to the happily exclaiming local gentry who had just learned that Foxbridge was to be reopened. Mary was pleased that Lady Elliott was also well received by them. Darcy told them all that he would be expecting them at Pemberley for the Christmas ball.

Young David declared his approval of the fine pianoforte in the music room. "And Miss Georgiana played and sang for us the song Grandma used to sing. You would have loved it!"

As Lord Exbridge's eyes watered, Darcy hurriedly thanked him for interceding with the prince regent. "I have heard from Sir Darcy Fitzwilliam, who was overwhelmed at the unexpected honour, and I know such early results tell us how highly you are regarded at court." Lord Exbridge waved away the compliment. Mary noted that Darcy did not mention the Lady for whom the title had been sought. She was glad of it, for that seemed a pettiness that did not accord with so stately a man.

Darcy ordered dinner served in the ballroom that evening so that Elizabeth could attend and receive her guests. Mary reluctantly declined the invitation to join them; she would dearly love to have remained in Pemberley, now ringing with hearty laughter as festive as that of Christmas, but she retired to the cottage feeling that she had much to tell Lydia which may tempt her sister to shed the secrecy that Mary so abhorred.

NO MANNER OF COAXING COULD DISSUADE LYDIA FROM remaining hidden. She did, however, ply Mary with questions about Georgiana and the Exbridges, and at first, Mary answered readily enough. She described the visitors in detail and recounted Georgiana's delight in her new-found childhood friend. Mary mentioned the title accorded to Colonel Fitzwilliam, omitting the remote reason for it, but Lydia's only reaction to that was "Would it not be wonderful if Wickham could be knighted?" Mary did not think so, and she excused Lydia's lack of interest in the Colonel, recalling that Lydia had not attended her sisters' weddings and could not really know him.

The following day at breakfast, it seemed that Lydia wished to reopen the news about Pemberley's fashionable new neighbours. "How splendid it would be to live as they do: fashionable, happy, and merry! Did they have much lace on their gowns?" Mary detected the envy in Lydia's tone, and she again feared that Lydia may be comparing her own present situation with that of her more fortunate older sisters. Wishing to distract Lydia, Mary related some of her reading from *The Odyssey*, but Lydia soon dismissed that with, "Oh, books!" in a distinct tone of disgust. It served, however, to remind Mary that her reading had been curtailed on the previous day, and she determined to visit Pemberley early to read for awhile.

The day being stifling; she did not think she could remain long on the balcony, so she assured Lydia that she did not mean to stay away long. At Pemberley, she looked for Elizabeth in her sitting room before going to the ballroom for access to the balcony. Delia, adjusting fresh flowers in a vase on the mantel, greeted Mary. "The mistress returned to her bedchamber, Miss Bennet. She was uncommonly discomforted this morning."

Mary hesitated to disturb her sister if she wished to sleep, but she tiptoed to the chamber meaning to look in and, if Lizzy was awake, let her know where she would be. When she neared the door, she heard gasping and rustling movements of the bed. She stood still, listening, unsure as to whether she ought to open the door, when a shriek from within decided for her. She tapped on it and peeked in.

Elizabeth thrashed fitfully, twisting the bedclothes and teetering dangerously close to the edge of the bed as she reached for the bell rope. Mary flew to her side and stood holding her to the bed with her knees. She pulled the rope Lizzy could not reach. "Lizzy, what is the matter?" Mary noticed the damp linens as Elizabeth tore at her nightgown moaning in pain. "Callie!" Mary called toward the nursery as Delia rushed in.

"Yes, miss?" Callie came in, saw Lizzy, and understood better than Mary did. "Oh Lord, the baby's coming!"

Delia took hold of Elizabeth's hands and said to Callie, "Find Mrs. Kaye, can you? The surgeon-midwife is not even expected until tomorrow, but his room is ready. Miss Bennet, can you stay with Mistress while I see if the doctor may be fetched?"

Fearful as she was to be left in such a situation, Mary took hold of Lizzy's hands as Delia had done, feeling their powerful jerking, and she held on tight. Delia reached the door, almost running into Mrs. Reynolds. Relieved that she would not be alone with her distressed sister, Mary looked at that competent lady. "Does Lizzy need the surgeon, ma'am?"

Mrs. Reynolds looked, nodded, and sent Delia running to the stairway. When the door opened, Darcy could be heard from the lower stairway. "The Bennets have arrived. Where is Mrs. Reynolds?"

Mrs. Reynolds stepped to the open chamber door and called out, "Please send Mrs. Bennet up right away, and help Delia fetch the surgeon. Mistress needs him today!"

Darcy reached the top of the stairway, sent Delia to summon Mrs. Bennet, and said he would go for the surgeon immediately. Meanwhile, Mary struggled to keep Elizabeth on the bed, pushing with her knees while holding her writhing sister's hands. Lizzy's fitful jerking seemed always to hurl her to the bed's edge, her hands clenching harder with each jerk. As intermittent shrieks escaped through Lizzy's clenched teeth, Mary felt tears rising, and she fought them off. Lizzy's face, bathed in sweat and contorted in pain, made Mary long to bathe it with a cool, damp cloth, but she had neither cloth nor a free hand to hold it. Mrs. Reynolds tried to still Elizabeth's legs, saying, "There, there, Mrs. Darcy," and she held one foot down while raising the thin gown covering her mistress's legs. Mary, seeing blood, turned away and could not look more. She concentrated on her sister's pain-wracked face and fought her own panic. What could she do to relieve her? All the while a terror within her warned: if this is childbirth, she should have no part of it. She would certainly tell her father she had no wish to marry, not ever. She was sure of that now.

Mrs. Bennet arrived breathless, unpinning her bonnet and dropping it on the low bench just beside the door. "Oh my! Lizzy, do not make such a clamour! Think of my poor nerves!" She stepped forward with practised competence, however, and took Lizzy's hands from Mary. "Good girl, Mary. Oh, she is squeezing hard; it is surely her time." She stopped Mary from escaping by saying, "See if you can find a damp cloth to bathe your sister's face." Then she turned to Elizabeth. "Be strong now, Lizzy." Mary looked around for some cloth. Mrs. Reynolds was using the bed linens to wipe Elizabeth's legs, and Mrs. Bennet said, "God bless you, Mrs. Reynolds."

Delia came in with a basin and towels, and Callie followed with Mrs. Kaye, who took one of the ewers of water Callie carried and poured it into the basin Delia had placed on the night stand. She then sent Callie to enquire after a wet nurse. Delia stood wringing her hands, saying, "Oh I do hope Mr. Darcy finds the surgeon in time!" Mrs. Reynolds asked her to bring more water, and she picked up the empty ewer and left. Mary grabbed a towel and plunged it into the basin, wringing it out while Callie stood at the door watching the proceedings.

Finally, as Mary moved to Elizabeth's face with her towel, Callie shrugged and said, "I will go ask my mum. She might know someone."

Mrs. Kaye, without looking up from Elizabeth or removing her hands from where Mary supposed the baby was, called, "Callie, try Carrie Langtry. She recently gave birth again." The midwife continued to feel for the baby's position, frowning slightly, which frightened Mary. Callie nodded, seeming to know where to go, and she left. The midwife still frowned, Mary still worried, and Lizzy still clenched her mother's hands tightly. As Mary wiped her sister's face with the soft towel, she felt that Lizzy clenched her face in fitfulness as well. Mary thought her screams had less volume, and she began to pray fervently that Elizabeth's strength would hold up. Before she left to refresh the towel, she whispered, "Mama, is Lizzy going to die?"

Mrs. Bennet, seeming to squeeze her tormented daughter's hands in a regular rhythm, burst out, "La, child. Lizzy will be all right. This is just the way it is. You should have seen me with Jane—and with Lizzy it was worse. My poor nerves have never been the same since, though it's little Mr. Bennet ever cared."

Mary took heart and returned to her task with a will. Mrs. Reynolds remained with the midwife, using a towel to wipe away fluids Mary refused to look at. She turned all her attention to Lizzy's tense face. "Dear, brave Lizzy." Elizabeth responded to her mother's urging to inhale deeply and in steady rhythm. Occasionally, though, she still gasped and groaned.

Suddenly, Elizabeth called, "Mama!" in a hoarse voice.

Mrs. Bennet's gentle "Hush, child, inhale deeply" seemed to ease her somewhat. Mary realized with surprise that her mother, despite her "poor nerves," remained calmly encouraging in this stressful situation.

Mrs. Kaye, probing with skillful fingers, frowned and said, "It is a boy," but still no baby emerged. *How did she know that?* Mary wondered while she continued trying to cool Lizzy's face and arms, hardly noting her own sweaty face and arms until she saw drips from her chin stain the bed linens. She determined not to fear the worst, with so many experienced women showing no alarm. But her prayers continued. "Lord, please do not let Lizzy die!"

After what seemed another age, with still no progress that Mary could see and Lizzy's wails again more frequent, Darcy appeared with the surgeon. Mrs. Reynolds admitted the doctor and begged Darcy to leave, but he refused to do so. He plunged down onto the bench, narrowly missing the bonnet, his eyes on the doctor.

The surgeon washed his hands and took over for Mrs. Kaye, who stood nearby. He deftly felt the child, commended Mrs. Kaye, and asked for fresh water. Mary saw the basin as Mrs. Kaye took it out and she paled at its crimson hue. She wondered if she could freshen her towel when the clean water came, but she hesitated to do so, sure that the doctor wanted that water for his own reasons. As soon as it came, however, Mrs. Reynolds rinsed her towels in it, changing its colour. Mary was shocked at such a flow of blood, and Darcy seemed to notice as well, for he averted his eyes and turned ghastly pale. Mrs. Reynolds looked at him with what an astonished Mary noted was amusement. She looked at her mother and saw Mrs. Bennet share the joke, shaking her head as she caught Mrs. Reynolds's eyes. Mary ventured to look at the doctor again, who handed a blotchy bundle to Mrs. Kaye. That lady methodically cleaned the babe and wrapped it in a clean, soft cloth.

*All over*, Mary thought, and began to relax. Elizabeth, however, winced and screamed still, and seeing Darcy in the room she yelled, "Get him out of here!"—the longest string of words Mary had heard from her that day. No one heeded her, but Darcy looked as though he would gladly have been elsewhere. Mary blessed his being there, because he seemed to be praying every bit as fervently as she was. Still, the doctor probed Lizzy, most indecently, Mary thought, until he produced a blob of something she could not look at. She had seen cows calve, and she should have expected afterbirth, but strangely, she had not expected a single thing she saw that day. Lizzy quieted a degree then, but remained tense and groaning occasionally. Dreamily, Mary continued her ministrations, wondering how long they had been at the ordeal. She glanced at the easterly window, surprised to find that the sun had moved from it. Was she hungry? No, but her stomach complained and her arms ached. She looked for weariness in the others, but she saw only pride in Mrs. Kaye's face as she presented the bawling bundle to Darcy. Darcy perked up as he held his new son. Mrs. Reynolds went on, efficient as ever, sending Delia for Mr. Shepard, ordering footmen to lift Mrs. Darcy, and bidding Callie to bring fresh linens for the bed.

Mary wondered what the doctor was still doing when she saw her mother, whose eyes were on the doctor, suddenly lurch and gasp. Automatically, Mary turned to look too, just as an alarming fountain of blood spurted up. Mary watched in a trance as regular rhythmic spurts shot forth. Lizzy kept groaning and shrieking in pain, in time with the spurts. Darcy, concerned with the howling child, mercifully missed the doctor's alarmed look as he snatched a towel and returned to his task, staunching the flow. Finally, he removed the towel, watched long and tensely, and then smiled as no more blood gushed forth. He washed his hands, and Mrs. Kaye came to clean and soothe Elizabeth's now quieter limbs. As the doctor wiped his hands, he moved into the relieved mother's view and said, "You have a boy with excellent lungs, Mrs. Darcy. And yours are not so bad either. The pain should subside soon, as things move back into place. Try to get some rest. Mrs. Reynolds may give you a sedating tisane if you wish."

Elizabeth, her face still taut, gave him a disgusted what-does-a-man-know look and turned her face away. The doctor addressed Darcy. "Is there a wet nurse available for the child?"

Mrs. Reynolds answered, "Callie went for Mrs. Langtry."

"Good." The surgeon asked for the carriage to take him home. "I am sorry to have missed the pleasant vacation of waiting in one of your fine rooms this time. This baby was in a great hurry."

Mr. Shepard arrived with two footmen who raised Elizabeth gently while Mrs. Reynolds and Delia swiftly changed the bed linens, and then just as gently, Elizabeth was lowered onto the clean bed. Shepard ushered the surgeon to the carriage, Callie presented Mrs. Langtry, who took the baby, and a strange, almost eerie silence prevailed. Elizabeth smiled wanly at her son, and Darcy approached her bed. In a hoarse whisper, she asked, "Shall he be Fitzwilliam?"

Darcy made a face. "Please, Lizzy, can we not leave that name for my cousins to perpetuate? May we not, to honour your fine and helpful family, call him Bennet?" Lizzy smiled and settled down tiredly. Mary looked around and realized that this was now like the scene she had witnessed after Charles was born, all calm and lovely. But now she knew the whole of it, and what a cruel lie that picture that was! The terrible ordeal deliberately made to look sweet would never deceive her again. Marriage must be a wonder indeed to make such suffering bearable, and even to rejoice in it! Would Stilton require even this of her? Impossible. She could never undergo anything like it. She would unsay her request as soon as she saw her father.

As if on cue, Mr. Bennet appeared at the door. "I saw the doctor leave. What a long time you have been at it!" He admired the perfect little boy, satisfied himself that Elizabeth would be fine, and fixed a stern gaze on Mary. "What on earth are you doing here?"

Mrs. Reynolds spoke up. "It was Miss Mary found her, Mr. Bennet, and most fortunate she did, or the Mistress would likely have miscarried, and God knows what would have become of her."

Mr. Bennet wondered much, but frowned still as he beckoned Mary and bid her follow him. Mary followed meekly. She was hot, tired, and sweaty; she might also be hungry, but only an occasional rumble from her stomach told her that. She dreaded this interview for quite another reason. How could she tell her father that now more than ever she wished she had never written that letter? She most certainly never wished to marry, never wished to undergo such torture. She thought fleetingly of poor women having to give birth without any help at all, and of Mr. Bennet's conjecture that Stilton would be poor within six months. That poor woman would be herself! On the upper stairway, she took courage. Surely Papa's answer would remain a steadfast no. But how she wished she had never asked or that he had written his denial! She had no wish to face him and explain. She stood at the top step, knowing that she must disappoint one of her parents. If her father relented, he would do so only as he also lost respect for her judgement, and she would agree with him. If not, and she remained as she was, how often would her mother remind her of her obstinacy? Marriage! Why must that be a woman's lot? Mr. Bennet still said not a word, but awaited her in the middle of the stairway. Marriage! She resumed her slow descent. Oliver's sermon on Cana flitted through her mind. He had stressed the strange, strong, and confident prayer of the Lord's mother: "They have no wine."

Mr. Bennet paused at the library door, and Mary took each step deliberately, slowing her progress. She breathed, "Lord, I have no sense." As she neared Mr. Bennet, further words of that Gospel came into her head: "Whatsoever he saith unto you, do it." Unaccountably restored in strength, Mary faced her father, confident that at least some decision must result from this conference.

## Chapter 19

Mr. Bennet closed the door to the dim library. He indicated a chair near the cold fireplace for her, and she sat facing him, though he remained standing. He fixed an exasperated stare on her, took her letter from his pocket, and brandished it before her in the half light. "Mary, what do you mean by this request?" Lessening the menace of his tone he went on. "Have you come to love this man?"

"No, Papa." Mary's earlier regrets compounded and mingled with the fright of the scene she had just witnessed above. Only with a struggle had she made her meager reply firm and free of tears.

"Then what does this mean?" She could think of no sensible reply, and it came to Mr. Bennet that this daughter might conceivably sacrifice herself for another. "Have you come to believe that he loves you?"

"No, Papa."

Bennet stuffed the letter back in his pocket, pulled out a chair from the table behind him, and sat, more puzzled than ever. "Then why ask to marry him? How can you hope for any happiness in a loveless marriage with a selfish wastrel?" She still struggled for an explanation, and Bennet attempted another surmise. "You do not make a mission of him, do you? Do you plan to reform him?"

"No, Papa." She wanted somehow to make him aware that she rescinded her request. "And I never looked for any happiness in marriage. I merely asked if you would release me from my promise. But if you will not…" She shrugged, as if she considered the matter closed.

Bennet erupted. "Of course I will not! You have no reason to marry this ne'er-do-well with his horses and his foppishness and his daft family who wish to make you his sorry guardian! Not even a saint could keep this man out of trouble, and the two of you would be penniless in six months' time." He inhaled deeply and began again in a tone to match her matter-of-fact one. "I more readily gave Lydia to Wickham than I could give you to Stilton, and God knows I debated long over that affair."

The mention of Lydia steeled Mary's resolve. She raised her head high and faced him. "Papa, he told me he has given up the races and his life of speculation."

"Then he is a liar as well. Darcy saw Stilton at Lambton's horse fair not long ago, where he won five hundred pounds on a wager with a horse breeder."

"He has begun to repay his father."

"If he has done so, it is out of his winnings. Tell him to finish what he has begun, and he will not need you. How could you, who have loved truth all your life, abide a liar as husband?" Bennet stood again and walked a few steps, then turned back to her. "And he would laugh at you, as he laughs at his parents, every time you attend a church service. Could you endure that?"

Mary felt defeated. "Papa, it is not as if I wished to marry Stilton. But he keeps asking, and he seems desperate, and…" She held her tongue, as her actual reason almost emerged.

"And what?" Bennet leaned over her. "What earthly reasons have you to accept a husband even worse than Lydia's? I never thought you capable of such nonsense!"

Mary heard the disappointment in his tone. She bent forward, her face in her hands. "Lydia," she began softly but could not continue.

Mr. Bennet shook his head impatiently. "Oh yes, I know that Lydia stays at your cottage. Has she talked you into such a thing?"

Mary stared at him even as she shook her head in reply. "How did you find that out?"

"Mr. Darcy wrote of it, even before you wrote, knowing I would worry about her."

"Mr. Darcy knows?" Mary, crestfallen, could already hear Lydia's accusations in her mind.

"Naturally Mr. Darcy knows what goes on around Pemberley. He is loved and respected by servants and tenants. How could he not know? And why is Lydia so bent on secrecy? Is she afraid of Wickham? I never thought him vicious, only foolish."

Mary felt obliged to describe Lydia's plight when first she arrived, her protestations that Wickham never harmed her, her gradual improvement at the cottage, and her growing jealousy of Mary's life there. "I thought if I left it to live with Stilton, she might be allowed to stay there."

Mr. Bennet touched her shoulder gently. "My dear, Lydia is my responsibility and Wickham's, but certainly not yours. Her husband came to Longbourn seeking her and, of course, money. I told him I would find her and ascertain the degree to which he had allowed her the pin money he had agreed upon, and that I would then consult with Mr. Philips about whether to consider divorce. He filled the room with his promises then and as much as admitted that he had deprived her but would treat her generously in future.

I sent him away to find a situation. I mean to deal with Lydia next. But first, you must know that I will never consent to see you tied to an immature, prodigal freethinker. Your new-found compassion is touching, but whatever became of your prudence?"

"But, Papa, he said we could be married in church—"

A howl trumpeted from the dark corner under the balcony overhang and rang through the library and beyond. "A fine concession! If everyone treated a church as nothing but a romantic venue for a wedding, there would not *be* any churches! Miss Mary Bennet! Is this the friend who meets God on his own without benefit of ritual or congregation? And you would *marry* him? Marry a man who does not open your heart? Yoke yourself to a liar? What fellowship is there between devotion and scorn? What harmony links Christian with unbeliever? What commonality between honesty and manipulation? Child, you are the temple of God! Can you join yourself to a gamester? You, who should be kept from every contamination!" Mr. Oliver left off his preaching volume and came forward pleadingly. "I respected your choice and forbore courting you because you wished not to marry. I laboured to establish you to live independently because it was all you left for me to do for you."

By this time, the roar of his opening had drawn Darcy into the library where he stood near the door, a surprised half-smile on his face.

Oliver approached Mr. Bennet and apologised for overhearing some of his discourse and for interrupting him. "Sir, if your daughter will accept to choose matrimony, would you allow me to court her?" He turned to face Mary, who stood transfixed before him. His voice broke sorrowfully. "I withheld no affection from you; yet you contrive to marry one who has none for you. How could you?"

Mr. Bennet looked questioningly to Darcy, who nodded and beckoned. Wordlessly, Bennet took Oliver's hand and placed it in Mary's, noting that she did not draw away. He slipped off to join Darcy, and they quietly withdrew, shutting the door behind them.

Mary felt herself grow younger by degrees, and when she spoke her voice squeaked high and thin. "But, sir, you and Kitty... I thought... I wanted you to marry her."

"Catherine? Your sister? Why wish her for me?"

"I wanted the best for you. You were sure to favour her: she is younger, prettier, charming, she—"

"'Favour is deceitful and beauty is vain,'" Oliver quoted. "And my dear, I wish a virtuous woman that feareth the Lord; one with the strength to try a position before she knows she can do it, and then with God's grace completes it. Miss Bennet, did you never see how I loved you?"

She shook her head solemnly. A great light turned on within her, and a cool, deep calm, refreshing as a mountain pool, welled up in her deepest soul. "I thought... the closest to you I had any hope for... was sister." Suddenly, she knew what made a woman accept even the pain of childbirth for love.

Oliver squeezed her hand and pulled her close. "When you were considering marriage, my dearest, I wish you had told me. I need you near me. I need your transparency, your guilelessness."

As warm as the day had been, Mary moved happily into his embrace, which tightened, unleashing a feeling totally new to her— one she had not even dreamed of. Mr. Oliver murmured into her ear, "I fell asleep in *Inferno*, and the candle went out. I awoke in *Purgatorio*. But all the light is on now. I have found *Paradiso*."

## Chapter 20

Mr. Oliver led Mary out to the parlour where Mr. Bennet and Darcy chatted. The couple held hands as if the condition was permanent, and one look at Mary's radiant face made official Bennet's acceptance of Steven Oliver as Mary's fiancé. Darcy laughed, saying, "Lizzy told me over a year ago that this would happen. I am not sure I appreciate my wife's knowing things on our estate so much sooner than I do."

Mrs. Bennet came down from the nursery to learn the happy news. "Oh, my dear, you will be so happy! I thought Kitty wanted him, but I believe she will be content with Mr. Grantley. And you know, Mary, I never did look forward to becoming related to Mrs. Long. I would have had to take an interest in her tiresome nieces. Now I daresay she will keep all her relatives to herself."

Catherine had slipped over to Mary's cottage before ever learning of Mary and Oliver. Lydia had written to her the "great secret" of her whereabouts, and Kitty went over to tell her about Bennet Darcy and of many other things. But when she actually saw Lydia, she asked, "What happened to Wickham's getting Hunsford? Why are you here?"

With Catherine, Lydia could only be saucy and smug, and she tossed her head. "You must know that the mourning over Lady Catherine puts it off for at least a few more months. Money got tight, and nobody gave us credit any more, so Wickham took Darcy's offer to support him at Oxford, though it did not include me. Wickham sent me to Longbourn, but I was furious with him for going without me and furious with Darcy for offering such a thing. Mary was my only salvation." Lydia showed off the dress that Catherine recognized as Mary's, remade in the expensive and daring fashion Mary would never have admired. Catherine decided she preferred the dress as it was on Mary at the Nottingham ball. She deliberately did not warn Lydia that her father meant to come claim her. She just sat down and let Lydia tell her how Mary spoiled her with berries and clotted cream for breakfast, Sundays at Kympton and that handsome Mr. Oliver, walks in the enclosed cottage garden even at night, barefoot, and in her nightgown! Catherine encouraged every disclosure, smiling quietly, knowing more of Lydia's future than Lydia did. Of course, she did announce their new nephew Bennet, and Lydia crowed as if he had been named for her.

When Mr. Bennet arrived, Kitty slipped away as Lydia, shocked to see him, stormed pettishly about what she termed "Mary's betrayal."

Mr. Bennet waited for her to finish, surprised at the length of her mean-spirited diatribe. She had learned much from living with Wickham, he deduced. Then he calmly assured her that Mary had kept faith with her and that she was an idiot if she thought she could keep anything at Pemberley from Darcy's knowledge. "Mr. Darcy wrote me of it almost as soon as he returned home. He knew I would worry about you. Now get your things together and return with me to Pemberley until we leave shortly for Longbourn. Your husband has been there asking after you."

Lydia smiled broadly. "He has?"

Bennet scowled and continued. "He hoped you had some money for him. His source of funds at Oxford abruptly dried up, once Mr. Darcy wrote Mrs. Younge that the scoundrel had left his wife behind. She is too smart a woman to support Wickham against Darcy's wishes."

Lydia showed her disbelief. "But it was Darcy who supported him at Oxford."

Bennet laughed. "Darcy indeed! When Betsy reported that to him, he guessed immediately why your husband did not want you with him. Mr. Darcy might have supported his study as an attorney. He said there are scheming attorneys enough that Wickham would fit in, but scheming preachers Mr. Darcy would never encourage."

Lydia's eyes widened, and her bravado dissolved. "What am I to do?"

Bennet softened to her. "Come to Longbourn. If your husband does as I advised and takes a post as an attorney's clerk—even Mr. Philips could use him, I expect—then you can return to him and stay as long as he allows you to keep your money. Your husband will never grow up if you keep on bailing him out. Mary assures me Wickham has never touched you in anger. Is that true?"

"Yes, Papa."

"Then Mr. Philips and I will watch him, and when he can support you, you may return to him."

Lydia sunk in misery. "If he has money, he will never want me." She left to collect her few things.

Mr. Bennet tried to avoid either encouraging or disheartening her. "We will see."

Mr. Bennet and Lydia set out with what few possessions they could carry, but Darcy approached them with horse and cart, making the short move easier. About halfway to the manor, James Stilton met them on his way to Mary's cottage. He pulled up beside the cart and announced to Mr. Bennet his intention to speak for Mary, and in his humblest manner, he requested Mr. Bennet's blessing. Bennet shook his head. "I am sorry for you, son; I gave my daughter Mary to her betrothed but a few hours ago." As he looked up, he saw Mary and Oliver walking leisurely behind the stable area, approaching the coppice.

Lydia exclaimed in amazement, "Mary engaged? Papa, why did not Kitty tell me?"

Stilton laughed. "No, Mr. Bennet. I see you are putting me on. Am I to think some knight in shining armour rode in and swept her off her feet and her sister does not know it? Tell me another tale." His sneering tone confirmed Mr. Bennet's delight that Mary had escaped this bounder.

"Young man, it happened not as you suggested. Rather, a young man of shining character walked in and swept her off her feet." Mr. Bennet spoke with deliberation, in a soft and serious tone.

Stilton's tone did not change. If anything, his sharpness increased as if he felt himself the butt of a joke. "Oh, come now, Mr. Bennet. Gentlemen are not suddenly standing in line for your plain and prudish daughter, unsung and unloved all this time."

Bennet invited Stilton to direct his gaze to the trees behind the stable, where Mary walked with her beloved. Mr. Stilton saw a smiling, not-so-plain-looking Mary with her face dangerously near a gentleman bending to her—the same gentleman he had seen with her at Nottingham! "Why, that sneaking little liar! She said he was her pastor and her employer."

Mr. Bennet alighted from the cart, stood before the young dandy's horse, and fixed a stern gaze up at him. "Mr. Stilton, my daughter may have been at times unwise, perhaps even uncharitable, but as far as I know, she has never been untruthful, and to my certain knowledge, she has never been unloved."

Lydia craned her neck to see the couple. "Mr. Oliver! So that is why he did so much for her!" Bennet noted the tinge of envy in her voice.

"Mary told you the truth about him at the time. He is her pastor and her employer, and for the past hour or so, he has been her betrothed as well. My daughter Mary has her faults; at times, she displays a tiresome gift for stating the obvious; but she takes no liberties with truth. I trust any business you may have had here is at an end. Convey my sympathies to your parents and your aunt. Since hearing your estimate of my plain daughter, I cannot imagine that you require any for yourself."

Stilton's manner crumpled into abject self-pity. "What am I to do? I cannot wait until I am thirty-five for my inheritance."

Bennet climbed back into the cart. "Nor should you, young man. Show your parents your independence of them. Since you feel that occupation is beneath you, you must marry some wealthy woman and forget the inheritance. Perhaps your parents may use it to satisfy your creditors."

Darcy spoke then for the first time. "I have just the wealthy woman for you, young man! There is a maiden lady with a fine estate near Lambton; enquire at the Inn after Miss Alicia Johnstone. I daresay she will welcome your attentions."

Stilton stared at Darcy in puzzlement. Then he seemed to take his words as serious, thanked him, and rode off.

Darcy turned to Bennet, smiling. "Let him find out what plain and prudish looks like!"

Lydia still watched the happy couple, twisting around as the cart again jogged ahead. "Such a fine, tall man. And handsome! I never thought a clergyman would make a good husband, but he is so gentle, and I would bet he will not ask her for money. Does Kitty know?"

"By now, I expect so," said Bennet.

"Oh, I do hope not. I would love to tell her that her beloved Mr. Oliver is taken."

Bennet, happy to remove such a mean pleasure from his bitter young daughter, said, "You will be surprised to learn that Kitty has a beau of her own at Hertfordshire, and I do not think she will mind at all having a brother like Steven Oliver."

"A beau? She did not tell me. Who is he?"

They pulled up at the side entrance to Pemberley. Bennet stepped down and helped Lydia, while Darcy directed the footmen to take her baggage. Bennet shook his head sadly at the daughter he really did not know what to do with. "Her beau is a fine and serious young man. He seemed at first interested in Mary, but when she moved permanently to Derbyshire, he transferred his affections to Kitty."

Lydia's eyes widened. "La! Mary of all people was wanted by *three* young men? Who would have thought it?" Mr. Bennet said nothing, though he could readily believe that a man of sense would appreciate a quiet wife.

Mary and Oliver reached the glade where she had once seen Oliver painting, but the deepening dusk caused them to turn toward Mary's cottage. They had walked aimlessly in companionable silence most of the time. Mary, confused by the turmoil of feelings the day had wrought in her, savoured the happiness that had settled on her, though she had neither expected nor sought it. She sighed, conscious of the immense blessing of loving and being loved by so fine a man.

Oliver guided her deftly through the trees, which deepened the darkness. "Do you know that you interested me profoundly before I ever saw you?" He smiled down at her as she showed her wonder at this. "Picture my surprise when I fell into this fine living at Kympton and learned that my patron's wife, named Elizabeth, was with child and that a kinswoman named Mary was soon to visit. I felt I had been planted right into Saint Luke's gospel! I eagerly looked forward to meeting you, and I was not disappointed."

"But I hardly said three words to you!"

"Precisely. You kept all sayings in your heart. You did not display great wit nor did you prattle away. Your interests were music, books, and religion. Rather soon I knew that you suited me more than any woman I had previously met." They reached the path where trees no longer deepened the darkness. He took her hand and drew her to face him. "Are you reconciled to marrying? You did not wish to marry, and I would not force myself on you."

"Yes, indeed. You are so much finer than any future I dared wish for."

"Will not your other young man be terribly disappointed?"

Mary laughed heartily. "Oh yes, because he will be deprived of his inheritance for a few years. By this time, God only knows how many." Mary's thoughts took a serious turn when the mention of inheritance reminded her of her own poor portion. "But you must know that my father can offer little in the way of dowry. You did not imagine me as rich as Lizzy, did you?"

Oliver put his arm around her waist as they walked the path slowly. "You are all the riches I could wish for. But to answer your question, I once did regard you as wealthy, and therefore much beyond me. But one day Mr. Bingley told me laughingly how Mr. Darcy once warned him not to marry the eldest Miss Bennet because she had neither money nor connections. How joyously I welcomed that news! But soon after that, my hint of hope was dashed from me when you announced that you would not marry. I had myself talked into remaining unmarried also, until I awoke in the library to hear that you had changed your mind. Then I silently prayed for your father to forbid that marriage."

They reached the cottage door, where Betsy waited to tell of Lydia's departure. "There is plenty for dinner if your young man wishes to stay."

Oliver declined sadly, before Mary could ask. "Mrs. Birch will have my dinner ready for me. Perhaps some Tuesday, on her day off?" They agreed that Tuesday dinners would be shared at the cottage until all dinners would be at the manse.

If Mary feared Catherine's reaction to her news, she soon found relief. The next day when she visited to learn how well Elizabeth rallied after her ordeal, she overheard Catherine begging her mother for permission to stay in Derbyshire. "Mama, you know Mary does not think of clothes for herself, and she has given so much of what she had to Lydia. Lizzy will be busy with her baby, and someone should attend to Mary's trousseau."

Mrs. Bennet reminded Kitty, "You will be looked for in Hertfordshire. You do not wish to discourage Mr. Grantley."

"Oh, Mama. I neither encourage nor discourage him. But he has a sadness that makes him move very slowly toward marriage, and I do not blame him. At any rate, I will go home with you after Christmas, I promise." When her mother seemed to accept this, Mary stepped in and asked if Kitty would like to stay at the cottage. "Yes, indeed. I will be able to see what you have and what you may still need."

On their very first evening at the cottage, Mary approached the subject of her seeming to usurp Kitty's place with Oliver. "Kitty, I am so sorry. I know how you liked Mr. Oliver, and believe me, I never thought to interest him in myself."

Catherine laughed. "I know. Papa told me you even said that to him. I believe I like to think of him as a brother. In fact, by choosing you, he shows me the kind of woman a good man loves." Kitty spoke in deepest confidence. "I believe I owe it to you that Mr. Grantley takes a serious interest in me. He had thought me flighty until you told him I did not dance to attract men. He says he watched me at dances after that and took courage to ask me."

Mary recalled her first strange encounter with Mr. Grantley. "To tell the truth, Kitty, I believe he watched you at dances before that as well! Even when he first talked to me, his eyes were on you. But do you really like him? You do not find him melancholy?"

"I like him; but yes, he is sad. And he may never ask me to marry him. He told me his sad history." Mary did not wish to pry, so she said nothing to that. But Catherine went on, "Once he was married to a young lady he says I remind him of. She died in childbirth, along with the baby. He used to watch girls at dances, pitying them for their ambition to get husbands, knowing that for some it would be their deaths. I try to let him see that I am healthy like my sisters, but if he never asks me, I will know it is only because he wishes me long life. I am content to bring him some joy in friendship."

Mary greatly wondered at this knowledge, and at the new Catherine that emerged from the association. "Then, whatever happens, I wish you great joy. Papa says he is good for you."

"He only means that I am calm and patient, and that is partly because my older sisters show me the right way to go about finding a good man." Kitty embraced Mary in genuine sisterly love and gratitude.

Mary kept thinking of Mr. Grantley's experience, and she wondered what gruesome torment his poor wife endured, since it had gone so badly with Lizzy, who had rallied and had a healthy baby. How could anything go worse? She shook off the horrid image and turned to Kitty. "Your thoughtfulness as to my wedding clothes is so touching, Kitty. I really need little, but I must say I will have only whatever you are kind enough to make because, from now on, my needlework must go to make a surplice and stole for Mr. Oliver. They must be perfectly done, and that may take me until the wedding day."

Catherine's thoughtful offer took on increasing necessity when Mr. Oliver insisted on keeping Mary with him as much as possible. He involved her more and more in his visits around the parish; and her calm helpfulness, especially with the poor and sick, endeared her to the parish more each day. Whenever she met the girls of the choir, she feared their envy, but she hoped they would soon accept losing him. Tom told her one day that his brother loved her as soon as he heard of the betrothal. Mary was amazed until she learned that

Fred Hooks, who had been sweet on Emmaline, had been much ignored since the new vicar arrived.

Tuesday mornings still found the vicar pursuing his art while Mary joined Catherine in needlework. Afternoons still found them in Pemberley's library, though not so far apart as formerly. Any spare time involved them in arranging the space in the vicarage to suit them both, and they now shared the duty of preparing the church for services. In short, Mary found little time to think of her clothes, even had she been so inclined. Fortunately, Catherine enjoyed working with Letty on gowns and a pelisse, keeping Mary's modest preference in mind. Georgiana helped Catherine also, and together they sewed a new silk tunic, a lace tippet, and other more ordinary undergarments to replace what Mary had given away. Once Jane came to join them, and for a week, Mrs. Gardiner offered her services, suggesting that they add a few nightgowns as well. She often provided finishing touches, where her expertise produced just the finery a trousseau needed. By the time the Gardiners left, promising to return for the holidays, Mary could boast of a wardrobe more complete than that of any of her sisters, but Mary hardly noticed. Her attention remained fixed on the stole and surplice she had almost finished, and she learned from Mrs. Gardiner how to complete them to perfection. Even so, she adjudged her work not good enough for Mr. Oliver. When Georgiana asked, "But where are the linens?" Elizabeth smiled smugly.

"They are already at the manse. They filled a chest at the cottage, because very early I had hints of Mary's need for them, and I began with her two years ago on the work."

THE CHRISTMAS HOLIDAYS RANG WITH SPECIAL MERRIMENT, TO be concluded with the wedding on the day after the ball. To that grand ball, Sir Darcy Fitzwilliam brought his beaming Lady. He thanked Mr. Darcy for his wise advice and confided his own prospective fatherhood. "By summer, Caroline will give birth, and how right you were! Caroline's spirits, as you see, are fully restored."

"And you, sir, are given the recognition that you deserve for your valour." Darcy could not help being reminded of the other reason for Lady Caroline's joy.

Fitzwilliam looked down. "I should no more be a knight of the crown than Sir Michael, perhaps less. The honour truly belongs to the French women who followed the battles to tend their fallen and who taught me their secrets only because they refrained from treating the wounded British. But for Caroline's insistence that she wished to emulate her sister Lady Helena in every way possible, I would have declined the honour."

For much of the evening, Sir Fitzwilliam studied Jane Bingley and Elizabeth Darcy, convinced that motherhood produced the serenity and precious contentment they exhibited. He approached

Mr. Oliver on the subject, pointing out his observations. "Have you observed among the women of Kympton that special joy that motherhood brings?"

"I fear I have not noticed," said Oliver. "Perhaps in a year or so, I may have better information." And he returned his attention to Mary, from whom it had not wandered for a full minute since the ball opened.

Lady Caroline glowed as she greeted her dear sister Jane—who would never be called Lady. She also smiled benignly on her dear cousin Elizabeth—who would be similarly deprived. She actually contrived to bestow pity on them. Her noblesse oblige produced the most fulsome tolerance that she had ever conceived as a substitute for love. She stressed, while gushing her greetings, their lowly titles of Mistress, not even imagining how genuinely both Jane and Elizabeth prized that title more than any the realm could bestow. Caroline's haughty benevolence extended graciously to Miss Anne de Bourgh with special sympathy because she had not inherited the title which her mother had borne like a sceptre. Miss de Bourgh returned her condescension in like sympathy, knowing Lady Caroline's wealth could never approach hers. Mary received Lady Caroline's exuberant greetings as blindly as she received all others, her rapt smile radiating her new-found love, which extended to everyone.

Lydia, however, Caroline studiously ignored as beneath contempt, having wed the man Darcy would abhor above all, and for some reason Darcy's approval still meant something to the lady.

Jane rejoiced heartily to see Caroline in such fine spirits, and Elizabeth amused herself watching the great lady. She found special hilarity in Lady Caroline's broad hint that her noble father-in-law had applied for the knighthood. Elizabeth fervently hoped that the Earl would not disabuse her of the notion. Having Caroline's happiness now closely entwined with that of Darcy's genial cousin bolstered Elizabeth's genuine concern for Lady Caroline's wellbeing.

Darcy's wonderment fell mainly on another cousin at that ball. Having cast mourning aside, Miss de Bourgh presided over the ball as if she were the guest of honour. Her enthusiasm for the dance astonished Darcy, who, at his wife's request, led Miss de Bourgh into the grand march. She danced then with Mr. Bingley, Sir Fitzwilliam, the Lords Exbridge elder and younger, and many other gentlemen present. Only Mr. Oliver did not approach the grand lady, as he danced only with Mary. However, when Anne learned that he and Mary were to travel to Kent right after the wedding to see his family, she insisted they stay at least a few days at Rosings, promising to return in haste to receive them.

Darcy watched the dance, marvelling at Anne's endurance and wondering how she had managed to learn all the steps with such mastery. His imagination gave credit to Witherspoon, but the lady never mentioned him nor did she appear to miss him. All except Lady Caroline, who did not notice, reckoned Anne the belle of the ball. Georgiana and Lord Exbridge made much of Miss de Bourgh, reminding her that she, as well as Georgiana, had often visited in town as young girls. She remembered more than Georgiana could recall, particularly of the departed Lady Exbridge, with whom she had visited while Georgiana played with young David. While this brought Lord Exbridge close to tears, he felt the healing joy of speaking of her at last.

The Reverend and Mrs. Wynters remarked the smiling Anne, having seen her at previous balls, but never so high-spirited. This couple had come expressly to officiate at the next day's wedding and to serve the parish again for the fortnight when the Olivers would sojourn in Kent. Mary wrapped herself in the joy of this day and the day following, but she feared meeting Steven's brothers. She could actually come to terms with the possibility of undergoing childbirth with more equanimity than she could summon to meet face-to-face with the brothers who, as Steven had told her, lived only to tease.

## Chapter 23

THE WEDDING, AT WHICH THE BRIDE AND GROOM EXHIBITED solemn contentment, rendered Mrs. Bennet positively giddy. To see the daughter who had perversely insisted that she need not marry actually win a husband gave her unspeakable relief. Why, four-fifths of her main task in life was completed! The new couple left directly from the church to visit the groom's family in Kent, and Darcy escorted Miss de Bourgh from Kympton while Elizabeth rode to Pemberley with the Bingleys. Darcy took advantage of the short ride to enquire about Anne's plans. "If you are considering marriage, I assure you I support your choice. I have become a great proponent of following one's heart."

Anne shook her head. "I know far too much about a woman's property rights after marriage. I will not likely sacrifice both consequence and control for the dubious compensation of a husband."

"You surprise me," Darcy replied as the carriage started up. "I trust this reflects your fondest desires and not mere financial prudence."

"Financial prudence is never mere, Cousin, and someone must display it. My substantial property may one day benefit your children, who may well be numerous—the usual consequence of marrying a charming and healthy woman. I will do what I can to provide for them, no matter how cavalierly you dismiss the need." She waited for Darcy to hand her out at Pemberley. "And when the Collins family moves to Longbourn, you may have a son in orders who desires a place."

Darcy laughed as they entered the splendid front hallway. "I do intend to raise my sons to be useful, but if one chooses to serve the church, I can find livings closer than Hunsford."

"But Reverend Wynters tells me you have given Kympton to the Olivers in perpetuity, a most generous wedding gift indeed. Someone must tend to the welfare of your sons, when their father casts off his most productive benefice. And who is to say you will not have a son who wishes to remove far from Pemberley?" She stood in the entrance looking up at him almost defiantly but with an unaccustomed twinkle in her eye.

Darcy presented a deliberately stern countenance. "I appreciate your concern, but I insist that you act strictly on your own desire. I had heard of a certain verger who had caught your fancy. Do not sacrifice love, even for my poor deprived children."

Anne laughed long and heartily, amazing Darcy even more. "A mere entertainment!" she finally managed. "To marry such a one would be sacrifice indeed—of my property, of the living at Hunsford to a blackguard, and of my own wits. Witherspoon's aspirations were my greatest amusement, along with his obsequious endearments. Now that Mr. Collins affords me the attentions he once accorded Mama, he will be sufficient amusement for me. Collins must dismiss the cunning verger, who knows by now that his intrigues for himself and his rogue ally are for naught." Anne smiled wryly. "Of late he has grown tiresome and has taken to whining about my domineering attitude."

Darcy returned her smile, grateful that Wickham's manipulations came up against the new-found iron will of Miss de Bourgh. Collins and Mrs. Jenkinson may have felt they had a new Lady Catherine to answer to as well. She may not have inherited the title, but she seemed fully intent on inheriting the deference. How well the doctor had assessed the situation, transferring his allegiance even before Lady Catherine's death! Others' allegiance would follow as convenience and profitability demanded. As the two progressed slowly to the parlour, Darcy thought again of Witherspoon, to whom the loss must be material, and of Wickham, deprived of his hoped-for living. Did Wickham suspect this when he sent Lydia off to fend for herself?

They entered the great parlour where family wedding guests talked of the new Mrs. Oliver. Mrs. Gardiner remarked the bride's radiance despite her simple attire. Elizabeth said, "Mary never felt comfortable in lace or jewelry."

"Once I expected Mary to remain at Longbourn. She seemed not to desire anything more." Aunt Gardiner went to the generous repast and selected some fruit from the tray on the table.

Elizabeth, after thanking Mrs. Reynolds for pouring tea, showed her agreement with Mrs. Gardiner. "Who ever knew what Mary desired, beyond books and music? In fact, if I understood Mr. Darcy right, she surprised even herself to find that she loved Mr. Oliver."

Darcy seated himself next to his wife and helped himself to a scone from her plate. "Did you not see it that way, Mr. Bennet?"

Bennet agreed immediately. "Indeed, yes. She had just allowed that she looked for no happiness in marriage, and Mary did not forsake the truth knowingly."

Elizabeth smiled. "How glad I am that happiness looked for her. She is a good soul, and she deserves it."

Catherine, more thoughtful than usual, nodded. "Lizzy, does it not seem as if Mary, of all of us, fell into the most striking romance?

She had not developed a great liking for him from the first, as Jane did Mr. Bingley"—Jane blushed at this—"nor did she develop a dislike to him that would turn to love later, as someone we know did." She fixed her teasing look on Lizzy, who cast her eyes down as Darcy pulled her close. "And she certainly did not lose her mind over him, as Lydia did over Wickham." Even Lydia smiled at that. "Her love for Mr. Oliver must have hidden deep inside of her until he called it out."

"Howled it out is more like!" laughed Darcy.

"I wonder which way I will find love, if ever I do." Kitty continued thoughtful.

Mr. Bennet asked teasingly, "And if you have your choice, which would you choose?"

"I do not believe I can choose," said Kitty. "Perhaps, with the grace of God, it will just happen." Mrs. Gardiner exchanged admiring looks with Jane and Elizabeth. Kitty would mature after all.

Mrs. Bennet entered the parlour from the nursery. "Our little Bennet is such a gem. He does not cry in the bath as he did when Mr. Oliver christened him. I must say that those ministers would have an easier time of it if they warmed the water and tested it on their elbows, as we do when bathing babies. Mary must enlighten her husband on these things."

Darcy addressed Mrs. Bennet, "Did Lizzy tell you that she knew two years ago that Mary was destined for Oliver?"

"No!" She turned on Lizzy, frowning. "Why did you never tell me? And me worrying all the time about that worthless coxcomb Stilton being her only chance!" Mrs. Bennet shook her finger accusingly, while Jane, Catherine, and Mrs. Gardiner exclaimed over the revelation.

Elizabeth shrugged. "How could I even tell Mary? It showed in the vicar's face but never in hers. He could even distinguish her playing from Georgiana's when we heard it from the parlour. When Darcy suggested that he accompany Mary to Longbourn, you should have seen the joy in his face, but Mary evidenced no elation or anxiety, either before or afterward."

Lydia spoke up dreamily, "I never thought to marry a clergyman, but what a nice thing it would be if Wickham took orders and we could be so nicely settled."

Again Mrs. Gardiner exchanged looks with Jane and Elizabeth, but with a wry smile. Lydia would always relate any topic to herself. Miss de Bourgh interjected, "But then, Mrs. Wickham, you would have to visit the sick and the poor. I am glad it will not be the case." She did not say she was glad on behalf of the poor, though her look implied it. Lydia took no offence.

Georgiana had been entertaining the Exbridge family in the small parlour, but at that moment Lord Exbridge, Martha, and Susan came in, preparatory to taking their leave. Exbridge whispered to Darcy, who excused himself immediately and left the room as Lady Elliott walked in smiling. Soon, Darcy and Georgiana walked in with David, and they all bid the departing guests a genial farewell. When the Exbridges and Lady Elliott had gone to Foxbridge, Darcy told Elizabeth and the others that spring would bring another family wedding. He was pleased that his sister had found her peace in David, yet he held Georgiana close and knew that losing her would be very like losing a daughter.

THE RETURNING OLIVERS, PASSING THROUGH LONDON, STOPPED at the Bell, recalling how they had once encountered Wickham and Witherspoon there. After dining, they walked around Hanover Square, and the rector of Kympton pointed out the little bookstore where he had purchased Mary's wedding gift. He apologised for its drawbacks. "The binding was poor, but I strengthened that. I could not find the whole work and likely could not have afforded it if I did. My choice was between the first two books of Augustine's *City of God* or the final two. It was all I could find in English."

Mary thanked him anew, even more grateful now that she had read it than when he gave it to her. "I am glad you chose the end, as it was about heaven. Did you know that?"

"Not at all. I have dabbled in that work but never reached the end. It is prodigiously long. I found the part about the demons being like sponges though, as I told you." They spent some time looking in the window at the fine leather-bound volumes, and then walked on hand-in-hand in companionable silence. As they started back to the post inn, Oliver looked at her seriously. "Was it so terrible an ordeal, meeting my brothers? They are simple labourers and rough-spoken, and I have always tried to shield you from humour such as theirs. I should have known they would consider a new bride fair game for bawdy jokes. I am sorry."

Mary hastened to assure him that she had come to appreciate their open and honest ways. "I have one brother whose lack of those characteristics you have already sampled. And you know, Mr. Martin sought me out on our final morning to apologise for their remarks."

Oliver laughed. "I think that you rather disappointed him by neither blushing nor laughing. And you did not blame them nor look mumchance, but only smiled at them. I commend you for that."

"Oh, but their japery made me prize the treasure of your gift all the more! I sincerely pitied them, for it seemed they could not properly value what Augustine calls 'a spouse's ministry to the spouse's physical pleasure.' I greatly pitied their dear wives too. They are missing so much!"

Oliver's arm went around her as he helped her into the coach for the long ride to Derbyshire. "Dearest, how you amaze me. I should have read the book while I rebound it. It shall be a central part of our small library."

On the return journey, they also spoke much of the kindness of Miss de Bourgh, who had hurried home to receive them herself. Mary greatly enjoyed seeing the Collins family, holding Louisa, and seeing Lucas so proudly keep watch over his little sister. Miss de Bourgh had spent much time with Mr. Oliver, and as he recalled it, he told Mary, "From her questions about the work, I believe Miss Anne will attend the poor and the sick with a true charity. She had many questions about it because she fears that Mrs. Collins will lack sufficient time for it for many years." Mary pictured them when they left. Collins waved them off, Charlotte held Louisa, and Lucas bowed a gracious farewell to his friend "Miz Oliver."

## Chapter 25

SOME WEEKS AFTER THE OLIVERS RETURNED TO KYMPTON, Elizabeth received a letter from Charlotte Collins which recounted her pleasure at seeing Mary again. She enthusiastically acclaimed Mary's choice of husband.

I believe Miss de Bourgh has profited greatly from their visit. So many Hunsford townsfolk admit, with some surprise, that they now enjoy her visits. We never heard such remarks in Lady Catherine's day, but that poor lady was not in the best health. Miss de Bourgh let slip at dinner one day that she seriously intended using her influence as Sir Lewis de Bourgh's daughter to request from the regent the selection of a bishop sometime in the future. I fear Mr. Collins took this as a reference to himself, and he has begun bowing and calling Anne 'my grand lady,' which seems to amuse her. However, my guess is that she has Mr. Oliver in mind, though I do not say so. I would not wish to detract from Mr. Collins's obeisance nor from Miss de Bourgh's amusement at it.

Lizzy laughed heartily at the letter, both in picturing portly Mr. Collins performing such courtesies and in imagining Mary, who was the last to look for honours, one day outranking Lady Caroline.

In spring, when Georgiana became Mrs. Exbridge, Elizabeth observed to her husband that his sister would inherit a title one day that would rival Lady Caroline's. Darcy nodded. "But I assure you, she thinks of it not as honour but as heavy obligation. Georgiana told me how gladly she joined the household at Foxbridge, delighted to be close to us. And she admitted that she wished to have some years of observing Martha before taking on duties of mistress. From you and Mary, she said she learned the joy of having sisters, and having lacked a mother's guidance, she thought that Mrs. Exbridge is just the model she needs."

Elizabeth admitted that she would miss Georgiana. "But how Mary and Steven Oliver rejoiced that so illustrious a couple had chosen to be wed at Kympton Saint Giles!"

At Pemberley, young Charles accepted baby Bennet as enthusiastically as Beth did her brother William, but Charles had to be reminded daily that he could not expect his little brother to run with him for a while. Charles steadfastly refused to believe that he himself had ever been too young to run.

The young girls of Kympton followed Emmaline Langley's lead and resigned themselves to a married rector. They joined the elderly, the sick, and the poor of the parish in their wholehearted support of his ministry, and the living of Kympton grew in value yearly. By autumn of their first year together, Mr. Oliver had forbidden the creaky choir stairway to Mary, and Emmaline became organist. Though the almost-nineteen-year-old had some problems keeping the girls from their antics at practises, she did well for so young a girl. Parishioners did not think of the new Mrs. Oliver as plain, although she kept to her simple clothing and unbraided hair. Her burgeoning self-confidence and frequent easy smiles rendered her lovely in the eyes of her beloved villagers.

The Bennets, often including Lydia, visited the North frequently, spending a fortnight at Pemberley, a fortnight at the Kympton manse, and a fortnight at Otherfield. Having three daughters in the area lured them often from Longbourn, though Kitty sometimes requested inviting Mr. Grantley lest she miss Hertfordshire. It was a full five years before that gentleman overcame his fear of remarrying, and Kitty, who had certainly exercised patience, became the second Bennet daughter to live at Netherfield.

Mr. Wickham finally took Mr. Bennet's suggestion and apprenticed himself to Mr. Philips as clerk. His education sufficed for the duty of writing documents, and his ready charm brought clients into the office. Meryton had forgiven him for leaving debts, which had been subsequently paid, and merchants carefully warned their daughters about his insubstantial virtue. Consequently, he managed to live longer in the same flat at Meryton than he had done at any previous residence. By Mr. Bennet's strictures laid down in advance, Lydia stayed with Wickham only as long as he did not take from her the pin money she should have. If Mrs. Phillips observed that Lydia was without it, and her observation remained astute, her immediate report to Bennet sent him for Lydia as he had promised. Then Lydia remained with her parents until Wickham again swore he would honour his word. Thus Lydia lived at Longbourn almost as many months as she lived at Meryton, and she grew to accept the arrangement, especially while Kitty lived at Longbourn. When she later lived there with her parents alone—much as Mrs. Bennet doted on her—the lack of need for husband-hunting had drained so much pleasure from

Mrs. Bennet's social life that she looked to travel for excitement. This kept Lydia often far from her husband, but she grew to accept that as well.

A few years after Kitty's marriage, Henry Fitzwilliam succeeded to the earldom, and the holiday season included quite a round of balls: Pemberley's, one at Norwich Mills, and one reinstated at Foxbridge. Miss de Bourgh chose Michaelmas for a ball at Rosings Park, delighting the gentlefolk at Hunsford, who were unused to such doings. When Kitty became mistress of Netherfield, she started a midsummer ball, and by then Beth knew the dances and taught her younger siblings and cousins as soon as they wished to join in. Bennet Darcy, however, sneered at such a waste of time; he preferred a book. Lizzy teased that the child must have seen Mary first at birth and so took on her propensities.

One day, shortly after Miss Langley had married Fred Hooks and moved to Saint Albans, where the young man had found a position, Darcy reported to Elizabeth that the cottage would soon be occupied again. "It amazed me that Oliver insisted on paying rent all this time only because one day it would be needed. But apparently, he has found a choir master who needs a residence nearby. Let us hope we will enjoy our new neighbour."

Elizabeth teased, "I thought to give it to Bennet for his hermitage. He finds his little sisters too much company, you know. They talk too much."

Darcy rejoined, "And I thought Oliver kept it for the overflow of children from the manse! But actually, it is to house a musical gentleman from Nottingham whose father has tired of his running horses to death and has forced him to procure a paying post."

"Surely you must speak of a gentleman we know?"

"Indeed, I do."

"Perhaps the post will increase his self-discipline." After a pause, Elizabeth added, "But if the spurned Miss Johnstone should change parishes to be near him that might send him off again."

"Yes," Darcy said as he laughed. "As far as the farthest colonies."

# Acknowledgments

My sincere thanks to my friend, Margaret Cain, and her friends, the D'Arcys of Derbyshire, for their substantial assistance in providing information regarding all things British.

# About the Author

Eucharista Ward was born in Minneapolis and is a member of the Sisters of Saint Francis of Sylvania, Ohio. She is a retired high school English teacher with an M.A. in English. After retiring from teaching, she became a licensed nurse's aid and worked as a home health aide, and then as an assisted living aide in Sylvania, caring for the retired sisters of the Sisters of Saint Francis. She currently works in an assisted living residence at night. To pass the time and keep herself awake through the night, she writes sequels to the Jane Austen novels of which she is so fond.

# The Pemberley Chronicles

*A Companion Volume to Jane Austen's* **Pride and Prejudice**

*The Pemberley Chronicles: Book 1*

## REBECCA ANN COLLINS

"A lovely complementary novel to Jane Austen's *Pride and Prejudice*.
Austen would surely give her smile of approval."
—BEVERLY WONG, AUTHOR OF *Pride & Prejudice Prudence*

### *The weddings are over, the saga begins*

The guests (including millions of readers and viewers) wish the two happy couples health and happiness. As the music swells and the credits roll, two things are certain: Jane and Bingley will want for nothing, while Elizabeth and Darcy are to be the happiest couple in the world!

Elizabeth and Darcy's personal stories of love, marriage, money, and children are woven together with the threads of social and political history of England in the nineteenth century. As changes in industry and agriculture affect the people of Pemberley and the surrounding countryside, the Darcys strive to be progressive and forward-looking while upholding beloved traditions.

"Those with a taste for the balance and humour of Austen will find a worthy companion volume."
—*Book News*

978-1-4022-1153-9 • $14.96 US/ $17.95 CAN/ £7.99 UK

# The Darcys Give a Ball
## ELIZABETH NEWARK

"A tour de force." —MARILYN SACHS, AUTHOR OF *First Impressions*

### *Whatever will Mr. Darcy say...*

...with his son falling in love, his daughter almost lured into an elopement, and his niece the new target of Miss Caroline Bingley's meddling, Mr. Darcy has his hands full keeping the next generation away from scandal.

Sons and daughters share the physical and personality traits of their parents, but of course have minds of their own—and as Mrs. Darcy says to her beloved sister Jane Bingley: "The romantic attachments of one's children are a constant distraction."

Amidst all this distraction and excitement, Jane and Elizabeth plan a lavish ball at Pemberley, where all the young people come together for a surprising and altogether satisfying ending.

What readers are saying:

"A light-hearted visit to Austen country."

"A wonderful look into what could have happened!"

"The characters ring true, the situation is perfect, the conclusion is everything you hope for."

"A wonder of character and action... an unmixed pleasure!"

978-1-4022-1131-7 • $12.95 US/ $15.50 CAN/ £6.99 UK

# *Mrs. Darcy's Dilemma*
## DIANA BIRCHALL

"Fascinating, and such wonderful use of language."
—JOAN AUSTEN-LEIGH

### *It seemed a harmless invitation, after all…*

When Mrs. Darcy invited her sister Lydia's daughters to come for a visit, she felt it was a small kindness she could do for her poor nieces. Little did she imagine the upheaval that would ensue. But with her elder son, the Darcys' heir, in danger of losing his heart, a theatrical scandal threatening to engulf them all, and daughter Jane on the verge of her come-out, the Mistress of Pemberley must make some difficult decisions…

"Birchall's witty, elegant visit to the middle-aged Darcys is a delight." —PROFESSOR JANET TODD, UNIVERSITY OF GLASGOW

"A refreshing and entertaining look at the Darcys some years after *Pride and Prejudice* from a most accomplished author." —JENNY SCOTT, AUTHOR OF *After Jane*

978-1-4022-1156-0 • $14.95

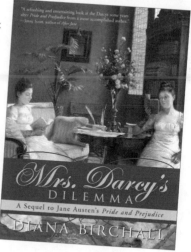

# Mr. Darcy's Diary
## Amanda Grange

"A gift to a new generation of Darcy fans and a treat for existing fans as well." —Austenblog

### *The only place Darcy could share his innermost feelings...*

...was in the private pages of his diary. Torn between his sense of duty to his family name and his growing passion for Elizabeth Bennet, all he can do is struggle not to fall in love. A skillful and graceful imagining of the hero's point of view in one of the most beloved and enduring love stories of all time.

---

What readers are saying:

"A delicious treat for all Austen addicts."

"Amanda Grange knows her subject... I ended up reading the entire book in one sitting."

"Brilliant, you could almost hear Darcy's voice... I was so sad when it came to an end. I loved the visions she gave us of their married life."

"Amanda Grange has perfectly captured all of Jane Austen's clever wit and social observations to make *Mr. Darcy's Diary* a must read for any fan."

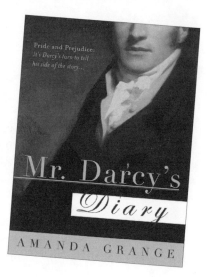

978-1-4022-0876-8 • $14.95 US/ $19.95 CAN/ £7.99 UK